G.J. KEMP

THE ACRE SERIES

Juno and the Lady Book 1

First published in 2021 by SilverWood Books
SilverWood Books Ltd
14 Small Street, Bristol, BS1 1DE, United Kingdom www.
silverwoodbooks.co.uk

This edition published in 2022 by TB5 Publishing
Copyright © G.J. Kemp 2021

The right of G.J. Kemp to be identified as the author of this work has been asserted in accordance with the Copyright, Designs and Patents Act 1988 Sections 77 and 78.

All rights reserved. No part of this publication may be reproduced, stored in a retrieval system, or transmitted in any form or by any means, electronic, mechanical, photocopying, recording or otherwise, without prior permission of the copyright holder.

This is a work of fiction. Names, characters, places and incidents either are products of the author's imagination or are used fictitiously. Any resemblance to actual events or locales or persons, living or dead, is entirely coincidental.

ISBN 978-1-915379-00-9 (paperback 2nd edition)
ISBN 978-1-915379-01-6 (ebook 2nd edition)
ISBN 978-1-915379-02-3 (hardcover 1st edition)

For Jess

Acknowledgements

I wrote most of this book in a room at the Angel View Inn, Gateshead, with a view of the Angel of the North and its protective wings spread over the area. To the then owners of the Inn, Tori, Stu and Mom, who looked after me through some trying times; your warmth, smiles and banter (and excellent meals) I will never forget.

To Jess, Nanna and Lara, who read the drafts of this book and gently helped me understand the struggles women have faced to get their rights. Thank you.

To Alice, Viki, Enya, Helen and the rest of the SilverWood team. Thank you all for helping me through the long publishing journey. Your support has been utterly fantastic. Andrei, your book cover is immense. And finally, to Davie boy, I finally got to writing. Thank you, brother, for your years of encouragement.

THE ACRE SERIES

Thank you for your interest in The Acre Series. I recommend you read the major books in order as the characters and the story grow with the series. The novellas are prequels and sequels to the larger books. You can read them in any order you wish.

—-

The Acre Series:
Juno and the Lady (An Acre Story Book 1)

Valen and the Beasts: A Juno and the Lady Novella(An Acre Story Book 1.1)

CHAPTER 1
FLYING PEARS

Juno caught the apple in her left hand. She checked the fruit for ripeness, then tossed it into her wicker basket. The basket, her pride and joy, she had made herself out of strong reeds she had harvested from the river that ran at the bottom of the school. A voice sounded through the fruit trees. She tilted her head and listened intently.

'Kick it, Travis,' a boy said at the back of the orchard. 'It's just a worthless stray. Stop being such a baby.'

Juno crept through the orchard and hid behind a pear tree.

'I am not a baby,' Travis said with a curled lip. He stepped deeper into the tall grass and kicked his leather boot at the roots of an old, gnarled tree.

A kitten snarled and hissed from in between the gnarled tree's roots.

Juno stepped into the open. 'What are you doing to her?'

'Well, what have we here?' the thinner boy said. 'Look, Travis, a little girl who wants to save the stray kitty.'

Juno slid the wicker basket off her shoulders and placed it against a tree. 'Leave her be. She has done nothing to you.'

Travis, the larger, more muscular boy, cocked his head. 'She is pretty, Simon. Very pretty,' he said, showing a toothless grin.

Simon snorted. 'Way too pretty for a simpleton like you, Travis.'

A third boy stepped out from behind the gnarled tree. 'Simon, Travis, leave her alone. It's time we went back home.'

'Shut up, Billy,' Simon said, with a dismissive wave. 'Come here, fruit picker. Let's see if we can fit you into that wicker basket,' he said, facing Juno.

The kitten sprang out of the roots. She sank her thin, razor-sharp teeth into Travis's ankle, and her needle-like claws dragged down the side of his calves. Travis yelped and shook his leg, sending the kitten flying through the air and back in between the roots.

Simon scooped up a rock. 'Horrible diseased stray. You will pay for hurting my friend,' he said, aiming the rock at the kitten.

Juno grabbed a pear from a low branch and threw it with all her might. It tumbled through the air and exploded on Simon's nose. Spots of blood splashed from his nostrils onto his clothes.

Billy walked over to Simon and grabbed the rock from his hand. 'I said leave her alone, Simon.'

'She broke my nose,' Simon said, through blood-covered fingers. 'This girl needs to know her place.'

Travis, hopping from foot to foot, cackled with glee. 'The girl is beating you, Simon. Beaten bloody by a fruit-picking girl.'

Simon snarled. 'At least I didn't get bitten by a stray. You're diseased now, Travis.'

Travis stalked to the gnarled tree. 'Come here, you filthy stray rat,' he said, parting the grass with his boot.

A ripe pear tumbled through the air and hit Travis on the side of the head. His eyes wide, he wiped the bits of pear from his cheek.

'That's enough,' Billy said, standing in between Juno and the two boys.

'Or what?' Simon said, walking up to Billy. 'Are you going to take us both on? Remember who you are, herb boy.'

Billy wagged a finger at Simon. 'This girl goes to the ladies' school on the hill. If Mr Hargreaves finds out that we are here, it's six lashes for all of us.'

Simon's jaw clenched. He turned to Juno. 'You haven't seen the last of us, fruit picker. We will come back for you.'

The two boys hopped over the fence and walked down the cobble path towards the village at the bottom of the hill.

Billy gave Juno a lopsided grin as he climbed over the fence. 'Close one, fruit picker,' he said with a wave.

Juno took in a few deep breaths to still her shaking hands. The kitten poked her head out of the tree roots, then stalked to Juno, her tail up in the air.

Juno knelt. 'What are you doing out here?' she said, extending a hand. 'Did those boys hurt you?'

The kitten looked at Juno with red-flecked amber eyes. Her round ears danced with each sound in the orchard. With a meow, she swatted Juno's hand with her paw.

Juno pulled her hand back. 'Where is your mummy? You shouldn't be out here alone.'

The kitten stalked around Juno then sprang into her wicker basket. With a last look of disdain at Juno she curled up around the pears, placed her head on her paws and closed her eyes.

'You can't come to my school,' Juno said, tentatively reaching into her wicker basket. 'Miss Petra does not allow animals at the school.'

The kitten's eyes snapped open, and with a growl she swiped a paw at Juno's outstretched hand.

Juno furrowed her brow. 'That wasn't very nice.'

The kitten sneezed, then placed her head back onto her paws.

The school bell clanged. 'That's the school wake-up bell, and I don't have enough fruit for breakfast,' Juno said, pulling the wicker basket onto her back.

The winding dirt path ran next to the cobblestone path. Just before the school, the dirt path broke away and led up to the school side gate. The cobblestone path continued south to the village. Juno looked across the cobble path and shivered at the dark forest, which rustled and swayed with each gust of wind. She pulled her wicker basket tighter onto her back and continued up the dirt path into the school courtyard, where the fountain bubbled and gurgled.

'We are going to go through the side entrance,' she said, swinging the basket off her back and onto one shoulder. 'It's closer to my dorm, where I have a place you can hide.'

The kitten opened an eye, looked up at Juno and yawned. Juno slid in through the west entrance and hurried down the corridor until she reached her dormitory.

Harriet, Juno's fourth-year prefect, looked up from her desk. 'Aren't you supposed to be in the kitchen?' she said, folding her arms.

'I need to drop something off at my bed,' Juno said, walking through towards the back of the dorm.

'Juno? What is going on?'

Juno carefully placed her wicker basket next to her bed and walked back to Harriet. 'There were three boys in the orchard. Boys I have never seen before.'

Harriet stiffened. 'What were they doing there?'

Juno shrugged. 'I don't know. They were not very friendly.'

'Did they do anything to you?'

'They were going to stuff me into my wicker basket, so I threw pears at them. One of the boys eventually stopped the other two.'

Harriet tapped her pen on her chin. 'Boys from the village know they shouldn't be in the orchard. I am going to have to report this to Miss Petra. Come back to my desk after breakfast so we can write a report.'

Juno nodded, then walked back through the dorm to her bed. She crouched and peered into her basket. 'I have just the hiding place for you, but you need to promise that you will stay there and be quiet.'

The kitten's nose twitched. Her amber eyes stared, unblinking. Juno glanced over her shoulder and, with the dorm clear, she lay on her stomach and crawled under her bed, where a net covered a hole. Juno unclipped the net and placed it to one side.

'Come here, little one,' she said, shaking the basket.

The kitten walked out of the wicker basket and crawled into the hole. She spun and scratched at the ground to make a bed. Satisfied, she curled up into a ball and rested her head on her paws.

'I will leave this hole open so you don't get trapped. There are lots of people that come and go in this dorm, so behave yourself,' Juno said with a wag of her finger.

Juno crawled out from under her bed, collected her basket and hurried off to the kitchen, where rows of girls sat sorting, cleaning and cooking an assortment of fruit and vegetables. Miss Petra, the school principal, glanced over at Juno with a raised eyebrow.

'Sorry, miss, there was a problem with some boys at the orchard,' Juno said, pulling out pears from her basket.

The girls along the tables stopped working and looked at Juno. 'Back to work,' Miss Petra said, clapping her hands.

The girls lowered their heads and hurriedly got back to work.

Miss Petra sat down next to Juno and placed a hand on her shoulder. 'Have you spoken to Harriet about what happened?'

'Yes, miss. I am to report to her after breakfast. Am I in trouble, miss?'

Miss Petra gave Juno a tender look. 'Boys should not be in our orchard. Give your report to Harriet, and once I have read it we will chat.'

'Okay, miss.'

'What is the problem, ladies?' Miss Petra said, clapping her hands again. 'I don't hear any sorting, washing or preparing.'

'Sorry, miss,' the girls said in unison.

Juno lowered her eyes and continued sorting pears into the baskets. The pears continued their journey from the baskets to the cleaning pots. After that, girls peeled and pipped the pears, then placed them in baking trays and boiling pots.

Tilly, Juno's best friend, slipped onto the bench beside Juno and said, 'I hear you were late. Everyone is talking about it.'

'Trouble in the orchard,' Juno said, checking a pear before placing it into the right sorting pot.

Tilly stared wide-eyed at Juno. 'Trouble? What do you mean, trouble? Are you okay?'

'I can't tell you now. Everyone is staring and whispering and I need to finish sorting,' Juno said, grabbing a pear from her basket and dropping it into a sorting basket. 'I am okay, Tilly, I promise. Let's talk later.'

'Herbs, please, Tilly,' Miss Petra said from the cooking stations.

'Yes, miss,' Tilly said, jumping up and running over.

Miss Petra took a bundle of herbs from Tilly, placed them onto a chopping board and furiously chopped them into tiny bits. Tilly skipped back along the tables and sat down opposite Juno.

'Help me put the remaining pears into the pantry,' Juno said. 'Make sure you wrap them properly this time.'

Tilly rolled her eyes. 'Okay, miss bossy.'

The school bell clanged, signalling the start of breakfast. They left the kitchen and followed a stream of students into the dining hall, where they sat at their designated tables. Each year's prefect sat at the table's head so they could watch the girls eat with a trained eye.

'Remember, forks in the left hand, ladies,' Harriet said, tapping the bottom of her knife on the table. 'Tilly, other hand.'

Tilly swapped her cutlery, then poked Juno in the ribs with her elbow. 'Tell me what happened. I can't wait any longer.'

'Elbows, ladies. Keep them off the table. Brenda, don't tilt your head when you are drinking,' Harriet said, picking up her glass and showing Brenda how to do it.

'Three boys in the orchard stealing apples,' Juno said with a mouth full of food.

Tilly leaned forwards. 'Three boys? What did they look like? I have only seen one boy before.'

'Mr Hargreaves? He is hardly a boy, Tilly. He is a full-grown man.'

'No, not Mr Hargreaves,' Tilly said, her fork hovering an inch from her mouth.

Juno frowned at her friend. 'What boy, then?'

'Tilly, Juno, what is going on with the two of you?' Harriet said.

'Sorry, miss,' Juno said, glaring at Tilly.

The bell sounded for the end of breakfast, signalling for the first-year students to clear the cutlery from the tables. The second- to fifth-year students chatted quietly, their backs straight and their hands folded neatly in their laps. With the cutlery cleared, the prefects signalled to the students that they could leave the dining hall. Juno and Tilly walked back to their dorm and sat at Harriet's table, waiting for her to get back.

'The two of you had a lot to say at breakfast, didn't you?' Harriet said, sitting at her desk.

Tilly clasped her hands in her lap. 'Sorry, Harriet, I wanted to know about these boys.'

Harriet gave Tilly an exasperated look, then turned to Juno. 'Tell me what happened.'

Juno went over the events at the orchard, but decided to leave out the kitten.

Harriet, pursing her lips, said, 'Did any of them say their names?'

'Billy, Travis and Simon,' Juno said.

Harriet scribbled in her notebook. 'I have never heard these names before, which means they are not from around here. I will let Miss Petra know, but for now keep it quiet. We don't want gossip disturbing anybody's lessons.'

Juno and Tilly nodded.

'Off you go,' Harriet said, waving her hand.

Juno and Tilly made their way to their beds at the back of the dorm.

'You're not telling me everything, Juno. I know you too well,' Tilly said, sitting cross-legged on Juno's bed.

Juno lifted a finger to her lips. 'I will tell you later. We have to go to lessons.'

Tilly huffed and folded her arms. Juno grabbed her school bags and walked out of her dorm. She crossed the courtyard and walked into the classroom section of the school, with Tilly close behind.

'First lesson is with Miss Taylor, and you know how much I love history,' Tilly said, rolling her eyes.

'I love history,' Juno said, sitting down at her desk and opening her book. 'The battles of lands far away to save the City of Lynn sound so romantic. I hope one day a boy chooses me and takes me to the City of Lynn.'

'A boy is going to choose you for your expert fruit picking,' Tilly said, 'not because you can tell them about a battle that happened centuries ago.'

Juno rested her chin on her hands as she listened to Miss Taylor speak of cities and towns in the south. Tilly drew in a deep breath, puffed out her cheeks, then let it out slowly while rolling her eyes. The bell clanged, signalling the end of history class. Tilly grabbed Juno's hand and dragged her through the school towards the greenhouse for their next lesson.

'Can you slow down?' Juno said, huffing behind Tilly.

'I have my flowers to check on,' Tilly said. 'Miss Poppy says if I carry on with what I am doing she will let me run the greenhouses next term.'

'Herbalism is so boring, and Miss Poppy is crazy,' Juno said, twirling her finger around the side of her head.

'Running the greenhouse is a big deal, Juno. If I get it this term, I will be in charge of it for our last year.'

'Better you than me. That place is enormous and filled with bugs that love me more than anyone else.'

'Yet you have no trouble beating up boys,' Tilly said, smirking.

Juno gave Tilly an exasperated smile.

Miss Poppy rattled off the names of plants as she led the students through the greenhouse. Tilly saw to the watering and pruning of her flowers. The rest of the day dragged by with lessons in etiquette, home-keeping, language and weaving. When the last bell rang, they walked to the dorm and collapsed onto Tilly's bed.

Tilly crossed her legs and poked Juno in the arm. 'Tell me everything.' Juno scanned the dorm, leaned in close and told her about the kitten.

Tilly's face contorted with anger. 'How can anyone hurt a kitten?'

Juno waved a hand in her face. 'Keep your voice down.'

Tilly covered her mouth with both hands, and through her fingers she said, 'Sorry.'

Juno scanned the dorm again, checking for any eavesdroppers. 'She is under my bed in my secret hiding place.'

Tilly's eyes turned into saucers. 'She is under your bed? If

Miss Petra finds out, she will punish us. You know the rules, Juno.'

Juno frowned. 'When have you ever cared about the rules?'

'I don't break the big rules,' Tilly said.

'I haven't told anybody but you, so keep it to yourself,' Juno said, placing a finger on her lips.

Tilly tapped a finger on Juno's forearm. 'Can we see her now?'

'Not now. There are too many people about,' Juno said, scanning the dorm again.

Tilly glanced over at Juno's bed. 'Okay, when? I really want to see her.'

'We can check when everyone is asleep.'

Tilly's fist pumped the air. 'Yes,' she said, her bright blue eyes shining.

'Quiet,' Juno said, raising her eyebrows. 'It's nearly time for dinner. We'd better behave tonight. I think Harriet will be watching us.'

Tilly slapped her hands over her mouth. 'Sorry,' she said through her fingers.

After dinner they entered the study rooms, which were next to their dorms. The rows of desks encircled areas of couches and cushions where groups of girls sat and chatted while working through their homework. Juno sat at a desk with the study room entrance behind her. She slid her books onto the table and flipped open her history book. Tilly sat opposite and chewed her pencil while working through names of plants in her herbalism book.

'We heard you were off with some boys in the orchard,' Erica, the school bully, said, standing behind Juno.

Tilly's head jerked up. Her eyes narrowing, she muttered under her breath. 'Go away, Erica.'

Juno spun round. 'They were stealing pears. I had to chase them away,' she said, her ears turning pink.

'Sure you did,' Erica said, winking at her friends. 'You are always up to something, Juno. That's the person you get when they don't have a mummy or daddy.'

Juno stood. 'Don't you ever speak about my parents. They sent me here a long time ago to become a proper lady.'

'Have you ever met them? Have you received any letters?' Erica said, holding up a letter from her father. 'Have you, orphan?'

Tilly scraped her chair back and stalked around the table. 'Back off, Erica,' she said, jabbing a finger at her.

Erica curled a lip. 'She has no parents. Orphans shouldn't be in charge of the orchard.'

Tilly took a step forwards. 'Juno deserves to be in charge of the orchard.'

Erica huffed. 'Juno only got the orchard because she is Miss Petra's favourite.'

Tilly's face scrunched up in anger. 'No, she didn't. She got it because she is a better fruit picker than you.'

Juno placed a hand on Tilly's shoulder. 'It's okay. Just ignore them.'

'Miss Petra is the only mummy you will ever have,' Erica said, her voice turning sing-song. 'We know she found you abandoned near the river. Poor little orphan girl with no parents.'

Juno gritted her teeth. 'You leave Miss Petra alone.'

'Whatever,' Erica said, waving a dismissive hand. 'Lowlife orphans don't belong in this school. You will never become a genuine proper lady.'

'We are not afraid of you, bully,' Tilly said, taking another step forwards.

Erica raised her hands in the air and took a step backwards. 'Let's go, girls. Remember, orphan, you cannot hide forever. I am always watching.'

'I am warning you, Erica,' Tilly said. 'Leave her alone.'

Juno sat and rested her head in her hands. 'Why does she hate me so much?'

'Because you are more of a lady than she will ever be.'

Juno took in a deep breath and smiled at her best friend. 'Thanks, Tilly.'

Tilly's grin beamed across the table. Her eyes widened as Harriet appeared around the door.

'Time to wrap up, ladies. Lights out in ten minutes.'

Juno packed up her books and followed Tilly into their dorm.

Tilly, dressing for bed, waved her hand at Juno. 'Hurry, I want to see this kitten.'

'Keep it down. We don't even know if she is still there,' Juno said, eyeing the dorm.

'I think she will still be there. Where would she go?'

Juno climbed into her bed and watched Harriet move through the dorm to blow out the torches that hung on the walls. She pulled the covers up to her chin and smiled at her friend, who lay fidgeting under her covers. The dorm quietened down as, one by one, the girls fell asleep. Juno chuckled as Tilly reached her hand out of her covers and gave Juno a slow, dramatic thumbs-up. Juno slid out of the covers and crawled under her bed.

'Move over,' Tilly said, crawling alongside her.

Juno slid an oil lamp in front of her and lit the wick. A soft light spread out under the bed.

Tilly's mouth fell open. 'She is beautiful, isn't she?'

Juno stroked the kitten's ears. 'Can you see how massive her paws are? They are bigger than any cat I have seen before.'

Tilly ran a finger along the kitten's paw. 'Look at her enormous eyes.'

Juno leaned in closer. 'They have those tiny red flecks in them.'

Tilly scrunched up her nose. 'She has caught something and eaten it. Look at the bones beside her.'

'Looks like a rat or a mouse. At least we don't have to worry about feeding her,' Juno said, poking the bones.

'What are you going to call her?' Tilly said. 'What about "The Huntress"? Or "Killer Queen"?'

Juno smirked. 'I don't know if we are even going to keep her yet. I am sure she belongs to someone.'

'She can't belong to a girl. Most of us are here at the school. Why don't we make signs and put them up around the village?' Tilly said. 'Maybe a boy has lost her.'

The kitten purred as Juno continued to stroke her under her chin. 'And say what? "Come to the school and pick up your kitten"?'

Tilly thought for a moment. 'This is not a smart idea, Juno. They will take the orchard away from you and the greenhouse away from me if they catch us hiding a kitten.'

'What do you suggest we do? I can't just throw her out of the school.'

Tilly sighed. 'I don't know.'

Juno jumped, and banged her head on the bed.

Tilly clapped her hand over her mouth. 'What happened? You scared me.'

'She bit me,' Juno said, sucking her bleeding finger while rubbing the top of her head.

Tilly shook her head at the kitten. 'Bad kitty, biting people.'

Juno looked at the two holes in her finger. 'That really hurt.'

Tilly looked Juno's finger over. 'You will be fine. I think we should get back to bed before someone sees us.'

'We will need to decide what to do with her,' Juno said. 'We can't leave her here forever.'

'I think we should tell Harriet tomorrow. She will know what to do,' Tilly said. 'We can say we found her under your bed, so it doesn't look like you brought her back.'

Juno gave Tilly a nod, then patted the kitten gently on the head. 'Sleep tight, little mouse murderer.'

'Killer Queen,' Tilly said, pulling a face at the pile of bones.

Juno climbed back into bed and pulled the covers up to her chin. She lifted her hand and frowned at the pins and needles that ran along her bitten finger. Her eyes growing heavy, she let out a sigh and fell sound asleep.

Juno shook Tilly awake. 'Tilly, wake up. Tilly, look at my finger.'

Tilly sat up and rubbed the sleep out of her eyes. 'What is that? Does it hurt?'

'No. I felt pins and needles in my finger last night, then I woke up this morning and this red mark was here.'

Tilly pulled Juno's hand closer and narrowed her eyes. 'It looks like a little flame.'

'Do you think I caught something from the kitten when she bit me?'

Tilly rubbed her fingers over the mark a little harder. 'I don't know.'

'The kitten did this somehow. It wasn't there before.'

'I don't see how,' Tilly said, frowning down at Juno's hand.

'I need to get to the orchard. I don't want to be late again,' Juno said, climbing off Tilly's bed. 'Miss Petra will get upset.'

Tilly pulled Juno back. 'You need to show Harriet. That mark isn't something you can ignore.'

Juno climbed off Tilly's bed and pulled on her fruit-picking clothes. She slung her wicker basket onto her back. 'I will show her when I get back. I promise.'

The kitten poked her head out from under the bed. She looked at Juno, then darted across the floor and sprang into the wicker basket.

Juno looked over at Tilly with her eyebrows raised. 'Looks like she is going with you.'

The kitten's nose twitched up at Juno. She licked her sharp teeth, then dropped her head onto her paws.

'What if she bites me again?' Juno said, glancing at her finger.

Tilly shrugged. 'Try to stay away from her, I guess. She is just a kitten, Juno.'

With a sigh, Juno made her way out of the school, through the courtyard and onto the dirt path towards the orchard. The kitten poked her head out of the basket, then sprang out onto the dirt path and walked alongside Juno. Juno gave her a weary look. The orchard gate swung open with a squeal. The kitten growled as she darted into the tall grass, her sharp claws extended. Juno chose a row of pear trees. Feeling each pear for ripeness, she plucked the ripe ones and tossed them into her wicker basket. The kitten's head popped up out of the tall grass. Her ears twitched as the sounds of the orchard danced through the morning light.

'Nearly done,' Juno said, moving to the last tree in the row.

The kitten stalked past Juno and growled with her teeth bared at a rustle in the grass. A bird shot up into the air, squawking in terror as the kitten pounced. The bird landed on the topmost branch of a pear tree and bobbed its head. Juno walked to the back of the orchard and sat with her back against the trunk of the gnarled tree. The kitten pranced up to her and purred as she rubbed her head against Juno's leg.

Juno stroked the kitten's head. 'Have you got something to do with this?' she said, showing the kitten the flame on her finger.

The kitten lowered her belly to the ground and growled, her hairs bristling along the length of her back.

'Oh look, it's the little girl with the kitten,' Simon said, hopping over the orchard fence.

Billy leaned on the other side of the fence. 'Leave her alone, Simon.'

Juno scrambled to her feet.

Simon gave Billy an exasperated look. 'Why do you keep following me?'

'To stop you from doing something dumb,' Billy said, spreading his hands.

'She will not get away with breaking my nose,' Simon said, pointing at the white tape over the bridge of his nose.

'We will both get lashes if we stay here,' Billy said with a tilt of his head.

Simon turned on Billy. 'You need to back off, Billy, or Travis and I will break your nose next.'

Billy held up his hand. 'Okay, but you know you're just going to get hurt again.'

Juno grabbed a pear out of her basket. The kitten, hissing and spitting, prowled between her legs.

Simon picked up a branch and stripped it of its dead leaves. 'I am going to teach this girl a lesson,' he said, slashing it in front of him.

Juno threw the pear as hard as she could, hitting Simon on the shoulder. Simon smirked. 'Missed,' he said, taking a step towards Juno.

The kitten sprang forwards and sank her teeth into Simon's ankle. Simon yelped, dropped the stick and kicked the kitten, sending her flying across the orchard.

'You mean, horrible boy,' Juno said between clenched teeth.

Simon laughed, then walked up to Juno and slapped the back of his hand across her face. Juno hit the ground and rolled onto her hands and knees. The kitten went up to Juno and stood in front of her with her claws extended. A sudden roar filled Juno's ears. The pins and needles in her finger turned to stabbing pain. A flash of yellow exploded in front of her eyes. Juno gasped and collapsed face first into the grass, her eyes closing as the darkness took her.

The kitten meowed and licked the side of Juno's face. Juno's eyes opened. 'What happened?' she groaned.

The kitten's nose twitched, and her tail swished from side to side.

Juno crawled to the kitten. 'Are you okay? That horrible boy kicked you hard.'

The kitten tilted her head and stared at Juno with unblinking eyes. The red flecks swam around her honey-coloured irises. Juno shook her head to clear the fog that filled her senses. Sitting back on her heels, she rubbed her hands together. Tendrils of white smoke floated up from the branch that had been in Simon's hands. Stumbling to her feet and resting her hands on her knees, Juno sucked in a few deep breaths.

'What is happening to me?' Juno said.

The kitten walked up to the smouldering stick and sniffed it.

Juno pressed her hands on her knees to straighten to a stand. 'Hello?' she said, scanning the orchard. 'Billy?'

The kitten meowed as she walked up to Juno's wicker basket and sprang in.

CHAPTER 2
THE REPLACEMENT

Juno stumbled into the dorm, dropped her basket and climbed onto her bed.

'What's wrong?' Tilly said, scooting to the edge of her bed.

Juno stared at the dorm wall. 'I think I hurt someone, Tilly.'

Tilly jumped off her bed and lifted Juno's chin. 'Why is your face red?'

'Those boys were there again and one of them hit me.'

'What?' Tilly said, her voice echoing through the dorm.

Harriet scraped her chair back and marched across the dorm. 'Tilly, you know the rules about shouting.'

Tilly scrunched up her face. 'Those boys hit Juno, Harriet.'

Harriet's eyebrows shot into her hair. 'Let me look.'

Juno's hand rushed up to her face to cover the red mark. 'It's nothing, Harriet, I will be okay.'

'It is clearly not nothing, Juno,' Harriet said, pursing her lips. 'Both of you, come with me.'

Juno closed her eyes, exhaled and shook her head. Tilly grabbed her arm and pulled her through the dorm after Harriet. Harriet marched through the corridors to the principal's office, where she rapped her knuckles on the door.

'The door is open,' Miss Petra said.

Harriet opened the door and ushered Juno and Tilly into the office.

Miss Petra, frowning, looked over her spectacles. 'What is going on?'

'The boys I told you about have returned to the orchard. They struck Juno in the face,' Harriet said, pointing a finger at Juno.

Miss Petra removed her glasses. 'Harriet, Tilly, please continue your duties. I will speak to Juno alone.'

'But, miss, what are we going to do about these boys?' Tilly said, wagging a finger in the air.

'Tilly, I will deal with it,' Miss Petra said. 'See to your duties, please.'

Tilly grunted, then stormed out of the office. Harriet stepped out and closed the door behind her. Miss Petra walked around the desk, placed her hand under Juno's chin and lifted her head.

'It's nothing, miss,' Juno said. 'I chased the boys away.'

Miss Petra shook her head. 'I will send word to Mr Hargreaves so we can find out who these boys are.'

Juno frowned while she rubbed her cheek. 'What is that on your finger?'

Juno jerked her hand away and slid it into a pocket.

'Juno?'

'It's just a scratch from working in the orchards, miss.'

Miss Petra suddenly turned pale. She lifted a hand to her forehead and caught the side of the desk with her other hand.

'Are you okay, miss?' Juno said, grabbing Miss Petra's shoulder.

Miss Petra waved Juno away. 'I am fine.'

'Are you sure, miss?' Juno said, letting go of her shoulder and taking a step back.

'I am okay. Mr Hargreaves will be here tomorrow with my medications.'

'Okay, miss,' Juno said.

'Tomorrow I want you to take Tilly to the orchard. If those boys return, forget about picking the fruit and come straight back to school.'

'What about the fruit for breakfast, miss?' Juno said.

'We have enough food in the pantry,' Miss Petra said. 'Now off you go. Get your fruit into the kitchen.'

'Thank you, miss,' Juno said, opening the door and walking out. She glanced back at Miss Petra, her face etched with concern. Juno ran down the corridor and into the dorm, where she retrieved her fruit basket. The wicker basket straps pulled against her shoulders as she hiked the fruit into the kitchen. She placed the basket on the table, and one by one she checked each pear before placing it into the sorting basket.

'What did she say?' Tilly said, sitting on the opposite side of the table.

'She asked that you come with me to the orchard tomorrow.'

Tilly groaned. 'You know how I hate mornings.'

'If the boys come again, Miss Petra says we should come back to the school.'

'After I have kicked them back to the village,' Tilly said with a grunt.

'As much as I would love to see that, Miss Petra says we need to come straight back,' Juno said.

Tilly let out a sigh.

'Tilly, Miss Petra isn't well. She was very pale when I left.'

Tilly looked up. 'Did she tell you what's wrong?'

Juno shook her head. 'No, but she was swaying on her feet. I am worried about her.'

Tilly stood and gave Juno a hug. 'I know she is like a mother to you. I am sure she will be fine.'

Juno squeezed Tilly, then continued with her fruit. Working together, the two girls cleaned the fruit then placed them in the sorting baskets. The breakfast bell rang, and they joined the chattering girls in the dining room. Harriet gave Juno a thumbs-up from the head of the table. Juno gave her a tight-lipped smile.

'Miss Petra isn't here,' Tilly said, looking over her shoulder at the head table. 'I have never known her to miss breakfast.'

Juno gave Tilly a worried look. 'Maybe I should ask Harriet?'

'After breakfast,' Tilly said with a nod.

The bell sounded for the end of breakfast. Juno scraped her chair back and headed back to the dormitory, where she waited on her bed.

'Can you two come here, please?' Harriet said from her desk. Juno and Tilly walked over and sat in the chairs opposite Harriet.

'After what happened to Juno this morning, I am giving both of you the day off. Don't wander too far away from the school.'

Tilly's fist pumped the air. 'Let's go to the orchard and pick tomorrow's fruit. Then we don't have to get up so early tomorrow.'

Harriet raised an eyebrow. 'I said you could have the day off, Tilly. Picking fruit is Juno's job.'

Tilly paused. 'Sorry.'

Juno chuckled. 'That's okay. I think it is a good idea.'

'Off you go, then,' Harriet said, waving a hand.

Juno cleared her throat. 'Harriet, after you left, Miss Petra didn't look well.'

Harriet inclined her head. 'She is fine, Juno. She just needs her medicine, which Mr Hargreaves will bring.'

'Okay,' Juno said, biting her lip.

Tilly jumped up and ran back to their beds. 'Let's get the kitten and take her with us.'

Juno pulled her wicker basket off the wall. 'Come on. In you get, little girl.'

The kitten darted from the hole and jumped into the basket.

Juno slung the wicker basket over her shoulder. 'She is getting bigger,' she said, following Tilly out of the side exit.

Tilly skipped down the dirt path past Juno. 'It's been a long time since I have been in your orchard,' she said over her shoulder.

Juno crouched and tipped the wicker basket. The kitten sprang out and ran off towards the orchard. 'Nothing has changed in the orchard. Except the fruit trees are older.'

Tilly skipped back up the path and hooked her hand through Juno's arm. 'I didn't tell you everything about this morning,' Juno said, looking at her friend.

Tilly gave Juno a surprised look. 'What do you mean?'

'Let me show you,' Juno said, opening the gate to the orchard. She walked down to the gnarled tree and crouched next to the ashen stick. 'The boy, Simon, tried to hit me with this stick.'

Tilly growled under her breath. 'I hope Miss Petra and Harriet do something about this.'

Juno pulled Tilly down into a crouch. 'It's not a stick anymore. It's a pile of ash.'

Tilly frowned. 'What are you saying?'

Juno sat down and crossed her legs. 'I don't know what happened. I remember him coming at me with that stick, and then the kitten bit him. He let go of the stick then slapped me. I was on my hands and knees, and then it felt like my finger exploded.'

Tilly gave Juno a confused look.

'I sound crazy,' Juno said, closing her eyes and shaking her head.

Tilly placed a hand on her arm. 'You know I don't think you are crazy. Can you remember anything at all?'

Juno shook her head. 'I woke up with a nasty headache, no boys, and a smouldering stick on the ground.'

The kitten, growling, darted past them and pounced into the tall grass. Tilly looked over and chuckled.

'Don't know what to do with her now,' Juno said, peering at the kitten.

Tilly let out a sigh. 'We are going to have to ask Harriet.'

'Okay. Shall we just say we found her today?'

'Good idea,' Tilly said.

Juno and Tilly lounged around the orchard for the rest of the day. The kitten, bored with its hunting, curled up next to Juno and slept under the afternoon sun.

'I think we'd better fill my basket and make our way back,' Juno said, sitting up and stretching. 'The sun is going down.'

Tilly darted from tree to tree and threw the pears over to Juno. Juno caught them and placed them into her wicker basket.

'That's it,' Juno said, counting the pears.

'Just in time,' Tilly said, looking at the last sliver of the setting sun.

The kitten hopped through the wooden fence and followed Juno and Tilly up the winding dirt path towards the school. In the distance, the street candles in the village flickered to life as the lamplighter extended his pole into the wicks.

As they approached the school's east entrance, Tilly looked over her shoulder at the kitten. 'How do we do this?'

Juno handed Tilly her basket, bent down and picked up the kitten. She kicked the door open, entered and walked up to Harriet's desk.

'What have we here?' Harriet said, reaching over the desk and scratching the kitten behind the ears.

'We just found her in the orchard,' Juno said.

Harriet smiled. 'She is a darling. And also very big for a kitten.'

'What do we do with her?' Juno said, turning the kitten around and looking into her amber eyes. 'Are we allowed to keep her?'

'You know the rules, Juno,' Harriet said. 'No animals in the school.'

Juno bent over and let the kitten go. 'Okay, but we can't just throw her out.'

Harriet watched the kitten run to the back of the dorm. 'We will need to ask around the village. Someone might have lost her.'

'We can do that tomorrow,' Tilly said, smiling at Juno.

'If nobody claims the kitten, we will need to speak to Miss Petra,' Harriet said.

'Okay,' Juno said. 'Tilly, let's get this fruit to the pantry.'

Tilly nodded and walked out of the dorm and down to the kitchen. Dinner came and went, the girls chatting among themselves about the whereabouts of Miss Petra. Juno and Tilly left the dining room, sat on their beds and finished the homework that Harriet had collected for them during the day. At bedtime, Harriet walked through the dorm and extinguished the torches on the walls. Juno climbed into bed and pulled the sheets up to her chin. A smile spread across her face as the loud purrs of the kitten drifted up from underneath her bed.

Juno woke, sat up in her bed and rubbed the sleep out of her eyes. 'Tilly? Where are you?' she said, looking over at Tilly's empty bed.

Tilly, dodging through the beds, came running through the dorm and stopped in front of Juno. Her eyes wide, she looked wildly across the dorm.

'What's wrong?' Juno said, sliding out of bed and grabbing her shoulders.

Tilly took a few deep breaths and said, 'Something is wrong with Miss Petra. Harriet has asked us to wait by our beds.'

'I knew it. I should have done something yesterday,' Juno said, sitting back down on her bed.

Tilly paced between the beds. 'What do you think is the matter? The school seems very quiet.'

The dorm door opened and Harriet, her eyes red, walked over to their beds.

Juno frowned. 'What is going on, Harriet?'

'Miss Petra,' Harriet said. 'She died during the night.'

Tilly stopped pacing and stared at Harriet. Juno's mouth opened and closed with no sounds coming out.

'I am sorry,' Harriet said, spreading her arms and pulling them both into a hug. 'I am so sorry.'

Juno pulled away. 'How?' she said, her voice a hoarse whisper.

Harriet dragged a sleeve over her eyes. 'I don't know.'

Mr Hargreaves rapped his knuckles against the dormitory door. 'You have all heard of what has happened to Miss Petra. Please can everyone make their way to the dining hall.'

'Yes, Mr Hargreaves,' Harriet said, walking back over to her desk.

Mr Hargreaves left the room, leaving the girls in a stunned silence.

'I know this is sudden,' Harriet said, her voice cracking. 'But we need to get to the dining hall. Follow me.'

The girls moved out into the corridor and down into the dining hall. Silence filled the room. Mr Hargreaves, tall and lanky with a twitching moustache, walked into the dining hall and stood at the head table.

He cleared his throat. 'I am sorry to announce such bad news. Miss Petra passed during the night. We will hold a ceremony this afternoon near the orchards. Your prefects will advise you on the details. Miss Petra's replacement will join us tomorrow.'

Mr Hargreaves scanned the room, gave a nod, then left.

'Is that it?' Tilly said, looking up the table at Harriet. 'Why are they not telling us what happened?'

'Tilly,' Harriet said, shaking a finger at her.

Tilly sat back in her chair and folded her arms.

The head girl moved to the front of the head table. 'Today

there will be no lessons. Your prefects will pass on any information that we get from Mr Hargreaves. Dismissed.'

The corridors echoed with whispers and murmurs. Juno and Tilly, on their way to their dorm, walked straight into Erica and her friends.

'Nobody to protect you now, orphan,' Erica said with a wicked sneer.

Juno continued walking. Tilly turned her head and opened her mouth to say something.

'Don't,' Juno said, dragging Tilly with her. 'It's what she wants us to do.'

Tilly flashed Erica a snarl. Juno entered the dorm and sat on Tilly's bed. She looked down at her hand and rubbed the mark on her finger.

Tilly wrapped her arms around Juno. 'We should get out of here. Shall we go to the orchard?'

Juno nodded. 'Okay.'

'I can't believe she has gone,' Juno said, walking next to Tilly on the dusty, winding path. 'I am scared, Tilly. Everything is going to change. Miss Petra ran everything in our school.'

'I am scared too,' Tilly said, kicking a stone down the path. 'I still can't believe they have found a replacement already. Something odd is going on and I can't get it out of my head.'

They entered the orchard and followed the pear trees to the old gnarled tree.

Juno froze. 'We forgot the kitten.'

Tilly slapped her forehead. 'Shall we go back for her?'

'She will be okay,' Juno said, walking up to the gnarled tree. 'She can find us if she wants to.'

The gnarled tree's twisted branches rustled in the slight breeze. Tilly sat with her back to one of the tree roots and rested her head onto her folded arms. Juno, sniffing away the tears, sat next to her and draped her arm over Tilly's shoulders. A growl reverberated from somewhere in the orchard. An amber cat padded out from behind a tree, her tail in the air.

Juno lifted her head. 'Tilly,' she said, elbowing her.

'What?' Tilly said, her head still resting on her arms.

'The kitten,' Juno said. 'Look how big she is.'

Tilly lifted her head and gasped. 'What the hell? How did she get that big?'

The cat, purring from deep down in her chest, padded over to Juno and Tilly with her tail high in the air.

'She is the size of a cat,' Juno said, a confused look spreading across her face.

Tilly reached over and stroked the cat's head. 'Are you sure it's the same one? This could be her mother.'

Juno picked the cat up and placed her on her lap. 'No, this is the same one. The red flecks in her eyes are in the same place.'

Tilly held up the cat's paw. 'She is going to grow bigger still. Her paw is the size of my palm.'

Juno scratched the cat under her ear, sending her into purrs of pleasure. 'Miss Petra told me about a cat she had when she was young,' Tilly said.

'Her name was Chax,' Juno said. 'She was also a stray.'

'Chax,' Tilly said. 'I like it. Let's call her Chax.'

The school bell clanged, breaking the peace of the orchard. Juno hauled herself up and dusted off her clothes. She extended a hand and helped Tilly to her feet. Chax looked up at the school, sniffed the air and snorted.

'We need to get going,' Tilly said. 'It's breakfast time.'

'Not really hungry,' Juno said. 'I am going to skip breakfast.'

Tilly grabbed a pear from a low branch. 'This will keep me going,' she said, biting into the pear. 'I can skip it too.'

They looped their arms together and walked back to the school. At the courtyard entrance Chax sniffed the air and snorted again. Juno removed her arm from Tilly and walked back to Chax and tried to pick her up. Chax took a step back, turned and stalked back down the dirt path.

'Do you want to go after her?' Tilly said, placing her hands on her hips.

Juno watched Chax disappear down the dirt path. 'No. I think she will stay in the orchard.'

'Okay,' Tilly said, turning Juno round and leading her back to school.

Juno walked into the eerily silent dorm and sat cross-legged on her bed.

Harriet, her eyes a light pink, walked over and sat on the end of Juno's bed. 'Not hungry either, I see?'

Juno shook her head.

'We are all going to make something to leave with Miss Petra at the ceremony this afternoon.'

Juno rubbed her eyes with the heels of her hands. 'I don't have anything I can leave with her.'

Tilly climbed onto Juno's bed. 'We can make something from the greenhouse. A lot of my flowers are blooming.'

'I think she would like that,' Harriet said.

Juno and Tilly spent the rest of the morning picking colourful flowers in the greenhouse. Early in the afternoon they wove the flowers to create a wreath. The last touches done, they lay on their beds and waited.

'It's time,' Harriet called from her desk. 'Follow me and keep together.' The girls walked through the courtyard and down the dirt path. They turned left at the orchard and worked their way to the river that wound its way past the back end of the school. A small bridge over the river led to a graveyard filled with multiple-sized headstones. At the centre of the graveyard stood a crypt, where the school had buried previous principals. A brand new plaque with Miss Petra's name shone in the late afternoon sunlight. One by one, the girls walked past and placed what they had made at the foot of the crypt. Juno, arm in arm with Tilly, walked up to the crypt and laid their multi-flowered wreath against the wall.

'Thank you for everything you have done for me,' Juno said. Their arms still hooked together, Juno and Tilly walked back through the graveyard and over the bridge.

They entered the school and returned to their dorms, where Juno climbed into her bed and pulled the covers up over her head. She placed a hand over her mouth to stop the sounds of her sobs echoing through the dorm.

The Saturday morning sun shone brightly through the windows of the dining hall. Juno and Tilly sat waiting for breakfast. Nervous whispers bounced off the walls as they waited for Mr Hargreaves's entrance. The dining hall doors banged open and Mr Hargreaves strode in. Gasps filled the hall as everyone set eyes on the woman following Mr Hargreaves to the head table. Her long, blonde, wavy hair reached down to the middle of her back. Sky-blue eyes spread wide apart smiled whenever she smiled. A flowing gown sparkled as she walked through the rays of sunlight from the windows. She walked up to Miss Petra's seat, sat and folded one leg over the other, placing her hands in her lap.

Mr Hargreaves stood at the head table. 'This is Miss Lady,' he said, with his eyes darting in her direction. 'She is Miss Petra's replacement. She has just finished her role in the institute of teaching in the City of Lynn and is now following her dream of being the principal for our esteemed school. I am sure you will all welcome her with open arms.'

Miss Lady stood and placed her hands behind her back. 'Thank you, Mr Hargreaves, and good morning, ladies. I am so glad to be here and to be your next principal. I hope I can fill the shoes of Miss Petra, who I know you all loved very much. Today I will meet with the head girl and prefects, and then I hope I will get to know you all.' Miss Lady sat back down, crossed her legs and, with a smile, inclined her head in Juno's direction.

Juno, shivering, wrapped her arms around herself and placed her hands under her armpits.

'Thank you, Miss Lady,' Mr Hargreaves said. 'I trust you will treat Miss Lady with the same respect you treated Miss Petra. Please continue your daily activities as per usual. Thank you.'

Mr Hargreaves offered Miss Lady his hand and escorted her out of the dining hall.

'She looks wonderful. Like a princess,' Tilly said. 'I can't wait to meet her.'

Juno flexed her hands. 'Something doesn't seem right to me.'

Tilly rolled her eyes. 'Come on, Juno, you don't know her yet.'

'Did you not feel the air turn cold when she walked in?' Juno said.

Tilly shook her head. 'What are you talking about?'

'I thought you were suspicious of someone replacing Miss Petra so soon?'

'I know, but look at how beautiful she is. She will teach us how to be proper ladies.'

Juno gave Tilly an exasperated look. She scraped her chair back and made her way back to their dorm.

'I am going to go to the greenhouse,' Tilly said, walking into the dorm. 'Do you want to come with me?'

Juno rubbed her temples. 'I think I am going to rest for a bit. I will come and find you soon.'

Tilly threw her arms around Juno and gave her a tight squeeze. 'I can stay if you want.'

'No, it's okay,' Juno said. 'Go. I will be fine.'

'Okay. You know where to find me,' Tilly said.

Juno climbed onto her bed and rested her head on her pillow. She lifted her finger and rubbed the tiny red flame. Pins and needles throbbed out from it. She sighed, rolled onto her side and placed her hands under her head. The cold of the dining room began to disappear as she snuggled deeper into her bed. Her eyes gently closed.

'Wake up, sleepy head, it's dinner time,' Tilly said, shaking Juno by the shoulder.

Juno sat up and stretched. 'Dinner time? Have I slept the whole day?'

'Yes, you must have needed it. We are having a feast tonight to welcome Miss Lady. It's going to start in a few minutes. I have put your clothes on the end of your bed.'

'Thanks, Tilly,' Juno said, slipping out of her bed.

They left the dorm and walked through the corridors to the dining room. Juno scraped her chair back and took her place at the dining room table.

Miss Lady strode in and took her place at the head table. 'Good evening, ladies,' she said.

The schoolgirls, their eyes bright with expectation, replied with their own good-evenings.

'Miss Petra has let the discipline of this school relax a little too much. If I were a well-to-do gentleman and I wished to choose a proper lady, my choices would be unsatisfactory,' Miss Lady said with a stern face.

The girls sat silently, their eyes staring at Miss Lady.

'Miss Petra was probably a lovely lady, but from this point on I will be teaching you how to be proper ladies.'

Tilly elbowed Juno. 'You see? I told you.'

Juno wrapped her arms around herself.

The first-year students walked out of the kitchen holding trays piled high with sweet-smelling food. They slid the trays into the centre of the dining tables.

'Presented before you is a feast. A feast I expect you all to cook before you leave this school,' Miss Lady said, waving a hand across the tables. 'Prefects, you may begin.'

Harriet raised a hand and signalled to the girls on her table to begin.

Tilly reached over and forked food onto her plate. 'Everything is going to be fine with Miss Lady. She seems strict, but it will be for our benefit.'

'Tilly, it's happening again. The air is turning cold,' Juno said with a shiver.

Tilly stopped forking food onto her plate. 'I can't feel it at all. Are you sure you are okay?'

Juno glanced at the new principal. Miss Lady turned her eyes on Juno. Her pupils expanded into her crystal blue irises. She stared unblinking at Juno with black and white eyes. Juno ducked her head down and looked at Miss Lady through her eyebrows. Miss Lady lifted her hands and spread her fingers. Words Juno had never heard before escaped Miss Lady's lips. Tendrils of dark grey smoke snaked from her fingertips and floated down over the students.

Juno nudged Tilly. 'Can you see that, Tilly? Can you see the smoke coming out of her fingers?'

'What are you on about?' Tilly said, scooping another fork of food into her mouth. 'Eat something, will you?'

Juno gritted her teeth. The mark on her finger pulsed pins and needles down it.

Miss Lady's fingers waved more tendrils of smoke over the students. The smoke sank, then darted into the girls' ears.

'Tilly,' Juno said, 'the smoke is going into everyone's ears.'

Tilly, staring straight ahead, reached for another piece of food. Her bright blue irises receded as the blackness of her pupils expanded out. Juno's eyes darted across the rest of the dining room. The students sat straight and rigid. Silent and staring. Smiles spreading across their faces.

'They are all mine now, young Juno,' Miss Lady said, making Juno jump. 'They will all do as I say.'

Juno's chair flew out from underneath her as she jumped up. She glanced at Tilly, who hadn't even flinched as the chair clattered to the ground. Miss Lady stood and started walking towards her. Juno turned and fled out of the dining room.

'Where are you going, young Juno?' Miss Lady said, her voice echoing through the corridors.

Juno ran through the passageways into her dorm and to her bed. Miss Lady's footsteps echoed down the corridor. Her tinkling laugh bounced off the walls. The dorm room banged open. Chax, growling, padded over to Juno.

'We have to get out of here. There is something wrong with Miss Lady,' Juno said.

Chax cocked her head and bared her teeth. Juno grabbed her jacket and ran out of the dorm and into the corridor.

Miss Lady, striding up the corridor, flashed a beautiful smile at Juno. 'Come to me, young Juno. You have nothing to be afraid of.'

Chax growled and dropped to her haunches. She bared her teeth and stalked towards Miss Lady. With her hands raised, Miss Lady sent grey tendrils of smoke through the air.

'Let's go,' Juno said, running to the side entrance.

Chax stopped her stalking, turned and ran towards Juno.

Juno yanked the door open and ran off into the night.

'Go and get her,' Miss Lady shouted.

CHAPTER 3
THE RESCUE

Juno hid behind the gnarled tree and listened for signs of the girls. Chax circled the tree, her muscles rippling down the length of her back. She lowered her head and snarled up at the school.

'Quiet,' Juno said, waving her hand. 'They are going to find us.'

Chax sat down next to Juno and scanned the orchard.

Juno dropped to one knee and pulled Chax towards her. 'What are we going to do now? We can't leave Tilly behind with those monsters.'

Chax lifted a paw and rested it on Juno's knee. She turned her head sharply and snarled.

'She is probably in the orchard,' Erica said from the dirt path.

Juno peered around the gnarled tree then jerked her head back as Erica and her friends opened the orchard gate. Juno crawled to the orchard fence and climbed over. Crouch-running across the cobble path, she darted into the dark, eerie forest, where she lay on her stomach behind a hedge. Chax poked her head through the hedge and meowed.

'Quiet,' Juno said, grabbing her and pulling her through.

Erica's black eyes scanned the orchard. 'Anyone see her?'

Her friends shook their heads. The school bell clanged. Erica took one more look around the orchard, then signalled for the girls to leave.

Juno waited for the girls to disappear up the dusty path. She crouch-walked across the cobble path, hopped over the orchard fence and sat with her back against the gnarled tree. As the sun faded and the breeze picked up, Juno shivered. Chax sniffed around the bottom of the gnarled tree, then snapped out her claws and climbed up into the branches. She looked down at Juno and meowed.

'I suppose you want me to climb up too?' Juno said.

Chax peered down with her big amber eyes. Juno reached up, grabbed the lowest branch and pulled herself up into the branches. Hand over hand she climbed to where Chax sat on a thick, forked branch. Juno placed her back on the tree trunk and wedged her legs into the branches. Chax jumped onto her lap and curled up into a ball.

'What is going on, Chax?' Juno said, shaking her head.

Chax turned her head towards the school and growled.

'We need to go and get Tilly in the morning,' Juno said, stroking the top of Chax's head. 'We are not leaving without her.'

Chax closed her eyes and purred loudly.

Throughout the night Juno would fall asleep then wake up with a jerk. As the thin beams of the morning sun broke through the branches, she rubbed her eyes with the palms of her hands. Opening her eyes, Juno closed her hand over her mouth. Chax stood on the end of the branch, her amber eyes staring at Juno. The red flecks surrounding the black vertical slits of Chax's irises danced and licked like flames in a fireplace. Fangs the size of pins poked out of her mouth and down over her chin.

'What are you?' Juno said through her fingers. 'This is not normal.'

Chax, now the size of a bobcat, walked along the branch and nudged Juno's knee.

Juno took a breath and, with a trembling hand, touched the top of Chax's head. 'How are you so big?'

Chax licked Juno's finger, then jumped out of the tree and into the tall grass. Juno unhooked her legs and scrambled down the trunk. Chax rolled over onto her back and waved her paws in the air. Her tail swished from side to side across the tall grass. Juno ran her fingers over Chax's neck, feeling the thick bristles of her tawny coat. Her fingers tingled with pins and needles as the heat from the mark spread out from her index finger. Juno turned her hands over, palms facing up. A fire mark sat on each finger between the knuckles. She flexed her hands as the pins and needles pulsed.

'Now I have a mark on each finger,' Juno said, frowning at Chax. 'What have you done to me?'

Chax, rolling onto all fours, tilted her head and meowed.

Juno gasped as another wave of pins and needles shot out of the flame marks and through her fingers. The clanging of the school bell rattled down into the orchard. 'That is the wake-up bell,' Juno said, worry etched across her face. 'Time to go and get Tilly.'

Chax bared her teeth at the school.

'We can sneak up along the riverbanks. Nobody should be out this early,' Juno said, walking towards the southern fence of the orchard.

Chax ambled into Juno's path and butted her head against her shins.

'I am going, Chax,' Juno said. 'I am not leaving her.'

Chax shook her head and let out a soft snort.

Juno walked around Chax and to the end of the orchard. She climbed over the low fence and walked across the dirt path. Down the small bank, the river gurgled over the outcrops of rocks littered in its bed. Juno slid down the riverbank and onto the river's edge, where she picked her way north along the moss-covered rocks until she reached the grounds of the school. She climbed the riverbank and lay flat in the dirt, her head peering over the bank edge. The well-kept lawn stretched from the river to the greenhouse. The morning dew sent sparkles across the lawn.

'Stay here,' Juno said, running her hand over Chax's head. 'I will be back with Tilly as soon as I can.'

Chax grunted, her whiskers twitching.

Keeping low, Juno ran across the open grass to the greenhouse. She lay flat against the greenhouse windows and listened. Tilly's humming floated through the air. Juno slid along the glass panels and stopped at an opening in the plants that lined the greenhouse. Inside, Tilly sat on her bench with her back towards Juno. Juno rapped her knuckles on the window until Tilly swung round.

With a wave, Tilly skipped along the path to the greenhouse door. 'Where have you been?' she said, stepping through the door. 'Miss Lady is looking for you.'

Juno brushed the hair out of Tilly's face to check her eyes. The blue of her irises shone clear and bright. 'You need to come with me,' Juno said, glancing through the door into the greenhouse. 'It is not safe here.'

'What do you mean? Everything is fine. Miss Lady is waiting for you indoors.'

Juno grabbed Tilly by the shoulders and shook her. 'Miss Lady is evil, Tilly. Come with me, please.'

The greenhouse door that led into the school swung open, and in marched Erica and her friends. 'Tilly, where are you?' Erica said. 'We are creating a search party to find Juno.'

'Tilly,' Juno said, hiding behind her. 'Come with me, please.'

'She is here with me, Erica,' Tilly said, waving through the glass pane. The greenhouse door behind Erica slammed open and in marched Miss Lady, chanting under her breath. The blue irises of Tilly's eyes receded into blackness. Tilly shook Juno's hands off her shoulders and grabbed Juno by the arm. 'Miss Lady would like to see you now,' she said, her voice turning thick.

Juno wrenched her arm out of Tilly's grip and took a step backwards.

Erica and her friends marched through the door and surrounded her. 'Miss Lady,' Erica said, rapping her knuckles on the greenhouse window. 'She is back here.'

Miss Lady hitched up her long, flowing dress and walked towards the greenhouse door. Juno felt the pins and needles in the little flame marks grow more intense. Her hands ached as the heat spread from her fingers into her palms.

'Take Juno to my office,' Miss Lady said, peering around the greenhouse door. 'Don't let her leave until I get there.'

Tilly took a step forwards with an outstretched hand. Juno took a step back and bumped into Erica, who wrapped her arms around her shoulders. Juno gritted her teeth and, with a growl, stamped on Erica's toe. With a curse, Erica let go. Juno bashed another girl out of the way and ran for the river. Chax's small, round ears poked above the bank. Shouts filled Juno's ears as Tilly, Erica and her friends chased her across the grass. The bank appeared, and Juno slid down past Chax and into the river. Chax hissed at the top of the bank, her tail swishing angrily.

Juno scrambled to her feet and hopped from rock to rock, following the river back towards the orchard. 'Chax,' she said over her shoulder. 'Follow.'

Chax scrambled along the riverbank. Her ears flat and her tail up, she bounded over branches and rocks.

'She is going to the orchard,' Erica said, running along the top of the bank.

'Check the gnarled tree at the back,' Tilly said. 'It is her favourite place.'

Juno continued in the river until she reached the small bridge, where, using her hands, she scrambled up the bank. To her right, the south fence of the orchard led her to the cobblestone road, where she leaned her hands on her knees to catch her breath.

'The gnarled tree is over there,' Tilly said, opening the orchard gate.

Miss Lady strode through the orchard gate and barked orders at the girls who were following her. Juno's hands continued to ache with heat pulsing from the small flames. Chax wove around Juno's legs while baring her teeth at the orchard. More girls streamed through the northern gate and began searching the rows of pear trees. Chax nudged Juno in the shin, then padded towards the dark forest. She stopped at the tree line, turned and looked back. Tilly walked around the gnarled tree, searching for her friend. Finding nothing, she looked up with black eyes and glared right at Juno. The air turned colder. Juno took one last look at Tilly, then bolted over the cobble path and into the forest. Branches scratched and scraped her arms as she wove through the closely packed pine trees. Clouds of insects made her gag as the odd one slipped past her lips. Birds fluttered away with a squawk as Chax, taking the lead, ran in front of Juno.

'Slow down, Chax,' Juno said, breathing hard. 'Where are we going?'

Chax looked over her shoulder and slowed her pace to a trot. They stumbled into a clearing filled with bright sun and clouds of insects. Juno blinked rapidly, trying to remove the sudden red sunspots that swam across her eyes. Swarms of insects divebombed her as she rested her hands on her knees and gasped for breath.

'I need to rest, Chax, I can't go any further,' she said, swaying on her feet.

Chax tilted her head and listened in the direction they had just come from. The grass parted as Juno sank to her knees. She hissed with pain as sweat intermingled with the cuts and scrapes she had received from running into branches and thorn bushes. Chax dropped to her haunches and growled.

'What is it?' Juno said, moving into a crouch.

Chax lay flat on her stomach, her tail swishing violently from side to side.

'She went this way,' a girl shouted.

'I guess we need to keep moving,' Juno said, laying a hand on Chax's head.

Chax's whiskers twitched as she smelt the air. She opened her mouth and hissed.

'Come, let's go.'

Chax turned away from the voices and prowled through the grass and into the dark forest. Her thighs burning, Juno followed Chax into the forest. Ferns tugged at her shoes as she picked up speed behind Chax. Ahead, a long row of hedges slowed Juno to a trot. She sank to her hands and knees and crawled up to the rows of interwoven thick plants.

'We are at the south of the village,' Juno said, taking in deep breaths. Chax, lying on her stomach, looked up at Juno and meowed quietly.

Juno peered over the hedge. The village store, with its outside fruit and vegetable market, lay silent. An old lady moved down the cobble street, her cane tap-tapping with each step. Juno moved onto her stomach. 'I am going to go to the village library. Miss Dean works there. She is good friends with Miss Petra.'

Chax's ears pricked up at the voices whispering through the forest.

Juno peered back over the hedge. 'Let's go.'

Chax looked up at Juno, meowed, then shot off into the forest.

'Where are you going?' she said, scanning the trees.

'This way,' a girl's voice shouted.

A flash of brown hair passed through the pine trees as the girls followed Chax away from Juno.

'Be careful, Chax,' she whispered.

The hedge gave way as Juno fought through it. The old lady glared at her from the fruit and vegetable stand. Trickles of sweat dripped down Juno's forehead as she walked through the quiet village to the library.

'Hello, young Juno,' Mr Ryan, the village guard, said. 'What brings you to the library today?'

'I need to see Miss Dean, please, Mr Ryan.'

Mr Ryan reached over and opened one of the library doors. 'Miss Dean is in the back. Nobody's here today, just like most days,' he said sadly.

'Thank you,' Juno said, then entered the library. Not taking time to browse, she walked through a long line of bookcases until she reached the open door of Miss Dean's office.

'Whatever is the matter? And why do you look like you haven't bathed and changed in days?' Miss Dean said, tutting from behind her desk.

Juno bit her bottom lip to fight back the tears. 'Something really bad is happening at the school, Miss Dean.'

Miss Dean walked around the desk and enveloped Juno in a hug. Bits of twigs and leaves fell to the ground as she smoothed Juno's hair. 'You are safe here now,' she said. 'Let me go and get some hot tea for the both of us.'

Juno sat on the couch against the office wall. She wiped her torn, dirt covered sleeve across her face and gagged as the dirt entered her mouth.

In the kitchen, Miss Dean clinked teacups onto their saucers. 'Where is Tilly? Unusual for you to come to the library without her.'

Juno hesitated. 'She is not well, Miss Dean.'

Miss Dean walked into her office with two cups of steaming tea. 'Is she with the school nurse?' she said, sitting down on the couch and handing Juno her tea.

Juno took a sip and sighed at the warmth of her first hot drink in days. 'Miss Petra passed, miss. Miss Lady, the new principal, has taken over, and everything is changing.'

Sadness etched across Miss Dean's face. 'I have heard, yes. Very sad about Miss Petra.'

Juno's eyes widened. 'Sorry, Miss Dean. I forgot she was your friend.'

The teacup tinkled into its saucer as Miss Dean stretched out a hand and patted Juno on the knee. 'That's okay, dear. I know she was like a mother to you. Now tell me, what is wrong with Tilly?'

Juno let out a long sigh. 'I don't know, miss. She isn't herself. Miss Lady did something to her, and she tried to hurt me. Erica and her bullies chased me down into the orchard.'

Miss Dean stopped blowing into her tea. 'Tilly is your best friend. Why would she ever try to hurt you?'

Juno bowed her head, fighting hard to keep back the tears. 'I know it doesn't make any sense, miss,' she said. 'Miss Lady did something to her. I don't know what, though.'

Miss Dean frowned. 'I am not sure I understand. What do you mean, Miss Lady did something to her?'

'I don't know what she did,' Juno said, and she picked up her teacup and took a sip.

'Where did you get those marks?' Miss Dean said, her eyes squinting at Juno's hands.

Tea sloshed out of Juno's saucer and onto her clothes. 'Sorry, miss,' she said as Miss Dean pulled out a cloth and dabbed Juno's wet knee.

'That's okay. So where did you get those marks?' Miss Dean said, with a gentle smile.

'I found a kitten in the orchard. She bit me, and these marks appeared shortly after.'

'*A* kitten?' Miss Dean said with another frown.

Juno nodded. 'Yes, miss.'

The library door banged open. Juno jumped, sending the teacup and saucer sliding off her lap and clattering onto the ground.

'Miss Dean, you have a visitor,' Mr Ryan said from the front door.

'Wait here,' Miss Dean said, walking out of her office and closing the door.

'Good day, Miss Dean,' Miss Lady said. 'I am so pleased to meet you.'

'And who may you be?' Miss Dean said.

'I am Miss Lady, the school principal.'

'Ah yes. Miss Petra's replacement. How can I help you today, Miss Lady?'

'One of my star pupils, Juno, has gone missing. I am wondering if you have seen her.'

Juno sprang off the couch and stood next to the door, her back to the wall.

'I have seen Juno today, but she has left already,' Miss Dean said. 'May I ask how her friend Tilly is doing? Juno expressed concern that her best friend is not well.'

'Tilly is doing just fine. Working in the greenhouse where she belongs. Did Juno tell you where she was going?'

'No. I assume she returned to the school.'

'Thank you, Miss Dean,' Miss Lady said, spinning on her heel and heading towards the exit. 'Have a good day.'

Juno rested her chin on her chest and let out a sigh of relief. Miss Lady's footsteps stopped. The ticking of the wall clock in Miss Dean's office suddenly sounded all too loud.

'Can I help you, Miss Lady?' Miss Dean said.

Juno spun and peered through the office window. Miss Lady stood at the library entrance with her hands on her hips. She tilted her head to one side. 'Juno has befriended a cat. I am not sure if you are aware that the school has a *no pets* policy. The cat is rather large and looks dangerous. So much so that the other pupils are afraid. Tell me, did Juno have a cat with her?'

Miss Dean raised her chin. 'As I am sure you are aware, the library has a *no pets* policy. If there was a cat with Juno, she certainly didn't bring it in here.'

Miss Lady's eyes narrowed. 'I don't think you are telling the truth, Miss Dean.'

'Juno is not here, Miss Lady,' Miss Dean said, walking to the library entrance. 'If she returns, I will send her back to the school.'

Juno turned the handle of the office door. She winced at the lock as it clicked open to release the door. A quick look through the shelves revealed Miss Dean and Miss Lady deep in conversation outside the front door. Her back flat against the wall, Juno slid out of the office and along a wall until she found an open window. She scrambled up onto the window ledge, climbed out and fell onto the grass below. Climbing to her feet, she placed her back to the library wall. The jagged stone wall ripped at her back as she sneaked along to the corner of the library.

'Juno, where are you?' Miss Dean said from inside the library. 'Miss Lady is here to take you back to the school.'

Pins and needles sparked down Juno's fingers, with heat spreading into her palms.

'She was here a minute ago,' Miss Dean said, exiting the library.

Juno shot a glance around the corner of the library and gasped at Miss Dean's black and white searching eyes. Counting to three, Juno darted down the street, along past the houses and towards the hedge. Shouts, followed by the pounding of boots, reached her ears. The hedge tugged at her clothes as she battled through it. Chax jumped out from behind a tree and snarled.

'Run,' Juno said, panting hard.

Chax took the lead, darting and weaving through the fern-covered undergrowth. Shouts from the village broke through the sounds of snapping twigs and branches. The ferns parted as Juno, crashing through them, gasped for air. Chax came to a stop and sniffed in the direction from which they had come. Echoes of men shouting met their ears.

Juno stood and looked in the same direction as Chax. 'They aren't stopping this time, Chax.'

Chax looked up at Juno and curled a lip. She turned and darted across through the forest.

'They are gaining on us,' Juno said, ducking under tree branches and hopping over rocks.

Chax huffed and picked up the pace, her tail swishing from side to side as she dodged through the pine trees. Juno came to a stop, placed a hand on a tree trunk and frowned at the thundering sound ahead of her. In the distance, through the darkness of the trees, a wall of bright sunlight meant the end of the forest. She ran until she broke through the tree line. With a gasp, she flailed her arms to stop herself from falling off the cliff that had suddenly appeared. Water from a roaring river splashed high into the air, the mist from it soaking into her clothes. Chax turned south and ran along the cliff with her tail in the air to keep her balance. Juno followed until the cliff turned into a hill, where she skidded down until she reached the pebbled bank of the river.

'Stop, miss!' a man said, crashing through the tree line atop the cliffs.

Juno weaved through boulders and decaying tree trunks. Pebbles sprayed up from Chax's paws and Juno's shoes. Chax rounded a bend in the river and stopped as another looming cliff appeared in front of them. Juno, panting hard, stopped and rested her hands on her knees. 'Which way, Chax?'

Chax snorted at the cliff.

Three men appeared around the bend. 'Miss Dean has asked us to bring you back, little lady,' one said, eyeing Chax.

53

Chax snarled. Her claws extended as she prowled around Juno, hissing and spitting.

'We will take care of that beast,' a man said, slapping a wooden bat against the palm of his hand.

Juno took a step in front of Chax. 'Leave her alone.'

'Move away from her, little miss,' the man said.

Juno bent down and picked up a pebble. Her eyes narrowed. 'One step closer, mister.'

The man took a step forwards and raised his bat. Juno hissed as pins and needles shot heat down into her palms. Bright lights popped in front of her eyes. Her knees hit the pebbled bank as her legs gave way. Sharp, stabbing pain pulsed harder through her hands. The surrounding air sizzled and popped. Juno screamed. Her forehead fell forwards and hit the pebbles as the blinding red light slowly turned to darkness.

Chax licked the side of Juno's face. Her purring roared through Juno's head. Juno opened her eyes, then squeezed them shut as the pounding in her head took hold. She licked her dry lips and coughed at the dryness in her throat. Chax nudged the side of her head and let out a soft meow.

Juno struggled to a sitting position. 'Where are they?' she said, gritting her teeth at the continued throbbing in the base of her skull.

Chax started walking the way they had come, then stopped and looked back at Juno. The muscles in her jaw tensing, Juno struggled to her feet and pulled herself straight. The pounding in her head turned to a slow throb as she stumbled after Chax. Chax rounded the bend, climbed the hill and darted into the trees away from the river.

'Chax, slow down,' Juno said. 'Where are we going?'

Chax popped her head through the ferns and meowed softly.

Her ears twitched as she turned and continued south. The ground underneath Juno began to rise as they made their way up a second cliff. Shouts echoed through the forest. Chax turned her head to the north and snarled.

'I don't know how much longer I can keep going,' Juno said, her legs growing heavier.

The pine trees thinned. Juno broke out onto a fern and grass-covered cliff. The river raged and roared through the narrow path it had cut through the rock. Another steep drop to the south ended in a sandy beach. Chax scrambled down the grass bank, turned and looked up at Juno.

'Probably not going to be able to catch me, are you?' Juno said under her breath. She pulled herself closer to the steep bank, then with a push of her hands she slid then tumbled onto the beach.

Chax padded over and licked Juno across the nose. Her cheeks filling with air, Juno grunted and fought to her feet.

'There she is,' a man shouted from the top of the cliff.

Chax snarled and hissed, the bristles on her back standing on end.

Juno broke into a run along the sandy riverbank. 'Over there, Chax,' she said, pointing to a thin log that lay across the river.

Chax gingerly placed a paw on the log, which swayed as she placed another paw onto it. Her tail level and her head lowered, she stepped carefully across the log. With a spring, she landed on the other side of the bank.

'Don't do it, miss,' a man said, holding up his hands. 'You won't survive this river.'

Juno took a step backwards. 'Leave us alone.'

'Come back home, miss,' the man said, taking another step forwards.

The end of the log hit the back of Juno's foot. She turned and ran across the bending log, her hands flailing out by her sides. Chax darted out of the way as Juno sprang the last bit and rolled onto the grass. With a creak, the log behind her bent. The man walked along the log with his arms stretched out.

'Come on, Chax, let's get out of here,' Juno said.

Chax padded to the log, extended her claws and swiped at its end, sending splinters into the air.

The man stopped walking and sneered. 'Wait till I get my hands on you, witch.'

Chax swiped her claws at the log. The man picked up speed. Fury spread across his face. Juno picked up a rock and, after heaving it high above her head, she smashed it against the log. Splintering and cracking, the log broke free from the bank and crashed down into the river below. The man screamed, then tumbled into the water.

'We will find you, witch,' the man shouted as the river whisked him away. Juno shook her head. Chax purred as she rubbed her head against her leg.

'They called me a witch, Chax,' Juno said. 'Why would they call me that?'

Chax meowed then padded south along the river.

Juno checked the angle of the sun. 'Mid-afternoon, Chax. We are going to have to find some food soon.'

Chax looked over her shoulder and licked her lips.

The river to Juno's right began to widen, with the rushing water now slowing into a calm, wide expanse of water. She stopped at a trail of stepping stones that led across the river. 'Those men can get across here, Chax.'

Chax poked her tail in the air, snarled at the rocks, then continued south.

'What is that noise?' Juno said, eventually catching up and walking alongside Chax.

Chax darted around an overhanging willow tree. Juno followed, and with a gasp she froze as the world in front of her disappeared. To her right, the river tumbled over the cliff in a wide, thundering waterfall. A lake of green-blue water swirled in a pool at the waterfall's bottom. Stretched out in front of her, hundreds of yellow fields swayed in the wind. Thick forests with enormous tree trunks lined the yellow fields to their right and left. The paths that surrounded the fields led to a town with a lone spire in its centre, which rose up into the sky. Trails of smoke escaped the chimneys of houses within its walls. A moat filled with the same coloured water as the lake surrounded the thick high walls. North of the town, a single wide road snaked up and over the horizon. The sky far to the north swirled with a layer of thick black clouds.

Juno sat on the edge of the cliff and let her feet dangle over the side. Chax sat next to her and licked her paws, showing no interest in what lay before her.

Juno bumped her shoulder into Chax. 'Are those orchards to the east of the town?'

Chax lifted her head and sniffed the air. With a growl, she stood and faced north. Juno tilted her head and sighed at the shouts of men echoing down the river. She turned and gazed out across the lands below. Chax meowed next to her.

'Yes, Chax,' Juno said, placing a hand to her brow. 'That's where we are going.'

CHAPTER 4
THE SEWER RATS

Juno left the roaring waterfall behind her. She jogged along the edge of the cliff with the forest to her left and the expanse of open farmlands down to her right. A long, mournful howl whined through the dark forest. Moments later a second howl, equally mournful and eerie, answered the first. Chax faced the trees and growled.

'Wolves?' Juno said, placing a hand on Chax's shoulder.

Chax's nose twitched with each sniff of the air. She bared her teeth at the trees.

'There is a valley up ahead. Maybe we can get down there,' Juno said.

The hairs on Chax's back calmed as she turned and trotted along the cliff edge. Another long, calling howl echoed through the trees. Chax broke into a run. Juno, sucking in gulps of air, picked up speed to keep up with Chax. The thin pine trees of the valley up ahead grew larger the closer they got, until suddenly the sunlight disappeared behind the canopy of treetops.

Another howl wailed down through the trees. 'That is a lot closer, Chax,' Juno said.

Chax looked over her shoulder and curled a lip over a fang.

With a snarl, she continued running down the valley. Another howl ripped through the trees. Juno stopped and looked up the path into a set of pale yellow eyes and a set of ivory-white fangs.

'Wolves,' Juno said, backing away slowly.

The black-haired wolf appeared on a boulder and snarled at Juno. He lifted his snout and howled up into the trees.

'Run,' Juno said, turning and sprinting down the valley. Branches and leaves whipped by her face as she concentrated on Chax's bobbing tail ahead of her. With a look to her right, Juno's heart beat faster as a white wolf, her tongue hanging out, danced through the trees, growling and snarling. A glance to her left, and the black wolf, dodging the tall, thin pine trees, showed his fangs then snapped his jaws together. The valley flattened and the trees began to thin. Juno pumped her legs harder as the tree line of the forest grew closer. Sunlight slammed into her eyes as she broke the tree line and ploughed into a wheat field.

The thick rows of wheat slowed her progress to a walk. 'Where are you, Chax?'

Chax poked her head out of the wheat, her mouth blowing quick plumes of hot air.

Juno sat next to Chax and sucked in deep breaths herself. 'Do you think they will follow us in here?'

Chax tilted her head and let out a silent meow. Her breathing slowing, Juno poked her head out of the wheat and checked for wolves. Seeing nothing, she stood and gazed over the wheat at the town that lay to the north. To the south of the town, down a long path through the wheat fields, a red barn with a small windmill stood alone.

'Let's get to that barn and see if we can get a better view of the town.' Parting the wheat with her hands, Juno moved from field to field until they

reached the path next to the barn.

'What do you think?' Juno said. 'It looks quiet to me.'

Chax darted across the path to the barn door.

'I guess that was your answer,' Juno said, darting across the path. The water trough filled with ice-cold water made Juno sigh with relief as she scooped up a handful and drank deeply. Chax stood opposite her, lapping up the water and sending it splashing over the trough's edge. Juno walked up to the barn door and pulled the wooden handle. The door creaked open. Chax darted in and prowled around the barn walls, checking for any signs of life.

'Is it all clear?' Juno said, her eyes slowly adjusting to the light.

Chax appeared between hay bales in the loft at the back. Juno walked to a wooden ladder and climbed up to find Chax sitting on a bed of hay between stacked bales.

The hay felt soft on Juno's hands and knees as she crawled up next to Chax. Moonlight crept through the windows as she lay on her back.

'What do you think the town is like?' Juno said.

Chax, turning in a circle, made little puffs of hay that floated into the air as her claws ripped out a new bed. With a yawn, she dropped her head onto her paws and fell fast asleep. Juno sighed and gazed at the barn roof. Sleep came slowly. But finally, with the gentle snores of Chax in her ears, Juno's eyes closed, and stayed closed.

'Is the trailer loaded, son?'

Juno's eyes popped open. She held her breath as footsteps shuffled below her.

'Yes, Papa,' a young boy said.

Chax's tail swished angrily from side to side. The shuffling feet moved to the front of the barn. The barn door slammed shut. Juno exhaled and wiped her sleeve over her brow. She crawled to the end of the loft and peered over to check the ground floor.

'It's clear downstairs,' Juno said, standing up and stretching. 'Time to go and see if Mr Hargreaves is in town.'

Chax bounded down the hay bales to the ground floor and waited at the barn door. The ladder creaked as Juno climbed down it. She opened the door a crack and peered out. Chax shoved her head against the door, swinging it open.

'Be careful, Chax, people will see us.'

Chax padded up to the road, turned and looked at Juno. 'Where are you going?'

Chax gazed south.

Shouts from the town rang through the morning air. Chax looked at Juno one more time before bounding off through the fields towards the forest. Juno took a step forwards, then hesitated. Chax's tail disappeared into the southern forest. The pounding of boots crossing the town drawbridge made Juno spin round. A horn sounded from the town walls. Juno hurried back into the barn, where she climbed the ladder and lay flat behind the hay bales.

Footsteps thumped past the barn. 'Did you see that cat?' a man said.

'A fine trophy it would make,' another man said. 'We will need to put a hunting party together.'

Juno lowered her chin onto her folded hands. 'Why did you leave me all alone, Chax?'

The pounding boots passed the barn and disappeared into the distance. Juno sat cross-legged and placed a hand on her growling stomach. With a shake of her head Juno stood, climbed back down the ladder, exited the barn and walked along the path to the southern gate. A long drawbridge stretching over a wide moat led into a bustling marketplace. Down below, stagnant green murky water cast her image back at her. Juno continued over the drawbridge and walked through the southern gate.

'What have we here?' a man said, grabbing Juno roughly by

the collar. 'Hey, Dec, it looks like one of those sewer rats has lost her way.'

'Trouble they are, Jon,' Dec said. 'Unusual for them to be out in the open.'

'Let me go,' Juno said, trying to twist out of Jon's grip. 'I am looking for Mr Hargreaves.'

'And what would a sewer rat like you want with the town mayor, eh?' Jon said. 'He doesn't deal with the likes of you.'

'Splendid fellow, that Mr Hargreaves,' Dec said. 'I ain't heard of him caring about a sewer rat, though.'

'Get out of here,' Jon said, shoving Juno to the ground. 'You stink. Nobody wants to smell you in the marketplace.'

Juno looked down and pursed her lips at her shredded picking clothes.

'Little girl, what are you looking for?' a woman sweeping between the stalls said.

'I am looking for Mr Hargreaves, miss,' Juno said.

'Hargreaves ain't going to have anything to do with you looking like that,' the woman said.

'Get back to work, Greta,' Dec said, throwing an apple core at the woman.

Greta scowled. 'I do not work for you, little man,' she said.

Dec rose from his seat. 'Know your place, woman, or end-of-day food scraps will be lighter than usual.'

Greta, muttering under her breath, shuffled in between the market stalls and continued sweeping.

'Can you help me, Greta?' Juno said.

Dec and Jon looked at each other and broke out into howls of laughter. 'The sewer rat wants Greta to help her,' Dec said.

'Greta can't even be helping herself, let alone a sewer rat,' Jon said. Greta caught Juno's eye and flicked her head towards an alleyway.

Juno walked past the stalls and into the alley.

Greta followed Juno and shoved her face right up to Juno's nose. 'What you be wanting Mr Hargreaves for, then?' she said. 'Mr Hargreaves ain't one for speaking to a sewer rat.'

'I am from the school up above the cliffs. The one Mr Hargreaves owns,' Juno said.

'That there finishing school for ladies?' Greta said, jabbing her finger into Juno's chest. 'You be messing with me, sewer rat?'

Tears sprang into Juno's eyes. 'I am not messing with you. My friend is in trouble and I need to speak to Mr Hargreaves.'

Greta pulled a dirty rag from a hidden pocket and handed it to Juno. 'No tough sewer rat be crying like you do. You not from around here, are you? Go speak to Angela. She is in the house with a pale blue door up in the weaving district. Follow the signs at the top of the street.'

'Thank you, Greta,' Juno said, handing the rag back to her after she had wiped her face.

'By the way, Angela only be helping for coins. Be sure to have them ready,' Greta said over her shoulder as she shuffled out of the alley.

'I don't have coins,' Juno said.

With a cackle, Greta walked back to the marketplace.

Juno exited the alley and walked up the street to the signposts. The weaving district sign pointed to the right. Juno walked along the cobble streets and stopped at each signpost to find the right direction. Men dressed in fine, flowing clothes sneered at Juno, while less well-dressed men grumbled and took a wide berth with their heads bowed. Several signposts later, Juno found the weaving district archway. The winding street after the archway greeted Juno with shop windows filled with multicoloured clothing draped on headless mannequins. Smaller streets led off the winding cobble street, which Juno back-tracked from when hitting a dead end. The houses in the second winding street she came to each had differently coloured doors. Nestled in a corner, the pale blue door looked older and in need of a coat of paint. Juno looked up and down the street then knocked. The peephole slate slammed back and a woman frowned through the gap.

'What do you want?' she said.

'I am looking for Angela, miss,' Juno said. 'Greta in the market told me to come here.'

A man's eyes appeared through the gap. 'Are you a sewer rat?'

'No, mister. My name is Juno. I am from the school above the cliffs. I am looking for Mr Hargreaves.'

'Let her in, Phil. The poor girl looks like someone dragged her through a hedge,' Angela said, slamming back the peephole slate.

Bolts scraped, locks turned and the pale blue door swung open. Angela reached out, grabbed Juno by the scruff of her torn clothes and pulled her into the house.

'Are you sure you are not a sewer rat?' Phil said, scanning Juno up and down. 'It doesn't look like you have come from a finishing school.'

Juno scanned the small living room. 'I don't know what a sewer rat is, mister.'

Phil looked at Angela and frowned. 'Why is she all the way down here and not at school?'

Juno's stomach growled. She wrapped her arms around herself.

'Leave her be, Phil.' Angela tutted while wrapping an arm around Juno's shoulders. 'Come on, let's get you cleaned up. We can talk about it over something to eat.'

Angela guided Juno through the living room, down a long, small passage and into a white-tiled room. 'Sit,' she said, pointing to a low bench that ran along the tiled wall. Angela busied herself around the room, grabbing towels out of a cupboard, a brush from a mantle and soap out of a drawer. Phil, grumbling to himself, walked in with two large kettles and poured the steaming water into the bath. The muscles in Angela's arms strained as she lifted a kettle of cold water and poured it into the tub. 'That feels about right,' she said, dipping her finger into the water. 'In you get, young Juno. I will be back in a few minutes.'

The steaming bath released the strain in Juno's muscles. With a sigh, she grabbed a bar of soap and scrubbed every inch of her cut and bruised body.

'Can I come in?' Angela said, knocking on the door.

'Yes,' Juno said, rinsing the last of the soap off.

Angela looked Juno up and down and gave a nod. 'We need to sort that hair of yours out. I dare say it has all manner of dirt in there.'

A white liquid squirted onto Angela's hands, which she rubbed into Juno's hair. She dumped Juno's head under the water, rinsed her hair, then applied more of the white liquid. Three times more and the water ran clear.

'We might have to cut some of this hair,' Angela said, tugging at the matted strands. 'Out you get.'

With a towel wrapped around her, Juno sat on a bench while Angela dragged a brush through the knots.

'Do you know Mr Hargreaves?' Juno said.

'He is the town mayor, but he is not in town at the moment,' Angela said. 'I have a friend who will look after you until he comes back.'

Juno flinched at the snip-snip of scissors behind her. Great lumps of knotted hair fell onto the surrounding floor.

'Cannot save any of this,' Angela said. 'Your hair will be a lot shorter for a while.'

'Who is your friend, miss?' Juno said.

Angela draped a towel over Juno's head and rubbed the rest of her hair dry. 'There are clothes for you over there on the bench. They are not much, but I think they will fit. Get dressed and come and join us in the kitchen.'

Juno waited for the door to close and pulled on the new clothes. The soft, plain white cotton trousers fitted snugly with a drawstring. The white cotton shirt with long sleeves was slightly too big, but that was hardly noticeable. Small white lace-up flat shoes fitted perfectly.

Phil and Angela both looked Juno up and down as she walked in. 'Pretty after you have washed up, aren't you?' Phil said.

'I like your new spiky hair,' Angela said. 'Sit and have some stew. Our friend will be here in a while.'

Juno sat at the table and took a small bite of the home-made bread. Her stomach rumbled.

Phil's forehead creased underneath his hair. 'Get stuck in. Nobody can beat my Angela's cooking,' he said, glancing at his wife with a smile.

Juno spooned the stew into her mouth, followed by thick chunks of freshly baked, buttered bread.

'Hungry little thing, isn't she?' Angela said, spooning more stew into Juno's bowl.

Swallowing the last of her food, Juno yawned.

'There is a couch there for you to lie on,' Angela said. 'We will wake you when our friend gets here.'

Juno curled up into a ball on the couch. She watched Angela busy herself with cleaning the table. The food in her stomach felt heavy as her eyes closed.

'Come on, little lady, it's time we got going,' a man dressed in fine silks said.

Juno jerked awake. 'Where are we going?' she said, sitting up and rubbing her eyes.

'I have a house with rooms where you can stay. There are other girls there your age,' he said with a smile.

'This is Donte. He will look after you, Juno,' Phil said, sitting at the kitchen table.

Donte reached out a jewel-encrusted hand. Purple, blue and pink rings surrounded his thick, chubby fingers.

Juno pushed herself deeper into the couch. 'I don't know who you are. Can I see Mr Hargreaves, please?'

'I told you Mr Hargreaves isn't in town at the moment,' Angela said.

'I own a place for young girls that don't have a home,' Donte said. 'As soon as Mr Hargreaves gets back he will come to see you.'

'Go with Donte, Juno,' Angela said. 'If the town guard catch you here, Phil and I will get into a lot of trouble. You can trust him.'

Juno stood and followed Donte to the front door. 'Thank you for looking after me. You are very kind,' she said over her shoulder.

Donte led Juno up the narrow road of coloured doors and up to a wagon drawn by a small pony. 'In you get. We have a distance to go,' he said.

Juno climbed into the plush, red-cushioned wagon and sat next to the far window. The wagon pulled off with a jerk, clattering over the cobblestone road. Her head leaning against the window, Juno watched the lamplighters turn the street lamps on as dusk enveloped the town. The wagon came to a stop and the side door swung open. Donte led Juno up to a door, which he rapped on twice with his knuckles. The door swung open and a woman wearing a set of overalls reached out and pulled Juno into the house.

'I will send payment through the usual means,' she said over her shoulder. 'I thought this was Donte's place for girls,' Juno said.

The woman smiled over her shoulder, then shoved Juno into a room. 'Don't believe everything you hear, sewer rat,' she said. 'I will be back for you later.'

Juno swung round, her hand shooting up to her mouth. Four

young girls wearing overalls sat on small cots along the room's walls. Juno rattled the door handle.

'They lock it. You cannot get out,' one girl said.

Juno spun round, her back firmly pressed against the door. 'What is this place?' she said.

'It is Donte's house,' a girl said. 'We work in the factory on the side.'

Juno moved away from the door, sliding herself along the wall until she reached an empty cot. She sat down and scanned the cold, windowless room for an exit.

The lock on the door scraped open and the woman walked in. 'Come with me,' she said, pointing at Juno. 'I have work for you.'

'Where are you taking me?' Juno said.

'No questions. Come with me,' the woman said, walking over and grabbing her.

The woman marched Juno down a long corridor of closed doors. At the end of the corridor, the woman pushed open a door to where a man wearing dark purple robes sat. The woman pushed Juno into the room and closed the door behind her.

'Hello,' he said, sitting on a plush purple couch. 'Welcome to Donte's house.'

'What do you want with me, mister?' Juno said, taking steps back until her back pressed against the door.

The man grinned, showing one gold tooth among his yellow rotting teeth. He opened up a big black book and licked the end of a pencil. 'The town of Fairacre needs workers. Street cleaners, window washers and lamppost polishers. What work have you done in the past?'

A flicker of light caught Juno's eye. Looking up she saw a small open window, lit up by the twinkling moonlight and letting a light breeze of cold air into the room.

The man lifted his chin. 'I asked you a question.'

Juno took a step sideways and bumped into a table, knocking a fruit basket onto the ground. Apples, pears and oranges spilled onto the floor, rolling in all directions. 'I would like to see Mr Hargreaves,' Juno said, bending down and gathering the fruit.

The man stood and raised his hand to strike Juno. 'I asked you a question. If you do not answer me, there will be no food tonight.'

Juno hissed as the pins and needles popped from the marks into her palms. Spots of red and yellow swarmed across Juno's eyes. With a gasp, Juno fell to her knees, the darkness taking her. Tendrils of smoke filled the air. Juno crawled to the door and grabbed the handle to pull herself up. The big black book spat charred black pages onto the floor. His eyes wide and his mouth opening and closing, the man lay plastered against the far wall.

Juno shook her head. The pins and needles subsided as she grabbed the end of the table and pulled it under the small window. The table swayed as Juno climbed on and pulled herself through the window. With a thud, she fell into a heap on the ground outside. Cold, fresh air hit her lungs, clearing the musty stink of Donte's house.

'Where did she go?' the woman shouted from inside the house.

'Window,' the man said, gasping with pain. 'She burned me.'

Juno rolled onto her hands and knees and used the wall to pull herself to her feet.

'She is around the side of the building,' the woman said. 'Get her back here.' Donte's front door slammed open, and footsteps and the chinking of metal sounded down the street.

Juno willed one foot in front of the other, and using the wall as support she walked in the opposite direction to the footsteps.

'Cut her off at the other end of the alley,' a man shouted.

Juno broke into a jog and glanced down perpendicular alleys as she passed them. Behind her, the thrum of boots echoed along the shop and house walls. In front of her, the flashes of lantern lights held by advancing men twinkled and shook. Juno jogged down another alleyway and halted at the next alley cross-junction. She chose another alley and sprinted in the opposite direction to the pounding boots. Bright street lights ahead slowed Juno's run. The alley turned to cobbles as Juno walked to the end of the building and peered into the street.

'Are you sure she said she was from the school?' Miss Lady said.

Juno cupped her hand over her mouth and, with a gasp, slammed herself against the alley wall.

'That is what she said, and she matches the description you have given, apart from her hair, which we had to cut,' Phil said. 'We handed her over to Donte.'

The pins and needles popped into Juno's palms as she crept back down the alleyway.

Miss Lady peered down Juno's alleyway and tilted her head. 'Spread out and bring her to me immediately.'

'Yes, my lady,' the man said, spinning round and signalling to his men. Juno continued to creep along the wall away from the street.

'Send someone down there,' Miss Lady said, pointing at Juno's alley. 'I can feel someone hiding in the darkness.'

Juno scuttled further back into the shadows. A hand snaked itself around Juno's face and gripped her tightly around her mouth. Juno tried to yank the hand away from her mouth.

'Keep quiet,' a girl said, relaxing her grip. 'I am a friend.'

Juno spun round and looked into dark brown wide-set eyes. Black clothes hugged the girl's body from head to toe. A snaking dreadlock fell out of her hoodie and down over her chest. She placed a finger over her lips. 'Follow me.'

'Who are you?' Juno said, glancing back down the alleyway.

'No time,' the girl said, creeping further into the alley. 'Stick close and do exactly as I do.' She turned in to another alley and knelt next to a wired grate nestled in the wall. The grate clattered to the floor. The girl lay on her stomach and slithered through, feet first. 'Hurry. They will be here any moment.'

Footsteps echoed from every alley. Juno stared down into the hole at the whites of the girl's eyes.

'The choice is yours. Come with me or get captured by those men,' she said up through the hole.

Juno lay on her stomach and slid feet first into the hole, landing with a splash into shallow water.

'What is that smell?' Juno said, her voice echoing off the walls.

'Keep your voice down,' the girl said while placing the grate back. 'We are in the sewers.'

'Are you a sewer rat?' Juno said, taking a step back.

The girl placed a finger on her lips and pointed at the grate.

'Have you checked the other alley?' a man said, standing next to the grate in the wall.

'Nothing here. Search the garbage cans in that alley. She couldn't have gone far.'

The girl beckoned Juno to follow her through the dark, foul-smelling sewer. 'Keep up, and don't stand in the water. They will hear the splashes through the grates.'

'What is your name?' Juno said.

The girl wound her way through the sewers and slowed at each grate that led to the surface. At a crossroads, she sank to one knee and pulled Juno down next to her.

'My name is Chloe. I am going to have to blindfold you now,' Chloe said.

Juno stood and took a step back. 'Why? Why should I trust you?'

'I don't see another option for you,' Chloe said, cocking an eyebrow. 'I am a friend. You can trust me.'

Juno ran the back of her hand across her brow. 'Okay, Chloe. It's not like I have much choice.'

Chloe whipped out a thick piece of cloth and tied it around

Juno's head. 'Here is my arm,' she said, grabbing Juno's hand and placing it onto her forearm. 'We don't have far to go.'

Juno gripped Chloe's arm and stepped forwards gingerly.

'I have got you,' Chloe said, laying a hand over Juno's hand. Juno took a breath and nodded.

After what seemed like hours, they eventually came to a stop. 'We are here,' Chloe said. 'I am going to let you go now. Don't move.'

Juno gave her another nod, then winced as metal grating on metal echoed through the sewers.

'Mind your step,' Chloe said, as Juno jabbed her toe against hard steel. 'There we go. Now, stand still.'

Juno felt the knots of the blindfold loosen.

'Welcome to the sewer rats,' Chloe said.

CHAPTER 5
LITTLE HEDGEHOG

Heads swivelled and eyes stared. Girls of all ages sat on couches, chairs and cushions. Chloe released the drawstring around her throat and flicked the hoodie off her head. Tracks of woven locs cascaded over her shoulders. The mask that covered her face fell away and she grinned, showing pure white teeth against her black skin.

'What is this place?' Juno said, scanning the room.

'It is one of our many meeting places,' Chloe said. 'Before we continue any further, you need to meet our leader, Naomi.'

'She is down in her office, miss,' a young girl said.

'Follow me. It's a bit of a walk through the tunnels,' Chloe said.

Juno hesitated. 'I am looking for Mr Hargreaves. Can you take me to him?'

'Mr Hargreaves?' Chloe said with surprise. 'Nobody here likes that man, Juno. Let's speak to Naomi and see what she says.'

Juno lowered her head.

A girl stood and walked over to Juno. 'You are safe here,' she said, with a shy smile. 'Miss Chloe and Miss Naomi are very nice.'

Juno gave the girl a thin smile, then gave Chloe a nod. The corridors wound through the sewers, lit by the flickering flames of the torches on the walls. Girls chatting, smiling and laughing filled the rooms.

Chloe stopped at a door, knocked twice and then shoved it open with her boot. 'Naomi, this is Juno.'

Naomi looked up at Chloe with a creased brow. 'At least let me say you can enter, Chloe.'

With a smirk, Chloe dropped into a chair and threw a leg over the armrest.

'Pleased to meet you, Juno,' Naomi said, extending a hand.

'Pleased to meet you, miss,' Juno said.

'Please call me Naomi. We prefer first names down here.'

'Or a nickname if two people have the same name,' Chloe said, bouncing her leg on the armrest. 'How goes it, boss?'

Naomi's eyes swivelled to Chloe then back to Juno. 'You will learn, young Juno, that Chloe is a bit of a maverick. Disobedience is her middle name.'

Chloe stuck out her tongue at Naomi, then rolled her eyes at Juno.

'Have a seat, please, Juno,' Naomi said, waving her hand at the chair next to Chloe.

'Found her in the alleyways, boss,' Chloe said. 'She was being chased by Donte's boys.'

Naomi's eyebrows shot up. 'You escaped from Donte's house? That is unusual. Care to share how you did that?'

Juno clasped her hands in her lap and used the long sleeves of the cotton shirt to cover her hands. 'I escaped out of a window.'

'A bit too proper to be an orphan, isn't she?' Chloe said, nudging Juno's chair with her foot. 'Where did you come from?'

Juno glanced at Chloe, then raised her chin at Naomi. 'I am here to see Mr Hargreaves. I need his help to save my friend.'

Tapping a pen against her teeth, Naomi frowned at Chloe. Chloe shrugged.

Naomi dropped her pen, then leaned forwards and placed her elbows on the table. 'Mr Hargreaves is a man we are not very fond of down here, young Juno.'

Juno jerked her head back in surprise. 'Mr Hargreaves has always been kind to me.'

'Where do you come from, Juno?' Naomi said, her eyes narrowing.

Juno lowered her head and remained silent.

'Juno, you are quite safe here. The sewer rats are a haven for orphan girls of this city,' Naomi said, with a quick glance at Chloe.

'And orphan girls from outside the city,' Chloe said, pointing a finger at her own nose. 'Seen many black people before, Juno?'

Juno shook her head.

Naomi let out a sigh, then grabbed a thick book from the desk drawer. 'I think some food and rest will do you good. Maybe after that you can tell us more. Let's see where we have some space.'

'I can make some space in my room,' Chloe said.

Naomi flicked through her book. 'That's not what we do around here, Chloe.'

'I know. But there is something intriguing about our young Juno,' Chloe said. 'I am sure you can bend the rules for me.'

Naomi pursed her lips. 'She is your responsibility, then. Get her settled and come and see me after she has rested.'

Chloe sprang up, her locs bouncing around her head. 'Yes, boss,' she said with a salute.

Naomi gave Chloe an exasperated look.

'Come on, Juno,' Chloe said, offering a hand. 'Let's get your cot ready and get some food down you.'

'You didn't tell me what this place is,' Juno said as she followed Chloe out of Naomi's office and into the corridors. 'Why are there so many passageways and rooms underneath the town?'

'It's the old town, which they called Farmacre,' Chloe said over her shoulder. 'They closed off these tunnels and rooms when they built the sewers for Fairacre, the new town.'

'Where do all these orphans come from? There are so many,' Juno said, walking double-speed to keep up with Chloe.

'*A* large majority are from unmarried women who have had children. Some are orphans from outside the town,' Chloe said, swinging open a door. 'Here is my little home.'

'I have never had my own room,' Juno said, taking in Chloe's cot and desk. 'What is behind these doors?'

'That is a wardrobe where I keep all my clothes,' Chloe said. 'Help me move things around so we can get your cot out.' Chloe scraped her cot against the far wall, then opened a wardrobe and pulled out a smaller cot. With the cot in place, she pulled out a pillow and bedspread and laid them out. She opened the second wardrobe and pulled out some brown pyjamas. 'Probably a bit too big for you, but they will do for now. Get dressed and throw those clothes in the corner. I will be back in a minute.'

Juno undressed, threw her stinking clothes into the corner, then climbed into the oversized pyjamas and sat at the end of the bed.

Chloe walked in with a tray of food. 'Compliments of our amazing cooks.'

Juno picked up a hardtack biscuit and dunked it into the watery broth. 'Hot,' she said, waving her hand at her mouth.

Chloe took a bite. 'Chilli broth,' she said as beads of sweat dotted her brow.

Juno finished what was on the tray, then washed it down with ice-cold water.

'Those marks,' Chloe said, glancing at Juno's hands. 'Are they birthmarks or tattoos?'

Juno sat on her hands. 'I don't want to talk about them right now.'

Chloe shrugged. 'Okay. In your own time. It has been a long day. I suggest you get some sleep.'

Juno climbed onto her cot. 'Thank you, Chloe.'

Chloe pulled the heavy bedspread over her and tucked the corners in. 'Sleep tight, little Juno.'

Juno's eyes fluttered open. She jumped and let out a gasp as two sets of identical eyes glared down at her.

'Another mouth to feed,' the first girl said, scrunching up her nose. 'More mouths, more food,' the other girl said, pouting.

'Why should we feed you?' the first girl said, jabbing Juno in the forehead.

'Gem. Jen. Leave Juno alone,' Chloe said, striding into the room.

'Porcupine,' Gem said, pointing at Juno's hair.

'Hedgehog,' Jen said, patting her palm on Juno's spiky hair.

'Out you go, the pair of you,' Chloe said, bumping them with her hip. 'We will be in the kitchen shortly.'

The twins spun on their heels and marched out of the door. 'Hedgehog. Little hedgehog,' they said in unison.

'Looks like the twins have given you a nickname,' Chloe said, grinning. 'Don't worry, it's only them that will use it.'

'Who are they?' Juno said, scooting herself to the end of the bed.

'They are the legendary cooks of the sewer rats. Even Naomi doesn't mess with them,' Chloe said, dropping a pile of clothes on the end of Juno's cot. 'Those should fit you.'

Juno climbed off her cot and slid out of the oversized pyjamas. The brown buttoned trousers and long-sleeved shirt fitted her perfectly. Next she put on thick, scratchy socks and leather tie-up boots. 'These aren't the same as the clothes you wear,' she said, smoothing down the clothes with her palms.

'There are very few of us that get to wear these clothes,' Chloe said, stretching out her arm and running a hand over the skintight material. 'I am part of the protection faction.'

'And my clothes?' Juno said, looking down at her brown outfit.

'Not all of us belong to a faction down here. Our weavers do what they can with the material they find,' Chloe said. 'Brown material is mostly what we find discarded.'

'At least I don't smell anymore,' Juno said, sniffing her sleeve.

'Oh, you stinky stank alright,' Chloe said, scrunching up her nose. 'Let's get some food, and then we are off to see Naomi.'

Juno stepped quickly behind Chloe through the maze of corridors. Girls smiled and waved at Chloe as she passed the small bedrooms.

'You will learn all these routes in due time,' Chloe said.

'So many orphans,' Juno said, glancing into the many open doors along the corridors.

'Too many,' Chloe said, with a look of sadness.

Long tables with wooden benches covered most of the room that they entered. Juno's nose twitched and her stomach rumbled at the smells that wafted from the cooking stations at the back of the kitchen.

'Welcome to Gem and Jen's domain,' Chloe said. 'We take a spoon measure of each type of food. Do not take any more than the measure. Remember, we are feeding a lot of girls.'

Juno followed Chloe to the buffet and mimicked everything she did. She moved to the bench opposite Chloe and sat with a straight back, her knife and fork placed neatly on either side of the plate. Delicately unfolding a tattered napkin, she placed the corner into her shirt. She picked up her knife and fork and carefully cut into her food, making small manageable bites.

Juno looked up and froze. 'What's wrong?' she said to Chloe and the twins. 'Why are you staring at me?'

'What school did you go to?' Chloe said, leaning forwards.

Juno hesitated. 'I told you. The one Mr Hargreaves owns above the cliffs.'

'No,' Chloe said, her eyes narrowing. 'You said you were looking for Mr Hargreaves. Not that you went to Mr Hargreaves's school.'

Gem and Jen walked up and stood on either side of Chloe. 'Mr Hargreaves is evil,' Gem said.

Juno rose out of her seat, her knife and fork clattering to the ground. 'Mr Hargreaves is not evil.'

'Very evil, little hedgehog,' Jen said, waving a knife at Juno.

Chloe raised both her hands. 'Enough, you two.'

Juno sat down, her hands trembling.

Gem dropped another knife and fork on the table. 'Be good, little hedgehog,' she said with a scowl.

'Shoo, you two,' Chloe said, waving her hands at them. 'Go on. Shoo.'

'Mr Hargreaves is not evil,' Juno said, her eyes narrowing. 'I need him to help save my best friend, Tilly.'

Chloe reached over and patted Juno's hand. 'Let's finish up and get over to Naomi.'

Juno continued to eat her food in the correct way. When she had finished, she placed her knife and fork together on the plate and sat quietly.

Chloe smiled at Juno as she picked up a chunk of bread and mopped up the remaining food on her plate. Once finished, Chloe led Juno to a row of trolley's. 'We place all of our cutlery in these trays,' Chloe said, sliding her plate onto a trolley. 'Always best to keep the cooks happy.'

They walked through the corridors and replied to the countless good mornings from the orphan girls.

Chloe knocked on Naomi's door and waited.

'Come in,' Naomi said.

Chloe slammed open the door. 'See, boss? I can do as I am told.'

Naomi let out a long breath. 'How are you feeling, Juno?' she said, waving at the seats in front of her.

Juno sat on her hands. 'Still a bit tired, but much better.'

'Fourteen hours of sleep will do that to you,' Chloe said, slouching in the chair next to Juno.

'Fourteen hours?' Juno said, her forehead crinkling.

Chloe stood and paced behind the chairs. 'Our young Juno here went to the finishing school owned by Mr Hargreaves.'

Naomi's brow furrowed. 'What on earth are you doing down here, then?'

'And who is that woman that's looking for you?' Chloe said, lowering her face next to Juno's ear. 'I thought you escaped from Donte's house?'

Juno bit the side of her lip and lowered her eyes.

'Have they sent you here to spy on us, Juno?' Naomi said, leaning forwards.

'No,' Juno said, her head snapping up. 'Miss Petra, our old principal, died and Mr Hargreaves brought in a new principal who hurt my friend, and I want Mr Hargreaves to get rid of her so my friend will be okay again.'

Naomi lifted a hand in the air. 'Okay. Let's take a breath here.'

Juno took a deep breath and slumped back into her chair. Chloe slouched back into the other chair and swung her leg over the armrest.

Naomi rubbed the bottom of her chin. 'And the woman you saw on the streets with Chloe is the new principal? And she has come all this way to get you?'

'Yes,' Juno said.

'The principal of the most renowned finishing school has travelled down the cliffs and to this town just to get one girl back?'

Chloe said, swinging her leg in Juno's direction. 'That is a lot of trouble to get one girl back, isn't it?'

'I don't know why she is chasing me,' Juno said, shaking her head. 'I just want to help my friend Tilly.'

Naomi lowered her head in thought. Chloe's leg continued thumping against the armrest.

Naomi sat back and looked at Juno. 'We cannot help you with Mr Hargreaves. He is the town mayor and he just about tolerates the sewer rats. And, to be honest, I don't think he will help you either.'

Juno rubbed her forehead. 'This doesn't make any sense.'

Chloe reached over and rubbed Juno on the shoulder. She turned to Naomi. 'What if I take Juno under my wing for a bit?'

Juno's mouth hung open. 'You are going to help me?'

'If Naomi agrees,' Chloe said, with amusement in her eyes.

Naomi spun her pen on her finger. 'Spend a few days with Chloe. Go to the surface and see what our town is truly like. Then if you would like to stay with us, I will agree to it.'

'Yes,' Chloe said, pumping her fist into the air.

A shrill whistle from the corridors echoed through the office. Chloe and Naomi both stood.

'Long time since I have heard that whistle, boss,' Chloe said.

Footsteps thundered down the corridors. A tall, olive-skinned girl burst through Naomi's office door. 'Trouble in the town, Naomi. The guard are congregating in the square.'

'Are all the girls home, Alexa?' Naomi said, her forehead crinkling in concern.

'We have one team in the weaving district,' Alexa said.

Naomi pursed her lips. 'Get them back right now, please.'

Alexa gave a sharp nod, then disappeared down the corridor.

'Chloe, assemble your team and go listen in,' Naomi said. 'Please be careful.'

'Yes, boss,' Chloe said, saluting. 'Come on, Juno, let's get you into some scavenger clothes.'

'She isn't ready for that, Chloe,' Naomi said, waving her pen at Chloe.

'This may involve Juno,' Chloe said, walking up to the door. 'I will look after her.'

Juno, half walking, half jogging, followed Chloe's long strides through the corridors.

'What do you mean, I am involved in this?' Juno said, breathing heavily.

Chloe walked through the door of her room and rummaged through her wardrobe. 'Here, put these on,' she said, throwing worn brown clothes onto Juno's cot.

Juno slipped out of her comfortable sleeping clothes and threw on the scavenger clothes.

Chloe pulled her protector's clothes off and climbed into her scavenger clothes. She ran an eye over Juno. 'Not bad. You should blend in quite nicely. Let's change your hair up.'

Chloe grabbed a jar of black gel from her wardrobe. She unscrewed the top and ran the gel through Juno's hair. 'Let's flatten those spikes out a bit before we go.'

'I am not going anywhere until you tell me why I am involved,' Juno said, wrapping her arms around herself.

Chloe stood in the doorframe. 'Nothing has happened in this town for years, Juno. You show up, and the town guard become active. It might have something to do with this woman who is looking for you.'

Juno smoothed her hair down further. 'Okay, tell me what to do.'

'In the town, we are street rats who are worthless and beg for food all day,' Chloe said, walking down the corridor. 'Just follow my lead, and whatever you do, don't leave my side.'

They made their way through the scraping metal door and

down through the dark sewers. Chloe pulled a grate out of the wall and went through into an alleyway. Juno lifted a hand and covered her eyes from the bright morning sun.

Chloe whispered into her ear. 'Hunch over and pick things up off the ground. I will do the talking if someone speaks to us.'

Juno hunched over and shuffled behind Chloe out of the alley and onto a wide cobblestone street. The marketplace behind them, they walked up the southern street until the tall spire of the town hall came into view. Guards standing in neat rows along the steps cast their eyes across the growing throng of men.

A portly man with a thin moustache climbed the steps and wagged his finger in a guard's face. 'Where is Mr Hargreaves? We demand to speak to the mayor.'

The guard placed his hand on the man's chest and shoved him down the steps. The crowd hissed up at the guards as they hauled the man to his feet. Juno and Chloe, shuffling on the outskirts of the town square, strained to hear any conversation.

'Penny for a starving girl, sir,' Chloe said, extending her hand to a man. 'Get away from me, you vermin,' the man sneered in disgust. 'This is men's business. Go on, get.'

Chloe bowed her head and shuffled away from the man. Juno ducked under the man's arm and stumbled forwards.

'Kicked him out of his own house, she did,' a man said. 'Something about her eyes all crazy-looking.'

Juno grabbed Chloe, pulled her close and put a finger to her lips.

'Old Ted be a bit mad in the head, though. You sure he isn't back on the wine?' another man said.

The man shook his head. 'Black and white eyes, he said.'

Juno's eyes darted across the crowd. 'We need to get out of here, Chloe.'

'What is it?' Chloe whispered into Juno's ear. 'What is going on? You look like you've just seen a ghost.'

Juno dragged Chloe down an alley. 'Juno, wait. What is it?'

'Miss Lady is changing girls in the town,' Juno said. 'She is doing to these girls what she did to my Tilly.'

Chloe whispered. 'What do you mean, she is changing girls?'

Juno rubbed her eyes. 'I didn't say anything because you are going to think I am crazy.'

Chloe placed a hand on Juno's shoulder. 'I feel like there is a lot more you are not telling me.'

'I was thinking of telling you, but then Naomi asked if I was a spy.'

'That's because Mr Hargreaves wants to know what we are doing every day,' Chloe said. 'We cause him trouble by fighting for our freedom.'

Juno looked back down the alley. 'We can't go back there, Chloe. Miss Lady will change you and then change the girls.'

Chloe bit her bottom lip in thought. 'If we go back to the sewers, will you tell me everything?'

'I have another friend I would like to check on,' Juno said. 'She is hiding in the barn south of the town.'

'The big red barn?'

'Yes,' Juno said. 'It's where I saw her last.'

'And this isn't Tilly?'

Juno shook her head. 'It's another friend. A cat.'

Chloe scrunched up her face. 'You want to go back to the barn to find a cat.'

Juno nodded. 'She is part of the story. Can we go there?'

Chloe hesitated, then lifted her head and let out a soft whistle.

'Yes, miss,' a girl said, appearing out of the shadows and making Juno jump.

'Tell Naomi we are off to search for Juno's friend,' Chloe said. 'Get another team to watch the town square, but make sure they do it from the roofs.'

The girl nodded and slunk off back into the darkness.

'Follow me,' Chloe said, moving southwards. 'As soon as this is all done, we are going to take some time to orient you.'

They twisted and turned through the alleys until they broke out into the eerily silent marketplace. The drawbridge stood unguarded, the guards being in the town square. Juno led them down the winding path to the barn, where she crouched and sneaked to the barn door.

'What are you doing?' Chloe said, standing on the path.

Juno placed a finger on her lips. 'I am checking if anyone is here.'

Chloe walked over and swung the door open. 'Practically everyone is in the town, young Juno.'

Juno let out a sigh. 'You are worse than Chax.'

'Chax?' Chloe said.

'Chax is the name of my cat,' Juno said, climbing up the ladder. 'This is where we slept.'

Chloe joined Juno in the loft. 'It doesn't look like she is here.'

'No,' Juno said, sitting cross-legged and letting out a sigh. 'She ran south into the woods. I was hoping she would be back by now.'

Chloe sat and spread her hands. 'So out with it.'

Juno told Chloe her entire story, from finding Chax through to Chloe finding her in the alley.

Chloe sat in silence, her mouth open as she played with her locs.

'Chloe?' Juno said.

With a shake of her head, Chloe said. 'I would say that's a great fable, Juno, but I don't think even you could make that all up.'

'Everything is true. Now can you see why I don't want you to tell anyone? I sound crazy.'

The barn door crashed open. 'We store the pitchforks at the back. Can you see the rack?' a man shouted from outside the barn.

Juno and Chloe lay flat on their stomachs.

'I see it,' a man shouted from under the loft. 'Have the trackers seen any sign of that cat?'

'Nah, but the wolves are quiet,' the man said. 'The tracker thinks they are quiet because she is close by.'

'Chax?' Chloe mouthed at Juno.

Juno nodded.

Chloe lifted her finger to her lips. 'Nothing we can do,' she mouthed.

'Got them,' the man said, slamming the barn door shut.

'Chax is in trouble,' Juno said, sitting up and wringing her hands. 'We need to help her.'

Chloe, her brow furrowed, rested her hand on Juno's knee. 'We need to tell Naomi. The two of us won't be able to do anything by ourselves.'

'She won't believe me,' Juno said, placing her head in her hands. 'I am surprised you believe me.'

Chloe ran her hand through her locs. 'I believe you, Juno.'

Juno looked up at Chloe with her mouth open. 'You believe me?'

'Yes, young Juno. Now let's get back to Naomi,' Chloe said, moving to the wooden ladder.

They made their way back into town and through the sewers. Chloe grabbed the handle of the big metal door and scraped it open. The chattering in the main room died down as all heads turned to look at Juno.

A young girl walked over. 'Naomi wants to see you in her office, miss.'

'Thank you,' Chloe said, ruffling the young girl's hair.

'Sounds like something is wrong,' Juno said while following Chloe through the corridors.

Chloe peered over her shoulder. 'Probably found out some information from the town square.'

Naomi's office door stood open.

'Boss,' Chloe said, walking in and dropping into a chair.

Naomi finished scribbling in her book. 'After you two left your posts, one of our teams listened in on a conversation in the square. It looks like the women of this town are finally fighting back.'

Juno glanced at Chloe.

'As you can imagine, everyone down here is excited. I, on the other hand, am wary. Why are they all of a sudden fighting back now?' Naomi said.

Chloe kicked the side of Juno's chair. 'You need to tell her, Juno.'

Naomi furrowed her brow and narrowed her eyes.

'You will kick me out onto the streets,' Juno said, rubbing her forehead with her hand.

Naomi walked around and sat on the corner of the table. 'I will not kick you out if you tell me, Juno. But if you withhold information which could harm anyone, then I will kick you out.'

Juno looked into Naomi's fierce, dark eyes.

'Okay,' Juno said, raising her hands up into the air. 'I will tell you everything I told Chloe.'

Naomi sat in silence with her arms folded. 'That is a tall tale, Juno,' she said, sitting back down in her chair.

'I saw the cat hairs in the barn, Naomi,' Chloe said, her leg bouncing. 'According to the crowds at the town hall, a few women have kicked their husbands out of their homes. Every one of those men mentioned black and white eyes,' Naomi said, scratching her nose with her thumbnail.

'This is not how we envisioned women standing up for themselves,' Chloe said, her brow furrowing.

Naomi rested her chin in her hand and closed her eyes. She stood abruptly and whistled down the sewer corridors.

'Yes, Naomi?' Alexa said, appearing in the doorway.

'Assemble your team and go to the southern forest. There is a hunting party looking for a cat. Get as much knowledge as you can,' Naomi said.

Alexa gave a nod and disappeared down the corridors.

'Chloe, assemble your team and track these women that the men in the square mentioned,' Naomi said. 'Juno, there are new clothes for you in Chloe's room. Get changed and stick with Chloe.'

Chloe jumped up and made for the door. 'Time to go a-hunting, Juno.'

'I don't think this is a good idea,' Juno said.

Naomi sat back in her chair. 'What are you saying, Juno?'

'I have seen how these women get infected. What if she does it to Chloe or one of the girls in her team?'

Naomi thought for a moment. 'That is a problem, but we cannot sit down here and hide.'

'We can stick to the rooftops,' Chloe said from the doorway. 'If Juno sees anything, we can get out of there quickly.'

Naomi looked at Juno. 'I agree with Chloe. Be vigilant, Juno, and if you see anything at all give Chloe the signal.'

'Okay,' Juno said as she stood. She stopped in the doorway. 'Thank you for believing in me, Naomi.'

Naomi inclined her head.

CHAPTER 6
EIGHT METAL LEGS

Juno pulled the stretchy material apart and watched in wonder as it sprang back into place. 'I have never felt anything like this before,' she said, glancing over at Chloe.

'We have talented tradeswomen down here,' Chloe said, smiling.

'Why are they down here and not working in the town?'

'That, young Juno, is exactly why the sewer rats are here,' Chloe said sadly. 'They don't conform to what men want them to be.'

Juno sat on her cot. 'I don't know if I can wear these. I can't do what you do, Chloe.'

Chloe sat next to Juno. 'You are a survivor, Juno. I wouldn't waste my time with you if I thought you couldn't be one of us.'

Juno sighed. 'I am so worried about Tilly and Chax and I feel that this distracts us from finding them.'

'This is all connected. If the Lady is here, then this is where we start looking,' Chloe said, bumping Juno with her shoulder. 'Get dressed and let's go and find out what is happening in our town.'

Juno shrugged off her old beggar's clothes and pulled the tight shirt and trousers on.

'Make sure the stirrups are secure around your feet,' Chloe said, waggling a bare foot at Juno. 'The same with the stirrups on the sleeves of your shirt.'

'Why are there pads on the elbows and knees?' Juno said.

'They will save your skin many times over. Same with your boots, which are at the end of the cot. They are tough, so not much gets through them.'

Juno slid her feet into the soft black leather ankle-high boots and tied the laces into a tight double bow.

'And now for the jacket,' Chloe said. 'Make sure you click the zip into place at your throat.'

Juno pulled the black zip up to her throat and felt the jacket close around her body. The soft, stretching material stuck to her every move as she flexed her shoulders and stretched out her arms.

'Flick the hoodie over, tie it in place, then snap the face covering into the fastener,' Chloe said, clicking her own face covering into place.

The hoodie tightened over Juno's head, squashing her spiky hair. She picked up the gloves from the bed. 'These gloves feel tight.'

'You will get used to them. They need to be tight so you can feel everything you touch,' Chloe said. 'Turn around and let me check that everything is in order.'

Juno extended her arms and turned on the spot. She stretched one leg out horizontally and felt the leather shoes gripping the ground, keeping her balanced in place.

'A couple of alterations to the hoodie and you will be perfect,' Chloe said. 'There is a mirror inside the wardrobe.'

Juno stood in front of the mirror and ran her hands over her arms and down her thighs. 'All I can see are my eyes.'

'That is the idea, young Juno,' Chloe said with a wink. Chloe swung open the second door of her wardrobe.

Juno leaned forwards. 'Those look dangerous.'

'Way too dangerous for you,' Chloe said, running her hand over the multitude of blades racked inside the wardrobe. 'Over time, we will find out which weapon suits you.'

'Have you ever had to use them on someone?'

Chloe pulled a long, sheathed blade from the rack, swung it over her back and clicked it into place. Two sheathed daggers snapped into holders on her thighs. 'I have never killed anyone, if that is what you are asking. We need to get going. Mimic my every move when we are topside. Understood?'

With a nod, Juno followed Chloe out of their room and down the maze of corridors to the metal door. A ray of dark orange dusk sunlight broke through a grate in the ceiling ahead of them. Juno jumped as three sets of eyes appeared out of the darkness.

'Just my team,' Chloe said. 'Ladies, this is Juno.'

The team members each gave Juno a quick nod. Chloe signalled to a team member, who reached up, dislodged the grate and then sprang like a cat through the hole into the alley above. Two hands reached down through the hole and dragged Juno out of the hole and into the alley.

Chloe sprang out of the hole. She grabbed Juno and pulled her into the shadow of a garbage can. 'Like sewer rats, the shadows are where we live. We stay silent, listening and learning. We never come out during high noon – only dusk, dawn or at night.'

Juno scrunched up her nose at the foul smell of rotting food. Chloe and her team darted from shadow to shadow. Juno mimicked the team's movements. At a stacked set of crates, Chloe signalled to her team to climb onto the roof.

'You're next,' Chloe said into Juno's ear.

Juno scrambled up the crates and winced at the noise she made. On the roof, a team member dragged her onto her stomach.

Chloe lay next to her. 'Not too bad. A bit noisy.'

Juno let out a sigh. 'I don't know if I can do this.'

'Practice,' Chloe said. 'Everyone had to go through this. You are not as bad as some girls I have trained.'

Juno looked into Chloe's smiling eyes and slowly relaxed.

'The rooftops are our other domain, and a good place to orient yourself in the town. Remember to use smell and sound, not just sight. Tell me what you hear and smell,' Chloe said, getting to her knees.

Juno rose to her knees. 'Shouting that way,' she said, pointing southwards.

'The marketplace where people sell their wares,' Chloe said. 'What else?'

Juno cocked her head and listened carefully. 'Clanging and banging that way,' she said, pointing east.

'The manufacturing district. Blacksmiths, cobblers, weavers, arts and crafts,' Chloe said. 'What else?'

'I hear nothing else,' Juno said, tilting her head to the other side. 'Oh, wait. Smells coming from that way,' she said, wrinkling her nose and pointing to the west.

'Well done,' Chloe said. 'The entertainment district. Dining houses, drinking taverns, theatres and bath houses.'

Juno turned northwards.

'See the steeple. That is the library and town hall. We are on the south side of the town,' Chloe said. 'If you are disoriented, climb onto a roof and use the steeple and the marketplace as your landmarks.'

Juno did a full circle while ticking off the four directions on her fingers. Chloe signalled to her team. The girls sprang in different directions, jumping from rooftop to rooftop.

'Keep close,' Chloe said, bolting along the rooftop and jumping over an alley.

Juno stopped and peered down into the alley. Chloe let out a soft whistle and beckoned her with a wave.

'Here goes nothing,' Juno said, taking a few steps back. The end of the roof came closer and closer, and with a leap Juno flew across the gaping hole. She hit the rooftop hard with her knees and rolled onto her back.

'Handy knee pads,' Chloe said, kneeling over her and smiling.

'I did it,' Juno said, a wide grin stretching across her face.

Her hand outstretched to pull Juno to her knees, Chloe grinned. 'Yes, you did, young Juno. Well done.'

They continued their journey towards the steeple in the centre of the town. On the third rooftop jump, Juno kept her footing. She sprinted hard and caught up to the heels of Chloe. Three roof jumps later, Chloe crouched over the edge of the building overlooking the town square. Juno crouched next to Chloe, peered over the edge and took in the sights and sounds of the bustling square. Rows of guards at the top of the town hall and library steps stood deathly still, the sun glinting off their shining armour and shields.

'I have never seen the guards lined up like that before,' Chloe said into Juno's ear. 'I wonder what they are protecting.'

'Does Mr Hargreaves live in the town hall?' Juno said.

Chloe shook her head. 'He has a house in the richer district in the north. The town hall is where he works.'

Juno pointed to a group of shambling girls in brown tattered clothes. 'Sewer rats?'

'Yes. Begging for money while listening for information,' Chloe said.

Juno moved a hand over her eyes as a commotion broke out at the bottom of the town hall steps.

'We demand an audience with Mr Hargreaves,' a man said, climbing the steps.

Two guards took a step forwards and bashed the man with their shields. The man's arms flailed before he tumbled back down. The crowd roared and punched their fists into the air. Fruit and vegetables landed at the feet of the guards. The guard captain, standing at the back of the guards, slammed the end of his spear into the ground. As one, the line of guards slammed their own spears, the sound echoing off the walls of the square. The crowd's shouts turned to whispers and then silence. The tall wooden doors of the town hall slammed open.

Juno let out a gasp, the muscles in her shoulders tightening. She flexed her hands as the pins and needles shot to her palms.

'The Lady?' Chloe said into her ear.

Juno shook her hands. 'I get pins and needles in my hands when she is near.'

'She cannot get you up here,' Chloe said, taking and squeezing Juno's hand. 'Take a few deep breaths and relax.'

Juno breathed deeply and relaxed her hands. The pins and needles pulsed and throbbed.

The Lady raised her hands and flicked her index finger at the crowd.

'Can you see that?' Juno said, shaking Chloe's hand.

'See what?' Chloe said, frowning.

'Tendrils of smoke coming out of her fingers. It's going towards the sewer rats.'

'I don't see anything,' Chloe said, staring at the Lady.

'You need to get them out of there,' Juno said. 'Right now, Chloe.'

'Something is wrong. That sewer rat is breaking away from her team,' Chloe said.

'She is being turned, Chloe. You need to get her out of there.'

Chloe whistled to catch the attention of her team. She pointed at the sewer rat and gave the signal to go help her. The sewer rats slid off the rooftops into the alleys.

'Come on,' Juno said. The pins and needles vibrated harder. 'Get her out of there.'

Three sets of hands appeared out of the alley, and the sewer rat disappeared.

'Let's go,' Chloe said, breaking into a run across the rooftops.

Juno ran hard to just about keep up with Chloe. The crates clattered and shifted, with Juno spinning her arms to keep her balance. A grate slid open and Juno followed Chloe through. They charged through the sewers and ran through the already open metal door.

Chloe, breathing hard, looked at a girl in the room. 'Have my team come through here?'

A young girl nodded. 'Gone down the corridor already, miss.'

They weaved through the corridors until they reached Chloe's team. 'Where is she?' Chloe said.

'We have locked her in a secure room down the corridor. Naomi is on her way.'

Chloe ran a concerned eye over her team. 'Go and get yourselves checked out in the infirmary.'

'Chloe,' Naomi said, striding up to them. 'Are you and your team okay?'

'Yes. It seems our little Juno was telling the truth. One of our girls has changed. We have her in a room down the corridor.'

They walked into a corridor of steel doors. Naomi shook her head at the sound of the sewer rat pounding her fists against the inside of the door.

'What is this place?' Juno said.

'The old town prison,' Chloe said.

Naomi opened the viewing hatch on the door, gasped and took a step back.

Two black and white eyes stared back. 'Let me out of here,' she snarled. 'You will pay for this.'

Naomi closed the viewing hatch. 'You saw what happened, Chloe?'

'I saw her change. Juno saw the tendrils of smoke.'

'The same tendrils of smoke that went into Tilly,' Juno said, still breathing hard. Juno cupped her ears as Naomi let out a deafening whistle.

'Yes, miss?' Alexa said, appearing out of the darkness.

'Shut us down,' Naomi said. 'Get everyone back here immediately.'

Alexa nodded and left down the corridor.

'Come to my office, you two,' Naomi said.

Juno and Chloe sat.

Naomi closed the office door and leaned against her table. 'These tendrils of smoke. They enter the girls through their ears?'

'Yes,' Juno said. 'She can direct it however she wants.'

Naomi walked around the table and sat. 'I have no idea what this is or how to stop it.'

The drumming of footsteps leaked through the cracks in the door as the girls closed down their home. Juno and Naomi jumped as Chloe sat up and slammed a hand on Naomi's desk.

'I have an idea. Permission to go topside, boss?' Chloe said.

'You know we are in lockdown. Where are you going?'

'To see a certain friend,' Chloe said, grinning.

'And what will he be able to tell us?' Naomi said.

'If there is someone in Fairacre that knows what is happening, it will be Valen,' Chloe said.

'I see,' Naomi said, rolling her eyes. 'Okay, go ahead, but take Juno with you. If she can see what this lady can do, she can keep you out of harm's way.'

Chloe kicked the side of Juno's chair. 'Come on, young Juno, we are off to the manufacturing district.'

Chloe crawled to the roof edge, then nudged Juno with her elbow. She placed a finger on her lips and pointed at a man sitting on a chair outside a shop. She dragged herself along the roof until she was above the man. 'Wait here,' she whispered into Juno's ear.

Juno watched Chloe disappear over the rooftop edge. A second later, the clattering of a chair and the gruff yell of a man filled Juno's ears.

Chloe's laughter tinkled through the air. 'You can come down, Juno,' Chloe said.

Juno swung her legs over and dropped in between the upturned table and chair.

'This is Valen, the owner of the town's arts and crafts shop,' Chloe said, looking up at a towering silhouette.

'Pleased to meet you, lass,' Valen said, extending a plate-sized hand.

Juno smiled up at the stubble-filled face of the young giant of a man. *'A* pleasure to meet you too,' she said, her hand disappearing into his palm.

The shop bell tinkled as Valen opened the door and stooped to go through. 'I think a cup of tea is in order,' he said, walking to the back of the shop.

Juno walked into the shop and stood with her mouth open. 'What are all these things?'

'My Valen is a bit of a genius,' Chloe said, standing next to Juno. 'He builds all manner of objects.'

The tip-tap of little feet whispered through the air. Nine red eyes appeared from behind a display cabinet. With a tap-tap, the eyes disappeared. Juno recoiled. 'What was that?'

'Come here, Henry,' Chloe said, lowering to her haunches. 'It's okay, little one.'

The nine red eyes reappeared from behind the display cabinet.

Chloe tapped her knee. 'Come and meet my friend. Her name is Juno.' The nine eyes scuttled out and ran to Chloe.

Juno moved behind Chloe and covered her mouth with her hand. 'Is that a spider?'

'It's Little Henry,' Chloe said, reaching down and rubbing the metal spider with her finger. 'He is the shop guard dog, or spider. He is harmless, but people don't know that.'

Henry's blunt fangs clacked together as he tapped in a circle under Chloe's finger.

'Tea is ready,' Valen said, from the back of the shop.

Little Henry fell over his eight metal legs as he scuttled over to Valen.

'Is he your boyfriend?' Juno said, nudging Chloe in the side.

Chloe flashed Juno a brilliant smile, then marched to the back of the shop.

Valen waved his hand at the tartan couch nestled against the wall of his office. 'To what do I owe this unexpected visit, lass?' he said, pouring steaming tea into mugs.

Chloe dropped onto the couch and swung her leg over the armrest. 'Unrest in the town of Fairacre, love. I assume you have heard? And you might have some news?'

Valen passed over mugs of steaming tea, then sat back in his oversized work chair. 'I have heard whispers. Women throwing men out of their homes.'

Chloe sighed. 'Yes. But not for the reasons you think.'

Valen raised an eyebrow. 'What reasons may that be?'

Chloe's leg bounced on the armrest. 'Time to tell your story, young Juno. You can trust my Valen.'

Valen sat quietly, listening. At the end of Juno's story he sat forwards and raised his eyebrows. 'That is a mighty tall tale, lass,' he said, looking over at Chloe.

'I have seen it myself,' Chloe said with a shrug. 'She has infected one of our girls.'

Juno's eyes darted to the armrest next to her. She whimpered and scooted over to Chloe. 'I don't like spiders. The orchard was full of them.'

Henry clack-clacked his mandibles, and his nine round red eyes stared at Juno.

'Get. Go on, get,' Valen said, waving his hand at Henry.

Little Henry jumped off the armrest and landed in a heap of metal legs. He dragged himself to his feet and scuttled under Valen's desk.

'How is he even alive?' Juno said.

Valen smiled. 'With the right ingredients, lass, you can bring life to anything.'

'I think he is a wizard,' Chloe said, waving her hands in an elaborate pattern. 'But he won't tell me anything.'

'Tell me about the tendrils of smoke,' Valen said, leaning forwards, inches from Juno's face. 'Why can you see it but my Chloe cannot?'

Juno cupped her hands in her lap and glanced over at Chloe. 'Show him,' Chloe said, nudging Juno.

Juno lifted her hands palms up. Valen took both of Juno's hands in his own and traced the small red marks with a massive finger.

'What do you think?' Chloe said, sitting forwards.

'I have never seen anything like this,' Valen said, releasing Juno's hands and scratching the bridge of his nose.

'Juno thinks it is why she can see the smoke,' Chloe said.

'Can you describe the smoke in detail for me?' Valen said. 'I need to know as much as possible.'

Juno closed her eyes and rubbed her forehead. 'It's grey. Snakelike. Pointy at the end.'

'Is it thick or thin?' Valen said.

'It is quite thick when it comes out of her fingers, but then goes thin when it gets to people's ears.'

'Do you see the person change?' Valen said.

'Nothing else happens, apart from the irises being eaten by the pupil. There is no colour left. Just black and white.'

Valen sat back in his chair and gazed up at the ceiling. Henry jumped off a bookshelf and landed on the desk, his mandibles clacking as he spun round in circles.

Juno shuddered.

Valen leaned forwards and placed a hand on each knee. 'I have an idea. A slim chance it may work, but an idea at least.'

'What are you thinking, love?' Chloe said.

A shrill whistle pierced the air. Chloe stood and cocked her head to one side.

'What is it, lass?' Valen said.

'Trouble,' Chloe said. 'We need to move, Juno.'

Valen wrapped Chloe in a hug, his enormous frame engulfing her. 'Come back tomorrow night. I should have something for you by then.'

Chloe pecked Valen on the cheek and strode out of the front door.

As Juno passed Valen, he laid a hand on her shoulder. 'Stick with my Chloe, lass. If there is one person who can find your Tilly, it is her.'

With a half-smile, Juno gave Valen a nod, then ran through the store to catch Chloe.

'What is it?' Juno said, coming to a stop next to Chloe.

Chloe searched the rooftops. 'I don't know. My team will be here any second.'

A girl's head appeared out of an alley and tweeted. Chloe jogged across the street and crouched next to her team, leaving a gap for Juno.

'What is it?' Chloe said.

'The sewer rat that changed has gone missing.'

'How?' Juno said. 'We locked her up.'

'Her eyes changed back, so we thought we could release her.'

'My Tilly did the same thing,' Juno said.

Chloe stood. 'She has all the secrets of the sewer rats. We need to get her back immediately. Get onto the roofs and search each alley. Juno, we are going to the town hall.'

The girls climbed onto the dark, flat rooftops and disappeared in different directions.

'Stick with me and keep your footing true. I don't want to be scraping you out of an alley,' Chloe said into Juno's ear.

Juno, her arms pumping hard, sprinted across the rooftops. She jumped over an alley then scaled a steep roof and slid down the other side using the padding of her trousers. At a wider alley she slowed, stretched out her arms and walked across a thin plank. Up ahead, the steeple loomed closer. Leaping across the last alley she crept to the rim of the roof that overlooked the square.

Sweat dripping down her forehead, she lay next to Chloe and shook her head at Chloe's even breathing and sweat-free brow.

'It won't take you long to get fit,' Chloe said, smirking.

Juno took in a few more deep breaths.

'Keep your eyes glued to all the alley entrances.'

'Two guards patrolling the top of the steps,' Juno said. 'Empty otherwise.'

'It will be hard to spot her with her training,' Chloe said, straining her eyes.

'She knows how to use the shadows.'

They lay in silence, the wind fluttering through their hoodies. Laughter and cheering from the entertainment district touched their ears every so often.

'Movement over there,' Juno said, pointing.

Chloe narrowed her eyes and followed Juno's pointing finger. 'That looks like her. I need you to wait here.'

'But I can help,' Juno said. 'What happens if you get turned?'

'If that happens, you get to Naomi as quickly as possible. And failing that, get to Valen's.'

Juno pursed her lips. 'Okay, but please be safe. I don't want to be alone in this town again.'

Chloe patted Juno on the forearm, then disappeared over the side of the house. Juno watched Chloe and her team move stealthily to the far end of the square.

A hand pressed between Juno's shoulder blades. 'Don't move. I don't want to have to hurt you.'

Juno gripped the side of the roof. 'What do you want?' she said through gritted teeth.

'I know you are one of the sewer rats. I have a message for the girl who came from the cliffs.'

Juno held her tongue.

'Tell her that Dr Viktor wishes to meet her. Do you understand?'

Juno turned her head, then grunted as the man increased the pressure between her shoulder blades.

'Do not look at me. Repeat what I just said.'

With the last bit of air in her lungs, Juno said, 'Dr Viktor wants to meet the girl from the cliffs.'

The hand released its pressure and Juno took in a gasp of fresh air. She scrambled to her knees and searched the roof but found it empty. A whistle floated through the air. Juno searched the adjacent rooftops until she found the girl waving at her. With a wave, she sprinted across the rooftops and skidded to a stop next to the sewer rat.

'Chloe has the other sewer rat,' the girl said. 'Follow me.'

They chose an alley, scaled down a drainpipe and slid through the hole that led into the sewer.

'We are not too far,' the girl said.

They ran through the sewers until they reached the big metal door. The girl placed her foot on the doorframe and pulled hard on the handle. The door screeched open and Juno walked into an eerily quiet room.

'All in their rooms during lockdown,' the girl said. 'Chloe is in Naomi's office.'

'Thank you,' Juno said.

The same eerie silence filled the corridors as Juno jogged to Naomi's office. 'Come,' Naomi said after Juno had knocked.

Chloe stood and wrapped Juno in a hug. 'You're okay?' she

said with a look of concern. 'We saw someone on the roof with you.'

Juno unclipped her mask and rubbed her forehead. 'It was a man. He held me down so I couldn't see who it was.'

Naomi leaned forwards, a frown creasing her brow. 'Someone held you down? What did he want?'

'He gave me a message. He said a Dr Viktor wants to meet the girl that came from the cliffs.'

Chloe stood up and paced behind the chairs. 'I shouldn't have left you. I am sorry.'

'She is your responsibility, Chloe,' Naomi said, raising an eyebrow. 'We agreed.'

Chloe growled under her breath. 'It won't happen again, boss.'

'From now on, someone accompanies Juno until we have given her the correct training. Understood?'

'I am fine,' Juno said. 'Do either of you know who Dr Viktor is?'

Chloe sat and threw her leg over the armrest. 'I have no idea.'

'Nor do I,' Naomi said, sitting back in her chair.

'Did we at least get the girl?' Juno said.

'Yes. We have her locked in the room. No sooner was she in there than her eyes turned back to normal.'

Juno sighed, and the sigh turned into an enormous yawn. She shook her head and rubbed her eyes with the heels of her hands.

'Bed. The both of you,' Naomi said, pointing her pen at the door.

'Naomi, we have news,' Alexa said, walking into the room. 'It is the lady who formed the hunting party. She is out looking for the cat.'

Chloe peered over at Juno then leaned across and chuckled as Juno let out a small snore.

'Get her to bed. No point worrying her about it now,' Naomi said. 'We can fill her in tomorrow morning.'

CHAPTER 7
BLOWN LOCS

'Why didn't you wake me up?' Juno said, swinging her legs off her cot.

'You fell asleep in Naomi's office,' Chloe said, while sorting through her clothes. 'You wouldn't have made it out of the sewers in your state.'

Juno reached for her clothes. 'Chax is out there. We need to go and get her.'

Naomi walked into the room and shut the door. 'Sit down, Juno, you are not going anywhere.'

Juno sat on her cot and folded her arms. 'I can't leave Chax out there alone with people hunting her.'

'My team is out there monitoring the hunting party,' Chloe said, sitting down next to Juno. 'We are going to join them, but we have to wait for the weavers to finish your new set of clothes.'

'Why do I need a new set of clothes?'

'We are going into the forest. You will stick out like a sore thumb in your beggar's clothes,' Chloe said, smiling.

'How long are they going to take? I am sorry, but I can't bear to think of Chax being hunted.'

'The weavers have worked through the night,' Naomi said, sitting on Chloe's cot. 'They will be ready shortly.'

Chloe tutted. 'You look tired, boss.'

'I spoke to the girl who is infected,' Naomi said, closing her eyes. 'It has been a long night.'

'What did she say?' Juno said.

'I poked and prodded, but she has a total blackout during the times her eyes are black and white.'

'We cannot trust her,' Chloe said. 'And we cannot cast her out.'

'We will keep her locked up until we find out more information,' Naomi said.

Chloe answered the soft knock on the door. 'Your clothes are ready,' she said, turning to Juno.

A young girl with long, wavy red hair walked in and placed the new clothes on Juno's cot. 'I have made slight adjustments to the hoodie, and I have made the face mask tighter.'

'Thank you,' Chloe said. 'You have outdone yourself creating this in one evening.'

The weaver smiled shyly. 'May I have the previous outfit to do the alterations?'

'They are in Juno's new section of the wardrobe,' Chloe said, swinging open the cupboard door and pulling out the black outfit.

The weaver draped the outfit over her arm and, with a nod, walked out of the room.

Juno ran a hand over her new forest camouflage outfit. 'She is my age. How can she create something like this?' she said, with a look of amazement.

'We are lucky to have her,' Naomi said, smiling. 'Another young girl with talent who got discarded.'

'Get dressed and let's join our team in the forest,' Chloe said, pulling her camouflage uniform from her closet.

After zipping up her jacket, tying up her hoodie and snapping her face mask into place, Juno followed Chloe down the winding corridors. They exited the steel door and turned south down the sewers. Juno shivered as the air turned colder. Each time a rumble sounded overhead, water dripped from the ceiling.

Chloe turned a corner and stopped at a rusted gate locked with an old chain. 'Outside is a main path that runs along the moat. Farmers use it constantly, so we need to pick the right time to get into the fields. If they spot us, we keep running until we hit the forest.'

Juno knelt and checked the laces on her boots. Chloe pulled the gates apart just enough for Juno to slip through. Juno crouched on the other side and watched Chloe bend and contort to get through the gates. They scrambled up the embankment and lay in the tall grass a few feet from the path.

'Mama, look,' a young girl said. 'It is so pretty.'

Juno held her breath.

'You have that butterfly already,' a woman said.

The butterfly forgotten, the girl stopped in front of Juno and stared wide-eyed. Juno pulled her face mask down, smiled and put a finger to her lips.

'Mama, there are people in the grass,' the girl said, pointing.

Chloe sprang to her feet. 'Time to go, Juno.'

Juno catapulted out of the grass and over the path. She crashed into the wheat fields and, dodging and weaving, she followed Chloe's bouncing locs.

'Keep low,' Chloe said, shouting over her shoulder.

They broke out of the first field and vaulted over the path and into the second field.

'Stop,' a farmer shouted, jumping out of Chloe's way.

Her legs turning to rubber, Juno dodged the farmer and vaulted into the last field.

'Oh no you don't,' a farmer said, grabbing Juno by the forearm and whipping her round.

'Let me go,' Juno said, lashing out with an elbow and feeling the crunch of bone.

Blood dripping from his nose, the farmer tightened his grip. 'Filthy sewer rat. It is forbidden to be in these fields.'

'You are hurting me,' Juno said, trying to pry the man's fingers open.

The farmer's body stiffened. His eyes blurred. Wheat parted as his body crumpled into a heap.

Chloe sheathed her dagger. 'Let's move.'

Juno took a step back from the man lying in the wheat. She shook herself, then ran through the field and into the forest. 'Did you kill him?' she said, staring at Chloe.

Chloe wrapped her hand around Juno's mouth and pulled her into a crouch. 'No, just knocked him out. Men nearby,' she said into Juno's ear.

Juno scanned the area. A tweet sounded from the branches above them. Chloe looked up and raised a hand.

Juno whispered into Chloe's ear, 'Who are you looking at?'

'Follow my finger,' Chloe said, pointing into the trees.

Juno followed Chloe's finger and stopped on a set of eyes that hovered in the branches.

'They have counted a full twenty-four guards and six trackers searching the forest,' Chloe said, her voice a whisper. 'The Lady is in the centre directing them.'

'Any sign of Chax?' Juno said.

'No. This forest goes all the way up into the valley. She could be anywhere.' Another tweet, and Chloe pulled Juno onto her stomach behind a rotting log.

Juno's hands burst with pins and needles. Heat spread across her palms. 'The Lady,' she whispered.

'Something is over here,' a guard said, walking out from behind a tree. 'Call the Lady.'

Juno caught her breath as the Lady, wearing trousers, a brown jacket and knee-high boots, appeared next to the guard.

'What is it?' the Lady said.

'I heard voices, my lady,' the guard said, scanning the forest. The Lady's eyes turned black and white. 'Girls' voices?'

'Yes, my lady.'

The Lady lifted her hands and sent grey tendrils of smoke out of her fingertips. 'Where are you, my young Juno?'

'Smoke,' Juno said into Chloe's ear. 'We have to get out of here.'

Chloe's tweet pierced the air. The Lady swung round, her narrowed eyes searching the area near the rotting log. Girls sprang from branch to branch, making their escape towards the town.

'Chloe, we need to go,' Juno said. 'Chloe?'

Chloe's head rocked from side to side. Her locs bounced around her shoulders as she slammed her hands up against her ears. A long groan escaped her lips.

'No,' Juno said, grabbing Chloe's wrists. 'Chloe, look at me.'

Eyes blinking rapidly, Chloe's pupils expanded across her irises. Juno's hands tingled with pins and needles as the crunching of the Lady's boots stepped closer. Deep in the forest, a roar reverberated.

'Find that cat,' the Lady said, turning to the guard.

'Fight it, Chloe,' Juno said. 'Keep your hands over your ears.'

Chloe groaned. She lifted her head and glared at Juno. Her pupils grew, then shrank, then grew again.

'I can hear you hiding, my dear girl,' the Lady said. 'There is nothing you can do for your friend. Come to me and I will not harm her or your cat.'

The heat grew in Juno's palms. Sweat beaded across her brow.

The tendrils of smoke poked at Chloe's ears, blocked only by her hands. 'Get me out of here, Juno,' Chloe said.

'Keep your hands over your ears. We are going to run for the fields. I will be right behind you,' Juno said.

'If you run, my dear, I will destroy everything you love,' the Lady said. 'Including your beloved Tilly.'

Juno froze.

'Juno, get me out of here,' Chloe said, blinking rapidly. 'Please, Juno.'

Juno shoved Chloe towards the wheat fields.

'After her,' the Lady said.

Boots crunched through the forest undergrowth. They escaped the searching tendrils of smoke. Chloe removed her hands from her ears and broke into a laboured run.

Juno stopped at the tree line. She turned and looked at the Lady. 'You leave my Tilly alone.'

'Come with me and you can see her,' the Lady said, striding through the pine trees.

The guards slowed to a jog and drew their weapons.

'You cannot do anything for Tilly, Juno,' Chloe said from the wheat field. 'Not if she takes you now.'

Juno broke the tree line and ran into the wheat field.

'Stay low,' Chloe said, crouching into the wheat.

Juno placed a hand on Chloe's shoulder and followed her, weaving through the wheat. The guards behind them hacked and slashed at the wheat. Chloe stopped and wrapped her arms around herself.

'Are you okay?' Juno said into her ear.

Chloe shook her head. 'I need to see Valen.'

Juno poked her head out of the wheat. The guards continued to search, but in the wrong direction. 'Let me lead,' she said, grabbing Chloe's hand.

The red barn grew in size as Juno worked her way through the fields. She stopped at the path opposite the barn and checked both directions. 'How do we get into Fairacre?'

Chloe shivered. Pain etched across her face. 'Go through the entrance. We can get to the alleys from the marketplace.'

'Hold on, Chloe,' Juno said.

They waited for the path to become deserted. Arm in arm, they left the wheat field and hurried along the path and over the drawbridge.

'Filthy sewer rats,' a man said. 'Get out of here.'

They hurried past the market stalls, then ducked into an alley. Chloe took the lead through the alleys and streets until they reached Valen's shop door. Juno rapped on the door, then tried the handle.

'Yes, yes, I am coming,' Valen said, his footsteps sounding through the shop.

'Are you okay?' Juno said, rubbing Chloe's back.

Shivering, Chloe nodded.

'Love,' Valen said, swinging open the door. 'Whatever is the matter?'

Chloe fell into Valen's arms, her hands wrapping around his neck. Valen picked her up as if she were a small doll, then marched through the shop and placed her gently on the couch. Henry sprang onto the armrest and clack-clacked his blunt mandibles at Chloe.

Valen sat next to Chloe and pulled her in close. 'What is going on?' he said to Juno.

'It was the Lady,' Juno said. 'We were in the forest and she sent out her tendrils of smoke. Some of it got into Chloe's ears.'

Chloe wiped her eyes, then laid her head into Valen's lap. 'It was so dark,' she said, her lips quivering. 'Like all hope was being drained from me.'

Valen lifted Chloe's head, stood, and with a growl he kicked his chair across his office. Sitting back down on the couch, he folded his arms around Chloe. 'You are safe here, lass,' he said, continuing to stroke her hair. 'I won't let anything happen to you.'

Chloe let out a sigh, closed her eyes and snuggled deeper into Valen's arms.

'What were you two thinking, going into the forest like that?' Valen said, frowning at Juno.

'It's all my fault,' Juno said, dropping her head. 'We went to find Chax.'

Valen let out a breath. 'You ladies take too many risks. I don't know what I would do without my Chloe.'

'I am sorry,' Juno said. 'I can't stand that Chax is being hunted.'

'It's not your fault. The sewer rats have always done it their way. Especially my Chloe.'

Chloe let out a long sigh. 'Can I have some tea, please, Valen?'

'Coming right up, lass,' Valen said, unwrapping himself and gently laying Chloe's head onto the armrest. 'I will be back here in the kitchen. Juno, can you swing the sign on the door to "closed", please?'

The sign turned, Juno returned to the couch. 'How are you feeling?'

'A little better,' Chloe said, rubbing her hands over her face. 'I never want to feel that way again.'

Juno hung her head. 'Does that mean my Tilly feels that way?'

Chloe lifted her head. 'Nobody deserves to feel that way. We will carry on looking until we find her, I promise you,' she said, curling a lip in anger.

Juno closed her eyes and thought of Tilly smiling and laughing in the greenhouse.

'Here we go, lass,' Valen said, handing out the mugs. 'I have added an extra sugar to give you some energy.'

Chloe blew gently on her tea, then took a sip. Nodding her head, she sighed, a smile creeping over her face.

Valen walked to the other side of his office and retrieved his chair. He sat and pulled a small velvet black box from a desk drawer. 'I am not sure this is going to work, so don't go relying on it, love.'

Chloe took the box and turned it over in her hand. She clicked it open and blinked at the two black devices sat nestled in a soft, velvet padding. 'Earplugs?'

'I started with an earplug, but then remembered the girls rely heavily on hearing. There is more to them than meets the eye, love.'

Juno plucked one out of the box and, twisting it in her fingers, she lifted it to the candlelight. She squinted through the small hole that ran through it. 'What are these metal bits deep in the hole?'

'Fans,' Chloe said, placing her cup of tea on the desk. 'Tiny fans.'

The corners of Valen's mouth curled up. 'Yes. The outside of the earplugs is soft and will mould to your ears when you insert them. The fans will stay still until they detect smoke, then they will activate.'

Chloe removed the earplug from the box and inserted it. She pressed the outside until it moulded to the contours of her ears. Juno handed her the other earplug, which she moulded into her other ear.

'How do they feel?' Juno said.

'They feel odd, but I can still hear,' Chloe said, tilting her head from side to side.

From a box on his desk, Valen pulled out a piece of incense. He struck a match and burned the end until trails of smoke snaked up through the air. With a gentle blow, the smoke floated towards Chloe's face.

Chloe's eyebrows shot up underneath her locs. 'I can hear them now. Like a soft whining.'

'Can you still hear me?' Juno said with a wide grin.

'I can just about hear you. Why are you grinning?'

'The fans are blowing your locs all over the place,' Juno said. 'Dancing locs. Jen and Gem have got to hear about this.'

'Don't you dare,' Chloe said, playfully punching Juno on the shoulder.

Valen moved in closer and cast a critical eye at the smoke being wafted away from Chloe's ears. 'They work with the incense smoke, love. I don't know if they will work against the smoke from the Lady.'

'I am sure we will find out sooner rather than later,' Chloe said, with a grim look on her face.

Valen sat back in his chair and frowned. 'You take too many risks.'

'The Lady will take over the entire town until she finds Juno. We cannot sit back and let that happen.'

Valen sighed, shook his head and folded his arms.

'Don't move, Juno,' Chloe said.

Juno froze.

'Valen, you'd better get that,' Chloe said.

Valen, leaning forwards, extended his hand to Juno's shoulder.

Juno's eyes widened. She covered her mouth with her hand. 'What is that?' she said through her fingers.

Valen turned the metal bug in his hand. 'My bumblebee. His name is Jay.' The bug spun in his hand and faced Juno. Its silvery wings lined with veins flapped into a buzz. Large, honeycombed eyes with tiny metal mirrors stared at her. Jay jumped into the air and, wings blurring, hovered over Valen's hand.

'Get it away from me,' Juno said, pressing herself into the couch.

'He is harmless, lass,' Valen said, waving a hand. 'Get, Jay. Go on, get out of here.'

Jay buzzed angrily towards Juno, then turned and disappeared into the kitchen.

Her body trembling, Juno said, 'Sorry. There are big bugs like that in my orchard, and they have a vicious sting.'

'My Jay won't sting you unless I tell him to,' Valen said, grinning.

Chloe smirked at Juno. She pulled the earplugs out of her ears and placed them back into the box. 'Can you make more of these?'

'Yes, love. As many as you want, but they take time.'

'For now, I need three more sets for my team and another two sets. A set for Naomi and another for Alexa.'

'Ok. Five earplugs will take me a day. I will send Jay to come and get you when they are ready.'

Juno's eyes widened. 'He can do that?'

Valen smirked. 'How do you think I get messages to Chloe?'

Chloe chuckled. 'I am exhausted. Can we stay here tonight?'

'Of course, love. Both of you have had a stressful morning. There is a small room off the kitchen if you would also like to rest, Juno.'

'I will stay here with Chloe,' Juno said, lying down next to Chloe.

Valen returned from his room and draped a large blanket over them. 'I will wake you at dinner time if you are both still sleeping.' He smiled at the two girls, who were already fast asleep.

Juno's eyes sprang open. A rough, large hand covered her mouth.

His face inches away, Valen put a finger to his lips. 'Quiet, lass. There is someone at the door. Get to the bedroom, the both of you.'

They clicked their face masks into place, fastened their hoodies and crept up the stairs to the bedroom above the store.

'Over here,' Chloe said, rolling up a carpet. 'We can lie down and listen through the cracks.'

'Who goes there?' Valen said.

A rasping cough followed by a cackle of laughter sounded from the darkness outside the shop door. 'Open the door, Valen. You know damn well who it is.'

'What do you want, Viktor?'

'Are you going to leave an old man out here in the dark?' Dr Viktor said. 'I raised you better than that, my boy.'

'The two goons behind you. Who are they?' Valen said.

'They will not harm you,' Dr Viktor said through another spluttering cough.

The bell above the shop door tinkled. 'Get in here, old man.'

A clunk sounded up through the gaps of the floor. Juno squinted her eyes and saw a man stooping over a cane, and two tall figures dressed from head to toe in dark cloaks.

'I am not the only one here. Any funny business and it will end badly for the two of you,' Valen said. With a hiss, Sia, a metal snake, slithered over Valen's shoulder and wrapped herself around Valen's neck.

'I see you have been putting your education towards trivial toys,' Dr Viktor said.

'I am happy here, Viktor. Why have you come?'

Dr Viktor hacked into his hand. He cleared his throat. 'Glass of water, perhaps?'

Valen growled and disappeared from Juno's view. 'You two sit on that couch and don't move,' he said from the office.

Juno and Chloe crawled along the bedroom floor. With just enough space under Valen's enormous bed, they slithered under and peered through the gaps in the floor. The clunk of Dr Viktor's cane fell silent.

'Careful,' Valen said, pointing a finger at one of the boy's.

'Have to remove my sword to sit, sir,' the cloaked boy said.

Juno watched the boy retrieve a long, thick sword from his back and place it across his legs. The second boy retrieved his staff from his back, sat on the couch and swung his leg over the armrest.

Dr Viktor slapped the boy's foot with his cane. 'Manners, my boy. We are guests in Valen's house.'

'Yes, sir,' the boy grumbled.

Valen pulled a chair over and offered it to Dr Viktor. 'Speak, Viktor. I am growing impatient with these theatrics.'

Dr Viktor wiped his mouth with a handkerchief, then placed it into his top pocket. *'A young girl from above the cliffs is roaming the town of Fairacre. You wouldn't know anything about that, would you?'*

Juno looked at Chloe with wide eyes. Chloe placed a finger on her lips. Juno closed one eye and continued watching through the gap.

'And what is this girl to you?' Valen said, sitting on his own chair and leaning forwards.

Dr Viktor rubbed his chin with his hand. 'She is in grave danger, my boy. A greater danger than you can imagine.'

Chloe pursed her lips and frowned at Juno.

'As if I didn't know that,' Juno mouthed, rolling her eyes.

'Your version of grave danger was not finding enough herbs for your potions, old man,' Valen said, waving a dismissive hand.

Dr Viktor slammed his cane into the floor. 'This is not a game, boy,' he said, spraying spittle at Valen.

Sia extended from Valen's neck and opened her mouth, showing two razor thin teeth.

'Not so much a toy, I see,' Dr Viktor said, sitting deeper into his chair.

Valen ran a finger over the top of Sia's head. 'It's okay, girl. Take it easy.'

Sia retracted around Valen's neck.

'What is this grave danger?' Valen said, tilting his head.

Dr Viktor spread his gnarled hands. 'Darkness. Untold darkness.'

Valen sat forwards. 'You'll have to be more specific than that, Viktor.'

'Don't play dumb, Valen. There is darkness in this town.'

'I will admit there is a presence in this town that I cannot explain.'

'Women acting out of place, yes?' Dr Viktor said, with a snort.

Chloe let out a low growl, then slapped her hand over her mouth.

The two boys stood in unison, drawing their weapons. 'Who is up there?' the taller boy said.

'Sit down,' Valen thundered.

The two boys looked over at Dr Viktor, who waved a hand for them to sit.

'Keep them in order, Viktor,' Valen said, sitting back in his chair.

Dr Viktor waved a hand at the two boys. 'These are the last of my pupils. They are like sons to me. Just as you were, Valen.'

Valen snorted. 'I never lived up to your expectations, Viktor.'

'I will ignore your hurtful retorts, Valen. Now tell me, where is the girl?'

Valen remained quiet.

'You could never lie to me, boy. You know where she is, don't you?' Dr Viktor said. 'I can help her.'

'For whose gain, Viktor? Your gain?'

'There is nothing to gain, my boy. If my assumptions are correct, she possesses a great power that she does not know how to control.'

Juno lifted her head and looked down at the flame marks on the underside of each finger.

Chloe shook both hands in front of Juno's face. 'O almighty powerful one,' she mouthed.

Juno rolled her eyes and slapped Chloe's hands away.

'How do you know of this power?' Valen said, leaning back and interlacing his fingers behind his head.

Dr Viktor retrieved his handkerchief from his pocket and wiped his mouth. 'Where is she, Valen?'

Valen rocked in his chair. 'It is not my place to tell you where she is. If she needs your help, she will find you herself.'

Little Henry scuttled across the desk, jumped onto Valen's knees and clacked his mandibles at the two boys sitting on the couch.

'So very lifelike,' Dr Viktor said, leaning forwards. 'Spreading your essence a little thin, my boy?'

'Easily retrieved,' Valen said.

Dr Viktor grunted. 'It is time for me to return home. You remember where that is, Valen?'

Valen gave Dr Viktor a nod.

'When you need my help. And you will. Either come to my home or contact one of my boys.'

Valen looked at the boys on the couch. 'How do I contact the boys?'

With a thump, Dr Viktor pressed his cane into the ground and struggled to his feet. 'They won't be far away.'

Valen hauled himself out of his chair and waited for the two boys to follow Dr Viktor.

'It was nice to see you again, my boy,' Dr Viktor said from inside the shop. 'And I am sure we will see each other soon.'

'Don't be so sure, Viktor,' Valen said, his snort floating up through the floor cracks.

Dr Viktor chuckled.

The shop door tinkled as they left.

'They are gone,' Valen said, shouting up the stairs.

Chloe double-stepped down the stairs and stood in front of

Valen with her hands on her hips. 'My boy? Your training? Your essence? We have a lot to talk about, Valen.'

Valen ran his hands through his hair and let out a sigh. 'I know, lass. And I promise we will. Right now you need to get Juno back to the sewers, where she will be safe.'

Chloe frowned. 'Is he that dangerous?'

'I don't think he would harm you. He would have to deal with me, and that, he knows, is a bad idea.' Valen grabbed three boxes from the desk. 'Three more sets of earplugs for your team. I will have Naomi's and Alexa's done by mid-morning.'

Chloe hugged Valen. 'Thank you, my love.'

Valen wrapped his arms around Chloe. 'Go now. It is not safe. Make sure you go down the closest drain to the sewers. He may be watching.'

'Thank you, Valen,' Juno said.

Valen pulled Juno into a three-way hug. 'Look after each other, will you? Now get.'

The doorbell tinkled as Juno and Chloe slunk into the night.

CHAPTER 8
YOU!

'Time to get up,' Chloe said, throwing Juno's black outfit at her. 'We need to update Naomi.'

Juno swung her legs over the bed and rubbed her eyes. She climbed into her outfit and followed Chloe down the corridors to Naomi's office.

'Morning, boss,' Chloe said, peering through the door.

Naomi waved them in. 'The twins have left food.'

Chloe placed the small earplug box onto Naomi's desk. 'We don't know if these will work. Valen tested them but has warned us to be cautious.'

Naomi snapped open the box, lifted an earplug and turned it between her fingers. 'Earplugs? How many do we have?'

'Enough for my team and two sets coming for you and Alexa. No point building more until we know they work.'

Naomi placed the earplugs back in the box. 'I was expecting a report last night but your cots were empty before I went to bed.'

Chloe shivered. 'I will let Juno fill you in, boss.'

Juno swallowed the last of her bread, then recounted the events of the previous day. Naomi scraped her chair back and stood in silence with her back to them.

'You okay, boss?' Chloe said after a few minutes.

Naomi's shoulders rose and fell with a sigh. She sat back down and folded her arms. 'Our way of life is at risk. If we cannot send our teams to the surface, we cannot feed our community.'

Chloe stood and paced behind the chairs. 'We cannot allow any girl to succumb to that darkness, boss. It is the most awful thing I have ever felt.'

Naomi's face softened. 'I agree. We need to ask Valen to make more of these devices.'

'What if they don't work?' Juno said.

'We don't have a choice, young Juno,' Naomi said. 'We have to feed our family somehow.'

'Can we speak to Mr Hargreaves?'

'He hasn't been back to his home since you have arrived,' Naomi said. 'Nor have we seen him enter or exit the town hall.'

'He wouldn't help anyway,' Chloe said with a scowl.

'Can you ask Valen to make more, Chloe?' Naomi said.

Chloe sat back into her chair and grunted. 'He isn't telling me how they work. I will ask him and see what he says.'

Juno lifted a hand. 'We have access to the farmlands through the storm drains. Can we not get food that way?'

'The town of Fairacre is a farming community and is the primary source of food for the City of Lynn,' Chloe said. 'If they catch any of our girls stealing from those lands, they throw them into prison for good.'

'It might be our only choice,' Naomi said.

Chloe shook her head. 'We ask too much of these young girls sometimes.'

A sharp rap on Naomi's door made Juno jump.

'Come,' Naomi said.

'The infected sewer rat has escaped,' Alexa said, after entering the office.

'Juno, Chloe, with me,' Naomi said, rising and striding out of her office.

'How did this happen again, Alexa?'

'A serving girl opened the door to hand her breakfast. The serving girl has ended up in the infirmary.'

Naomi changed direction towards the infirmary. 'How is the girl?'

'Pretty banged up,' Alexa said.

They strode into the infirmary and up to the young girl's bed.

The girl looked up with a black eye and bruised lip. 'I am sorry, miss,' she said, tears springing to her eyes. 'She hadn't returned the plate from last night's meal, so I went in to get it.'

'It's okay,' Chloe said, squeezing her hand. 'Our nurses will take good care of you. You have done nothing wrong.'

Naomi bent down, kissed the young girl's forehead, then looked up with eyes of steel. 'Chloe, Juno, get the team into town and find that sewer rat.'

Chloe strode out of the infirmary and sent an ear-splitting whistle down the corridors. 'Wear your beggar's clothes over the black outfit, Juno. We don't know how long we will be topside.'

A team member came up to Chloe. 'Yes, miss?'

Chloe placed the three boxes in her hand. 'Every team member uses these at all times. Understood?'

The team member took the boxes and shot down a corridor.

'Where do we start looking?' Juno said, slipping her beggar's clothes on.

'We check the alleyways from the rooftops,' Chloe said, snapping her sword to her back and daggers to her thighs. 'Ready to go solo?'

'I don't know all the hand signals.'

'A whistle will do,' Chloe said, tucking her locs into her hoodie and striding out of their room. 'Let's move.'

The metal door of the hideout slammed shut and, joining

Chloe's team, they made for the nearest grate, which they slid open, and climbed out. Chloe slid the grate back into place and gave her team their instructions. They started from the town hall and worked outwards towards the town edge, each taking a different district. Juno stood on a roof corner and scanned the length of the alleyway. She gave Chloe the thumbs-down, then ran horizontally to the next corner and peered over the edge. The deeper she went into the entertainment district, the stronger the smells of baking bread, stewing fish and boiling fruit drifted up into her nostrils. She scrambled up a steeper rooftop, held onto the chimney and cocked her head at the sound of marching boots echoing from the street below. The padded outfit protected her as she slid down to the roof edge. Hands gripping the edge, she peeped over and caught her breath. Juno slunk away from the roof edge, ran back to the top of the roof and scanned the town skyline, searching for Chloe's team. She slid down the roof, sprang across the alley and sprinted towards the town hall, waving frantically.

Juno let out a sigh of relief as Chloe's figure sprinted towards her.

Chloe knelt. 'Did you find her?'

Juno nodded. 'Guards. The same guards that stand at the top of the town hall steps. They are escorting her along the street.'

'How many?' Chloe said, a grim look spreading across her face.

'Eight guards,' Juno said. 'Four in front, four at the back.'

Chloe lifted her head and whistled. 'She will know we are coming after that whistle. When we go down, I need you to stay on the roof.'

'You're going to fight them?' Juno said. 'Can you take on that many?'

'We don't have a choice. If that sewer rat gets back to the town hall, she will compromise our entire home.'

'Please be careful,' Juno said, resting a hand on Chloe's

shoulder.

Chloe's team shed their beggar's clothes, clicked their masks into place and drew their short swords.

'The street narrows near the bakery shops,' Chloe said, peering over at a wide street. 'We take her there.'

The team bounded over the alleys and knelt on the rooftop overlooking the small bakery shop. The distant thump of marching boots grew louder.

'Remember to stay up here,' Chloe said, into Juno's ear. 'If I signal, go to Valen's. Are we clear?'

'Okay. Please be careful,' Juno said.

Chloe signalled for two of her girls to vault across the narrow street and wait on the rooftop opposite. Her hand raised ready to signal, Chloe listened to the thumping of the leather boots as they grew louder. Four guards appeared around the bend, their feet marching in unison, their hands resting on their swords. They shoved Fairacre residents out of the way if they got too close. The sewer rat followed, her black eyes searching the street and rooftops. The remaining guards, their faces set in grim determination, appeared at the rear. Chloe dropped her hand and sprang from the roof. She struck a guard on the top of his head with the pommel of her short sword. The girls plunged among the guards, their short swords high above their heads. The clash of steel on steel shattered the quiet street. Two guards fell, knocked to the ground, blood spurting out of their noses. The infected girl, stepping out of the fray, stood with her back against a shop window and folded her arms. Chloe spun under a slashing sword and swept the guard's feet from under him.

'The famous Chloe and her team to the rescue?' the sewer rat drawled. 'How pathetic.'

Juno's ears pricked up at the sound of guard's boots running towards them. 'Chloe, more are coming,' she shouted. 'Get out of there.'

Chloe spun her blade into the shield of a guard. She flicked her leg up and caught the guard's chin with the heel of her boot. 'You are not yourself, Joanne,' she said, ducking under a guard's sword. 'Come home with us.'

'The Lady has called me to her side,' Joanne said, lifting her chin. 'I will escape that rat-infested hole we call home.'

Eight more guards ran around the corner of the street and charged into the group.

'Back to back,' Chloe said, parrying a guard's sword with her blade.

'You cannot escape, Chloe,' Joanne said. 'The Lady's guards will cut you down and I will tell her about the sewers.'

The four girls stood in a tight circle and defended themselves from the swinging, slashing and prodding of the guards' swords.

'Get to Valen's,' Chloe said, shouting over the crashing of weapons. 'Go now, Juno.'

Joanne snapped her head up and caught Juno's gaze with her bottomless black and white eyes. 'The Lady wishes to see you,' she drawled, unfolding her arms and pointing. 'No harm will come to your friends if you come with me.'

'Don't listen to her, Juno,' Chloe said, snapping a fist out and breaking a guard's jaw. 'Get to Valen's.'

The pounding of boots echoed through the street as eight more guards, drawing their swords, ran around the corner.

'I cannot leave you here,' Juno said, a tear sliding down her cheek.

Chloe ripped her face mask off and pointed her sword at Juno. 'Do as I say, young Juno. We lose it all if they take you.'

Juno clenched her fists by her side. She turned, then jumped with fright as two flowing cloaks swirled past her, dropping onto the street below. The singing of steel from sword sheath rang through the street as the boy released his shining greatsword from his back. A gnarled staff spun through the air, twirling in great arcs, removing guards' helmets with sickening thuds. The guards fell one by one at the feet of the girls and the two boys as they worked together.

Joanne inched along the shop wall, looking for an escape down the narrow street.

'You are staying right here,' one of the boys said, catching Joanne between the eyes with the end of his staff. Joanne's eyes closed as she crumpled into a heap.

The taller boy lifted the chin of a guard with the end of his greatsword. 'Leave this place and take your fallen with you.'

The guard, wild-eyed, signalled to the remaining men to retreat with their fallen brothers. He picked up a guard and said, 'The Lady will hear about this.'

'I am counting on it,' the boy with the greatsword said. 'Now leave before there are none of you left to leave.'

Juno slid down a drainpipe and ran over to Chloe. 'Are you okay?'

'I think so,' Chloe said, checking herself over.

The boy with the staff walked over to Joanne and checked her neck for a pulse. 'She is alive but she will have a headache in the morning.'

Chloe sheathed her short sword and replaced her dagger. She walked up to the boy with the greatsword and said, 'Why are you helping us?'

The boy reached over his head and slid his greatsword back into its sheath. Folding his arms, he lifted his chin and remained silent.

'What boy doesn't want to help a lady in distress?' the boy with the staff said.

Chloe turned and jabbed her finger in the boy's chest. 'Don't patronise me. You appear out of nowhere to help. Have you been spying on us?'

The boy took a step back. 'I thought you would be happy with the help.'

Chloe let out a grunt and walked over to Joanne. 'We need to get her home before they send more people to get her.'

The boy with the staff stepped in front of Chloe. 'She is coming with us to Dr Viktor. He can help her.'

'Like hell she is,' Juno said, marching over and peering up at the boy. 'She is a sewer rat. One of our sisters and she belongs with us.'

The boy with the greatsword looked at the other boy. 'It seems you have angered the fire child, brother.'

The boy with the gnarled staff lifted a hand and took a step backwards. 'We mean no harm. Do you want your sister cured of this affliction or not?'

'First thing we do is get out of this street,' Chloe said, walking over to Joanne and heaving her up.

The boy with the greatsword walked up to Joanne and scooped her up into his arms. 'Lead the way.'

Chloe signalled to her team. 'Keep an eye on these two,' she said, marching down the street into a narrow alley.

They headed north. The sounds of the entertainment district faded behind them. Chloe twisted and turned through the alleys until she reached a small gate. She swung open the gate and walked into a garden that looked like paradise. A water fountain sitting against the town wall glinted with the sun's rays as water bubbled down its steps into the small pond at the bottom. Fish swam lazily along the surface of the small pond, their mouths opening above the water to suck in any unsuspecting insects.

'Where are we?' Juno said, looking around in amazement.

'Mr Hargreaves's back yard,' Chloe said, walking up to a bench. 'Put Joanne down here, please.'

The balconies of the three-storey house glinted with clusters of multicoloured flowers that grew in identical display pots.

'I have never seen a place like this,' Juno said, her mouth wide open. 'Tilly would love this.'

'Welcome to the trading district,' Chloe said, scowling. 'Rich men with their bought brides live here.'

Juno closed her eyes as her thoughts turned to the school above the hills.

'Yes, young Juno. You would have ended up here,' Chloe said, sensing what Juno was thinking. *'A* bought trophy.'

Juno sighed and shook her head. She turned and marched up to the two boys, who stood either side of the bench. 'What did you mean by calling me "fire child"? Why did you call me that?'

The two boys, their faces still hidden, stared at Juno. The shorter of the two boys glanced over at the taller boy.

'Tell me,' Juno said, taking a step towards the taller boy. 'What do you know that I don't?'

The boy raised his hands. 'Dr Viktor called you that. I don't know anything more.'

Juno narrowed her eyes and glared, unblinking, at the taller boy.

Chloe moved alongside Juno and laid a hand on her forearm. 'We need to deal with Joanne first.' She turned to the tall boy and said, 'You said you could cure Joanne.'

The boy clasped his hands behind his back. His dark eyes never leaving Chloe, he said, 'Dr Viktor said he could, yes.'

'I don't trust these two,' Chloe said, waving a dismissive hand at the boy. 'Let's get Joanne back home.'

Juno shook her head at the boys, walked to the bench and ran a hand over Joanne's forehead. 'What if they can help her, Chloe?'

Chloe let out a sigh. 'Even if they could, it is not up to us to make that decision.'

The boy with the staff reached inside his hoodie and unclipped his face mask. The mask fell away from his face. He turned to Juno. 'And what if Dr Viktor can help you, Juno?'

Juno swung round and froze. 'What is it?' Chloe said. 'Juno?'

'You!' Juno shouted, her face scrunching in disgust.

The boy cocked his head. A lock of blonde hair fell out of his hoodie as he gave Juno a lopsided grin. Chloe drew a blade from her thigh and pointed it at the boy.

'Steady now,' the boy said.

'This is Billy,' Juno said with a growl. 'He tried to kill my Chax, my kitten, in the school orchard.'

'I did not try to kill your kitten,' Billy said, pointing his staff at Juno. 'I was trying to protect it.'

Her hands balled into fists, Juno ground her teeth. 'When I found Chax in the orchard, there were three boys trying to hurt her. Billy was one of them.'

'Dr Viktor sent me to protect that kitten from those thugs,' Billy said, leaning forwards. 'Do you not remember me protesting?'

'You did little to stop them either.'

'From what I recall, you had that under control,' Billy said, his lopsided grin returning.

Juno turned away from Billy and knelt next to Joanne.

'And you,' Chloe said, pointing at the taller boy. 'Who are you, then?'

The boy unclipped his mask and ran his hand over a strong, slightly hooked nose and wide, thin-lipped mouth. 'My name is Miles.'

'Miles isn't much of a talker,' Billy said, removing the hood of his cloak. 'More the strong, fighting type.'

Chloe thought for a moment. She signalled to her team. 'Take Joanne home. Tell Naomi to meet us at Valen's.'

The girls walked over to Joanne and lifted her between them.

Miles stepped in front of them. 'Dr Viktor told us to bring the girl to him.'

'She will go where I say she goes,' Chloe said, shoving her face inches from Miles. 'We will talk to Naomi at Valen's.'

Miles's brow furrowed.

'Leave it be, brother,' Billy said, walking over and placing a hand on Miles's shoulder. 'Chloe is right. Let us do this the proper way.'

Miles grunted and crossed his arms.

Chloe signalled to the girls to move. 'We need to move too. The sun is setting and the rich will be returning home,' she said, snapping her face mask into place.

Juno, Chloe, Miles and Billy climbed onto the rooftops and sprinted south towards the manufacturing district.

Chloe tapped on the shop door, stood back and smiled at the clattering from inside the shop.

'What?' Valen said, ripping the door open and blinking rapidly.

'Valen, what have you done to yourself?' Chloe said, her mouth dropping.

He scratched the side of his face. 'What do you mean, love?'

Chloe placed her hand on his chest and gently walked him back into the shop. 'Sit, and I will make some tea.'

'Why are these two men in my shop?' he said, dropping into his chair. 'Are we playing with the enemy now?'

Miles and Billy removed their weapons and sat on the sofa with their hands on their knees.

'When last did you sleep, Valen?' Juno said. 'You aren't looking your best.'

'Busy with the devices,' he said, waving his hand at his desk.

Juno frowned at the rows of black boxes along the desk. 'How many did you make?'

'Around forty,' Valen said, stifling a yawn. 'Enough for ten teams.'

'We didn't ask for that many,' Chloe said, placing her tea on the table. 'Why do you look so tired?'

'He just needs a little sleep,' Juno said. 'He has been working all night and day.'

'He has parted with too much of his essence,' Billy said from the couch. 'Not a wise thing to do.'

Juno frowned. 'Too much of his essence?'

'How else do you think he gets these little machines to run around?' Billy said. 'Every machine has a part of him in it.'

Chloe cupped Valen's face in her hands and traced her thumbs down the sides of his nose. 'Is this dangerous?'

'It is okay, love,' Valen said. 'My essence will return to me if I tell it to.'

'It's dangerous,' Miles said.

'What my brother is trying to say,' Billy said, bumping Miles with his shoulder, 'is that Valen needs a good night's sleep.'

'What are you not telling me?' Chloe said, standing and placing her hands on her hips.

A sharp rap sounded on the front door.

'That will be Naomi. I will fetch her,' Juno said.

Chloe leaned forwards. 'Naomi is not someone you want to mess with. Remove your masks.'

Miles removed his mask and sat straight, placing his hands back on his knees.

'I trust this meeting is a wise choice?' Naomi said, striding into the room and eyeing the two boys.

'This is Billy and Miles. They helped rescue Joanne. They say a Dr Viktor can help her. He also knows what I am. I think we should speak to him,' Juno said, running out of air.

'Take a breath, young Juno,' Naomi said.

'Juno is correct. I, however, am not sure I trust this Dr Viktor,' Chloe said.

Valen jerked awake. 'What of Viktor? I will throttle that man,' he said, his voice booming across the room.

Billy cleared his throat. 'If I may?'

'Go right ahead,' Naomi said.

'Dr Viktor sent me to look after Juno before she came to the town of Fairacre. He has given the two of us strict instructions to bring Joanne and Juno back to him so we can help them both.'

'Study her, more like,' Valen said, wagging a finger at Billy.

Billy spread his hands. 'I do not think he wishes to study them.'

'Naomi, he knows what is happening to me,' Juno said, looking down at her hands.

Naomi clasped her hands together and steepled her fingers. 'How can this Dr Viktor help our Joanne?'

'Dr Viktor and I have experience in herbal potions,' Billy said. 'We may have the ability to chase this darkness from your friend.'

'And how does he know of what is happening to young Juno?' Naomi said, sweeping her hand at Juno.

'He spoke of the fire child when he sent me to the school above the cliffs,' Billy said. 'He imparted no other information.'

'Master Valen,' Naomi said. 'You have your reservations?'

Chloe rolled her eyes, then kicked Valen's chair. 'Wake up, my love.'

Valen snorted awake. 'Sorry, love, what was the question?'

'Naomi wants to know what your issue is with us taking Juno and Joanne to Dr Viktor.'

Valen narrowed his eyes. 'Viktor always has a second agenda. An agenda that suits him.'

Naomi turned back to Miles and Billy. 'Well?'

Miles raised his chin at Valen. 'Would you deny Juno and Joanne the possibility of being free of this darkness because of your personal vendetta with Viktor?'

Valen let out a growl, yawned, then fell asleep.

Naomi knelt next to Juno. 'What are your thoughts?'

Juno looked at the boys, then cleared her throat. 'If there is the possibility of finding out what is happening to me, I would like to go. But only if Chloe approves.'

Chloe looked at Naomi and gave her a nod.

Naomi stood and looked at the boys. 'Two sewer rat teams will escort you to Dr Viktor's residence. If anything happens to any of our people, you will have to deal with a far greater force than a few city guards. Are we crystal clear?'

Billy and Miles nodded.

'Eastern gate at sundown,' Naomi said. 'Chloe, Juno, stay here tonight and look after Master Valen.'

Valen started in his chair and sat up. 'The devices,' he said, with a wry smile. 'Don't forget the devices.'

Chloe reached under the desk and pulled out a cloth bag. She scooped the devices into the bag, knotted the top and handed it to Naomi.

'Gentlemen,' Naomi said, giving the boys a nod. 'You will leave here five minutes after I have. No sooner.'

'It has been a pleasure to meet you, Naomi,' Billy said, standing and placing a fist over his breast.

Miles stood. 'We will take good care of your two girls.'

Naomi gave the two boys one last look, then marched through the shop, out the door and into the night.

'Help me get Valen to his room,' Chloe said.

The stairs creaked as the four of them groaned and wheezed under Valen's weight. They laid him on his bed and returned to the shop.

'It was a pleasure meeting you, Chloe. And good to see you again, fire child,' Billy said, his lopsided smile spreading across his face.

Miles walked to the shop door and peered over his shoulder. 'Sundown.'

The shop bell tinkled, and the boys faded into the night.

CHAPTER 9
PARENTS

'This is so stupid. It's not doing what I want it to do,' Chloe said, her voice causing Juno's eyes to snap open.

Juno walked into the kitchen and pointed at the cooker. 'Chloe, it's burning.'

Chloe grabbed the pan and threw it into the sink. 'It's either too hot or too cold. How do Gem and Jen do this all day?'

Juno chuckled, picked up a damp cloth and wiped off the flour stuck to Chloe's face. 'You have more ingredients on you than in the pan. Your locs have turned white.'

Chloe slouched against the kitchen counter. 'So much for cooking breakfast for Valen.'

'Good morning, love,' Valen said, shuffling into the kitchen.

'You still look tired. Did you sleep?' Chloe said, embracing him.

'Very well,' Valen said with a wry smile. 'It will take some time for my energy to replenish.'

Juno pointed at Valen's office. 'Why don't you go and sit? We will bring you some tea.'

Valen's chair creaked as he lowered his enormous frame into it. 'Don't worry about the kitchen. I will sort it out later.'

Chloe scowled and whispered, 'He noticed.'

'Let's get some tea on the go. We need to find out why he is so tired,' Juno said. With two more extra lumps of sugar in Valen's tea, Juno walked into his office and handed the mug to him. She sat on the couch, then jumped. 'What the hell?' she said, slopping her tea onto the wooden floor.

Nine red eyes stared up at her. Little Henry clack-clacked his mandibles in disapproval.

'Shoo. Go on,' Chloe said, waving a hand at Henry.

Little Henry sprang from the chair onto the armrest, then onto the desk. He raised his two front legs and tip-tapped them together.

Juno shuddered. 'I will never get used to these creatures running about.'

'Harmless,' Valen said through a yawn.

Chloe sat on the couch and draped a leg over the armrest. 'Time you explained what is going on, love. Seeing you like this has us both worried.'

'Start from the beginning,' Juno said, wrapping her legs underneath her.

Valen raked his hands through his hair. He leaned back in his chair and sighed. 'My mother never married, so I was born to a woman who had no husband. My father, to deny the shame on his family, cast my mother out of Fairacre.'

Chloe shook her head. 'Women have endured this for hundreds of years.'

Juno's mouth hung open.

'And here in Fairacre it happens all the time,' Valen said with a shake of his head.

'What happened to your mother?' Juno said.

'My mother spent all day searching for food in the forest. There was not enough, so she sacrificed her food to feed me,' Valen said, his voice cracking. 'She lay down and placed me on her breast. The next morning I woke up in a strange bed, with no sign of my mother.'

'Dr Viktor?' Chloe said, her eyebrows jumping into her locs.

'One of Dr Viktor's students found me,' Valen said.

'And your mother?' Juno said, her eyes widening.

'She died that night in the forest,' Valen said. 'Dr Viktor had her buried at the back of his house.'

'That is so sad,' Juno said, biting her bottom lip.

'I am so sorry, love,' Chloe said, placing an arm around his shoulders.

'I think it is no different to what you two have experienced,' Valen said, resting his head on Chloe's shoulder.

Juno balanced her tea on the couch armrest. 'I never knew my parents. They left me near the river by the school. Miss Petra was like my mother to me.'

'My parents were slaves. Captured and brought here from the west. Eventually they outlawed the ownership of people, but by that time I was with the sewer rats, and my family left to go home,' Chloe said, standing and dropping back onto the couch.

'Did your parents not search for you before they went?' Juno said.

'If they did, I didn't know about it,' Chloe said. 'I was only a babe when the sewer rats took me in.'

'Alexa, and your three team members?' Juno said.

'Same story with all of them. We have grown up as sisters.'

Valen closed his eyes and dragged his hand over his face. 'Laws of the City of Lynn. They have a lot to answer for.'

'What happened at Dr Viktor's?' Juno said, breaking Valen out of his thoughts.

Valen opened his weary eyes. 'Dr Viktor took me in and raised me like a son. What Naomi does for the orphan girls in Fairacre, Dr Viktor does for the boys. There are fewer orphan boys because we use them for hard labour in the town. The girls, they discard.'

'Apart from Donte's house,' Chloe said, snarling.

Valen curled his lip in disgust. 'Donte has an arrangement with Mr Hargreaves.'

Juno's brow furrowed. 'The more I hear about Mr Hargreaves, the more I don't like him.'

Valen rubbed his chin. 'He is not altogether an evil man. He has to play by the rules of Fairacre. Rules set by the City of Lynn. And Donte comes from the city.'

'Did Dr Viktor teach you to bring these creatures to life?' Juno said, taking a sip of her tea.

Little Henry clack-clacked his mandibles while spinning in circles on the desk.

Valen smiled at his spider. 'Dr Viktor finds out what people are capable of and then teaches them through a strict regimen. He teaches each boy he takes in differently.'

'What of this essence?' Chloe said, looking at Valen through her eyebrows.

Valen waved his finger at Little Henry. Juno suddenly vaulted from the couch, through the shop and out of the front door.

'Juno,' Chloe said, running after her and catching her by the arm. 'Whatever is the matter?'

Juno, wild-eyed, pointed at the shop door. 'Valen.'

Chloe frowned. 'What about Valen?'

'Smoke,' Juno said, grinding her teeth. 'Smoke came out of his fingers, Chloe.'

Chloe's frown deepened. 'My Valen?'

'Like the Lady,' Juno said.

Chloe shook her head. 'Are you sure?'

Juno wrapped her arms around herself. 'I am sure.'

The shop door opened with a tinkle. 'Whatever is the matter? Can you come back inside?'

Chloe marched up to Valen and jabbed a finger into his chest.

'Juno says you have smoke coming out of your fingers. Just like the Lady.'

His mouth opening and closing, Valen squinted in confusion. 'I have no idea what you are talking about. All I did was an essence transfer.'

'Are you telling me you don't see the smoke either?' Chloe said, tilting her head.

Valen shook his head. 'No, love. I have never seen any smoke.'

Chloe grunted. She walked back to Juno. 'I think we should go back inside and see what Valen says.'

Juno shook her head. 'I don't want to go back into that place.'

'Juno, it's Valen. I have known him most of my life,' Chloe said, hugging her. 'He will never hurt you.'

'How do you know?' Juno said into Chloe's shoulder.

'Because I love him. And I know him,' Chloe said, releasing Juno from their hug.

Juno, eyeing Valen, took a wide berth and stalked back into his office where she sat down on the couch.

Little Henry lay sprawled on the tabletop, his glass eyes dark and empty. Chloe spread her hands. 'Well, Valen? Care to share what this essence transfer is?'

With a look of concern on his face, Valen peered over at Juno. 'I am sorry if I scared you, lass.'

Juno pressed herself deeper into the couch and gave him a nod.

'Dr Viktor taught me how to share my essence so I could bring life to objects. I didn't know that smoke comes out when I do it.'

'It's what the Lady does when she infects people,' Juno said. 'Her tendrils of smoke are a lot darker than yours, though.'

Valen scratched his chin and pursed his lips. 'I left Dr Viktor's before I learned anything more. We had a falling out about another boy.'

'How does all of this essence thing work?' Chloe said, her leg bouncing on the armrest.

'It is a piece of me that I give to something to give it life. Little Henry here has no essence. That's why he lies lifeless.'

Chloe stood and paced. 'Have you ever used it to control a person?' she said, stopping and placing her hands on her hips.

Valen spluttered. 'Of course not. I would never use it on people, even if I could. I don't even know what it would do.'

'Dr Viktor said you were spreading your essence too thin?' Chloe said.

'Each person has a certain amount of essence. The more I give, the less there is inside me.'

'And let me guess,' Chloe said, slumping back onto the couch. 'You used your essence on the earplugs?'

'A tiny bit,' Valen said. 'Enough for the small fans to spin when smoke gets near them.'

'A tiny bit works out to be a lot if there are that many, Valen,' Chloe said. 'I understand why you look so gaunt now.'

A grin spread across Valen's face. 'The essence will return to me when someone destroys a device. I can also order it to return to me.'

'There is no danger of it not returning?' Juno said, taking a sip of her tea. Valen scrunched up his nose and stared off into the distance.

'Valen?' Chloe said, nudging him with her foot. 'What are you not telling us?'

Valen moved the lifeless body of Little Henry around with his finger. 'If I pass away suddenly, there is no time for my essence to return.'

'What does that mean?' Chloe said, leaning forwards with a look of concern. 'That doesn't sound good at all.'

Valen bit the bottom of his lip. 'If you die suddenly and you have shared your essence, which is the spirit of your soul, it stays separated in parts in this world. It will forever roam in this world until your soul reclaims all the parts of its missing essence.'

Juno and Chloe sat in silence, the dripping of the kitchen taps growing louder, like the sound of the second hand on a clock.

Juno broke the silence. 'What does your soul become when parts of its essence are missing?'

Valen cleared his throat. 'You are going to see Viktor this evening?'

'To heal Joanne and find out information regarding young Juno,' Chloe said, resting a hand on Juno's shoulder.

Valen sat forwards. 'Viktor has more information. I left before my education was complete. He will be able to answer your question.'

'Why did you leave when you did?' Juno said. 'You mentioned another boy.'

A frown creased over Valen's forehead. 'Viktor educates with a heavy hand. I stood up to him with my size advantage. The boy could not, so I took him away.'

'Typical of my Valen,' Chloe said, looking at Valen fondly.

Valen sat back and pinched the bridge of his nose. 'It is difficult seeing that man again. The terrible memories are far stronger than the wonderful memories.'

'You have built a good life for yourself here,' Juno said. 'And found a lovely girl.'

'Aye, lass,' Valen said, blushing. 'For that I am very grateful.'

Chloe nudged Juno with her elbow. 'It's time for us to get back to the girls. Naomi will be planning tonight's escort of Joanne.'

Valen snapped his fingers, then held his palm facing upwards. Juno shuddered as a buzzing passed her right ear. She pushed herself hard back onto the sofa.

The metal bumblebee landed on Valen's hand and curled up into a perfectly round metal ball. 'I want you to take Little Jay with you. He will come back to me, and I will then know there is a problem.'

'You aren't coming with us?' Chloe said.

Valen rolled Jay into Chloe's outstretched hand. 'I will stay in town. I want Dr Viktor to concentrate on Juno and Joanne, and I will just be a distraction.'

'Okay,' Chloe said, deciding not to press further. 'How do I get Jay to come back to you?'

'Throw him as high as you can,' Valen said, using the desk as support to stand. 'I am going to go and get some more rest.'

Chloe stood and pecked him on the cheek.

'Young Juno,' Valen said, catching her before she walked through the front door. 'Do not trust Viktor. Trust your instincts first.'

'Thanks, Valen,' Juno said.

Naomi listened to the morning's events with her chin resting on her steepled hands. She picked up a pen, sat back and tapped her teeth. 'Can we trust this Dr Viktor?'

'No,' Juno said. 'But I need to find out if there is any way to help Tilly. And if we can help Joanne.'

'He has information about the Lady,' Chloe said, her leg bouncing off the armrest. 'It's a chance I think we have to take.'

Naomi continued to tap her pen against her mouth. 'I am going to add another team for the escort. We have enough devices.'

'That leaves you short here in the town,' Chloe said.

'Once Alexa has assessed the situation, she can send one team back,' Naomi said. 'We are much safer here in the sewers than you will be out there.'

'How is Joanne?' Juno said.

'Continuously asking why she is being held captive,' Naomi said, dropping her pen and shuffling papers into a neat stack. 'Do you think this lady is controlling her even when she is all the way down here?'

'I think so,' Juno said, inclining her head. 'I am hoping Dr Viktor will fill in the gaps.'

'What is the plan for the escort, boss?'

Naomi picked up a piece of paper. 'Three teams. One team to escort Joanne, another team on the roof and the last through the alleys.'

'Why don't we use the sewers all the way to the eastern gate?' Juno said.

'They are too narrow?' Chloe said, looking at Naomi.

Naomi nodded. 'Chloe is right. We are going to come out in the manufacturing district and work our way through the streets to the eastern gate. Every team will wear their beggar's outfits, with their black fighter's outfits underneath.'

'What about me and Chloe?' Juno said, glancing over at Chloe.

'You two lead the escort and keep an eye out for Viktor's boys. Once you are over the moat, it's double-time through the orchards and into the forest in the east.'

'Everyone has their devices?' Juno said.

'Everything is in order,' Naomi said. 'I suggest you get some food and some rest.'

Juno and Chloe left Naomi's office and made their way to the kitchen. They filled their plates and walked back to their room, where they sat cross-legged and ate dried fruit and morning-baked bread.

'When we get to Dr Viktor, can you stay with me?' Juno said, looking over at Chloe.

'I am not letting you out of my sight,' Chloe said, flashing her a wide smile. 'If something we don't like happens, we are both out of there.'

Juno placed her plate on the floor and stretched out on her cot. 'How long till we leave?' she said, closing her eyes.

'We leave just before sundown,' Chloe said, lying on her cot and propping her feet on the bed frame. 'Alexa will come and get us.'

'Ready, miss?' Alexa said, rapping on the doorframe.

Juno rubbed her eyes with the heels of her hands. 'I thought we had until sundown?'

'Looks like your young one needed her sleep,' Alexa said, smiling at Chloe.

'Time to go,' Chloe said, swinging her feet off the bed and opening their wardrobes.

They finished dressing and marched in silence through the corridors and sewers towards the manufacturing district. The tunnels narrowing, they turned a bend and slowed as the sewer rat team holding Joanne came into sight ahead of them.

'Everyone have their devices?' Chloe said, scanning the three teams. 'Yes? Good. Let's get to the eastern gate as quickly as possible.'

Alexa slid the grate aside and effortlessly climbed up through the hole. She extended a hand and pulled Juno into the waning sunlight. One by one the girls sprang up into the alley and took their positions. Joanne, her eyes bright and clear, fell into her correct position and worked as a member of the team. Chloe ran an eye across the three teams, then signalled for one team to get onto the rooftops. A second signal, and the second team melted into the alleys. She gave another signal and her team walked out of the alley and into the street. They darted through the streets, keeping to the shadows. The last corner turned brought the eastern gate into view.

Chloe whispered into Juno's ear, 'Can you see the boys?'

Juno, scanning the area, shook her head.

'This gate is a lot busier than usual,' Alexa said over her shoulder. 'Merchants lining the streets.'

Chloe scanned the rooftops, looking for any danger signals. 'Everything is fine from above. Keep moving.'

Juno spotted a hooded figure standing on either side of the drawbridge. 'The boys are on the other side of the moat.'

Chloe upped the pace.

'Joanne!' Alexa shouted.

Juno spun round and gasped.

'Do not move, or your friend is no more,' a man said, holding a knife to Joanne's throat. With a shrug of their shoulders, the men shed their merchant coats. City guards circled the girls with their swords drawn.

Chloe reached for her sword. 'Let her go,' she snarled.

'I wouldn't do that if I were you,' a guard said, knocking Chloe in the back with the pommel of his sword. 'We have you surrounded.'

A man dressed in a smarter uniform walked up to Juno. 'I am the guard captain. The Lady wishes to see you. Come with us and we will not harm the girl or your friends.'

'What do I do, Chloe?'

'I am talking to you, not her,' the captain said, lowering his face next to Juno's. 'Come with us and we will not harm your friends.'

Juno raised her hands and narrowed her eyes. 'If you let my friends go, I will come with you.'

'This isn't a negotiation,' the captain said, grabbing Juno by the arm. 'Turn around.'

Juno felt the ropes wrap around her wrists. She winced as the captain knotted them tightly.

Joanne's black eyes bore into Juno. 'The Lady won't harm you.'

The captain shoved Juno in the back. 'Move.'

Chloe shook her head at the girls watching on the rooftops.

The people of Fairacre, their backs to the shop walls, whispered, pointed and shook their heads in disgust at the girls.

'Move,' the captain said, shoving Juno forwards again.

Juno's eyes darted from Chloe to the captured girls and then to the rooftops. She stepped in time with the guards' marching boots as they moved up the street and into the square. The town hall guards marched down the steps and dispersed the gathered men who filled the town square. The captain shoved Juno to the centre of the square. He stood next to her, waiting and watching the town hall doors. Murmurs flitted around the square as the surrounding men's chatter died down to a whisper. The town hall door creaked open. Dressed in a long, flowing coloured gown, black diamond earrings and a dark orb necklace, the Lady strode out of the town hall. She stopped at the top of the steps and stared at Juno. A wide smile crept over her beautiful features. Pins and needles sprang from Juno's marks and flooded her palms with heat.

'My young Juno,' the Lady said with a lilting whisper. 'You know you couldn't hide from me forever.'

Juno lifted her chin and ground her teeth to keep herself from saying anything.

'Cat got your tongue?' the Lady said, stifling a giggle with her jewelled hand. 'Where is your beast?'

Juno lifted her chin further and maintained her defiant stare.

The captain cracked the side of Juno's head with his elbow. 'The Lady has asked you a question.'

Juno bit the inside of her cheek as red spots exploded in her eyes.

'You will do well not to defy me, young Juno. I will have no issue with doing to your friends what I did to Tilly,' the Lady said, her face turning into a snarl.

Unable to hold her tongue any longer, Juno said, 'What have you done with Tilly?'

The Lady's face turned back into a wide smile. 'Tilly is safe. Would you like to see her?'

'It's a trap,' Chloe whispered out of the corner of her mouth.

Juno winced at the sickening thud of a shield striking the back of Chloe's knees.

'Chloe,' Juno said, tensing as the captain grabbed the back of her neck and forced her head to look forwards.

The Lady sighed. 'It looks like we are going to have to do this the hard way. Captain, bring her to the top of the steps so she can watch what her defiance has brought on her friends.'

The surrounding men's murmurs descended into silence as they all turned their heads towards the Lady.

'Let go of me,' Juno said, struggling against the captain's grip.

'You touch one hair on her head,' Chloe said, struggling to get back onto her feet.

The Lady threw her head back and laughed. 'I don't think you should worry about Juno. You should be more worried about yourselves.'

Chloe lifted her chin, only for a guard to strike her again.

The Lady lifted her hand and waved her fingers at the girls. With a frown, she tilted her head and waved her fingers a second time. 'Guards, bring one of them to me,' she said, her face creasing over with anger.

The fluttering of capes whispered through the wind. A soft thud of leather boots murmured off the cobblestones.

'I don't think so,' Miles said, his greatsword singing out of its sheath.

'Guards,' the captain shouted.

Chloe bent her arms, pulled the shiny sphere from her pocket and threw it into the air. The sphere sprang open and Jay buzzed away angrily towards the manufacturing district. Juno struggled against her rope bonds. Heat pulsed through the palms of her hands. Chloe's whistle pierced the air. Girls from the rooftops landed in the square, their short swords drawn.

Billy strode towards the captain. 'Time to let her go, sir,' he said with a lopsided grin.

The square exploded with the ringing of steel as sewer rats fought guards.

The Lady chuckled gleefully down at Juno. 'I will stop this if you come to me. If you don't, you will watch all your friends die.'

The lumbering thud of boots from the southern street broke the sounds of fighting. Valen roared as he burst into the square with his heavy club swinging in wide arcs. Guards flying through the air like rag dolls landed with a crunch on the cobblestones. The captain whistled. Guards streamed into the square from the surrounding streets. Billy spun his staff and caught the captain under the chin. Juno felt the hold on her bonds release.

Miles strode past, and with a flick of his greatsword he sliced through the ropes that bound Juno. 'You have to get out of here, young Juno,' he said calmly.

'I am not leaving anyone,' Juno said, dodging a stabbing pike.

'There are too many of them,' Chloe said, blood dripping from a wound in her right arm.

Valen took a club to his jaw. He spat blood onto the square, swung his club and lifted three guards into the air and out of the fight.

'Circle Juno,' Miles said, standing side by side with Chloe.

Juno looked down at her hands. The ten marks, one on the inside of each finger, pulsed a bright orange.

'Any ideas?' Chloe said, dodging a sword.

His face set in calm determination, Miles shook his head. 'You are right, there are too many.'

A terrified, high-pitched scream screeched from the southern street. Juno flexed her hands as the marks pulsed. Pain shot down her fingers, making her gasp. A second scream from the southern street pierced the air. The captain struggled to his feet and moved up the steps. His eyes widened as he peered over the fighting in the square. Great plumes of steam blasted from an enormous mouth filled with razor-sharp teeth. Muscles rippled down tawny-coated shoulders and legs ended in paws with nail-like claws, which clicked on the cobblestone street. A long, thick, tufted tail whipped behind her angrily. Amber eyes dotted with red specks shone bright with murderous rage. Chax's roar rattled the shop windows.

The captain hollered, 'Guards, stop that beast.'

'Stay where you are,' the Lady said, waving a dismissive hand at the captain. 'Let her come to me.'

Chloe, her mouth hanging open and her eyebrows in her locs, turned to Juno. 'Chax?'

Juno ground her teeth as the flames grew hotter and brighter. Chax stalked into the town square. The guards and sewer rats, forgetting their quarrel, scrambled away from the advancing cat. Juno tentatively held out a hand as Chax ambled up to her.

'So much power,' the Lady said, her voice a whisper. 'Bring her to me, Juno.'

'She stays with me,' Juno said, placing a hand on Chax's shoulder.

Her face turning into a sneer, the Lady extended her hands. 'I am done playing these games. Bring her to me or I will cut your friends down.'

Chloe pointed her sword at the Lady. 'You heard Juno. They are going nowhere.'

The Lady murmured under her breath, then flung out a hand. Juno gasped and fell to her knees. A thin black blade protruded from her shoulder. Chax stumbled and roared with pain, her right front leg going lame. The thin material on Juno's hands disappeared in a puff of smoke. The red marks pulsed and throbbed with every beat of her heart.

'I don't need you, Juno,' the Lady said. 'Your cat is what I am after. You will die now for not obeying me.'

Pain jolted through Juno's chest. She looked down wide-eyed at another thin black blade that had slammed into her chest. Her legs giving way, she fell to her knees. Vision blurring, she lifted her hands and blinked at the marks swirling around her fingers.

Another blade slammed into her chest.

She shut her eyes and opened her mouth in a silent scream. A blast of yellow light burned through her eyelids.

'Juno!' Chloe screamed.

Juno collapsed face first into the cobbled town square.

CHAPTER 10
DEAR JUNO

'Where am I?'

'Lie still, fire child,' Dr Viktor said, coughing into his handkerchief.

'Chloe? Where is Chloe?' Juno said, wincing at the light as she opened her eyes.

'Here, let me darken the room,' Dr Viktor said, pulling the curtains closed. 'I don't know where Chloe is.'

Juno lifted her head off the pillow, then sucked in air through her teeth. She filled her cheeks with air, propped herself with her elbow and breathed out gradually.

'A little stiff, I assume?' Dr Viktor said with a cackle. 'That will last for a while.'

Juno pushed herself into a sitting position. She looked down and hesitantly touched her chest.

'Your wounds have healed,' Dr Viktor said, lowering himself gradually into a chair. 'Your abilities are remarkable.'

'They don't feel like they are healed,' Juno said, rotating her shoulder.

'Stiffness and internal bruising which will disappear in time,' Dr Viktor said, stuffing his handkerchief into his pocket.

'I don't understand,' Juno said. 'I saw the blades in my chest and I felt them go through me.'

'Did I not ask you to come to me earlier? Did I not say I would explain all of this to you?' Dr Viktor said, waving a dismissive hand. 'We could have avoided some of this if you had.'

'I don't trust you,' Juno said, wincing. 'So I assume I am at your house?'

Dr Viktor pulled out his handkerchief, covered his mouth and coughed. 'Yes, you are at my house. And why do you not trust me?' he said, replacing the handkerchief.

Juno stared at him through her eyebrows.

'Ah, you are talking about Valen. It was my first teaching attempt, and I was perhaps too harsh.'

'He lost his mother,' Juno said. 'And you beat a friend of his. Teaching wasn't the only problem.'

Dr Viktor grunted. 'Men run this world. There is no space for weaklings. I was toughening them up.'

Juno curled a lip. 'Where is everyone? How did I get here? How long have I been here? And you still haven't told me how I healed.'

'So many questions. Billy and a girl in a black outfit dropped you off. They returned to Fairacre. You have been here for a few weeks.'

'A few weeks?' Juno said, her mouth hanging open.

Dr Viktor nodded, grabbed his cane and struggled to his feet. He shuffled to the window and opened the curtains. 'Winter has hit early. The snow is up to the windowsills.'

Tree branches, covered in white, bowed under the weight of the sparkling white crystals.

Juno pulled the soft white cotton sheets up to her shoulders. 'What about Chax?'

Dr Viktor pointed at Juno's hands. 'You have the marks on your hands, which means she is still alive.'

Juno opened her hands and took in a sharp breath. 'They have grown. Each one is now the length of my finger. Do you know what they are?'

Dr Viktor shuffled to the side of Juno's bed and sat on the end. 'It is the mark of the fire elemental.'

'Fire elemental? What is it? And why did it choose me?'

'I cannot answer why it chose you. Once you've rested, I can tell you what I know.'

'I want you to tell me the rest now.'

With a grunt and a wave of his hand, Dr Viktor walked over to the door. 'There is a letter for you on the side table next to your bed.'

Juno waited until the door had clicked closed. She reached for the letter and ripped it open.

Dear Juno,

We hoped that you wouldn't need to read this letter. But if you are, it means you have awoken before we have returned.

Everybody is alive, which is a miracle. The town of Fairacre needs our help, so Miles and I have gone back.

Listen to Dr Viktor. I know you don't trust him, but he will have answers for you.

Stay warm, Billy

Juno folded the letter and placed it on the side table. She laid her head back on the pillow and gazed at the ceiling. A few minutes later she let out a sigh, sat back up, and wincing she swung her legs over the side of the bed. The buttons on the soft white robe she wore opened easily enough. Juno ran her finger over the smooth skin where the black blades had pierced her. She buttoned up her robe and placed a foot onto the floor. It felt firm under her feet as she stood. She took a step towards the door and caught herself on the bedside table, her head swimming. A shake of her head and the fog cleared. Pushing her shoulders back, she took small steps to the bedroom door and swung it open.

'You should be resting,' Dr Viktor said, his voice echoing from the floor below.

'I am fine,' Juno said, swaying a little.

Dr Viktor coughed noisily.

Juno walked through the bedroom door and placed a hand on the banister of a wide horseshoe staircase. 'So beautiful.'

'What is?' Dr Viktor said, from the entrance hall.

'This house. I have seen nothing like it.'

Dr Viktor grunted. 'It is old. Older than the town of Fairacre.'

She walked along the carpeted floor towards the steps while holding on to the banister.

'Take it slowly, fire child,' Dr Viktor said, gazing up at her. 'If you fall, I cannot get you back into your room.'

Juno placed a tentative step on the staircase to test her weight. A step at a time, she moved down the steps to the entrance hall. 'I am hungry,' she said stepping off the last step.

'Definitely on the mend,' Dr Viktor said, smiling. 'Follow me. You should be able to keep up with this old man.' He shuffled towards a large wooden door, which he pushed open with his cane. 'The pantry is at the end of the kitchen. I am not much of a cook, so help yourself.'

Juno walked into the kitchen and traced her finger along the blue marble countertops. Knives stuck to thin magnetic strips, and pots and pans connected to hooks hung above the solid steel cooker. 'Gem and Jen would love this place,' she said, swinging open the pantry door.

Dr Viktor pulled a stool out and hauled himself onto it. He retrieved his handkerchief and, coughing loudly, covered his mouth.

Juno returned from the pantry, grabbed a pot and started a soup on the cooker. 'Are you going to tell me about this fire elemental now?'

'What did Valen tell you?'

'Nothing about a fire elemental. He told us about sharing his essence. That's all.'

'Silly boy left before his education was complete,' Dr Viktor said, his shoulders slumping.

'He said that if he passes suddenly, his soul will remain on this plane until it finds all of its essence.'

Dr Viktor grunted. 'An unfortunate event, yes. Dangerous to spread his essence so thin. You have heard of spirits? Ghosts?'

Juno tapped the wooden spoon on the side of the pot and placed it on the counter. 'I have heard stories. Fairy tales. The girls in my school used to tell them after lights out.'

'Souls that remain on this plane are spirits trying to put themselves back together. They must search for the essence they have either given or lost.'

Juno pulled out a stool and sat opposite Dr Viktor. 'I have never seen one of these spirits. Do they really exist?'

'Yes, fire child. There are many spirits that walk this plane. They are here because their essences have separated during life. Some spirits are friendly, some are evil. No matter which, they are all lost.'

'What makes a spirit friendly or evil?' Juno said, resting her chin on her hand.

'It depends on how their essences get separated. If good intentions, the spirit is good, if bad intentions, the spirit is evil.'

Juno massaged her aching shoulder. 'I only know of Valen who can separate his essence. How are there so many spirits? It all sounds like the tales the girls used to tell.'

Dr Viktor smiled, showing off his yellow teeth. 'We all share our essence, do we not? Giving something of ourselves when we love someone. Losing a little of ourselves when we lose someone. All join up at the right time to make spirits whole again, but sometimes we lose our essence, and our spirits wander in this world looking for it.'

Juno wrapped her arms around herself. 'I loved Miss Petra. I felt like I lost something when she passed.'

'Miss Petra?' Dr Viktor said.

'My mother. Well, she wasn't my mother, but she brought me up as her own,' Juno said with a sorrowful smile. 'She died one night when I was at school.'

'I am sorry about your mother,' Dr Viktor said, clasping his hands together. 'It feels like someone has ripped something out of you, doesn't it?'

'It does,' Juno said. 'I miss her more every day.'

Dr Viktor stared at the kitchen wall, his eyes distant.

Juno cleared her throat. 'I can see smoke when Valen does this essence transfer, and I can also see smoke when the Lady does it.'

'That, young Juno, is one of the abilities the fire elemental has bestowed on you.'

'Why has it chosen me?'

Dr Viktor shrugged. 'The elemental spirits only show themselves during times of great direness. Why they choose and how they choose people, I do not know.'

Juno walked to the cooker and stirred the soup. 'I didn't ask for this.'

Dr Viktor gripped the countertop through another hacking cough. 'It need not ask. It chooses who it wishes to choose.'

The two bowls Juno pulled from the cupboard clinked together.

She filled them with the steaming soup and placed a bowl in front of Dr Viktor. She took her seat opposite and lightly blew on a spoonful. 'I can see this smoke because of Chax?'

'Yes,' Dr Viktor said. 'You are both vessels for the fire spirit. The elemental spirits are too powerful for one vessel, so it must use two.'

Juno sipped her soup. 'I can feel Chax when she is near. And when she is not near me, I feel like something is always missing.'

'Two halves make a whole,' Dr Viktor said, clearing his throat once he had stopped coughing.

'Is the Lady using her essence to control people? Is that why their irises turn black?'

Dr Viktor's face creased with worry. 'She is using her essence. Only the darker souls, the evil souls, have the power to control people. The lighter souls can transfer to objects, but don't have the power to control people.'

Juno finished her soup and dabbed her mouth with a paper towel. 'How do we stop her?'

'How do you stop her, you mean?' Dr Viktor said, raising an eyebrow. 'That is your journey. All we can do is help you prepare.'

Juno scooped up the two bowls and placed them in the sink. 'Where did you get all of this information from?'

'Mostly handed down through generations. They say there are volumes of text in the City of Lynn that contain these teachings.'

Juno placed her hands on the sink and sighed heavily.

'Time for rest,' Dr Viktor said, creaking as he stood.

Juno faced Dr Viktor. 'I would like to talk more.'

'It is near impossible to travel the eastern forest during the winter. We will have lots of time to talk,' Dr Viktor said, pointing his cane at the kitchen exit.

'You will come and wake me if any of my friends return?'

'Ha,' Dr Viktor said, starting another coughing fit. 'I don't think I could stop them waking you.'

A smile stretched across Juno's face. She exited the kitchen and climbed the stairs to her room. The bed creaked as she climbed in. With the covers pulled up to her chin, Juno watched the snow fall against the window. Her eyes fluttered closed as the warmth from the soup spread through her body.

'Is she awake?' Billy said, standing next to the window.

'Sound asleep,' Miles said from the doorway.

'Entering my room without my permission,' Juno said, her eyes still closed.

Miles chuckled. Juno snorted at the sound of a drinking glass hitting the bedroom carpet.

'I am sorry,' Billy said, picking the glass up and placing it onto the table. 'Didn't mean to be rude.'

Juno opened her eyes and smiled at Miles, who was rolling his eyes at Billy.

'You are back,' Juno said, jumping out of bed and throwing her arms around Billy.

Billy cleared his throat and patted Juno on the shoulder. 'Yes, we are back.'

'Dinner will be ready in ten minutes,' Miles said, disappearing through the doorway.

Juno released Billy from their hug. 'Where is Chloe?'

'She is still with the sewer rats,' Billy said, his face a light pink. 'Get dressed and come to the dining room.'

The stiffness made Juno wince as she pulled on her beggar's outfit. She walked gingerly down the stairs to the dining room.

'Young fire child. Glad to see some cheer in your face,' Dr Viktor said. 'Please come and join us. The boys have been hard at work.'

She sat next to Billy and cast her eyes over the many dishes of assorted food. Fork in hand, she picked a single piece of food from each dish and piled it onto her plate. 'Well?' she said, with a mouth full of food.

Miles looked at Billy. 'Looks like someone who can eat as much as you.'

'Impressive,' Billy said, spooning some potato soup into his mouth. 'I think we had better give her the news before she turns those fire-throwing hands on us.'

'Fire-throwing hands?'

Miles placed his fork on his plate and said, 'You don't remember?'

'Remember what?' Juno said, putting her fork down.

'All in good time, my boys,' Dr Viktor said. 'Let us start with the update first.'

Billy cleared his throat. 'Everyone is alive and well. However, a lot has happened. The sewer rats are no longer in Fairacre because the guards raided the sewers, with information from Joanne.'

Juno's mouth hung open. 'Where have they gone?'

'They went south but didn't tell us where. Naomi refused.'

'We need to go and find them,' Juno said, rising from her chair. 'What if they need our help?'

Miles wagged a finger at Juno. 'Let Billy finish.'

Juno sat and looked at Billy expectantly.

'Chloe went with them and assured us they would be safe. She told us to tell you that everything is okay.'

'Did she say if she is coming here?'

'A tall order during winter,' Miles said. 'I think we can expect her in the spring.'

'So I am stuck here with you three,' Juno said, shaking her head in disbelief.

'Yes, fire child,' Dr Viktor said. 'And a perfect time to start your training.'

'What training?'

'Fire-throwing hands,' Miles said, reaching for a bread roll. 'You need to learn how to control it.'

Juno growled. 'I don't know what you are talking about. I don't remember any fire-throwing.'

Billy raised a hand at Miles and Dr Viktor. He swivelled in his chair and faced Juno. 'You honestly don't remember?'

Juno shook her head. 'I remember falling to my knees. And feeling the pain from those things that the Lady stuck into me.'

'Show me your hands.'

Juno pulled her sleeves up and placed a hand in each of Billy's palms.

'These marks,' Billy said, tracing a finger along them. 'Fire comes out of them. Or at least, we think this is where it comes from. It seems to happen when you are in danger. I saw it happen in the town with the Lady, and in the orchard when the two boys came back for you.'

Juno balled her hands into fists, then opened them. 'They get hot,' she said. 'That's the last thing I remember before everything goes dark.'

'You cannot control it at the moment, so the fire goes everywhere. You haven't hurt anyone, but you will if you don't learn to control it. That is where Dr Viktor will help.'

'The entire town saw what you can do,' Miles said. 'You cannot go back there. The men think you are some kind of witch.'

Juno dropped her hands into her lap. 'I am not a witch and I definitely don't want to hurt anybody.'

'The time will come when you have to,' Miles said, matter-of-factly. 'It is your choice if you want us to train you so you are ready for it.'

Juno looked down at her hands and shook her head.

After a few minutes, Dr Viktor cleared his throat. 'If you want to see Tilly, and defeat the Lady, I suggest you let us teach you, young fire child.'

Juno finally nodded. 'I will learn. I will learn if you help me defeat the Lady and help me get Tilly back.'

A wide, lopsided grin stretched across Billy's face. 'We will help.'

'What training will I need to do?'

'Weapons for fighting,' Miles said, picking up another roll and wiping his plate clean.

'Herbalism,' Billy said. 'I am going to teach you how to prepare medicine.'

'And I shall teach disciplines of the mind,' Dr Viktor said. 'I cannot teach you how to control this gift but I can teach you how to control your mind.'

'Why do I have to learn all these things if all I need to learn is how to use this gift?'

Dr Viktor let out a snort. 'The fire child thinks she can master the mind with a few lessons from me once a day.'

Juno glared at Dr Viktor. 'My name is Juno.'

'Don't mind Dr Viktor,' Billy said, blowing air out of his cheeks. 'You will get used to his bluntness.'

'To master the mind, you need to discipline the mind,' Miles said. 'To discipline the mind, you need to discipline the body.'

Juno shook her head. 'He talks funny sometimes.'

Billy stifled a chuckle. 'What he means is you are going to get beaten up by Miles every day. I will teach you how to make draughts that sometimes go bang, and Dr Viktor is going to make you sit and chant and hum stuff you don't understand for many hours each day.'

'You start tomorrow,' Dr Viktor said, grabbing his cane and walking to the dining room door. 'I am breaking my rule for you, young fire child. Do not make me regret it.' The door closed gently behind him.

'What rule?' Juno said, her gaze darting from Billy to Miles.

'He never trains women,' Miles said, his dark, unblinking eyes staring at Juno.

Juno looked at Billy and frowned.

Billy shrugged his shoulders. 'He regards this as men's work.'

'Oh, really? And what do you two think?' Juno said, her brow furrowing. Miles scraped his chair back and stood. With a curt nod, he walked out of the dining room.

Billy, draping his arm over his chair, shook his head at the dining room door. 'Fools, the both of them.'

Juno bit the bottom of her lip. 'Do you think I will be able to do everything they ask of me?'

Billy gave another lopsided grin. 'I know you will. But I am warning you. They will not go easy on you, because they will try to prove themselves right.'

'I will think of Tilly,' Juno said, determination setting across her face. 'When it gets hard, I will think of her.'

'There you go,' Billy said, punching her lovingly on the arm. 'Let's do that tour of the house, shall we?'

They left the dining room and walked into the marble entrance hall. The glass chandelier above spun lazily, glittering dots of light all over the room.

'The house has six key parts. You have seen the bedrooms, dining room and kitchen,' Billy said, placing his hands behind his back as he walked. 'Behind the dining room is our lounge.'

Juno followed Billy and stopped at a painting depicting a battle scene. 'Is this an actual battle?'

'Dr Viktor says it is. He will no doubt give you a history lesson.' Billy ushered her into a cream-coloured room with shadows of flames licking up the walls. 'Take your shoes off when you come into this room. The carpets suck up dust, and yours truly must keep this room clean.'

'A fireplace,' Juno said, smiling.

'We use this room to relax. We either read or just watch the fire.'

Juno scrunched her toes into the thick white carpet. 'So soft. I haven't felt anything like this.'

They walked out of the living room, under the spiral staircase, and stopped in front of two doors that stood next to each other.

'The door to the right leads to the medicine and herbal room, where I do all of my work. The left door is Miles's sparring room, where all of us gain lots of bruises. I will show you my room once we tour through the greenhouse.'

Juno stopped and placed a hand on the staircase banister.

'What's wrong?' Billy said, placing a hand on her forearm.

'Nothing,' Juno said, biting the bottom of her lip.

Billy folded his arms. 'Let it out.'

'Tilly's favourite place was the greenhouse,' Juno said. 'Sorry. I didn't realise you had a greenhouse here.'

'We don't have to visit it now, but you will need to when we begin your studies.'

'It's okay,' she said. 'Lead the way.'

Billy opened a large wooden door behind the staircase and walked down a wide corridor.

'What's this door?' Juno said, pointing at a door carved full of writing.

'That is Dr Viktor's area. You only go down there when he invites you.'

Juno raised both her hands. 'Okay. No entering without the doctor.'

Billy smirked. Juno continued walking down the corridor.

Billy cocked his head and came to an abrupt halt. 'Someone is at the front door,' he said with a frown. 'Stay behind me.'

Juno followed Billy back up the corridor, under the spiral staircase and into the entrance hall. Billy slowed when he saw Miles's outstretched hand.

Miles placed his hand on the hilt of his sword and pressed down on the door handle. 'Who goes there?'

'Let me in, you silly boy.'

'Chloe,' Juno shouted, running around Billy. 'Let her in, Miles.'

Miles swung the door open and caught Chloe as she stumbled in.

'Didn't think you would see me so soon, did you, young Juno?' Chloe said, collapsing onto the marble floor.

'Chloe, what's wrong?' Juno said, kneeling down next to her. 'Billy, she is bleeding.'

'Dr Viktor,' Billy shouted. 'You two, get her to Juno's room. Hurry.'

Miles lifted Chloe and carried her up the stairs.

'Why all this noise?' Dr Viktor said, his cane thumping up the corridor.

'Someone has injured Chloe, and Miles has taken her to Juno's room,' Billy said, opening the door to his herbal room.

Dr Viktor barked at Billy, 'Get to work, boy.'

Billy exited his herbal room and double-stepped up the winding staircase into Juno's room.

'She is freezing,' Juno said, holding Chloe's hand. 'She can't say anything with those teeth chattering.'

'Juno, climb in next to her. She needs your body heat. Miles, go and make a hot drink.'

Juno climbed into bed next to Chloe. She wrapped herself around her friend and rubbed her hands along her arms.

Chloe's eyes fluttered open. 'Good to see you, young Juno.'

'Where are you injured?' Billy said, his concerned eyes scanning the length of Chloe.

'Back,' Chloe said, her teeth still chattering.

Billy rolled Chloe over and tutted. He uncorked a bottle of yellow salve and poured it into a thick bandage. 'This is going to hurt,' he said, applying it to a long deep wound on her back.

Chloe's body stiffened, then she trembled violently and let out a scream through clenched teeth.

'Sorry, Chloe, but I have to do this,' Billy said, muttering under his breath.

'Chloe, can you hear me?' Juno said.

'She has passed out. How she has survived this I will never know,' Billy said.

Dr Viktor walked into the room and glanced at Chloe's wound. 'She won't make the night,' he said, grimly.

'She will,' Juno said, a tear falling down her cheek. 'You watch. Just you watch.'

Billy applied another thick layer of salve to Chloe's back. He grabbed a thick gauze and placed it along the wound. 'I have done everything I can, Juno. Let's all hope and pray.'

Juno squeezed Chloe tightly. She looked at the boys and said, 'Leave us. Now.'

CHAPTER 11
BLACK SNOW

'Wake up, Juno.'

Juno jerked awake. 'Don't move, Chloe. I am going to get Billy.'

Chloe sucked in air until her cheeks were full, then, pursing her lips, she let it out slowly.

Juno ran out of the room and leaned over the banister. 'Billy, Chloe is awake.'

Billy's door slammed open. 'Tell her to remain still.'

Juno moved a chair to the bed and sat. 'Billy says not to move. How are you feeling?'

'My back is really hurting,' Chloe said through gritted teeth.

'Truly remarkable,' Billy said, walking through the door. 'Stand aside, please, Juno. I need to check Chloe's back.'

'How long have I been out?'

'A few days,' Juno said, biting her lip. 'We thought you were going to be okay, but then you caught a fever.'

'I am going to roll you over now,' Billy said.

'Be careful, please, Billy,' Juno said.

Billy rolled Chloe over and pursed his lips at Chloe's gasp. He gently pressed his fingers against the skin around the wound. 'How badly does that hurt?'

'Not too bad,' Chloe said, taking slow, deep breaths.

'The infection that caused your fever has gone,' Billy said. 'You are out of the woods.'

'I told you she would make it, didn't I?' Juno said, a wide smile playing across her face.

'Time to start your training, Juno,' Miles said from the doorway. 'No more excuses.'

'It can wait, Miles,' Juno said, waving a hand at him.

'Miles is right,' Chloe said, reaching over and grabbing Juno's hand. 'I cannot train you, so let Miles do it.'

'I don't want to leave you.'

'Billy says I am going to be fine. Besides, I am going to be testing you when I am back on my feet.'

'Looks like you need some training yourself, Chloe,' Miles said, arching his eyebrow. 'You can't be that good after seeing that wound on your back.'

Chloe narrowed her eyes at Miles but remained silent.

'What happened after we left?' Juno said, touching Chloe's forehead with the back of her hand. 'How did this happen to you?'

'Time to roll over again,' Billy said.

Chloe let out a sigh as the salve worked its way into the wound. Billy finished and rolled her onto her back.

'How does that feel?' Juno said.

'Much better,' Chloe said, her eyes fluttering closed. 'Now go on, young Juno. It's time to start your training.'

'The salve has cured the infection, but she is still a bit hot from the fever,' Billy said. 'She is going to be asleep for a while.'

Juno squeezed Chloe's hand. 'She will be okay, though?'

'She will,' Billy said, wiping his hands clean of the salve.

Juno stood. 'So training it is. What happens now?'

'You are with me now, Miles in the afternoon and Dr Viktor in the evening,' Billy said.

'That's the schedule for each day,' Miles said, leaning against the door with his arms folded.

'I am done,' Billy said, packing up his medicine bag. 'Follow me, Juno.'

Juno closed the door softly behind her and followed Billy down the stairs and up to the two doors.

'Don't be late,' Miles said, walking into his room.

Billy ushered Juno into his room and closed the door behind her.

'That smells awful,' Juno said, scrunching up her nose.

Billy grinned. 'You will get used to it. Some plants need to rot to get the ingredients I need.'

Juno walked to the centre of the room, turned and took in the equipment sitting on the two long benches against the walls. 'Is this where you make the stuff you put on Chloe?'

'It's a simple healing salve,' Billy said, nodding. 'Lavender, which we grow in the greenhouse. Beeswax and honey, which we get from hives at the back of the house. Olive oil, which we make ourselves from our olive trees.'

Juno picked up a jar of healing salve and unscrewed the cap. 'Smells very sweet.'

'It won't be long until you can make your own.'

Juno replaced the cap and placed the jar on the table. 'What do you need me to do?'

Billy pulled up a stool for Juno to take a seat. 'Dr Viktor mentioned an antidote that may help with the infected. Our job is to figure out how to make it. We know the ingredients, but we don't know the combination.'

'You mean, how we mix it?'

'Yes, and it can be dangerous. We will need to build a suitably safe area to try different combinations.'

Billy pulled out a slim black book from a drawer and handed it to Juno. The cover displayed a picture of a skull. Purple smoke tendrils leaked out of the skull's eyes. Juno shivered as she opened the book and ran her finger down the list of ingredients.

'According to the book, the antidote should be purple when it's done,' Billy said.

On the next page, Juno frowned at a picture with detailed measurements surrounding it. 'You know how to build this?'

'Yes, that part I have already built. The safety box is what I have to finish. You are responsible for getting the ingredients.'

Juno turned back the page and ran her finger down the page. 'I don't know what these are.'

Billy walked to a bookcase and ran his fingers along the spines of the books. He stopped at a thick book, pulled it out and handed it to Juno. 'It's all in there with pictures. Follow each one properly as some we need fresh, some we need dried and some we need mixed.'

Juno sat and flipped through the pages, taking in the hand drawings of the plants. 'This is going to take some time.'

'A herbalist's most important skill is patience,' Billy said, reaching into another drawer and pulling out a notepad and pencil. 'We work together slowly and methodically until we can make this antidote. I think lives will depend on it.'

Juno took the notepad and pencil and, starting with the first ingredient, she flicked through the thick book until she found each one. She continued through the morning marking plants and ingredients on separate pages of the notebook. A sharp rap sounded on the door.

'Miles is calling you,' Billy said with his lopsided grin. 'Good luck.'

With the book, notepad and pencil sitting neatly in a drawer, Juno left the herbal room and followed Miles into his room.

'Shoes off, please,' Miles said, pointing at a shoe rack. 'The door to your right is the changing room. Get changed and join me in the centre.'

Juno scuttled into the changing room and changed into the cotton trousers and button-up shirt that hung from the wall. The door clicking quietly behind her, Juno joined Miles at the back of the room.

Miles gave Juno a half-smile. 'Any weapon that takes your fancy?' he said, waving his hand at the weapon rack that spanned the length of the wall.

Juno worked her way along the rack. 'Chloe uses a weapon like this,' she said, running her hand over a short sword.

'You are too short,' Miles said. 'Chloe is tall, so her reach makes that weapon useful. Try another.'

Juno huffed. 'I am not that short.'

'Try another,' Miles said.

'You're the expert, what do you think?'

Miles grunted and walked along the weapon rack. With a nod, he picked up a long pole. 'We call this a Bo. It is one of the best weapons for defending and attacking.' He walked into the centre of the room and twirled the Bo around in long, sweeping arcs. On the last twirl he caught the pole at one end and pointed the other at Juno. 'Try it.'

Juno grabbed the Bo and tested the weight in her hands. She turned it around, placed one end of the pole on the floor and scanned the length, which towered above her.

'It is too long,' Miles said, walking over to her. 'Give it back.'

Juno handed the Bo back.

Miles placed it back on the weapons rack and grabbed a shorter pole. The pole spun effortlessly in his hands, and on the last spin he pointed the end at Juno. 'We call this a Jo.'

'It's thicker and heavier,' Juno said, balancing it in her palm.

Miles twisted another Jo from the weapons rack and walked to the middle of the room. He took a deep breath, spread his feet and began a series of slow, deliberate movements, which sent the Jo in wide arcs and spins. After each set of movements, he sped the series up until his Jo whined through the air.

Juno stared wide-eyed. 'I don't think I can do that.'

Miles slowed the movements of his Jo. 'I am going to teach you the basic movements. Over time you will be able to do what I have just done.'

Juno joined Miles in the centre of the room.

'Ready?' Miles said.

Juno nodded. She followed each step, taking note of Miles's hands and feet. 'Very good,' Miles said. 'Again.'

Juno spun, stabbed and swept the Jo over and over again.

'Again,' Miles said, stalking around her with a critical eye.

The muscles in her forearms popping, Juno let out a growl, willing herself through each movement.

'Again,' Miles said.

Juno gritted her teeth as blisters formed and burst on her hands. Small streaks of red coated her Jo.

'Enough,' Miles said. 'Wash your hands in the bucket over there. It has salt water to help the blisters.'

Juno dunked her hands in the bucket and grunted as the pain shot into her palms.

'You have done well. I will see you tomorrow,' Miles said, opening the door. 'Dr Viktor is waiting for you. Knock on the door and enter only when he asks you to.'

Juno left the training room and made her way under the staircase and down the corridor. She knocked lightly on Dr Viktor's door.

'Come,' Dr Viktor said.

Juno slipped in and shut the door behind her. She walked into the centre of the room and marvelled at the bookshelves that filled three walls of Dr Viktor's room.

'Staring is rude, fire child,' Dr Viktor said. 'Take a seat.'

Juno sat at the antique table and watched Dr Viktor turn a page of an enormous book. The book sat on a pedestal in the centre of the room. He picked up a feather and scribbled notes on the thick yellow pages of the book. Juno sat and listened to the scratching of the quill as it dragged across the page. Dr Viktor dipped the quill into an ink-pot, wiped the sides of the quill and continued writing.

Her arms aching and her eyes getting heavy, Juno's head fell forwards. Her chin bounced off her chest, jerking her awake.

'You may go now,' Dr Viktor said.

Juno shook her head. 'I thought I was here to learn something.'

Dr Viktor waved a hand. 'I will see you tomorrow, fire child.'

Juno stalked out the door and into the corridor. Walking into the entrance hall, she made her way to Billy, who stood looking out of the window next to the door. 'What are you looking at?'

Billy sighed. 'Black snow.'

'Why is it black?' Juno said, peering out of the window.

'Come to the living room,' Billy said, pulling the curtains closed.

'I will be there in a second,' Juno said, double-stepping up the staircase. She opened the door and crept over to Chloe's bed. Little beads of sweat ran across Chloe's forehead. Juno picked up a cloth, dipped it into a bowl and ran it across Chloe's forehead.

'Valen,' Chloe said, her eyes still closed.

Juno smiled down at her friend. 'You will see Valen soon.'

Chloe let out a sigh.

Juno dropped the cloth into the bowl and left the room quietly. She entered the living room and felt a flood of warmth rise up through her body. Miles sat cross-legged on the carpet next to the fire. With a crackle and spit, the fire sent showers of sparks up the chimney. Juno stepped over Miles and sat cross-legged.

'How is she?' Billy said, lifting his head from the book he was reading.

'Calling for Valen,' Juno said, picking at her hands. 'How long will she be like this?'

'She is tough. She will be awake any day now,' Billy said.

Juno rested her chin on her hands. 'She looks so weak. I am used to her being strong and full of life.'

'She should not have survived that wound,' Miles said, flipping a page of his book.

'No, she shouldn't have,' Billy said. 'She is still with us because she is strong.'

Juno stared at the flickering flames in the fireplace. She looked down at her hands and traced her finger over the marks on the inside of her fingers. They glowed the same colour as the flames in the fire.

'The black snow,' Juno said, shaking her head to clear her thoughts. 'Why is it black?'

Billy stared into the fire. 'Dr Viktor tells stories of gigantic machines in the north of the City of Lynn. Machines that pour clouds of black smoke into the air. During the summer the wind blows north. In the winter the winds blow south, bringing smoke that mixes with the snow.'

Miles closed his book and placed his hands on his knees. 'Dr Viktor calls them factories. They produce metal goods for the city.'

'It destroys the forests and the animals that live in them,' Billy said, shaking his head. 'One day the wind will blow over Fairacre and destroy the farmlands.'

'Your plants will grow again,' Miles said. 'They do every year. Stop fussing, Billy.'

'What will happen to your precious City of Lynn when Fairacre cannot feed it?' Billy said, looking over at Miles.

Miles stood and raised his chin. 'The City will survive. It has for centuries. I am going to bed. Goodnight.'

Juno watched Miles walk out of the living room. 'What is it with him and that place?'

'His dream is to be a member of the queen's guard. They say they are the greatest fighters to have walked our world.'

'Why is he living here, then? Shouldn't he be in the city?'

'Only the sons of nobles automatically become members of the guard,' Billy said. 'Miles, unfortunately, is an orphan.'

Sadness crossed Juno's face. 'Must be horrible knowing you can never achieve a dream.'

Billy shrugged. 'There is a way, but it is dangerous. Dr Viktor has forbidden it.'

'Tell me,' Juno said.

'In the eastern lands, the barracks choose four soldiers to send to the city. The way they select these soldiers often results in death. Miles wants to take part in the rituals.'

Juno lifted a hand. 'I don't want to hear about it.'

'I see Miles is treating you well,' Billy said, casting an eye over Juno's hands.

Juno picked at her blisters. 'If this helps me in saving Tilly, then I will do as I must.'

'Stick with it,' Billy said. 'Miles is an incredible teacher.'

'I will. I am going to bed. See you tomorrow.'

'Goodnight, young Juno.'

Juno walked up the marble stairs while trailing her hand along the banister. She opened the door quietly, walked over to Chloe and placed a hand on her forehead.

Her eyes fluttering open, Chloe grimaced and said, 'Young Juno, you are still here.'

Juno smiled as she sat on the chair and rested her chin on her folded hands. 'I am not going anywhere.'

'How does my back look?'

Juno pursed her lips. 'It's going to leave a big scar, but it is healing.'

'Battle scars,' Chloe said. 'We need to get back to the sewer rats.'

'We can't leave now. The eastern forest is covered in toxic black snow.'

Chloe's forehead creased over. 'Black snow?'

'Yes, black smoke from the City of Lynn. It looks beautiful and horrible at the same time.'

Chloe placed an elbow on the bed and attempted to lift herself up.

'Rest,' Juno said, placing her hand on Chloe's cheek. 'I will tell you everything when you feel better.'

Chloe closed her eyes and let out a sigh. Juno sat back in the chair and pulled a blanket over her. She draped a leg over the armrest and let it bounce. With a smile, she closed her eyes and let the deep, even breathing of Chloe lead her into sleep.

'Chloe, where are you?' Juno said, unwrapping her blanket and scrambling to her feet. 'Chloe?' she said, double-stepping down the stairs.

'In the kitchen, Juno,' Chloe said.

Juno slammed open the door. 'Why are you out of bed?' she said, walking around the counter.

'The wound is holding, so I gave her permission to get up,' Billy said, taking a sip of his tea.

'I doubt she needed your permission,' Juno said, pulling up a stool and sitting next to her friend.

Billy rolled his eyes and smiled his lopsided grin.

'Chloe was about to tell us how she managed to get here during the winter,' Miles said, returning from the pantry.

Chloe raked her hands through her locs. 'I can't remember much, but I think I have your Chax to thank.'

'Chax is okay?' Juno said, hugging herself.

'You know she is just fine, Juno,' Billy said.

Juno nodded at Billy. 'Yes, she is alive, but I don't know how she is.'

'I think she led me here,' Chloe said. 'I wouldn't have found this house otherwise.'

'I hope she is okay in all of this snow.' Chloe glanced at Miles and Billy.

'What?' Juno said, scanning the three of them.

'With that amount of fire, Chax will be fine in the snow,' Miles said while spreading out the fruit from the pantry.

'They didn't tell you, did they?' Chloe said.

'Tell me what?' Juno said, frustration etched on her face.

'We thought it was best we wait for you, Chloe,' Billy said.

Chloe looked at Juno. 'Chax helped us get out of the town.'

'Well, Chax and Valen,' Billy said, grinning. 'I never want to get in the way of that club.'

Miles nodded. 'Truly dangerous.'

Chloe placed a hand on Juno's forearm. 'There was a lot of fire. We don't know if it came from you or Chax, but it scattered the soldiers. We were able to get you and leave through the eastern gate.'

'Miles and I brought you here,' Billy said.

Juno gave Chloe a gentle hug. 'I am so happy you are okay. What happened to the others?'

Her brow furrowing, Chloe scratched her chin. 'They got hold of Joanne. Not long after that, they raided the sewers. We were ready for it, but it was still a shock. The girls escaped south and are in the caves under the great waterfall.'

'If they have one of your sewer rats, they will know where the caves are,' Miles said, peeling a piece of fruit.

'Only a few of us know about the caves,' Chloe said. 'It was always a fallback option in case something like this happened.'

'Good thinking,' Miles said.

'A compliment from Miles,' Chloe said with a snort.

Billy chuckled. 'What of Valen?'

'He is still in Fairacre,' Chloe said, worry etched on her face. 'It must worry him sick not knowing where I got to.'

'Won't the soldiers go after him?' Juno said.

Chloe shook her head. 'Bonking heads together is not his only ability. The rumours of metal snakes in his shop keep them well away.'

'That may change with the Lady, though,' Billy said.

'He will get out of there if he needs to,' Chloe said.

'What happened to you? How did you get that wound?' Juno said.

'My team of girls led the chasing of Fairacre's soldiers to the orchards while the rest of the girls were escaping south. We scattered, and I thought I was in the clear.'

Miles let out a grunt.

Chloe lifted an eyebrow. 'I reached the tree line of the eastern forest and someone hit me from behind. I didn't see who it was.'

'And Chax found you?' Juno said.

'I think it was her. I just followed her in a daze.'

Everyone fell silent at the thumping of Dr Viktor's cane. He entered the kitchen and frowned. 'Why are you not training?'

'We were just leaving,' Billy said. 'Come on, Juno, we have work to do.'

Juno huffed and stalked towards the kitchen door. 'One day off wouldn't make any difference.'

'Get to work, young fire child. You want to save your friends, don't you? And, Chloe, you get back upstairs and back into bed. You will not survive another infection.'

Chloe's knuckles turned white as she gripped the kitchen counter. She stepped off the stool and carefully made her way out of the kitchen. Juno beckoned Chloe over to the window next to the front door. She held the curtain open and pointed at the black snow glinting in the morning sunlight.

'I have never seen anything like that,' Chloe said. 'Have you gone outside?'

Juno shook her head. 'Not allowed to. Dr Viktor gets angry.'

'Come on, Juno,' Billy said, reaching over her shoulder and pulling the curtain closed. 'You can see Chloe later in the living room.'

Juno, being careful of Chloe's wound, gave her a hug, then followed Billy to the herbal room.

'Are you ready for our first try at this antidote?' Billy said, closing the glass window on the safety box.

'I have yet to get all the ingredients.'

Billy grinned. 'I retrieved all of them. You can help me get the next batch. I have updated your notepad.'

Juno placed her notebook on the table and flipped through the plant book to cross-reference which plant was which. Once ready, she began passing the requested ingredients into Billy's outstretched hand. Billy placed the ingredients into small mixing pots inside the safety box. Sizzles, pops and bangs sent out putrid smells of burning plants and smouldering wood. The safety box, its inside turning a dull grey, remained safe. After each attempt Billy, his face set deep in concentration, wrote down the sequence of ingredients and the method of how he had mixed them.

Juno jumped at the sharp rap on the door. 'Miles,' Billy said. 'Get going.'

Juno got changed in the small changing room. She grabbed her Jo from the weapon rack and began the same sequence of basic movements on the training mat. She ignored the pain from the skin ripping off the tops of her blisters. Hours later, sweat soaking her cotton clothes, Miles grabbed the Jo and flicked his head at the door. 'Dr Viktor is waiting.'

Juno knocked and waited for the signal to enter. She sat in the same chair and watched Dr Viktor scribble and scratch into the enormous book.

Hours later, Dr Viktor said, 'You may go now.'

Juno stood and marched out of the room, slamming the door behind her. She double-stepped up the stairs and, walking into her room, she looked Chloe over as she slept, her face peaceful. Juno wrapped the blanket over herself and winced at the coarse material rubbing against her blisters. The chair creaked as she curled her legs underneath herself. She rested her head on the armrest and watched her friend sleep.

A quiet knock on the door made Juno spin her head round. 'Come with me, fire child,' Dr Viktor said.

Juno unwrapped the blanket, pulled on her sandals and tiptoed out the door. 'Where are we going?'

His staff clumping on the floor, Dr Viktor grabbed the banister and made his way slowly to the ground floor. 'I need to take some measurements.'

A frown creased Juno's forehead. 'Measurements? For what?'

Dr Viktor pulled out his handkerchief just in time to catch another coughing fit that racked his body. He walked down the corridor and entered his room. Following Dr Viktor into his room, Juno stopped at the table and rested her hands on the back of her chair.

Dr Viktor slid open a drawer and pulled out a tape measure. 'Stand on that block and hold your arms out straight.'

'What are you measuring me for?' Juno said, taking a step back.

Dr Viktor tapped his cane on Juno's forearm. 'Get on the block and hold your arms out.'

Juno climbed onto the block and stood with her arms horizontal to the ground.

Dr Viktor scribbled notes into a book after each measurement.

'Why do you cough so much?' Juno said, trying to break the silence.

'Too many years working on the machines in the city,' Dr Viktor said. 'Hold still.'

'What do the machines do?'

'Metal,' Dr Viktor said, scribbling another measurement in his book. 'I am done. You can go now.'

Juno dropped her arms. 'What are the measurements for?'

Dr Viktor, hacking hard into his handkerchief, waved Juno away. Juno shook her head and left Dr Viktor's room. She climbed the staircase, entered her room and checked on Chloe. The pitter-patter of snow on the window grew faster and louder. Juno pulled the curtain across and scrunched up her eyes at the sharp silver reflection of the moonlight bouncing off the black snow. She let the curtain close, walked over to her chair and wrapped herself in her blanket. Chloe mumbled in her sleep. Exhausted, Juno fell asleep.

CHAPTER 12
BLAST, DAMN, DANG

Juno opened the curtains and covered her eyes as the light streamed across the bedroom floor. She looked back into her room and smiled at her friend, who was leaning over and tying her shoelaces.

'What you smiling at?' Chloe said.

'It's good to see you moving about,' Juno said, letting the curtain drop. 'It feels like we have been in this place for years, but it's only been a few months.'

'I know,' Chloe said, standing up and stretching. 'Winter is nearly over.'

'How does your back feel?'

'I don't feel pain anymore,' Chloe said. 'I use some of Billy's salve when it gets tight.'

'Do you think you can spar today?'

'That is the plan. Billy has given me the go-ahead.'

Juno sat on her bed to put her shoes on. 'I am going to work with Billy. We still haven't figured out this antidote.'

'We need to figure it out before we go to the caves. There may be some infected people that need it,' Chloe said.

Juno grabbed a brush and pulled it through her shoulder-length hair. 'Billy thinks we are close, as we only have a few more combinations to try.'

Chloe tied up her locs and walked over to the door. 'I am going to go and find Miles. I will see you after you and Billy have finished.'

'Wait for me,' Juno said, tying her last lace. She followed Chloe out of the room down the wide stairs and stopped at the two doors. 'Be careful with Miles,' she said. 'He packs quite a punch.'

'I look forward to it,' Chloe said, smiling.

Juno knocked on Billy's door and entered.

'Ready to try these last combinations?' he said, glancing over at her.

She nodded, pulled out the book from the drawer and turned to the last page she had written on. Billy slid the window of the safety box open and placed the ingredients into the jar. With a hiss, the liquid in the jar bubbled and spat. Billy jumped back as the jar exploded, sending its contents all over the safety box.

Juno sighed. 'We only have a few more combinations left.'

'Have faith, young Juno,' Billy said, with a lopsided grin.

Juno drew a line through the previous combination. She lined up the ingredients and passed them to Billy, who placed them in a new jar. The liquid turned a bright pink, bubbled, then turned a dark red. Billy looked at Juno with his mouth open.

'Do you think that's it?' Juno whispered.

Tentatively opening the safety box, Billy stooped forwards to get a closer look. 'I think we are onto something here, Juno.'

With a bang, the jar exploded. Small showers of liquid splattered onto Billy's face.

'Blast, damn, dang,' Billy yelled, kicking the safety box. 'I was so sure we had it.'

Juno snorted through her nose, trying not to laugh.

'What are you laughing at?'

Juno grabbed a cloth, wrapped the end around her finger and

wiped Billy's eyebrows. 'They have gone red.'

Billy took the cloth from Juno and scrubbed his face. 'Gone?'

'No,' Juno said, her eyes watering from trying not to laugh. 'You look good with red eyebrows.'

Billy threw the cloth into the corner of the room. 'Miles is not going to let this go. Next combination, if you please.'

Juno drew a line through the previous combination. Billy took the ingredients one by one and placed them into the jar. He placed the last ingredient in, closed the safety box, stood back and wiggled his red eyebrows at Juno.

Juno smirked.

She looked at the safety box and held her breath. The liquid turned bright pink, then a dark red.

'Not again,' Billy growled.

Juno, waiting for the explosion, closed one eye and scrunched up her face. Billy leaned in to get a closer look.

'Do you think that's it?' Juno whispered.

'I think that's it,' Billy whispered.

'Why are we whispering?'

Billy's lopsided grin stretched across his face. 'Let's have a look, shall we?' He wrapped a cloth around his hands, slid back the window and pulled out a jar of deep purple liquid. Placing it onto a wooden tray, he sniffed at the small tendrils of purple smoke. 'I think we have done it,' he said. 'Months of trying and we have finally done it.'

Juno clapped her hands together and grinned at Billy. 'How do we know if it will work?'

'We don't. We have followed what instructions we have, so all we can do is hope,' he said, his face turning serious. 'Can you bring me that box over there?'

Juno fetched the box and placed it on the counter. She opened the top and ran her finger over the rows of tiny glass-corked bottles. 'Aren't these bottles a bit small?'

'No, the antidote is strong. Two drops per person will be enough,' Billy said. 'Use this spoon to fill these bottles up. Be careful, please.'

Juno took the spoon, dipped it into the cauldron and filled a bottle to just under the cork. 'This jar will fill all of these.'

Billy grunted. 'I will make another one just in case.'

Juno jumped at the sharp rap on the door. 'That's Miles. If you don't get this finished by the time I am done, I will come and help you.'

'Go. Get out of here,' Billy said. 'You know never to be late for Miles.'

Juno handed Billy the spoon and ran to Miles's room. The door banged closed behind her. 'I think we have done it.'

'Done what?' Chloe said, wiping the sweat from her forehead. 'The antidote. I think we made it.'

'That is good news,' Dr Viktor said.

'A bit of a crowd today, Miles,' Juno said.

Miles walked to the weapon rack, picked up Juno's Jo and tossed it across the room to her. He reached behind his greatsword and pulled out a wooden practice sword. The mat creaked under his weight as he moved to the centre. With a nod, he invited Juno to join him. Juno walked to the centre of the mat, spun her Jo and settled into her ready stance. In a series of swift moves, she defended herself from the flurry of attacks Miles unleashed on her.

'You're exposing your left side,' Miles said. 'Bring your Jo around higher to protect it.'

Juno nodded, then rested back into her ready stance. Miles darted in with a sharp jab, followed by an overhead cut. Juno danced across the mat while deflecting each attack.

'Enough,' Dr Viktor said. 'It is time to draw her out, my son. Chloe, remain where you are.'

Miles inclined his head at Dr Viktor, then settled into his ready stance. He lifted his sword and gazed down the length of the wooden blade at Juno. With a feint, he darted to the left, spun his sword and rapped it hard against Juno's arm.

Juno gasped. 'That hurt.'

Miles stepped to the right and slammed his practice sword into the side of Juno's head. Spots exploded across her eyes. Miles hunched down and, blade blurring, struck Juno's knees, making her buckle to the ground. He brought his sword around and slapped the flat side of the blade on the back of Juno's head.

'You are hurting her, Miles,' Chloe said, taking a step forwards.

Miles extended the hilt of his sword and thumped Chloe back against the wall.

'Remain where you are,' Dr Viktor said with a hiss. 'Continue, son.'

Miles jabbed out his sword and struck Juno along the length of her back. Juno fell onto all fours and screamed. Pins and needles shot out of the marks and into her hands. With heat building through her palms, she lifted her head and snarled at Miles.

'Stop it,' Chloe said, pushing herself off the wall.

'One more step and I will put you down,' Miles said, pointing his blade at her.

'There she is,' Dr Viktor said, interrupting everyone. He climbed out of his chair and hobbled across the mat to Juno. 'Do you see the red flecks in her eyes?'

Miles took a step back and, resting his sword across his forearms, glanced at Dr Viktor.

Dr Viktor knees cracked as he lowered himself to the floor. He cupped Juno's face with his gnarled hands. 'Look at me, fire child.'

Juno bared her teeth and let out a long, guttural growl.

'You need to control it,' Dr Viktor said, squeezing her face. 'Emotions bring it out. Like the pain you are experiencing right now. Learn to control it.'

Juno snarled.

'Control it,' Dr Viktor shouted, his face inches from Juno's.

Juno coughed. She looked down at her hands and watched the flames spring out.

'Yes. That's it,' Dr Viktor said. 'Imagine the marks are fire. Turn them on, fire child.'

Juno concentrated on another mark and gasped at the heat that tore into her finger. With a soft pop, a flame sprang from the mark and wrapped around her finger.

'Remarkable,' Dr Viktor said, leaning back and clapping his hands.

Juno's eyes grew heavy. The flame disappeared and Juno fell forwards into Dr Viktor's arms.

'Animals. The both of you,' Chloe said, jabbing her finger at Dr Viktor and Miles.

'This will one day save her life. Take her to her room,' Dr Viktor said, nodding at Miles. 'She will need a lot of rest.'

'Don't you dare touch her,' Chloe said, cutting Miles off. She picked Juno up and carried her out of the room and up the stairs. Kicking the bedroom door open, she laid Juno across the bed and tucked her in. Chloe sat on the chair next to the bed, pulled the blanket over her and watched her friend sleep.

'Wake up, Chloe,' Juno said, shaking her friend.

'How are you feeling?' Chloe said, stretching her long legs out from underneath her.

'You know you are sleeping in my chair,' Juno said.

Chloe chuckled. 'Dr Viktor said you will need a lot of rest. I was expecting you to be out for a few days.'

'I haven't felt this good in a long time,' Juno said, holding her hands out and turning them over. 'It feels like a dark place in my mind has some light shed across it.'

'Do they hurt?' Chloe said, taking Juno's hand and tracing a finger along a mark.

'No, but I can feel the heat just below the surface.'

Chloe pulled her hands away. 'I can actually feel the heat.'

Juno looked at her hands as the pins and needles flooded heat into the marks. 'I think I can control them.'

'They are glowing,' Chloe said, poking Juno's palm with her finger.

Juno dropped her hands down by her side. 'I can feel the heat, but I haven't tried the fire trick yet. I am going to speak to Dr Viktor about it first.'

'A good idea. There are a lot of things in this house that could catch fire.'

'Want to come with me?' Juno said, pulling her shoes on.

Chloe scowled. 'I find them disrespectful. Dr Viktor and Miles have no respect for women. I don't know if I want to see them right now.'

'Dr Viktor said he didn't know why the elemental had chosen a girl.' Juno said.

'See what I mean?' Chloe said.

'I need his help. If he's offering, I need to take it.'

Chloe pursed her lips. 'Don't expect me to hold my tongue, though.'

Juno laughed. 'That is something I would never ask you to do.'

A knock sounded on the door. 'Can I come in?' Billy said. 'I have brought you some food, Chloe.'

'Come on in,' Juno said.

Billy walked in holding a tray of food. 'So much for you needing rest. I would have brought you some food if I had known.'

'We can share it,' Chloe said, taking the tray from Billy.

Billy propped himself against the windowsill. 'Did Juno tell you about the antidote?'

'Yes. Do you think it will work?'

'We think so. We will only know once we test it on somebody.'

'Let's get to the caves, then. The snow has melted, so we can get through the forest.'

'Not so fast. Juno needs to finish her training,' Billy said, raising a hand.

'There may be girls who are suffering. We need to go now.'

Juno rested a hand on Chloe's arm. 'We need to trust Naomi, Chloe. She would have sent someone if she needed us. I need a bit more time.'

Chloe sat down, placed her elbows on her knees and rested her chin on her hands. A few moments later, she sat up and gave Juno a nod. 'Okay, but let's hurry this along if we can.'

Juno smiled. 'Where is Dr Viktor?'

'Having breakfast with Miles. I suggest we go and join them in the kitchen.' They double-stepped down the staircase and entered the kitchen.

'Didn't expect to see me?' Juno said, sitting on a stool.

Dr Viktor pulled out his handkerchief and coughed into it. 'You should be resting.'

'I am fine. Just starving.'

Billy, on the way back from the pantry, grabbed a bread knife. The neatly cut slices of the freshly baked bread sent steam rising into the air. Juno spread jam and butter on her slice and devoured it in four big bites.

'So much for the finishing school,' Miles muttered.

Juno stuck out a tongue, then buttered another slice.

'Our young fire child wasn't joking,' Dr Viktor said with a snort. 'It seems your abilities take a lot of energy.'

'Talking about abilities,' Juno said, finishing her slice. 'What is the plan for today?'

'After breakfast, you will join me,' Dr Viktor said. 'Miles and Billy have done all they can to get you ready.'

'What can I do to help?' Chloe said from the other side of the counter.

'Alone,' Dr Viktor said, waving a dismissive hand at Chloe. 'She will join me alone.'

Chloe scowled and dropped her fork with a clatter. 'What is your problem?'

'No problem. I am training Juno, not you. She will join me alone or not at all,' Dr Viktor said, his eyes narrowing at Chloe.

Chloe stared at Dr Viktor.

'It's okay. The quicker I do this, the quicker we get out of here,' Juno said, with a half-smile.

Chloe stalked out of the kitchen.

'Leave her with me. We can train more in my room,' Miles said.

Dr Viktor climbed off his stool, picked up his cane and hobbled out of the kitchen. Juno pushed away from the counter and followed Dr Viktor out of the kitchen, under the stairs and into his room.

'Sit,' he said, waving at Juno's chair.

Juno sat in her usual spot, her hands folded in her lap.

Dr Viktor pulled out a chair and dragged it in front of Juno. He propped his cane against the backrest of his chair and said, 'I have one more thing to show you. After that, it is up to you to work the rest out.'

Juno lifted her hands, palms up. 'I can bring heat to the marks. Nothing happens after that.'

Dr Viktor took one of Juno's hands and placed it, palm up, in his own. 'Show me.'

Juno closed her eyes and willed the pins and needles to the marks. A yellow glow shone out from the marks as the heat grew.

'You are learning,' Dr Viktor said.

'What is the last thing you need to teach me?' Juno said, resting her hands in her lap.

He grabbed his handkerchief and coughed loudly. 'Do you recall me saying that emotions bring the fire out?'

Juno looked down at her hands. 'When I am angry, I feel the heat rise.'

'Raise your hands,' Dr Viktor said. 'Concentrate on an emotion. Not anger, but another emotion you feel strongly.'

Juno shifted in her seat, then straightened her back. She stared at the marks and thought of Tilly, her best friend. Waves of love sang through her body, bringing the familiar pins and needles to her hands. Heat rose sharply, making her take in a sharp breath.

'The pain you will get used to,' Dr Viktor said. 'Don't let it break your emotions.'

With a picture of Tilly in her mind, Juno concentrated on the marks on her hands. A small pop and a bright yellow flame sprang from a mark on her finger. She concentrated on another mark, and with a pop a yellow flame sprang from it. One by one, the yellow flames popped from her marks.

'Enough, Juno,' Dr Viktor said urgently. 'You need to learn to extinguish them.'

Juno willed the flames away, but they burned stronger. 'I can't turn them off,' she said, wild-eyed.

Dr Viktor grabbed her by the cheeks. 'Let go of the emotion you were thinking of.'

Juno cleared her mind of any thoughts of Tilly. The flames fluttered, then disappeared.

Dr Viktor leaned back in his chair and showed a rare smile. 'My knowledge of this is now at its limit. I suggest you practise with different emotions and see what happens. But please don't do it in my house.'

Juno sat back and rubbed her forehead. 'What is wrong, fire child?'

'I might hurt someone with this.'

Dr Viktor leaned forwards. 'Do you want to see your sisters

consumed by the evil that runs through Fairacre?'

Juno shook her head. 'I will do anything to help Tilly, Chloe and the girls. But I don't wish to hurt anyone.'

Dr Viktor grunted. 'The very reason the elemental should have chosen a man.'

Juno curled a lip. 'We don't need to settle every issue with violence, Dr Viktor.'

Dr Viktor leaned in closer. 'And we cannot settle some issues with talking. Do what you must, young fire child. It is your road to walk.'

Juno folded her arms and remained silent.

Dr Viktor stood, turned and walked towards the door at the back of his room. 'Follow me. I have something for you.'

'I think I will go now,' Juno said, turning towards the exit.

With a thump of his cane on the wooden floor, Dr Viktor glared at Juno. 'It is a gift. Please. Follow me.'

Juno unfolded her arms and followed him to the door at the back of the room. A silver key appeared out of Dr Viktor's pocket. He slid it into the lock, unlocked the door and pushed it open. The torch he grabbed cast flickering shadows across the walls.

'Come on in,' he said, beckoning Juno to enter.

Juno took a step into the room and peered at the mannequin standing in the middle. Dr Viktor grabbed a brush from a desk and expertly flicked it across the clothes draped over the mannequin. Juno ran her eyes over the pitch-black outfit. The material, not unlike her sewer rat fighting outfit, hugged the mannequin tightly. She extended a hand, gripped the end of the sleeve and rubbed. The soft material stretched delicately under her fingers.

'I have made this with a special flame-retardant material,' Dr Viktor said, brushing the dust off one sleeve. 'The shoes are in that box at the bottom.'

Juno picked up the box and slid the lid off. Two black lace-up boots with small heels sat snugly next to each other.

'Why have you done this for me?' Juno whispered.

'I do not agree with the elemental choosing a girl. But what the elemental wants, it shall have. I may judge, but I will still help where I can.'

Juno tilted her head and said, 'You will rue the day you underestimated me.'

Dr Viktor cackled, then beckoned Juno to the back of the mannequin. He reached up and pulled a short pole out of a magnetic clip. 'This is your Jo. It is collapsible. Here, take it and push the button in the middle.'

Juno took the short pole and spun it in her hand. She pressed down on the button, and with a snap the two ends sprang out. The Jo balanced perfectly in her palm.

'How does the pole feel?' Dr Viktor said.

'Like a part of me,' Juno said, spinning it around her hands. With a push of the button, the Jo snapped its ends back.

Dr Viktor walked towards the door. 'I am going to step out. Once dressed, join me in the other room.'

Juno stripped off her cotton clothes. She peeled the trousers off the mannequin and pulled them over her feet. Next, the jacket, which she pulled her arms through and zipped up to her throat. At the bottom of the jacket, she clipped the zip onto the trousers and zipped it around her waist. The two items of clothing joined snugly together. She pulled the face mask over her face, flicked the hood over and pulled the drawstrings to tighten them both around her head. Her feet slipped comfortably into her new boots. Juno took a step away from the mannequin. She reached behind her back and snapped out her Jo. Her feet slid into the ready stance. The Jo sang around her as she performed the basic movements first and then moved to the more complex ones. With a smile, she cartwheeled across the room, ending in a handstand, her legs straight as arrows above her. She swung back onto her feet and walked through the door into Dr Viktor's room.

Dr Viktor ran a critical eye over her. 'How do you feel?'

'It's like a second skin,' Juno said, beaming from ear to ear.

'You haven't given it the important test yet.'

Juno looked down at her hands, closed her eyes and brought up images of her friend Tilly smiling in the greenhouse. Pins and needles flowed into her palms. Her jaw clenched as the pain burst around the marks. Flames, dancing out of the five marks, engulfed her hands.

'Run them under your forearms,' Dr Viktor said.

Juno extended her arm and ran the flames along the underside of her forearm.

'Hold the flame in one position,' Dr Viktor said. 'Dragging the flame along will not test it properly.'

She extended her arm, locked her elbow into place and held the flame under her forearm.

'It's not burning the clothes. It just feels warm.'

Dr Viktor thumped his cane onto the floor. 'Then, young fire child, I have done my job.'

Juno extinguished the flames and, placing her hands together, she gave Dr Viktor a small bow. 'Thank you. I shall never forget this generous gift.'

Dr Viktor coughed. 'Think nothing of it. Now get out of here,' he said, waving his hand.

Juno walked over to the door, turned the handle, then stopped. She spun round, ran back to Dr Viktor and grabbed him in a fierce hug. 'Thank you for everything,' she said.

Dr Viktor cleared his throat. 'Go away, fire child.'

Juno pulled away and grinned. With the door closing behind her, she stopped and listened to Chloe's, Billy's and Miles's voices, which floated out of the living room.

Juno swung open the living room door and said, 'Time to go home.'

CHAPTER 13
IT TAKES TWO

'Well?' Juno smiled. 'Are we going?'

Chloe, her mouth hanging open, walked over to Juno. 'Where did you get these clothes?'

'Dr Viktor made them for me. He said I needed fireproof clothes. What do you think?'

Billy slapped his thigh. 'So that's what Dr Viktor has been up to.'

'You look incredible,' Chloe said, rolling the material between her finger and thumb.

Miles gave Juno a withering look. 'Dr Viktor made that for you?'

'Yes,' Juno said. 'These clothes won't burn.'

'Miles, she needs clothes,' Billy said, with a look of concern.

Miles shook his head and, pushing past Juno, he stormed out of the living room.

'What's wrong with him?' Juno said, looking at Billy.

Billy walked past her and stopped at the door. 'He is angry because Dr Viktor has made you clothes and not him.'

'I didn't ask for them,' Juno said, shaking her head.

'It's not your fault. I will go and speak to him. Can you get the antidotes ready for transport?'

Juno grabbed Chloe's hand. 'Come and help,' she said, leading her into Billy's room.

'Miles can be so childish,' Chloe said, rolling her eyes.

'It must hurt him, though. I suddenly appear in their lives and Dr Viktor makes clothes for me.'

'I suppose,' Chloe said. 'Are these the antidotes?'

'Yes. We need to place them in those boxes and then into that satchel,' Juno said, signalling towards a large bag on the floor.

'They are tiny,' Chloe said, holding a small bottle between her fingers.

'Billy says it will only take two drops to cure the infected people. That's if it works.'

Chloe pulled down another wooden box from a shelf and, opening the lid, she counted out ten slots.

'Lift that layer,' Juno said. 'There are ten more slots underneath the one you have just counted.'

Chloe pulled the top layer out and began placing bottles of antidotes into the lower layer of slots.

'We need five boxes, with twenty bottles in each,' Juno said, securing the lid of the first box with a small latch. 'One hundred antidotes.'

'Are we ready?' Billy said, walking into the room. 'Miles is waiting at the front door.'

'Is he okay?' Juno said.

Billy walked over to the table. 'Yes. He will be fine.'

'I need to get my stuff from the room,' Chloe said.

'Last box,' Juno said, placing the top layer into the box and filling it with bottles of antidotes.

Billy lifted the satchel and placed it on the table. He slid the last box in, pulled the drawstring, checked the strap's length and gently pulled the satchel onto his back. He gathered his long, flowing cloak and his green gnarled staff and walked out of the door. Juno followed Billy out of the house and down the steps into the sunshine. A ray of sunlight broke through the trees, warming her face. She smiled at Chloe, who raced out of the front door, jumped from the top step and landed next to her.

'What trees are these?' Juno said, staring at the thick, twisted trunks.

'Kapok trees,' Billy said. 'It rains a lot here.'

'I will lead,' Miles said. 'Chloe, I suggest you cover our backs. Juno, you stick with Billy in the middle.'

'We know how important these antidotes are,' Billy said, looking at each of them in turn. 'Let's make sure we get them to your friends in one piece.'

Miles walked to the front to lead the way.

'What is that smell?' Juno said.

'After the black snow has melted, it leaves a thin layer of gunk all over the place,' Billy said, with a look of sadness across his face. 'It's disgusting.'

'How does this forest survive covered in this stuff?'

'Summer rains wash it away. Once it's gone, the forest turns green again,' Billy said.

'And this stuff is from the machines Dr Viktor used to work on? Do you know what he did?'

'He helped build them,' Billy said. 'He doesn't talk about it much.'

The overgrown path wound south through the black-tarred forest. Juno tilted her head and listened for any signs of animals. Birds high in the tree canopy called for their mates. Below the canopy there was no rustling of bushes, no buzzing of insects or grunts and growls from little animals. The forest felt and sounded dead. Juno wrapped her arms around herself and shivered. After hours of silently walking through the forest, Miles suddenly hissed, lifted a hand and crouched. Juno squatted and pulled her Jo from her back.

'What is it?' Chloe whispered.

Miles placed a finger on his lips. Juno tilted her head and strained her ears.

Miles pulled them together in a circle. 'There are soldiers to the south. I think I hear at least six of them.'

'Can we let them pass?' Billy said.

'They are searching,' Miles said. 'We need to get off the path and hide.'

A thin layer of black rubbed onto Juno's clothes as she parted the plants to get off the path. She gagged, grabbed her mask and pulled it into place.

'Disgusting,' Chloe whispered, pulling her own face mask up.

They wound through the black-covered bushes and stopped at the trunk of a large kapok tree. Juno inched her head above the bushes and counted six heads. The searching men's voices trickled through the trees.

'One of those soldiers is not from around here,' Billy said, tilting his head.

'He is from the City of Lynn,' Miles said. 'I can tell by his accent.'

The loud snap of a branch sent the four of them to their bellies. Juno held her breath.

'If they see us, Chloe and I will hold them back. Juno, you get Billy out of here. Stay off the path but follow it south,' Miles whispered.

Juno looked over at Chloe. 'You okay with this?'

'Yes. Make sure the antidotes get to Naomi.'

The stench of tobacco and alcohol drifted into their nostrils. A man cleared his throat then stopped and folded his arms. 'Anything?'

'Nothing,' another man said, stepping out of the bushes. A

third man hacked at the undergrowth with a wicked-looking curved blade.

A tall, thin man appeared behind them. His back perfectly straight, his hands behind his back, he walked slowly while scanning the bushes. 'Keep moving,' he said, waving a hand to the north.

The men spread out from the path and continued north while hacking and slashing at the undergrowth.

Miles waited for the forest to turn quiet. 'It looks like they have gone. Get to the path and move as quickly as you can.'

They scrambled to their feet and doubled their speed along the path. The forest thickened, with branches of the trees spreading across the path creating a tunnel.

'The black is getting less,' Juno said, moving up alongside Billy.

'Not much snow, but a lot of rain falls down south,' he said. 'If it did snow this far south, Fairacre would be in serious trouble.'

'Fairacre is in serious trouble,' Chloe said.

Billy grunted. 'Yes, you are right. But if this black snow hits the farmlands, starvation will hit everyone, including the citizens of the City of Lynn.'

'Nothing new for the girls,' Chloe said, scowling. 'Leaving forgotten orphan girls to starve while feeding the town and the city's rich people.'

Miles peered over his shoulder and gave Chloe a withering look. 'Orphan girls produced by unmarried women.'

Chloe growled, 'Takes two to make a child, Miles.'

'Can we rest and eat?' Juno said, sensing a fight.

'Good idea,' Billy said, giving Juno a grateful look. 'We will need to get off the path.'

'There is a fork in the path about an hour from here,' Miles said. 'It is a safer place to stop because we can see most directions from there.'

Juno, panting hard, kept her eyes on the heels of Billy's boots as they trudged along in silence. After half an hour, Juno slowed down so that she walked side by side with her friend. 'Miles doesn't know any better.'

'No excuse,' Chloe said, her eyes boring holes into Miles's back. 'He should at least try to educate himself.'

'His actions are contradicting what he says, though,' Juno said. 'Why go to all this trouble to help the girls?'

Chloe shrugged. 'Dr Viktor's orders? Or maybe he doesn't like the fact that the Lady might be in charge of Fairacre?'

Juno nodded. 'That may be so, but he is helping us help the girls. We need all the help we can get.'

Chloe gave Juno a reluctant nod. 'Let's see.'

Juno threw her hand over her eyes as they broke out of the thick trees.

Miles held up his hand as he peered left along the path that led to the eastern land and right along the western path that led to the waterfall. 'Let's get off the path,' he said.

Juno fought her way through the thick undergrowth until she broke into a clearing with one large kapok tree in the middle.

'We should be safe here,' Miles said, turning a full circle to check all angles.

'Can you get the food out of the pack?' Billy said, turning his back to Juno.

Juno pulled out a small leather pack from the large satchel. She sat cross-legged and fished out the food supplies, which she divided into four and passed around. They sat with their backs to the tree and ate in silence. Miles, taking a draught of water, suddenly froze. He cocked his head and frowned. A branch snapped. Miles jumped to his feet and slid his greatsword from its sheath.

'What is it?' Juno said.

'Trouble,' he said. 'Up, everyone. Billy, get behind me and keep your back to the tree.'

Juno snapped out her Jo and Chloe drew her short sword.

'I can't hear anything,' Chloe whispered.

'That is the problem,' Miles said. 'The forest birds have gone quiet. Too quiet.'

There was a flash of sunlight glinting off steel. 'Over there,' Juno said, pointing her Jo.

'And there,' Chloe said, pointing her sword in the other direction.

'Surrounded,' Miles said, moving Juno to his right side and Chloe to his left.

A mountain of a man walked into the clearing. His breath smelled of alcohol and tobacco. Tattoos and scars covered the length of his arms. He reached behind him and pulled out a two-sided battle-axe. The steel glinted in the sunlight. Behind him, the thin man with his close-set eyes and a beak of a nose stood with his hands clasped behind his back.

He turned his eyes to Juno. 'You must be the child of fire.'

Juno's nostrils flared as she lifted her chin.

'The Lady has a bounty on your head. A bounty I am going to collect,' the thin man said, his smile widening.

'She isn't going anywhere,' Chloe said, lifting her short sword and pointing it at the man.

The man chuckled. A snap of his fingers, and four more soldiers appeared out of the forest.

'Mercenaries,' Miles said with a growl.

'Yes, mercenaries,' the thin man said, looking down at his hands while picking his nails. With a disinterested sigh, he said, 'You can come with me now, fire child, and I will make sure the end comes swiftly and humanely for your friends.'

A whisper of a smile appeared on Miles's face. He pointed his sword at the thin man. 'If you are going to end us, why would we let the fire child go without a fight?'

The thin man lowered his eyes at Miles. 'I was expecting nothing less,' he said, taking a step back. 'Gentlemen, you may proceed.'

The tattooed man roared and sprang at Miles with his axe sweeping around in a wide arc. Miles ducked, spun, and with a whine of steel he watched the man crumple to the floor.

The thin man chuckled. 'Bravo, you brave boy. Bravo.'

Chloe shoved Juno behind her and joined Miles with her sword at the ready. 'The man to your right has a hidden blade.'

Miles narrowed his eyes and caught the hilt of the knife in the man's belt. The mercenaries rushed the group, their weapons slashing and hacking. A whip of sword, a whine of greatsword, and two mercenaries' knees buckled as their lifeless bodies slumped to the ground.

'Enough,' the thin man said, whipping up his hands and releasing two thin daggers.

'Miles,' Chloe shouted, swinging her blade and deflecting one dagger.

Miles grunted and staggered backwards, a blade protruding from his shoulder. The thin man took a step forwards and flung out two more black blades. Juno twirled her Jo, deflecting one dagger. Chloe, slashing out with her blade, deflected the other.

'Your pathetic weapons are no match for a knife slinger,' the thin man said. Two more blades appeared in his hands. 'Come with me, fire child. You do not have to see your friends fall.'

Juno brought forwards her emotions and felt the heat grow in her hands. A bright yellow bolt of fire sprang out of her marks and hit the knife slinger in the face. His eyes widening, he staggered back and desperately slapped his cheeks. The knife slinger snarled at Juno, his face black, his eyebrows and eyelashes gone. He signalled to the remaining mercenary and stepped backwards into the forest. 'I will be back for you, fire child. And next time I will make your friends pay for what you have done to me.'

Juno spun her Jo and pointed it at the knife slinger. 'Tell the Lady I will never come to her.'

The knife slinger growled as he disappeared into the undergrowth.

'We have to move. He will be back with more,' Miles said, his face etched with pain.

'We need to take care of that blade first,' Billy said.

Miles waved his hand. 'Move first.'

'Sit,' Billy said, pointing to a rock at the edge of the clearing. 'It will take a minute. Chloe, Juno, can you stand guard, please?'

A look of resignation on his face, Miles sat on the rock with his greatsword spread across his knees. Juno stood next to Chloe and scanned the tree line that surrounded the small clearing.

'This is going to hurt,' Billy said. 'I will count to three.'

Miles grabbed the hilt and, with a grunt, pulled out the dagger in one fluid movement.

'Well done, tough guy,' Billy said, placing a thick cloth over the wound. Chloe looked at Juno and rolled her eyes. Juno smirked. The muscles in Miles's jaw twitched as Billy removed the cloth and placed a salve-soaked cloth back on the wound.

'Keep the pressure on it. I will need to look at it properly when we have the time,' Billy said. 'Try not to move it too much.'

Miles got to his feet and looked at Chloe. 'You could be formidable with some proper training.'

Chloe shook her head. 'Looks like I need to train you.'

Miles snorted.

'I think that is Miles's way of saying thank you,' Billy said with a lopsided grin.

'You're welcome,' Chloe said, nodding at Miles.

Juno clicked her Jo back into place, then stared down at her hands.

Chloe frowned at the look of worry on Juno's face. 'Are you okay?' she said, placing a hand on Juno's shoulder.

'I don't like hurting people.'

Chloe lifted Juno's head by the chin. 'That man was trying to kill us, Juno.'

'They taught us never to hurt anyone at my school,' Juno said, her breath catching in her throat.

'They taught you how to be a wife at your school too,' Chloe said, scowling. 'The world is not what you think it to be, young Juno.'

Juno pulled her lips into a thin line and looked away.

'We need to move,' Miles said. 'They will be back with a lot more mercenaries.'

'Come on,' Chloe said, giving Juno a small shake. 'You did what you needed to do.'

Juno steeled herself and followed Miles out of the clearing, through the bush and onto the eastern path. Pine trees replaced the kapok trees and to her left stood the smooth grey cliff. Juno breathed heavily as Miles kept up a gruelling pace. The forest grew thicker with pine trees, and the bushes below grew thinner. The sunlight dwindled as the canopy of pine trees closed in above.

Chloe let out a hiss.

Miles spun and looked at Chloe. 'What is it?'

Chloe lifted her head and mimicked the tweet of a small bird. A second later, the same tweet sounded from the trees. A wide smile stretching across her face, Chloe said, 'Sewer rats. I will take the lead, Miles.'

Miles stepped aside and waved Chloe through. Juno looked up into the trees and saw nothing but a thick blanket of green. Another tweet from above. Chloe left the path and crashed through the undergrowth. In the distance, the thunder of the great waterfall echoed through the forest. Another tweet and Chloe dropped to her haunches.

Juno's eyes searched the trees. 'Chloe. Up there,' she said, pointing.

'I can see you, Alexa,' Chloe said.

Alexa sprang out of the branches and landed on her feet. Her black skin was covered by a green outfit, the same colour as the trees. 'You are alive, miss,' she said, embracing Chloe.

'You know I am not that easy to get rid of.'

'Juno, Billy, Miles,' Alexa said, nodding her head. 'Please follow me.' Alexa wound through the tightly packed trees and, using animal tracks, she led them through the thick fern undergrowth. The surrounding air turned fog-like as the mist from the waterfall rolled gently through the forest.

'A bit hard to breathe,' Juno said.

'Feels like you are drowning, doesn't it?' Billy said. 'I am sure we will get used to it.'

They broke into a large clearing with a large lake of crystal-clear water. The waterfall crashed into the lake and sent waves outwards until they lapped against the water's edge. Small rainbows danced along the waterfall just before the water crashed into the lake.

Alexa cupped her mouth and shouted over the thunder. 'This way. The entrance is on the other side of the pool.'

Juno frowned as she searched the smooth cliff face for an entrance. Alexa walked along the wall and then suddenly vanished.

'An illusion,' Billy said, chuckling. 'I can see why Naomi chose this place.'

Juno, walking away from the waterfall, ran her hand along the cliff face. 'There is no opening.'

'Keep going,' Billy said, his lopsided grin growing in amusement.

The cliff wall disappeared from Juno's touch.

'There is a gap,' Billy said. 'The cliff wall overlaps itself so you cannot see it from the outside. Hard to find if you don't know what you are looking for.'

Juno walked around the lip of the rock and into pitch-blackness. Her hands out in front of her, she slowed her walk to a snail's pace.

A hand reached out and grabbed her. 'Come on. It's just a short way,' Chloe said from inside the darkness.

One hand on a wall and the other in Chloe's hand, she twisted and turned down a series of tunnels. Another turn, and the walls widened into an enormous cavern. The chattering in the cavern died down as faces turned and stared.

'Sisters, brothers,' Naomi said, as she strode towards them.

'Naomi,' Chloe said, spreading her arms. 'It is so good to see you, boss.'

Naomi embraced Chloe and smiled at Juno. 'I was sure you were okay. Come, we have a place for you in the smaller caves.'

Juno followed Naomi across the cavern and into a small cave. Girls sat and chatted on beds of hay lining the walls.

'Over there.' Naomi pointed to a clear spot in the hay. Juno walked over and dropped onto the hay.

'Food is out here in the cavern, Juno,' Naomi said.

Chloe tilted her head. 'Juno?'

Juno's chest rose and fell in the rhythm of someone fast asleep.

Juno, lying on her hay bed, stretched her stiff arms and legs. The entrance to the enormous cavern flickered with the light from the cooking fire that sat in its centre. She slid her Jo out from underneath a pile of hay and clicked it onto her back. The sound of her boots thudding on the ground echoed gently through the small cave as she walked into the cavern.

Naomi waved her over. 'It is good to see you, young Juno.'

Juno sat on a log and stared into the flames that licked the bottom of the cooking pot. 'Where is everyone else?'

'Sleeping,' Naomi said. 'Chloe wanted to report but she couldn't keep her eyes open. Billy took Miles to another cave to sort out his shoulder.'

'Food time,' Jen said, making Juno jump.

'Yes, hedgehog, food time,' Gem said, spooning thick porridge into a bowl and handing it to Juno.

'I don't look like a hedgehog anymore,' Juno said, smiling at the twins. 'My hair has grown.'

Gem and Jen pouted simultaneously over their shoulders as they walked to the back of the cavern and into another cave. Juno smiled after the twins.

'What news have you for me, young Juno?' Naomi said. 'I see you have upgraded your outfit.'

'A gift from Dr Viktor, would you believe,' Juno said.

'Oh, really?' Naomi said, reaching over and rubbing the clothes between her fingers.

Juno grinned at Naomi's surprise. 'Billy thinks we have created the antidote to cure the infected.'

Naomi froze, her mouth hanging open. 'I wasn't expecting that. What incredible news. Are we sure it will cure them?'

'We don't know. We haven't been able to test it. But it was the only antidote that didn't explode in Billy's face,' Juno said, grinning.

Naomi chuckled. 'I would have liked to have seen that.'

'You can still see some purple in his eyebrows,' Juno said, giggling into her hand.

Naomi stood and paced around the fire. 'In the big escape, we lost four girls to the Lady. We couldn't attempt a rescue, because bringing them back to the caves would have told the Lady where we are. Having the antidote means we can execute our rescue plan.'

'Chloe knew you would plan a rescue,' Juno said.

Naomi sat back down. 'We think alike, Chloe and I.'

'Good morning,' Billy said, walking up behind them. 'Could I perhaps trouble someone for some food?'

'In the pot,' Juno said. 'It's really hot.'

'Bowl,' Gem said, making Billy jump.

'Boys,' Jen said, scowling at Billy.

Billy took the bowl from Gem and filled it with porridge using the wooden spoon.

'How is Miles?' Juno said, looking up at Billy.

'He is fine. The blade missed all the important parts. He can already move his shoulder. How are you feeling?'

'Better now I have slept and eaten.'

Chloe, appearing out of a side cave, strode over to the group. She grabbed a bowl and presented it to Billy, who filled it up with porridge. With a groan, she sat and rubbed her legs. 'What's next, boss?'

'Juno here has just told me about the antidote. We have already created the plans for a rescue. We move before first light tomorrow morning.'

Juno rubbed the back of her neck. 'So soon?'

'The sewer rats are always prepared, young Juno,' Naomi said.

'How many are we rescuing, boss?'

'There are four missing,' Naomi said. 'That includes Joanne. Our spies have them living in a house next to the town hall.'

'Even after she has infected our girls, they have stuck together,' Chloe said, spooning the last of the porridge into her mouth.

Naomi nodded. 'Getting to them is the simple part. Escaping is where we are going to have a problem.'

Miles strode over to the pot, inclined his head at everyone, then sat next to Billy.

'It may not be that difficult if we can get the antidote into them before we escape,' Billy said. 'But, of course, we don't know if they work.'

'We plan for the worst. We may have to fight our way out,' Naomi said.

Miles rotated his arm and flexed his hand. 'I have a date with a certain knife slinger,' he said, his eyes narrowing.

'Not if I get to him first,' Chloe said, her lip curling.

'What do you need me to do?' Juno said, rolling her eyes at the pair of them.

Naomi glanced at Chloe. 'You get to stay here, young Juno. We cannot have another episode like the last.'

Her forehead crinkling in surprise, Juno said. 'I am not sitting around here while you go out there.'

Naomi said, 'The Lady is after you. Our plan is to get the girls back, not engage with the Lady.'

Juno stood, her fists balled by her sides. 'I will not hide anymore, Naomi. You need me to come with you. I can help.'

Chloe rested a hand on Naomi's forearm. 'She can control it now, boss.'

'Is that so?'

'Show her,' Chloe said, smiling at Juno.

Juno took in a deep breath and brought up images of Tilly. She grunted as the heat shot through the marks. With a pop, a flame burst from her hand.

Naomi sat with her mouth open. 'Remarkable. I have seen nothing like it.'

Juno willed the flame away. 'I am part of this team, Naomi. I couldn't bear it if something happened to any of you and I wasn't there to help if I could.'

Naomi eventually nodded. 'Okay. You may come, but you and Chloe will have a separate mission.'

'Assassinate the Lady? Free the women of Fairacre from oppression? Establish equality for all?' Chloe said.

Miles hmphed, then coughed as Billy's elbow found his ribcage.

Naomi gave Miles a withering look before reaching into her pocket and pulling out a round metal ball, which she handed to Chloe.

'Little Jay,' Chloe said, a smile spreading across her face.

'Valen left that with me. His instructions were to give it to you. He is beside himself with worry.'

'What has Chloe's love interest got to do with our mission?' Juno said, dodging a swift kick from Chloe.

'Valen has been making more devices. Your mission is to get Valen and his devices out of Fairacre.'

'Can't he just leave with them?' Billy said, frowning.

'A lot has happened since the autumn,' Naomi said. 'The men of Fairacre are being held hostage. The Lady and their infected loved ones have either kicked them into the sewers or have them locked in their houses.'

'Maybe they will understand what it is like, then?' Chloe said with a huff.

'That may be so,' Naomi said. 'But it is not what we are fighting for. Remember, your Valen is being held hostage too, Chloe.'

Chloe sighed. 'I apologise. I do not wish this on anybody.'

'How are the men being held hostage by the women?' Miles said, his face crinkling with confusion.

'The Lady has threatened to take the men's loved ones away from them,' Naomi said. 'They are falling into line with her demands.'

Billy growled. 'We need to stop her.'

Naomi scanned the group. 'I have further, more worrying news.' The group turned their heads in Naomi's direction.

'The Lady can infect men too,' she said. 'Our spies have told us of men with black and white eyes.'

'Impossible,' Billy said. 'Dr Viktor says it is not transferable between men and women.'

Naomi spread her hands. 'It is what we have seen.'

Miles stood and paced around the fire pot. 'Was that knife slinger infected?'

'No,' Juno said. 'His eyes were normal.'

Miles's brow creased over.

'What are you thinking, brother?' Billy said.

'The knife slinger is from the City of Lynn. Which means the Lady is getting support from the city.'

'You think the queen has a hand in all of this?' Naomi said.

Miles sat and rubbed his forehead. 'I don't know. But it is worrying.'

'One issue at a time,' Naomi said. 'Take some time now to relax and recharge. Tomorrow before dawn we move on Fairacre.'

As the group dispersed, Chloe grabbed Juno's hand. 'Come with me.'

Juno followed Chloe through the winding pitch-black tunnel. They scanned the area around the lake, then exited the cave.

'What are we doing?' Juno whispered.

Chloe pulled Jay out of her pocket. 'Time for you to go and wake up my Valen, little guy,' she said, throwing Jay into the air.

With a pop, Jay uncurled himself and buzzed off into the forest.

'You will see him tomorrow,' Juno said, wrapping an arm around Chloe's waist.

Chloe hugged her friend hard. 'That I will, young Juno.'

CHAPTER 14
A KNIFE SLINGER

Before dawn, the teams gathered around the cooking pot to eat and talk over the plan. Once done, they exited the cave in single file and followed the soft tweets from the girls in the trees. An urgent tweet from the forest canopy sent the three teams onto their haunches.

'Soldiers,' Chloe whispered into Juno's ear. 'This early in the morning, and they are still searching for you.'

Juno scanned the trees for movement. Her hand reached behind her back and rested on her Jo.

Naomi waited until the next tweet. She stood and led the teams through the trees, following the directions of the girls high in the canopy. At the forest tree line, the moon bathed light across the tilled wheat fields. In the distance, lights flickered from windows in the town of Fairacre.

Naomi knelt and called Juno, Chloe and Alexa into a huddle. 'We know the plan. Alexa, your team enters the sewers and clears a path. Chloe's team scales the wall near the manufacturing district and goes to Valen's shop. My team stays on the rooftops until we get to the house where the girls are.'

'We meet at the red barn before we head back to the forest,'

Chloe said, nodding at each of the team leads. 'If there is trouble, Alexa, our teams stay and Naomi's team takes the infected girls back into the forest.'

The girls pulled up their face masks and crouch-walked back to their teams. Naomi gave the signal to move out.

'Be careful, Juno,' Billy said, squeezing her hand. 'Don't get yourself caught.'

Juno squeezed Billy's hand then ran to catch up with Chloe. She slowed to a jog and glanced at Alexa's team, who were running for the hidden tunnels. Miles and Billy jogged behind Naomi, heading for the south entrance. The clink of glass tinkled in the darkness as Billy's wrapped-up antidotes knocked together.

Chloe threw a hand up and slid into a ditch on the south side of the road that ran along the moat. 'Patrol,' she whispered, pointing her chin at the road.

'Naomi is moving across the bridge,' Juno said.

'We follow once these guards have passed,' Chloe said, waving her hand for her team to flatten onto their bellies.

The guards walked by, chatting to each other. The stench of alcohol floated down into the ditch.

Chloe whispered into Juno's ear. 'Completely uninterested. We move when they walk past the bridge.'

The four team members moved into a crouching position and waited like tightened coils, ready to spring.

'Go,' Chloe said, her voice quiet but clear.

Juno ran hard to keep up with the three tall girls. As they turned onto the bridge, Juno caught the swish of Billy's cloak moving along the rooftops. At the end of the bridge, the team turned to the west, running along the outside of the wall. Chloe stopped short of the wall, turning north. She laced her fingers together and held her cupped hands out for the feet of her team. Juno, following the two girls, stepped into Chloe's hands, reached up, and grabbed their outstretched hands. She sat on the top of the wall and scanned the rooftops as the two girls pulled Chloe up. A small jump onto the closest rooftop, and they ran in single file above the manufacturing district.

Chloe jumped over an alley, ran across the rooftop, stopped and peered at the street below. 'Valen's shop is below us.'

'Looks like Naomi has reached the town hall,' Juno said, looking to the north-west.

'They will move once Alexa gives them the signal,' Chloe said.

'You stupid snake,' Valen shouted as something crashed onto the floor. 'I have told you not to lie around or I will trip over you.'

Juno smiled at Chloe. 'I think Valen needs saving.'

Chloe grinned, swung her legs over the roof and sank silently to the street below. Juno left the two remaining girls to keep watch and dropped next to Chloe.

'Last summer you would have damaged a limb attempting that,' Chloe said, nudging Juno with her elbow then turning and rapping her knuckles against the glass window.

'Who's there?' Valen said. 'It is after curfew.'

Chloe knocked once more. 'Open up, Valen.'

The door flung open, its windows rattling. 'Lass,' Valen said, reaching out and dragging Chloe into a fierce hug. 'I knew you would come. Little Jay told me you would.'

'Can't breathe,' Chloe said, slapping Valen on the back.

'Sorry, lass,' Valen said, a massive grin stretching across his face. 'Juno, come in, please.'

'How are you, Valen?' Juno said, giving him a hug.

Valen closed the door and walked past his office and into the kitchen. 'Sit, sit. I will get some tea on the go.'

'Valen, we have no time,' Chloe said. 'We need to move as quickly as possible.'

Valen peered around the kitchen door. 'What's the rush?'

'We are here with three teams to rescue the infected girls,' Chloe said. 'We will need to help in the escape.'

Valen walked back into his office and grabbed a large knapsack from under his desk. 'We can carry the devices in this.'

'How many do you have?' Juno said, a worried look etched on her face. 'How thin have you spread your essence?'

Valen moved to the side of his desk and lifted a large chest onto the table. 'I have made them, but haven't added my essence to them. There are too many for me to do that.'

Juno opened the chest. 'Can you tip the box? I will hold the knapsack.'

'Aye,' Valen said, picking up the chest.

As the last box clattered into the knapsack, Juno pulled the drawstring closed.

'There is no way either of you are going to carry that,' Valen said.

'We thought you might do the honours,' Chloe said, smiling at him. 'We need you in the caves with the girls.'

Valen stood with his mouth open. 'I thought the sewer rats forbid men to be among their ranks?'

'With everything going on, I think that rule is dead,' Juno said. 'Miles and Billy have been with us in the caves.'

'Sia, Jay, Henry, pack your bags,' Valen said, thumping his hand on the desk.

Little Henry clattered along the desk and spun in circles. Sia slithered out from behind the couch, her metal tongue searching the ground. Little Jay buzzed in front of Valen's head, dodging his attempts to catch him.

Chloe shook her head. 'I think you need to get your things, love,' she said, pushing him towards the stairs.

'Yes, yes, you are right,' Valen said, lumbering up the stairs. 'Sia, Jay and Henry don't have bags, do they?'

'I think he's delirious,' Juno said, eyeing Little Henry, who waved his two front legs at her.

'He has been here all winter worrying about us,' Chloe said. 'I think it's a weight off his shoulders.'

Valen's enormous feet thumped down the staircase and into the office. 'You three,' he said, dropping a small bag onto the floor. 'Get into the bag now.'

Little Henry dawdled at the edge of the desk. 'Stop sulking,' Valen said. 'Come on, move it.'

Little Henry disappeared into the small bag, followed by an angry, buzzing Jay and a winding, slinking Sia.

'Valen, this mission is to be quick and silent,' Chloe said. 'Do you have all your things?'

'Yes,' Valen said.

Chloe raised her hand, calling for quiet. 'What is it?' Valen said, straining to hear.

'Trouble,' Chloe said, striding to the front door and wrenching it open. 'Report,' she said to the girls standing outside.

'We have run into a problem,' a team member said. 'Sounds like fighting,' Juno said, walking up behind her.

'Fighting near the square,' Chloe said. 'We need to move now. Valen, get your stuff.'

Valen stuffed the smaller bag into the knapsack and slung it over his back. On his way to the front door, he grabbed his enormous club.

'Go with the girls, Valen,' Chloe said. 'Get those devices to the barn. Juno, you are with me.'

'But, love, I am not leaving you,' Valen said, his brow furrowing.

Chloe reached up and kissed him on the cheek. 'You need to trust me. Those devices are critical for our plans to succeed. I will see you at the barn.'

With a curse, Valen tore himself away from Chloe and walked towards the southern wall.

'Onto the rooftops,' Chloe said, sprinting over to a pile of crates.

Juno bounded up the crates and sprinted alongside Chloe. 'What do you think has happened?'

'Either the rescue has gone wrong or the guards have blocked the sewers.' At the town hall, Juno came to a halt and peered into the town square.

'I can't see anything.'

'It's gone quiet,' Chloe said, frowning. 'Let's look along the main street to the south.'

They bounded south across the rooftops and over the alleyways. Further south, near the gate, the sound of steel against steel rang out.

'Main southern street,' Chloe said. 'Come on.'

Juno reached behind her back and flicked out her Jo. 'Marketplace,' she said, jumping over another alley.

Chloe, a few strides ahead of Juno, pulled out her short sword and jumped off the roof into the marketplace. Juno pushed the button on her Jo's handle, and with a snap the ends extended. Sprinting to the roof edge, she dug the end into the gutter and catapulted herself upwards. After a single somersault, she fell, cat-like, towards the ground and slammed her Jo into the metal helmet of a guard. With a jab of her Jo she caught another guard between the eyes, sending him to the ground. City of Lynn and Fairacre guards battled Naomi and Chloe's teams between the stalls of the marketplace.

'Where are the infected girls?' Chloe shouted as she parried a long shining sword.

'Miles and Billy are taking them out the eastern gate,' Naomi said, her muscular limbs dancing around axes, swords and shields.

'We are a distraction?' Juno said, ducking under Chloe's armpit and slamming her Jo into the face of a snarling guard.

'A few more seconds and we go,' Naomi said, sucking in air as the tip of a sword nicked her forearm.

Juno spun her Jo, tripped up a guard then parried a short sword. She dug the end of her Jo into the ground and flicked a rock into the face of a guard.

'Impressive,' Chloe said, slamming the hilt of her sword into a guard, his helmet clattering to the ground.

Naomi let out a shrill whistle. The girls darted in between the market stalls, through the southern gate and over the bridge. Alexa's team appeared out of the rusted sewer gate and sprinted over to Naomi.

'Watch our backs,' Naomi said, glancing over her shoulder.

'They are not following,' Chloe said, a frown creasing her forehead.

Juno stopped on the path to the red barn, turned and faced the southern gate.

'Why are they not chasing?' Naomi said, sliding her sword back into its sheath.

'Let's get to the barn,' Chloe said. 'Valen, Miles and Billy will be waiting.' Juno jogged down the path and vaulted over the fence at the red barn. 'You made it,' she said, walking up to Valen.

'Yes, lass,' Valen said. 'But please don't ask me to climb another wall.'

'Where are Billy and Miles?' Naomi said, joining them.

Valen frowned. 'I haven't seen them.'

'Should they have been here by now?' Chloe said. 'Did we not stay long enough?'

'I gave it ample time,' Naomi said, turning and gazing at the southern gate. 'Should we go and check the east gate?' Juno said.

'Something is happening,' Chloe said, squinting at the southern gate. 'I can see movement.'

'No,' Juno said, her voice a whisper. 'They have got the boys.'

Chloe cursed and drew her sword. 'It's that thin man we fought in the woods.'

'I am going to get closer to get a better look,' Juno said, snapping out her Jo. 'Take Chloe and keep well away,' Naomi said. 'The rest of you, with me to the caves.'

'What if we need to get them?' Juno said, turning to Naomi. 'We cannot leave them there.'

Naomi gave Juno a sympathetic look. 'It will be a suicide mission, Juno. We will need to get back to the cave and get more girls.'

'But we can't just leave them,' Juno said, pointing her Jo at the southern gate.

Naomi placed a hand on Juno's shoulder. 'Juno, we don't know what is happening. We will get them back, but we cannot do it with our limited numbers.'

Juno sighed, vaulted over the fence and ran alongside Chloe up the path. Chloe pulled Juno down into a crouch. 'If they see you, they will use them against us.'

They left the path and ran through the tilled fields. At the bank they dropped to their bellies and gazed along the bridge.

'They have them,' Juno said. 'Bound and gagged and on their knees.'

'The four infected girls too,' Chloe said.

The thin man, hands behind his back, paced behind the six captives while staring out through the southern gate.

'The knife slinger,' Juno said. 'I should have finished him when I had the chance.'

'Quiet,' Chloe said, tilting her head. 'What is he saying?'

'Call them,' the knife slinger said, removing the gag off Billy. 'I know they are out there.'

Miles and Billy hung their heads and remained quiet.

'Are they watching? What were their plans?' the knife slinger said, continuing to pace.

'We have to do something, Chloe,' Juno said, willing the pins and needles into her marks.

Chloe whispered into her ear. 'If we go in there, he will kill them in front of you. He won't do anything to them now because he knows we will come back for them.'

'I am not leaving them behind,' Juno said.

'They will try to get our plans out of them. They will keep them alive,' Chloe said. 'Let's get back to the caves and discuss this with Naomi.'

Juno growled at the southern gate. 'Hang in there. We won't leave you behind.'

They crawled out of the ditch and, staying low, ran through the fields. The first signs of the sun, peeping over the eastern horizon, sent a warm glow across the Fairacre farmlands. With the southern gate a fair distance away, they stopped crouching and sprinted to the tree line.

They crashed into the forest, where Chloe knelt and put a finger to her lips. 'We wait for the signal.'

Juno flexed her hands at the pins and needles that still prickled through her marks. A sharp tweet from above, and they were moving again through the tall pine trees. The rolling thunder and cooling mists of the waterfall reached their ears and wet their outfits. Juno ran up to the cliff and slid in through the entrance to the caves.

'Love,' Valen said, a look of relief on his face, 'I have just heard from Naomi.' Chloe hugged Valen.

'We need to go back,' Juno said, walking to the logs and facing Naomi.

'Yes, young Juno,' Naomi said, rising and placing a hand on her shoulder. 'We will go back.'

'When? How long can we leave them there with that evil knife slinger?'

'Knife slinger?' Valen said, striding over. 'What did he look like?'

'Thin, close-set eyes and a beaky nose,' Chloe said, slipping her hand into Valen's.

'I have seen him around Fairacre. He ordered the curfew whereby all the men need to be indoors before sundown. Knife slingers specialise in keeping law and order.'

'Can you confirm the Lady is holding the men of the town hostage?' Naomi said. 'Our spies are reporting that this is the case.'

Valen sat on a log and waited for everyone to sit. 'It is indirectly the Lady. The women of the town are holding their own men hostage. They are all infected.'

'Every single woman?' Chloe said, placing her hand over her mouth. 'Yes, love. Some men, after being kicked out of their homes, are sleeping on the streets or in the sewers.'

Naomi began pacing. 'Another worrying report, Valen, is that she has infected men.'

Valen sat deep in thought. 'Dr Viktor is who you need to speak to. From my limited knowledge, she can infect a man only if he allows it.'

'How does that work?' Chloe said.

'Different essence types,' Valen said. 'Men and women. For our essence to mix, both parties need to want it. As an example, if a man falls in love with a woman, they may share essence.'

'Why don't the women infect their men, then?' Juno said with a frown. 'Very few people can knowingly use their essence,' Valen said. 'Most of the time it happens organically. Love, trust and loyalty.'

'So the Lady knows how to do this, but the women of the town don't?' Naomi said.

'Yes,' Valen said.

'If she turns Billy and Miles, she will know where this cave system is,' Chloe said. 'Juno is right. We need to get them back immediately.'

'Easier said than done,' Naomi said. 'We do not have the element of surprise.'

'And the knife slinger is in the mix,' Juno said.

Naomi lifted a hand and waved towards the back of the cave. 'Alexa, can you come here, please?'

Alexa jogged over. 'Yes, miss?'

'Get your team into Fairacre. We need information on the two boys and the infected girls. But do not engage with anyone unless it's the last resort. Even with your devices, they can still capture you.'

Alexa inclined her head, then jogged back to her team. 'Food,' Gem yelled, making the entire group jump.

Jen walked over and dumped bowls next to the enormous pot. She removed the lid and filled the bowls with steaming porridge.

'Sorry, we have nothing more exciting,' Naomi said. 'Oats were the only thing we could save during the escape.'

Finishing his bowl, Valen placed it next to the pot and nodded his thanks. Jen picked up the bowl, spooned more porridge into it and held it out for Valen.

'Large boy. Eat,' Gem said. Chloe snorted.

'Thank you, Gem, Jen,' Naomi said, waving them away.

The twins pulled a face at Naomi, then stalked off to the back of the cavern. 'We need a plan,' Naomi said. 'Alexa will influence our decisions, but we should start putting one together.'

Valen stood, walked over to his knapsack and retrieved the smaller bag. Back at the fireplace, he opened the drawstring. 'Come on, you three. I have a job for you.'

Naomi took a step back and gasped. 'What? How?'

'Meet Sia the snake, Henry the spider and Jay the bee,' Chloe said. 'Remember that ball of metal you gave me? That was Jay.'

'I had a metal bee in my pocket for the whole of the winter?' Naomi said, clenching her jaw.

'Harmless,' Valen said. 'Well, unless I don't want them to be harmless.'

'How are metal objects alive?' Naomi said.

'It is why Valen knows so much about essence. He imbues objects with his own. It's how the devices work.'

Naomi sat down on a log and shook her head. Valen threw the metal ball into the air. Jay uncurled himself, then buzzed out the exit of the cave.

'Why have you sent Jay to them?' Chloe said.

'I am going to get them,' Valen said, rummaging around in the small bag.

'On your own?' Chloe said through clenched teeth. 'I think not.'

'Love, I am a man. Why would they suspect me?'

'He has a point, Chloe,' Naomi said.

Chloe glared at Naomi. 'First, there is a curfew. Second, the knife slinger will have them guarded. Third, we don't know if the antidote works.'

'I agree with Chloe,' Juno said. 'If something goes wrong, we will have lost Valen too.'

Valen stopped rummaging through his bag. 'We cannot leave them there, and we cannot get them in an all-out attack. I am going, and that is final.'

Chloe stood and stalked towards the exit.

'Love?' Valen said, turning to follow.

'Valen,' Juno said, grabbing his arm. 'Let me speak to her.'

Valen stared after Chloe. 'I want to help.'

Juno, walking towards the exit, peered over her shoulder with an exasperated look. She made her way through the winding, dark tunnel. At the exit, she shielded her eyes from the morning sunlight as she scanned the pool and the tree line. A sharp tweet snapped her eyes up to the forest canopy. A girl in a green camouflage outfit pointed east towards the valley in the cliff. With the cliff on her left, Juno walked into the forest. Another tweet from the canopy pointed Juno to the cliff face. She looked up, then smiled at the two long black legs swinging off a rocky outcrop.

'How did you get up there?'

Chloe leaned over the edge and pointed Juno to a tree.

Juno reached up, grabbed a branch and scrambled up the tree trunk until she reached Chloe's level. Juno jumped from the tree onto the ledge. She sat with her feet dangling over the side.

'Worried about Valen?' Chloe grunted.

'I can go with him. And burn the place down if someone hurts him,' Juno said, bumping Chloe with her shoulder.

'Thanks,' Chloe said with a half-smile. 'It's not just that, though, that's bothering me.'

'What do you mean?'

Chloe remained silent for a while. She dragged her hands through her locs. 'I mean, what is going to happen in the future? They do not allow Valen and me to be together.'

Juno gave Chloe a confused look. 'Why can't you be together?'

'I keep forgetting you don't know the full workings of this town. Men cannot take orphans to be their wives. If they do, Fairacre asks them to leave.'

Juno's confused look grew. 'That is so stupid. Is this where my school comes in? The men of Fairacre can only choose a woman from these schools.'

'One school of many, yes,' Chloe said, with a look of disgust. 'Why don't you and Valen just leave?'

'I don't know if you have noticed, but I am black. Daughter of a slave. We are not welcome in many places throughout these lands of ours.'

'Even in the west?' Juno said. 'Where you are originally from?'

'The inverse is true. Valen would not be welcome after they pillaged the west for slaves.'

Juno wrapped her arm around Chloe. 'I don't think you should give up. You and Valen will find a way.'

Chloe smiled. 'Always the optimist.'

'I get it from my friend Tilly. I hope you get to meet her one day,' Juno said. 'You said the last time you saw her was at your school?' Chloe said, playing with one of her locs.

'Yes. The Lady infected them. I haven't gone back since I escaped.'

'I think we should go and look. The Lady is in Fairacre. Maybe she left Tilly at the school?'

'You would do that for me?'

'Of course, young Juno.'

Juno lay back onto the warm rock. 'Will you tell me more about your home one day?'

Chloe lay back and interlaced her fingers behind her head. 'I know nothing about it. I was too young.'

Juno sighed. 'I know nothing either. I don't know who my parents are. Tilly and Miss Petra were everything to me before I met you and the sewer rats.'

Chloe let out a long sigh. 'Your story is the same for so many young girls. Don't forget you have a family now, young Juno.'

Juno reached over and grabbed Chloe's hand. Her eyes grew heavy as the warm sun's rays bathed her face.

CHAPTER 15
DOCTOR HENRY

A tweet made Juno snap her eyes open. A girl gave a flurry of hand signals then pointed to the caves.

'We need to go,' Chloe said. 'Alexa is back.'

Juno slid down the tree and followed Chloe along the cliff face. They walked through the entrance and down the tunnels and joined everyone at the fireplace.

'What's wrong?' Juno said, her forehead crinkling at Naomi's worried look.

'We have some bad news,' Alexa said.

'Our plans need to change,' Naomi said, shaking her head. 'Miles has turned.'

'What do you mean, he has turned?' Chloe said, her mouth hanging open. 'He has let the Lady infect him?'

'Chloe, we don't know the circumstances,' Juno said, taking a step closer to her friend.

'What circumstances?' Chloe said, picking up a bowl and throwing it at the cavern wall. 'He thinks women have no equal place in this world and then he lets her in.'

Valen raised an eyebrow. 'She has a point.'

Naomi raised a hand, calling for calm. 'The why does not matter right now. We need to decide what to do.'

'The cave is at risk,' Chloe said, swinging her foot at the bowl and sending it skidding along the cavern floor. 'We are going to have to move.'

'To where?' Juno said, picking up the bowl and handing it to a scowling Gem.

'There are the old ruins on the cliffs,' Naomi said. 'But we may not have to leave here just yet.'

'Miles will tell them, Naomi,' Chloe said. 'I knew we couldn't trust him.'

Naomi bit her bottom lip, deep in thought.

'What are you thinking, boss?' Chloe said.

Naomi turned to Valen. 'If we needed to block the entrance to the cave, how would we do it?'

'Wouldn't that trap us in here?' Juno said, arching an eyebrow at Naomi.

'There is another way out of this cave system,' Naomi said. 'Let me show you.'

Juno followed Naomi to the back of the cavern, where a narrow tunnel led into darkness. Naomi turned sideways and squeezed herself into the small gap. Juno followed through the tight tunnel until they broke out into a dimly lit cave.

Naomi pointed upwards. 'Water filled these caves a long time ago. The hole above us used to be the entrance to an old well. We can get out of the caves this way.'

'There is no time to get everyone out if the soldiers of Fairacre come for us,' Chloe said, climbing up some fallen rocks.

Naomi thought for a moment. 'I suggest we send the bulk of the girls to the ruins now. We keep who we need here for the rescue.'

'That's if we can close the entrance,' Juno said, turning to Valen.

'We will need rocks, ropes and a net,' Valen said. 'Can we talk about this in the cavern? I feel like this place is going to fall in on us.'

Chloe chuckled, grabbed Valen's hand and pulled him through the thin tunnel. Valen sat at the fireplace, pulled out a handkerchief and wiped the sweat off his brow.

Naomi paced around the cooking pot and muttered under her breath as she worked out plans in her head. 'First, we need to get most of the girls to the ruins. Second, we need to be able to block the cave's entrance at a moment's notice. Third, we need a plan to get the captured girls and the boys back from the Lady.'

'Thanks, Miles,' Chloe said. 'One plan now turns to three.'

'You mentioned ropes, rocks and a net,' Juno said, looking at the now relaxed Valen.

'I don't think getting rocks is a problem,' she said, waving her arm at the surrounding walls. 'But how do we get ropes and a net?'

'We make them,' Naomi said, putting her fingers to her lips and blowing a sharp whistle.

Team leaders streamed out of the joined caves and stood attentively in front of Naomi.

'Everyone here? Good,' Naomi said. 'We need rope, and a lot of it. Break up and go and search the surrounding farmlands. The rest of you, collect as much plant fibre as possible. Alexa, can you stay behind, please?'

The dispersing team leaders barked out orders to their team members. A flurry of activity echoed throughout the cavern.

Naomi turned to Alexa. 'Once we have enough rope, please take charge of getting everyone but the fighting teams to the ruins.'

'Yes, miss,' Alexa said, hurrying off to her team.

'How is this going to work?' Juno said, looking over at Valen.

Valen counted off items on his hand while he worked through his plan. He walked over to his knapsack and pulled out a thick piece of chalk. 'We use nets to hold rocks, which we collapse over the entrance. We also use the nets to capture the infected in Fairacre,' he said, scribbling a diagram on the cavern floor.

Juno stood over the diagram. 'That way we don't need to go all the way into the town square?'

'Aye, lass,' Valen said, stroking his chin. 'Miles and the knife slinger will stop us getting there. We need to get them to the alleyways, where the girls are most comfortable.'

Chloe stood next to Juno. 'How are we going to get the infected girls into the right places?'

'That, love, I will leave to you. I can, with the help of some girls, set the trap. It is up to you to get the infected girls to walk through those traps.'

'We need to set the traps before they know we are in Fairacre. If Miles knows we are there, he will use the infected girls against us,' Naomi said. 'We will need to get into Fairacre tonight and set them.'

'For now we concentrate on securing the cave,' Chloe said.

Juno gazed over at the entrance and watched rows of girls entering the cavern with arms of long dried grass. The weavers, humming a song in unison, sat in a long line and twisted the strands of grass together. They passed the single rope pieces down the line and wove them together, making them into longer, stronger pieces. The young weaver with the long red hair walked along the lines, giving quiet words of encouragement.

'Come and look at this,' Chloe said, grabbing Juno's hand and walking to the end of the weavers' lines.

A group of weavers sat in a circle tying strands of rope together, forming a large net.

The young red-haired weaver approached. 'With the current materials, we can make five nets, miss. This net is the larger one, to hold the rocks. The other four nets will be smaller, to fit in the alleys.'

'How long till they are complete?' Naomi said, walking over and sweeping her hand across the net.

'An hour more for this net. A few hours for the rest.'

'Thank you,' Naomi said, watching the young weaver walk back to the lines. 'We can move into Fairacre just after midnight.'

Juno frowned at the sound of hissing air through teeth. She turned and, raising a hand to her mouth, chuckled as Valen walked past carrying an enormous boulder. With a grunt, he dumped the boulder next to the entrance, sending echoes through the cavern.

'The plans are ready for our relocation, miss,' Alexa said, walking up to Naomi.

'Once we complete these nets, please execute the plan,' Naomi said. 'Juno, Chloe, I suggest you get some food in you and some rest. We will enter Fairacre early in the morning.'

The mention of food made Juno's stomach grumble. She walked over to the pot and spooned some porridge into her bowl, which she took back to the small cave she slept in. Dropping onto the hay, she smiled as Chloe entered the cave with a spoonful of porridge in her mouth. Juno finished her porridge, kicked off her boots and lay on the hay.

'How are we going to get the infected girls into the nets?' Chloe said from her cot.

Juno yawned. 'They want me, don't they?'

Chloe placed her bowl on the floor.

'What are you thinking, young Juno?' Valen said, peering through the entrance of the small cave.

Chloe placed a finger on her lips and pointed at Juno.

With a jerk, Juno sat up sharply and frowned at the empty cot opposite her. She slipped on her boots, laced them up and walked into the cavern. The eerie silence of the now empty cave was suddenly shattered by a booming yell from the cavern entrance.

'What happened?' Juno shouted from the cooking pot.

'Rock fell on his toe,' Chloe said from the cave entrance. 'My big man yelling because of a tiny rock.'

Juno walked to the cave entrance and looked up at the boulders bulging from the tightly woven grass net. Two strands extended down to the floor, where pegs held the net securely. The other two corners were nailed into the cave wall.

'It wasn't tiny,' Valen grumbled, sliding his foot back into his boot.

Chloe stood and folded her arms. 'About your idea in the cave. I assume you were going to use yourself as bait. We have a better idea, young Juno.'

'It was just an idea,' Juno said, holding up her hands. 'What time is it, anyway?'

'Just before midnight,' Chloe said, walking back to the cooking pot. Valen hobbled over and knelt in front of Juno. 'Young Juno. The Lady cannot in any circumstances capture you. If she gains the power you and Chax hold, there will be untold destruction brought on this land. So no more baiting, you hear?'

Juno's nostrils flared. 'I am not going to hide, Valen.'

'We don't expect you to hide, lass,' Valen said, his face softening. 'I have no doubt you will be front and centre in this fight. All I ask is you think clearly before you act.'

Juno held her hands up. 'Okay, okay. What is this other way that you have thought of, then?'

A smirk spread across Valen's face. 'Little Henry is going to bring Billy south of the square. We are hoping the infected girls will follow.'

'Will Billy know to follow Henry?' Juno said.

'I think Billy will be smart enough to get the message,' Valen said, rubbing his chin. 'And Little Henry can be very convincing if he wants to be.'

'It's nearly time,' Naomi said, striding across the cavern. 'Juno, your old clothes are in your cave. Time to get ready.'

Juno jogged over to the sleeping cave and picked up her old beggar's uniform. She kicked off her boots and dragged the shirt and trousers over her flame-retardant outfit. Next to her hay bed was the pot of black oil. She picked it up, unscrewed the cap, dipped her fingers in and rubbed the oil into her hair. Back at the cooking pot, she sat and laced up her boots.

'We have four nets in these drawstring bags,' Naomi said, holding up a bag. 'We need to get them into the small alleys of the manufacturing district. The bags next to the nets are full of dried leaves that we will use to cover the nets.'

'How do these nets get triggered?' Juno said. 'Our girls will pull them taut from the rooftops.'

'Tonight's mission is not about fighting,' Chloe said. 'We sneak in, place the nets and sneak out with as little disruption as possible.'

'It's time to move,' Naomi said, nodding at the team leaders. 'Valen, you get to guard the cavern.'

With a glance at Chloe, Valen dropped his head with a huff. 'I will be fine, love,' Chloe said.

He dropped his hand into the small satchel and waited for Little Henry to jump into his palm. 'Time to hide, Henry,' he said, wagging a finger at the metal spider.

Little Henry jumped into the air, folded his legs and rolled into a ball. Valen rolled the ball into Juno's extended hand. 'Release Henry when you get into the town. He will go and find Billy. When the time is right, Henry will get Billy moving.'

'What about Jay?' Juno said, frowning. 'You released him earlier.'

'Little Jay told them that we are coming, but he won't lead them out. Henry, on the other hand, will.'

Juno placed the ball in her pocket, patted it and said, 'No funny business, Henry.'

'We are weavers delivering goods to the weaving district,' Chloe said to the assembled girls. 'Once we are through the gates, we get to the manufacturing district and we lay the nets. With the men being housebound, nobody should disturb the nets.'

Juno grabbed one of the bags, threw it over her shoulder and followed Chloe out of the cavern. Once out of the small clearing, they crouched under the trees and waited for the signal from the girls in the trees. The soft tweet sounded from the canopy, giving the teams the okay to move through the forest. They broke the tree line and joined the path that led to the southern gate. Juno kept her head down and followed in Chloe's footsteps as they made their way to the southern gate. The dirt turned to wood as they thumped along the bridge.

'What forsaken time do you call this?' a guard said, holding up his hand. 'Materials for the weavers,' Chloe said, shaking a bag at the guard. 'We have come from afar.'

The guard growled. 'There will be nobody awake to receive this.'

Chloe flashed him a wide smile. 'Fairacre is fair. We leave the materials outside for the weavers to retrieve in the morning.'

The guard strode over. 'Open it,' he said, pointing at Chloe's bag.

Chloe pulled the drawstring open and showed the guard the coloured material that hid the net.

The guard grunted. 'You have one hour. Drop your materials and make your way out of Fairacre or I will send someone after you,' he said, waving them through.

'Yes, sir,' Chloe said, saluting.

They walked into the marketplace, then ducked into the first alley. As one, they ducked and weaved past the weaving district and into the manufacturing district. At Valen's shop, Chloe signalled for her team to get onto the roof. Juno untied the drawstring, shook the net out and spread it across the alley. Chloe threw the capture ropes up to the waiting girls, who tied them securely to the roof gutters. Juno spread the leaves from the bag over the net.

'Done,' Chloe said, her voice a whisper.

Juno pulled out the small metal ball, crouched and placed it on the ground. 'Go on, Little Henry.'

Chloe's brow creased. 'Why is he not doing anything?'

Juno moved the ball with her finger. With a snap, Little Henry jumped up and waved his mandibles at her. Juno yelped and fell onto her backside.

Chloe chuckled. 'Jo-wielding fire child scared of a small spider.' Juno pulled a face and stuck out her tongue.

Chloe's team, dropping from the rooftops, joined Juno and Chloe as they jogged through the alleys to the weaving district. Juno slowed at each house and peered through the windows. 'Only women,' she whispered.

Chloe gave her a sharp nod. 'No men whatsoever.'

They entered the southern street and walked through the marketplace. Juno smiled at the guard, and with a wave they moved over the bridge and along the path. A quick glance over her shoulder, and Juno counted the three teams of girls moving on paths between the fields. They entered the forest and followed the sewer rat signals to the cave entrance.

Valen jumped up from the fireplace. 'How did it go, love?' he said, wrap- ping Chloe in a bear hug.

'Eerie,' Chloe said, pulling herself away. 'We only saw soldiers. We didn't see one trader, artisan or entertainer through the house windows.'

Valen sighed. 'They must have moved them to the sewers. Have we set the nets?'

'Yes, and I released Little Henry,' Juno said. 'He gave me a fright, and I think he did it on purpose.'

'He has a playful side,' Valen said with a smirk. 'He can also be quite deadly.' Juno shivered and wrapped her arms around herself.

'We have a few hours before we move back to Fairacre,' Naomi said. 'Get some rest.'

Juno picked up a log and threw it into the smouldering fire. She looked up at Valen and smiled at Chloe resting her head in his lap. Valen's soft gaze of adoration traced her face as he stroked her locs. Juno raised her hand and thought of Tilly in the greenhouse. The pins and needles sent heat over her hands. With a pop, she sent a small burst of fire into the fireplace. She looked up and chuckled at Valen's big mouth, which hung open. Juno laced her hands behind her head and sat staring at the fire.

'It's time,' Naomi said, shaking Chloe awake. 'Let's check each other's equipment.'

Chloe stretched, yawned and stood. 'Come here, young Juno.'

'Do we have the antidote?' Naomi said, as she slid her short blades into their holders on her thighs.

'Each team has four bottles, boss,' Chloe said, while checking Juno's Jo. Naomi waited for everyone to finish. 'We each know our jobs. We stick to the plan. Our one and only mission is to get our captured girls and the boys back. If you have the opportunity, feed them the antidote.'

Valen stood and wagged a finger in Juno's face. 'Any sign of the Lady, and you get yourself out of Fairacre. That is not negotiable.'

Juno crossed her arms and gave him a tight smile.

'Valen, station yourself at the southern gate,' Naomi said. 'You will cause too much attention going into Fairacre.'

Valen nodded and tapped his huge club against his palm. They exited the cavern and went out into the cool, moonless night. With each tweet from the treetops they switched direction until they broke the tree line. Like silent hunters, they ran through the fields until they reached the banks of the path that ran along the moat. Across the bridge, two guards sat facing each other, playing some sort of game. Four crouched girls ran silently across the bridge. A flurry of steel, and the two guards fell soundlessly to the ground.

'Let's move,' Naomi said, dropping her hand.

Juno followed Chloe across the bridge, their padded boots leaving no sound. Each team passed through the market stalls and disappeared into an alley.

'We make our way north until we get to the square,' Chloe whispered in Juno's ear.

Halfway up the southern alleys, Juno held up a hand. 'Fighting in the alleys of the southern street.'

Chloe snapped her fingers. Two team members scaled up the walls onto the rooftops. 'We continue. They will report back.'

Juno and Chloe continued through the alleys until they reached the bottom of the town square.

'It hasn't worked,' Chloe said, running her eyes across the square.

A dark figure slid beside Chloe. 'Miles and our teams are fighting on the other side of the street, miss. It is not going well.'

'We need to move, Juno,' Chloe said, climbing up onto the roof. 'I am not leaving Billy,' Juno said.

'Juno, you cannot stay here. You heard what Valen said.'

Juno kicked fresh air. 'Okay, I am coming.'

She scaled the wall and ran after Chloe. Mid alley jump, a flash of silver passed across her eyes. Her hand snapped out her Jo as she rolled onto the roof.

The flash of buzzing silver stopped right between her eyes. 'Little Jay,' Juno said.

Jay buzzed around her head, then flew north towards the town square. Clashes of steel rang through the air from the south.

'I have to help them,' Juno said.

Jay flew back, buzzed angrily in front of Juno's face, then flew north. 'What is it?' Juno said, throwing her arms up.

Jay buzzed in circles, then flew further north.

'This is not going to go down well with Chloe,' Juno said, sprinting after Jay.

Alley after alley flew past until Juno slid to a stop at the town square. Little Jay buzzed down into the square and waited for Juno to follow.

'You'd better know what you are doing,' Juno said. She slid down a drain and crept quietly after Jay. The little bee made his way to a house on the eastern side of the square. Juno crept up to a window and searched the dark room for movement. Little Jay buzzed around her head and flew to the windowsill on the other side of the door. Slowly moving across the path to the door, Juno reached the other window and looked into the candlelit room.

Slumped in a chair, gagged, bound and bruised, Billy sat unmoving. Two guards sat at a table. One slept with his head on his hands, while the other read a small book.

Juno caught a flash of metal scuttling across the floor. 'Little Henry.'

Little Jay buzzed towards the front door. Juno turned the handle until the door swung open. Light shone through the gap of the door on the right. Her ear pressed against the door, Juno held her breath so she could hear more easily. A second later, a man yelled. Juno turned the handle and kicked the door open. On the floor, a guard holding his ankle writhed around in pain. Little Henry clacked his mandibles at the second guard, who had his back pressed up against the wall.

'Get that thing away from me,' the guard said, his eyes wide with fear. Juno snapped her Jo forwards and caught the guard under the chin. His eyes closing, he slid down the wall and crumpled into a heap on the floor.

'Come on, Billy, let's get you out of here,' Juno said, untying the ropes around his wrists and ankles.

Billy grunted. 'You are here on your own?'

'Yes, and it's not going to go down well. Can you walk?'

Billy nodded, stood and stumbled. He took a breath and shook each leg to get the blood flowing. 'Can you get my stuff?'

'You look terrible,' Juno said, walking to the corner of the room to get Billy's staff and cloak.

'Superficial,' Billy said with a grin. 'They slapped me about, that's all.'

'You two,' Juno said, pointing at Henry and Jay. 'Home.'

With a scuttle and a buzz, the two metal creatures disappeared into the night.

'We need to move. Chloe and Naomi are fighting at the south entrance,' Juno said.

Billy followed Juno out of the house and across the town square. They jogged down the southern street, the market stalls appearing in the distance.

Juno gasped on seeing a group of girls dragging a large body across the bridge. 'Is that Valen?' she said.

'It looks like it,' Billy said.

Juno ran down the rest of the street, through the market stalls and onto the bridge.

'He isn't going to make it,' Chloe said, fear etched across her face.

Short, sharp, laboured breaths escaped Valen's mouth. Long open wounds crisscrossed his chest and arms.

'Move,' Billy said, moving a girl out of the way. He ran his hands over Valen, then peered up at Juno with a grave look.

'Do something, Billy,' Chloe said, pulling on her locs. 'Get him to the caves,' Billy said. 'As fast as you can.'

Juno grabbed Chloe and shook her. 'Where is Miles? Chloe. Look at me. Where is Miles?'

Tears streaking down her cheeks, Chloe shook her head. 'He is fighting Naomi's team. She led them into the alleys.'

Juno spun and scanned the south entrance.

'You are coming with us,' Billy said, grabbing Juno's collar. 'Naomi and her team can take care of themselves. Your friend needs you.'

Juno, looking at Chloe's grief-stricken face, clicked her Jo back into its holder and grabbed Chloe's hand. 'Come on. Let's get to the caves so Billy can work his magic.'

'We need more people to carry him,' Billy said. 'Chloe, send someone back to the forest to get the girls.'

Chloe signalled to one of her team members, who sprinted off into the night.

'It's not looking good,' Billy said. 'He has lost a lot of blood. We need to get those wounds closed.'

'Do what you can, Billy,' Juno said, laying a hand on his forearm.

Minutes later, girls appeared out of the darkness. They lifted Valen and ran down the path and into the forest. Throwing caution to the wind they made straight for the cave, where they pulled Valen through the tunnels and laid him next to the fireplace. Billy returned from a small cave with his medicine bag. He pulled out a jar of salve and dipped a thick, white clean cloth into it. Frantically ripping Valen's shirt open, he cleaned the deep wounds across his chest. He pulled out a needle and cotton from his bag. He dipped the needle into the salve, then, his eyes squinting, he held up the needle and deftly guided the white cotton through the hole. The buzz of wings and the clatter of metal feet echoed through the cavern. Little Henry scampered across the rock floor and jumped onto Valen's chest.

'Now is not the time,' Billy said, waving his hand at Henry.

His mandibles clacking together, Little Henry moved to the largest gash in Valen's chest. Metal legs rubbing together, he started producing thin, white glistening thread. Little Henry dug his jaws into a wound and began sewing it closed.

'Unbelievable,' Billy said.

The girls stared wide-eyed as Little Henry continued sewing further wounds closed.

Billy stood and placed a hand on Chloe's shoulder. 'He is susceptible to infection, which I cannot cure here. We have to get him to Dr Viktor's.'

Chloe gave Billy a quick nod.

'We need help here,' Naomi said, appearing at the cave entrance.

Juno ran over to the entrance, grabbed the hand of a wild-eyed girl and led her to the fireplace.

'What is happening, miss?' the girl said. 'One minute we were escaping the sewers and now we are in a cave.'

'Yes,' Juno said, grabbing a cup and filling it with water from a bottle. 'You are safe. Take this and drink. We will explain everything later.'

'My Valen,' Chloe said, her voice a choked whisper. 'My big, strong Valen. He isn't going to make it.'

Billy cupped Chloe's face. 'He will make it, Chloe. But we need to leave for Dr Viktor's right now.'

Naomi's voice thundered through the cave. 'Let's move.'

CHAPTER 16
MATILDA

Six girls, three on either side, carried Valen in a net through the morning sun's rays that bathed the southern forest. Naomi walked at the head of the train, following the tweets from high in the canopy.

'Was it Miles who did this?' Billy said, walking alongside Chloe.

Chloe shook her head and curled her lip in a snarl. 'It wasn't Miles. It was that knife slinger. He came out of an alley with two long thin daggers.'

'Stilettos,' Billy said under his breath. 'Deadly in the right hands.'

Juno jogged past Valen and stood next to Naomi. 'How are the girls that we rescued?'

'Confused,' she said. 'The antidote has worked, but they cannot remember anything throughout the time the Lady had them infected.'

Juno frowned. 'Joanne looked normal when we had her down in the sewers,' she said, rubbing her jaw.

'I don't understand it either,' Naomi said with a shake of her head. 'I haven't been able to speak to Joanne yet. She is on the trail behind us if you would like to talk to her.'

Juno stepped off the trail and waited for the girls carrying Valen to pass. The four rescued girls, their eyes darting nervously, huddled together as they walked up the path.

Juno stepped back onto the trail and walked next to Joanne. 'How are you feeling?'

Joanne stopped chewing her nails and glanced at Juno with worried eyes. 'I don't understand, miss. An entire part of my life is just black.'

'Can you remember being held in a room in the sewers?'

Joanne closed her eyes and shook her head. 'My memories are blank, miss. Can you tell me what happened?'

Juno placed her hand on Joanne's shoulder and gave her a reassuring rub. 'The Lady infected you, and we came back to get you. You are back home with us now.'

Joanne began biting her nails again. 'Did I hurt anyone?'

'No, you didn't. Telling the Lady our secrets was our biggest worry, so we made plans accordingly.'

Joanne hung her head and said, 'I am sorry.'

'It is not your fault,' Juno said. 'You were not yourself.'

'Valen would not be in trouble if we hadn't become infected,' Joanne said, peering ahead of her.

'We went to rescue all of you, including Miles, who she has also infected. We would have gone in for you regardless.'

Joanne pursed her lips and rubbed her hands together. 'Please tell Miss Chloe that I am sorry.'

'I will tell her. For now, though, take the time to recover. We are going to need all of our girls.'

Joanne breathed deeply, pushed her shoulders back and gave Juno a nod. Juno jogged back up to the front of the train. Her forehead creased with concern at the sweat dripping off the six girls who carried Valen. Naomi, sensing Juno's concern, lifted her hand

and brought the train to a halt. The six girls lowered Valen onto the path.

Billy knelt and ran a hand across Valen's forehead. 'He is stable for now,' he said, looking up at Chloe. 'I am worried about infection, which will bring on the fever.'

Chloe kissed Valen's forehead. 'We are here, love,' she whispered in his ear. 'We are all here looking after you.'

The group rounded a bend and came to a stop at the fork in the path.

'We need to rest,' Naomi said, stopping everyone. 'Get Valen off the path and into that clearing.'

Juno and Chloe walked up to Naomi, knelt and pulled food from the communal backpack.

Naomi knelt next to them. 'We are going to separate. Alexa's team will stay with you to share the carrying. I am taking the cured girls up to the ruins.'

With a mouth full of biscuit, Chloe said, 'What are the plans, boss?'

'Get as much information from this Dr Viktor as you can. He must know a way to help the men of Fairacre.'

'The men?' Chloe said with a look of surprise.

'We are helping Valen, Chloe,' Naomi said, spreading her hands. 'I can only imagine the pain the men of Fairacre are feeling after losing their loved ones. Plus they may be unlikely future allies.'

Chloe's face softened as she glanced through the bushes at Valen.

'I don't know how Dr Viktor is going to react when he hears about Miles,' Juno said.

'Not very well,' Billy said, walking out of the undergrowth. 'I will make sure we get as much information as we can, Naomi.'

Naomi nodded at Billy, then signalled for her team of girls to move. 'We will see you soon.'

Juno and Chloe hugged Naomi, then watched her disappear down the path. 'How is Valen?' Juno said, turning to Billy.

'His wounds are making his breathing laboured, and I have seen people like this decline rapidly. We should get moving.'

Chloe twirled her finger in the air, signalling for everyone to move.

Juno turned and waited for the carrying team to lift Valen. 'Is everyone ready?'

Chloe, resting her hand on Valen's shoulder, nodded.

Moving along the path, Juno scanned the trees, looking for movement. Alexa's team, high in the canopy, tweeted the all-clear.

'We should get there just after sundown,' Billy said, calculating the distance left.

'Can we send someone ahead?' Chloe said.

'It will have to be one of us,' Billy said. 'Dr Viktor won't answer the door to any of the girls.'

'I will go. Give me the signal when the time is right,' Juno said.

A sharp tweet sounded from the canopy. They all crouched and scanned the area.

Chloe grabbed Billy's hand and pulled him to a crouch. 'I forgot you don't understand the signals.'

With a lopsided grin, Billy mouthed a silent 'sorry'.

Crouch-walking up to Juno, Chloe said, 'What is it?'

'I don't know. One of your team members thinks she saw something.' Looking up into the canopy, Chloe gave a flurry of signals. After receiving a response, she brought her mouth close to Juno's ear. 'The forest has gone silent.' Chloe turned on her haunches and gave the signal to secure Valen.

The girls pulled Valen off the path, grunting with the effort.

Billy joined the girls. 'What seems to be the problem?'

Chloe placed a finger on her lips and shook her head.

They listened with tilted heads as they scanned the tree line. Looking up, Juno watched the girls signalling to each other.

'Can you smell that?' Juno said into Chloe's ear. 'The same smell when we were waiting for guards to pass on the path outside Fairacre.'

With what looked almost like an explosion of leaves, Miles jumped out of a hole and sprang onto the path. Shouts of soldiers broke the silence of the forest. Juno snapped out her Jo, faced the nearest soldier and snarled.

'I wouldn't do that if I were you,' Miles said, his black and white unblinking eyes staring at her. 'We have you surrounded.'

The knife slinger, his hands behind his back, sauntered onto the path and inclined his head in greeting. With a smile he said, 'We will harm none of your friends, fire child, if you come with us.'

'She isn't going anywhere,' Chloe said, her lip curling.

The knife slinger took a step forwards and said, 'How dare a western black slave speak to me without permission?'

Her face contorting in disgust, Juno fought back the rising heat in her hands. 'She is no slave.'

'Let me see those hands, fire child,' Miles said, pointing his finger at Juno. 'We know what you can do.'

The knife slinger peered into the bush and smirked. 'I see that bumbling mountain of a man is still alive. Too stupid to die quietly.'

'You leave my Valen alone,' Chloe said, her face contorted with rage.

The knife slinger snorted. 'A southern man consorting with an eastern black slave woman. This union is an abomination.'

Chloe drew her short sword, took a step forward, then stopped as three soldiers drew their swords and aimed them at her throat.

'You can save them all, fire child,' Miles said, his unblinking gaze still set firmly on Juno. 'Come with me.'

'I said she is not going anywhere,' Chloe said, lifting her chin as the sword points pressed into her throat.

The knife slinger drew a stiletto from behind his back, walked up to Valen and pointed the long, thin blade at his throat. 'He was lucky the last time we met. He will not be lucky this time around.'

'Okay,' Juno said, replacing her Jo and holding her hands up. 'I will go with you if you leave everyone alone.'

'Juno, you can't,' Chloe said, glancing at her friend. 'You heard what Valen said.'

Juno scanned the area and counted the soldiers. 'There are too many of them, Chloe,' she whispered.

'Smart fire child,' the knife slinger said.

Miles walked up to Juno and shoved her forwards towards the tree line. Juno, crashing through the undergrowth, walked with her hands up, the pins and needles burning in her palms.

A yell from behind made Juno spin round to see Chloe, Billy and the girls on their knees lined up in a row.

'What is he doing with them, Miles?' Juno said, facing him.

'What he does is none of my concern. The Lady wishes to see you.'

'You said you wouldn't hurt them.'

'I said I wouldn't hurt them,' he said, waving a dismissive hand. 'I am not going with you if he hurts them.'

His face contorting into a snarl, Miles slapped Juno in the face.

A guttural growl thundered through the forest. Spreading his feet, the knife slinger reached back and drew his second stiletto. Red-flecked amber eyes parted the bushes behind the knife slinger. Sharp ivory-white teeth clamped on the knife slinger's shoulder. With a scream, the knife slinger disappeared into the bush. Chloe let loose a piercing whistle. From the canopy, sewer rats fell onto the soldiers, their swords whistling through the air. Miles's greatsword sang from its sheath and swung in a wide arc. Juno ducked under the lightning-fast blade, the ends of the hair on the top of her head slicing off and falling to the floor. Stumbling backwards, Juno unsnapped her Jo and parried the shining thick greatsword. Her hand pushing on the ground, she hopped to her feet and twirled her weapon while looking for an opening. She jabbed forwards, missed, and felt the hilt of Miles's sword smash into the side of her head.

On all fours, she looked up at the smiling black-and-white-eyed Miles.

Miles, raising his sword over his head, said, 'The Lady does not need you. All she needs is that creature of yours. Tell me, will she come if I remove your head?'

Juno rolled onto her back and drew on her deep love for Tilly, Chloe and Valen. As the greatsword swung down, Juno willed the heat into her marks. Sucking air in through her teeth, she released a white-hot stream of fire at Miles's hands. Miles screamed, then jumped back, his greatsword jabbing into the dirt inches from Juno's throat. He took a step back, shook his hands, grabbed his sword, and ran for Fairacre. Juno rolled onto all fours and willed her breathing to slow down. With the pain in her hands subsiding, she stumbled to her feet. Soldiers with blood dripping from stabs and gashes ran out of the tree line and back to Fairacre.

'Juno,' Chloe said, running up to her.

'I am okay,' Juno said, her voice hoarse.

Chloe ran her hands over Juno and said, 'Are you sure?'

'Yes. We need to move. How are the others?'

'One stab wound and some minor scratches. Billy is tending to them.' Juno, walking back through the trees, inclined her head at the wide-eyed girls.

'How are we looking?' Chloe said to Billy.

'We need to move now before Miles brings back more soldiers.'

Chloe whistled and spun her finger in the air, calling for everyone to move out.

The train walked in silence, their ears and eyes trained for movement. They slowly reduced the distance to Dr Viktor's house. The last of the sun dipping over the horizon sent the forest into darkness.

'Let me lead,' Billy said, breaking the eerie silence. 'We are not far away now.'

The girls, swapping more frequently, blew long breaths as they struggled down the thin path.

Billy turned the last bend, rushed up to the door and used his staff to bang a flurry of knocks on the door. 'Dr Viktor, open up.'

'Yes, yes,' Dr Viktor mumbled, his staff thumping on the floor.

Dr Viktor swung the door open and stood with his mouth hanging open.

'Come on, then,' Chloe said from the rear of the group. 'What's the holdup?'

'How dare you bring these people to our haven?' he said, waving his staff in Billy's face.

Billy moved Dr Viktor to one side and waved the girls in.

'Get Valen upstairs into the room on the left,' Billy said, pointing up the stairs. 'It is the only room that has a bed that can hold his weight.'

The girls, grunting and groaning, doubled up to carry Valen up the staircase.

'Juno, come with me,' Billy said, walking under the stairs and into his room. 'We need to make the salve to stop the infection.'

Juno, following Billy's instructions, placed the ingredients into the glass beaker. 'How long will this take to make?'

'It's quick,' Billy said. 'We need to heat the ingredients so they infuse. Here is the last one.'

Juno placed the last ingredient into the beaker, lit the wick and closed the glass bulb. 'I am going to go and check on Chloe.'

Billy, still mixing the contents of the beaker, waved his hand for her to go. Juno left the room, bounded up the stairs, knocked on the door and entered.

She walked over to Chloe and placed a hand on her shoulder. 'He looks peaceful.'

'Billy is still worried. I get scared when Billy worries,' Chloe said, biting her fingernails.

'He knows that surviving an infection is difficult. Once he has his salve, Valen should be okay.'

Chloe picked up Valen's hand and laid a gentle kiss on his massive knuckles.

'Where are the girls?' Juno said.

'In the kitchen with Dr Viktor.'

Juno's forehead crinkled over. 'This should be interesting.'

Chloe flashed Juno a mischievous grin, then shrugged her shoulders.

Billy thumped the bedroom door open and strode in carrying a pot of light brown salve, which he placed on the bedside table. He used his thumb to signal to Chloe to get out of the way. He knelt next to Valen, stripped the bandages away and spread the salve over the wounds using a small, fine brush. Brow furrowed, hands steady, he worked methodically, not missing a cut or scrape.

Billy slid the brush back into the pot and sat down. 'I think we got him in time.'

Chloe wrapped her arms around Billy and whispered into his ear, 'Thank you, Billy. Thank you very much.'

Billy, his ears burning, unwrapped Chloe's arms and flashed her a lopsided grin. 'Time for me to go and deal with downstairs.'

'Who is going to tell him about Miles?' Juno said.

'I think Billy needs to tell him,' Chloe said. 'If it comes from one of us, it might not go down very well.'

'It won't go down well either way,' Billy said, rising and walking out of the room.

Juno followed Billy down the stairs and into the kitchen. The girls stood in a row against the kitchen wall, shoulder to shoulder, their face masks fastened and their eyes looking straight ahead.

Dr Viktor, staring at the girls, thumped his cane on the floor and said, 'Where is Miles?'

Billy sat down next to him, cleared his throat and met his eyes. 'The Lady has turned him.'

His face scrunching up in anger, Dr Viktor coughed violently into his handkerchief. Billy placed his hand on Dr Viktor's shoulder and waited for the coughing to subside.

'Impossible,' Dr Viktor said. 'That woman could not turn my boy.'

Chloe snorted. 'Well, he has. And he has tried to kill each of us. Including Juno.'

'Did Miles do this to Valen?'

'No. A thin man with stilettos and knives tried to kill him. Valen called him a knife slinger.'

Dr Viktor's eyes widened then narrowed. Grinding his teeth, he mumbled under his breath. 'No, no, no.'

'What is it?' Billy said, a look of concern etched on his face.

Dr Viktor ran his eyes along the people sitting around him. 'Knife slingers are operatives who specialise in law and order. If they are in the picture, this mess is coming from the City of Lynn.'

'From the Queen herself?' Billy said.

'I refuse to believe the Queen has descended into this dark world.'

'Yet she has sent a knife slinger to Fairacre,' Juno said.

Dr Viktor stroked his stubbled chin. 'Only the Queen gives orders to the knife slingers.'

'How many of them are there?' Juno said.

'I do not know, so I cannot tell you. But be sure there will be more. Where is this knife slinger now?'

'Chax ate him,' Juno said with a shrug of her shoulders.

They listened with tilted heads as they scanned the tree line. Looking up, Juno watched the girls signalling to each other.

'Can you smell that?' Juno said into Chloe's ear. 'The same smell when we were waiting for guards to pass on the path outside Fairacre.'

With what looked almost like an explosion of leaves, Miles jumped out of a hole and sprang onto the path. Shouts of soldiers broke the silence of the forest. Juno snapped out her Jo, faced the nearest soldier and snarled.

'I wouldn't do that if I were you,' Miles said, his black and white unblinking eyes staring at her. 'We have you surrounded.'

The knife slinger, his hands behind his back, sauntered onto the path and inclined his head in greeting. With a smile he said, 'We will harm none of your friends, fire child, if you come with us.'

'She isn't going anywhere,' Chloe said, her lip curling.

The knife slinger took a step forwards and said, 'How dare a western black slave speak to me without permission?'

Her face contorting in disgust, Juno fought back the rising heat in her hands. 'She is no slave.'

'Let me see those hands, fire child,' Miles said, pointing his finger at Juno. 'We know what you can do.'

The knife slinger peered into the bush and smirked. 'I see that bumbling mountain of a man is still alive. Too stupid to die quietly.'

'You leave my Valen alone,' Chloe said, her face contorted with rage.

The knife slinger snorted. 'A southern man consorting with an eastern black slave woman. This union is an abomination.'

Chloe drew her short sword, took a step forward, then stopped as three soldiers drew their swords and aimed them at her throat.

'You can save them all, fire child,' Miles said, his unblinking gaze still set firmly on Juno. 'Come with me.'

'I said she is not going anywhere,' Chloe said, lifting her chin as the sword points pressed into her throat.

The knife slinger drew a stiletto from behind his back, walked up to Valen and pointed the long, thin blade at his throat. 'He was lucky the last time we met. He will not be lucky this time around.'

'Okay,' Juno said, replacing her Jo and holding her hands up. 'I will go with you if you leave everyone alone.'

'Juno, you can't,' Chloe said, glancing at her friend. 'You heard what Valen said.'

Juno scanned the area and counted the soldiers. 'There are too many of them, Chloe,' she whispered.

'Smart fire child,' the knife slinger said.

Miles walked up to Juno and shoved her forwards towards the tree line. Juno, crashing through the undergrowth, walked with her hands up, the pins and needles burning in her palms.

A yell from behind made Juno spin round to see Chloe, Billy and the girls on their knees lined up in a row.

'What is he doing with them, Miles?' Juno said, facing him.

'What he does is none of my concern. The Lady wishes to see you.'

'You said you wouldn't hurt them.'

'I said I wouldn't hurt them,' he said, waving a dismissive hand. 'I am not going with you if he hurts them.'

His face contorting into a snarl, Miles slapped Juno in the face.

A guttural growl thundered through the forest. Spreading his feet, the knife slinger reached back and drew his second stiletto. Red-flecked amber eyes parted the bushes behind the knife slinger. Sharp ivory-white teeth clamped on the knife slinger's shoulder. With a scream, the knife slinger disappeared into the bush. Chloe let loose a piercing whistle. From the canopy, sewer rats fell onto the soldiers, their swords whistling through the air. Miles's greatsword sang from its sheath and swung in a wide arc. Juno ducked under the lightning-fast blade, the ends of the hair on the

Dr Viktor chuckled. 'Word of advice. If you encounter another one, run.'

'Unless you are Chax,' Chloe said.

Dr Viktor grunted. 'She may not be around when you need her. Do not take on a knife slinger under any circumstances.'

'Noted,' Chloe said with a curt nod.

Dr Viktor wiped his mouth, closed his handkerchief and placed it into his pocket. He looked at Billy. 'Did she try to turn you?'

Colour rising up his neck, Billy ran his hand through his hair. 'She tried, yes. I kept my mind on Matilda.'

'The girl from the cliffs?' Dr Viktor said.

Her breath catching in her throat, Juno spluttered, then fell into a fit of coughs.

Chloe slapped Juno on the back and said, 'Our powerful fire child choking on nothing. Are you okay, Juno?'

The coughing fit subsiding, Juno stared at Billy. 'Matilda?'

'Yes, Matilda,' Billy said, cocking his head to one side. 'She worked in the greenhouse. I was planning to choose her as my partner.'

'Tilly?' Juno said, standing up, her mouth hanging open.

'Her name is Matilda, not Tilly,' Billy said with a perplexed shake of the head.

'"Tilly" is short for Matilda.'

His mouth opening and closing, Billy stared at Juno.

'Did Tilly have a choice in choosing her partner?' Chloe said, curling a lip.

Billy gave Chloe a perplexed look, then dragged his hand through his hair.

'Enough,' Dr Viktor said, thumping his cane again. 'Miles being infected is a problem. He knows where this house is.'

'Worrying about your house more than your son,' Chloe said. 'Why am I not surprised?'

Dr Viktor turned on Chloe and snarled, 'This house has been a haven for young orphan boys before you were a light in your mother's eyes. A haven that your Valen grew up in. Don't test me.'

'What is the point of this haven if you are willing to sacrifice your own sons to this evil? We would go back for the very last girl,' Chloe said, her eyes narrowing.

'I do not have the luxury of having a small army, Chloe.'

Chloe spread her hands. 'All you have to do is ask.'

Dr Viktor grunted. 'Why would you help us?'

'I would help you because you have helped Valen,' Chloe said. 'And Billy I class as a friend.'

Dr Viktor closed his eyes and sat deep in thought. He sighed, opened his eyes and looked at Chloe. 'I am asking you now. Can you help save my son?'

'We have tried,' Chloe said. 'And we will try again.'

Dr Viktor's face softened before he gave a small nod.

'How long is Valen going to have to stay here?' Juno said.

Dr Viktor looked at Juno and said, 'If you wish to save Valen, you need to leave this place immediately. Miles is after you. If you are not here, he will not come here.'

'I am not leaving Valen,' Chloe said.

Billy walked around the kitchen counter and laid a hand on Chloe's shoulder. 'I will stay here with Valen. I need to make more antidote now that we know she has infected all women in the town.'

Chloe placed her head in her hands and breathed in deeply. She looked up at Billy and said, 'What if Miles comes here? How are you going to protect him?'

'I have a plan for that,' Dr Viktor said. 'There are places in this house my boys do not know about. I will show Billy where we can move Valen.'

'I need to think about this,' Chloe said.

Dr Viktor banged his cane on the floor. 'There is no time. You need to leave and show Miles that you are not here anymore.'

'How do we do that?' Juno said.

Dr Viktor shrugged and said, 'That I cannot help with.'

Chloe stood and paced along the side of the counter. 'On our way to the ruins, we need to find one of the Fairacre search parties. Let them chase us to the caves.'

'An excellent idea,' Dr Viktor said, nodding. 'Billy, pack a travel bag of food for the girls. The quicker the better.'

Billy walked to the back of the kitchen, opened the pantry door and grabbed dry foodstuffs off the shelves.

Juno grabbed a drawstring bag and joined Billy at the pantry. 'I didn't know about Tilly. She didn't tell me.'

Sadness spreading across his face, Billy cleared his throat. 'They must have forbidden her to say anything. I am sorry it was a shock to you.'

'Do you know where she is?' Juno said, placing some food into the bag. Billy stopped packing the food bag and faced Juno. 'I don't know. I don't even know if she is alive,' he said, wiping a tear off his cheek.

A frown creasing her brow, Juno said, 'Why haven't you gone to look for her?'

'The same reason you haven't. I think you know. If she is alive, she is with the Lady somewhere.'

Juno gave Billy a tight hug. 'I will go back to the school and look for her. Just in case. Make more antidote, as she will need it when we find her.'

Billy wiped his nose. 'I am sorry I haven't gone to look for her. I live with it every day.'

'We will find her. I promise,' Juno said, wiping a tear off his face. Billy smiled and continued passing food to Juno.

'Are you done?' Dr Viktor said. 'We need to move Valen to the bottom floor.'

Juno pulled the drawstring closed, walked to the entrance hall and watched the girls bring Valen down. They carried him under the stairs, through the corridor and into Dr Viktor's rooms.

Billy walked over to Chloe and gave her a quick hug. 'Take this,' he said, passing her a small metal ball. 'If you need my help, send Little Jay back.'

'How will you find the ruins?' Chloe said.

'I know where they are. I have explored most of the cliffs,' he said, smiling.

'Go now,' Dr Viktor said. 'Make sure you get the message to Miles that you are not here anymore.'

Chloe walked into the entrance hall. 'Let's move.'

Juno followed Chloe and the girls into the forest. They ran hard down the southern path.

'We are approaching the fork in the path,' Chloe said, over her shoulder. 'We need to find a Fairacre search team.'

The girls dispersed and flew up the trees into the canopy.

Juno crouched and said, 'So what is the plan?'

'We engage, then run for it. They will have a hard time keeping up. They have heavy armour.'

A few moments later, a soft tweet rang from above. They followed the tweets along the path into the southern forest. One by one the girls dropped from the trees to fall in line along the path. The last sewer rat, high in the canopy, blasted a shrill tweet.

'They are up ahead, sitting around a fireplace,' Chloe said. 'We need to get them to see you somehow.'

'How are we getting up to the cliffs?'

'We go up the valley,' Chloe said. 'No need to go through the cave.'

'Let's move around them so we can escape,' Juno said.

Chloe, signalling to the girls, moved in a wide arc around the soldiers and back onto the eastern path.

'How are we going to do this?' Chloe said.

Juno winked at Chloe then crouch-walked through the undergrowth. She moved a thick bush apart and counted four soldiers sitting around the fireplace. Juno closed her eyes and summoned up images of Tilly working in the greenhouse, followed by Billy's tears of love.

Juno stepped through the bushes and said, 'Good evening, gentlemen.'

Four heads turned and stared in confusion. The leader, snapping out of his surprise, jumped up and barked orders. Pain coursing through her hands, Juno pointed her palms at the fireplace. With a blinding flash, she sent a small ball of fire at the fireplace, causing it to explode. Bits of burning wood and coal blasted up into the soldiers.

Juno sprinted along the path and flashed Chloe a smile with a thumbs-up as she bolted past them.

'Okay then,' Chloe said, springing like a rabbit into a full sprint. 'I think that worked.'

Her legs pumping hard, Juno let out a whoop as she jumped over a fallen tree. With the wind rushing through her hair, she smiled at the whoops and cheers of the following girls as they ran up the valley.

Juno stopped at the top of the valley and leaned against a rock.

After a few minutes, Chloe turned to Juno and said, 'We have lost them. Let's take it easy from here.'

The girls settled into a brisk walk and followed the path leading along the cliff face. In the distance, the rushing water of the river feeding the great waterfall filled their ears.

Juno broke out of the trees, walked up to the cliff and gazed over the fields at Fairacre.

'We will get our town back,' Chloe said, standing next to her.

'I wonder if Tilly is there,' Juno said. 'She may have been there all along.'

Chloe threw her arm over Juno's shoulder and said, 'If she is there, we will find her.'

'We need to find her as much for Billy as for me. She was so happy the last days I was with her.'

'Then she is lucky. Not all women are fortunate with who chooses them.'

With the stunning view on their left, the girls followed the cliff until they reached the river. They turned north and followed the river until they reached the stepping stones. When the last girl had crossed the river, they moved west past the overhanging willow trees and through the thick undergrowth. Bird-calling every few minutes, Chloe listened for a response. A shrill tweet shattered the quiet early morning. Juno looked up and smiled at a girl hanging from a tree branch. They continued west until they broke out of the trees into a large clearing filled with old ruins. In the centre sat the cooking pot, surrounded by seating logs.

Naomi, striding over, spread her arms and gave everybody a hug. 'Welcome back, my sisters.'

CHAPTER 17
THE RUINS

Juno sat on her hay bed and pulled pieces of hay out of her hair. Courtesy of the weavers, awnings and tents made out of fabric lined the ruins. The warm glow of dusk spread across the ruins and into her small tent. Juno pulled her shoes on, stepped out from under the grass cover and reached her arms up in a stretch. Her mouth watering, she walked over to the cooking pot and searched for a bowl.

'Juno,' Chloe said, striding over. 'The bowls are coming. Gem and Jen are cleaning them.'

'I am absolutely starving,' Juno said, sitting down on a log. 'Have I been asleep the whole afternoon?'

'We all have,' Chloe said, sitting next to Juno.

'My legs hurt. We moved a lot last night and this morning.'

Chloe splayed her legs out in front of her. 'We need to speak to Naomi about getting Miles back.'

'Do you think she will help?'

'I think we will have to do a lot of convincing. For the first time in a while, the sewer rats are safe.'

'But the women of Fairacre are not,' Juno said, rubbing more sleep out of her eyes.

'I know. We need to use that as a second reason to go to Fairacre.'

'Bowls,' Gem said, making Juno jump.

'Hello, hedgehog,' Jen said, scrunching up her nose.

Gem held the lid of the pot while Jen spooned stew into a bowl. Jen opened a basket next to the pot, pulled out bread rolls and passed them to Juno.

Juno sat on a log, closed her eyes and breathed in the spices of the stew.

'This is so good,' Chloe said, spooning in a mouthful.

'First hot meal in days,' Juno said, dunking her roll in the stew.

'You two are amazing,' Chloe said appreciatively. 'The spices make me warm.'

'And the meat is so succulent,' Juno said, chewing heartily. 'What is it?'

'Rat,' Jen said.

'Sniff sniff, ratty rat,' Gem said.

Juno opened her mouth and let the piece of meat drop back into the bowl.

'Nothing wrong with rat, Juno,' Chloe said. 'You ate it all the time in the sewers.'

Her face turning green, Juno used her fingers to wipe the top of her tongue.

'Silly hedgehog,' Jen said with a snort. 'Go hungry, then.'

'Good evening,' Naomi said, stepping over a log and sitting down. 'Did you sleep well?'

Juno gave Naomi a weak smile. 'It has been a while since I slept that well.'

Naomi accepted a bowl of stew from Jen with an incline of her head. 'How is Valen?'

'He will survive. He will stay at Dr Viktor's with Billy,' Chloe said.

'That is really good to hear,' Naomi said, smiling at Chloe.

'We have other pressing issues to deal with, boss,' Chloe said.

'Miles,' Naomi said.

Juno cleared her throat and tried to get the images of rat out of her head. 'Yes, Miles. He knows where Dr Viktor's house is. We have shown him we are not there, but we cannot be certain that he won't go back.'

'Which puts Valen in danger,' Naomi said, finishing the last of her stew.

'That is not the only problem,' Chloe said.

Naomi gave her bowl back to Jen and faced Chloe.

Chloe ran through the events with Miles and the knife slinger. She ended her report with Dr Viktor's request to save Miles.

Naomi frowned. 'I will need to think about this tonight. The sewer rats have lost too much lately. Putting them back in danger so soon may be asking too much.'

'It is our town too, boss,' Chloe said, her voice softening. 'Women, and their men, are suffering.'

Naomi sighed. 'The Lady has infected all the Fairacre women. The men are being held hostage by their love for their infected wives and daughters. The Fairacre guard is answering to the Lady. Knife slingers from the City of Lynn are being sent by the queen. And lastly there's Miles, a master swordsman who knows too much about us for us to ignore.'

Juno stared into the fire. 'Too many obstacles for our small band of girls. We need to tackle each one separately.'

Naomi stood, placed her hands behind her back and paced around the cooking pot. 'What of the men who do not have loved ones in Fairacre?'

Chloe spread her hands. 'There are few men who do not care for someone. A mother, a sister, a chosen partner or a hidden lover.'

Naomi continued to pace. 'Did Dr Viktor shed any light on how we can help these men?'

'We didn't get to it. Too much going on when we were there,' Chloe said. 'He was not best pleased to have his house full of girls.'

Naomi shook her head. 'Dr Viktor still lives in the old ways.'

'As do most men in Fairacre,' Chloe said, nodding.

'What if we rescue some men from the sewer and bring them back here?' Juno said, looking up at Naomi.

'It is an idea my mind keeps coming back to,' Naomi said. 'I am hesitant, though, as it will expose our position.'

'We don't have to bring them back to the camp,' Chloe said. 'We can keep them separate.'

Naomi sat back down. 'Suggestions on where?'

'We can set up a new camp on the other side of the waterfall,' Juno said.

'And surround it with hidden guards,' Chloe said, glancing at Juno.

Naomi remained silent for a while. With a nod, she said, 'Sundown tomorrow. We go and rescue Miles and some men. Tonight we sort out the new camp.'

'Strategy, boss?' Chloe said.

'Three teams in total. Yours and mine will get Miles. Alexa's team will go and get some men from the sewers. I will increase the size of Alexa's team to handle any unforeseen issues.'

'What if there is another knife slinger?' Juno said.

Naomi grunted. 'That, young Juno, is someone you might need to deal with.'

Juno narrowed her eyes. 'Okay,' she said.

Chloe signalled to Juno to follow. 'Let's get this camp sorted out.'

Throughout the night the girls built the camp next to the rocks on the other side of the waterfall. Rows of hay beds placed under grass covers stretched across trees among the rocks. The girls dragged logs into the centre and placed them in a circle. They dug a hole in the middle and packed it with wood for a fire. Just before sunrise, Juno walked back to the ruins. She kicked off her shoes and collapsed onto her hay bed. With her hands under her head, she listened to the hustle of the girls doing their daily chores. Her eyes closing, her mind drifted to Billy and Tilly and the likely couple they could one day make.

'It's time,' Chloe said, shaking Juno. 'It's just gone midday.'

Juno pulled her shoes on and laced them up. She picked up her Jo and clicked it into place behind her back.

The three teams of girls stood ready at the fireplace. Chloe walked along the lines of girls while holding boxes of antidote. 'Two bottles for each of you. Do not hesitate to use them. We can make more if we need to.'

Juno took two bottles and slipped them into her hidden side pockets.

'Equipment checks,' Naomi said, striding over.

Juno spun to her left and checked the girl's equipment and then turned so the girl could check her own equipment.

'Let's go,' Naomi said.

As the sun set at their backs, the girls crossed the river, past the new camp and followed the trail down the valley. Darkness enveloped the southern forest as they settled into an easy jog down the valley and to the forest edge. Naomi held up her hand, bringing the three teams to a stop. Juno peered across the fields and watched the guards patrol the southern gate. The drawbridge lay open, with guards seated at the entrance to the market.

Juno whispered in Chloe's ear, 'They are being more careful.'

'I would be too,' Chloe said. 'I can only imagine the tales of the knife slinger's death have spread throughout the town.'

Naomi tweeted and pointed her finger towards the town, signalling for all to move. Silently leaving the woods, the three sewer rat teams crept out onto the fields. Halfway across, the teams split, with Alexa moving towards the grated sewer entrance. The two teams crouched and moved to the bank near the path, where they fell to their bellies.

'We monitor now,' Chloe whispered in Juno's ear. 'Our best time to strike is when there is a guard change.'

Juno rested her chin on her hands and listened to the calm breathing of the girls, the distant laughter of the guards and the women's chatter inside the southern gate.

'Movement,' Chloe said into her ear. 'Someone coming through the market.'

Juno frowned at the slender man standing at the south entrance. 'Chloe. That looks like the knife slinger.'

'It can't be. You saw Chax take him.'

'It's dark and we are too far away,' Juno said, squinting her eyes. 'But he looks like the knife slinger. He is definitely not from around Fairacre.'

'Go,' Naomi said suddenly.

Juno sprang to her feet, snapped out her Jo and ran along the path and across the bridge. Shouts and clashing of steel shattered the night air as they engaged the guards. Moments later, the sewer rats stood over the disarmed Fairacre guards, their swords trained on their chests. The slender man, his hands behind his back, stood inside the southern gate with a look of amusement on his face.

'Who are you?' Naomi said, pointing her sword at him.

The man smiled. 'This ragtag bunch of misfits bested my brother? How amusing.'

Chloe laid a hand on Naomi's forearm. 'Another knife slinger.'

The knife slinger chuckled and lifted a hand, showing long thin fingers. 'Yes, another knife slinger.'

Juno took a step forwards. 'We are here for Miles. Where is he?'

'The sword boy?' the man said. 'The Lady's pet?'

'He is our friend, and nobody's pet. Where is he?'

'Right here, fire child,' Miles said, striding out of an alley and into the lights of the south entrance.

'It's time to go home, Miles. Your brother Billy is waiting for you,' Juno said, lowering her Jo.

'I am home,' Miles said, a smile cracking his usually serious face. 'The Lady has promised me the highest position in the queen's guard. All I need to do is bring you to her.'

'You know that isn't going to happen,' Chloe said, her brow furrowing.

Miles's unblinking black and white eyes bore into the group of girls. He reached behind his back and drew his shining greatsword. The slender man, following suit, reached over his shoulder and drew a long, thick black pole.

'Blades on each end of his Bo,' Chloe said, warning the others of the slender man's weapon.

'This is your last chance, fire child,' Miles said. 'The Lady is waiting.'

Naomi took a step forwards and extended her sword. 'Let's make this quick.'

Suddenly, with a lightning burst of speed, the slender man sprang forwards, his Bo a flurry of movement. With a swift jab, he caught Naomi in the chest and sent her sprawling to the floor. Miles let loose a sharp whistle. Out of the alleys soldiers charged, their swords and shields at the ready. Chloe screamed a war cry, bringing the girls into action.

Naomi flipped to her feet. 'Separate them.'

Drawing on their years of training together, the girls beat back the Fairacre soldiers. Juno and Chloe engaged the knife slinger. They ducked and rolled under the whistling blades of his Bo. With a grunt, Miles staggered backwards as Naomi's elbow jabbed him in the ribs.

Naomi removed a vial of purple antidote, uncorked it and threw the contents at Miles's face.

Miles wiped his face with his sleeve. 'I have no time for your tricks,' he said, re-engaging.

Juno swept her Jo along the ground and caught the knife slinger's feet, sending him onto his back.

Chloe slashed her sword down and stopped inches from his throat. 'Move and I will end you.'

The knife slinger looked to his left and smirked. Juno's eyes widened. Naomi, her mouth moving without words, stood with Miles's sword protruding from her chest. Miles, looking over Naomi's shoulder, tilted his head and smiled. Chloe's ear-piercing scream turned the heads of the girls. She fell to her knees and screamed again, her hands balled into fists by the side of her head. The knife slinger sprang to his feet and swung his bladed Bo at Chloe's neck. Pins and needles burst into searing pain as rage pounded through Juno's veins. She opened her mouth and let out a guttural roar as blue and yellow flames shot from her hands. Blinking rapidly, she shook her head to clear the fog. She looked down and gagged at the pile of ash where the knife slinger had once stood. The sound of Naomi's body slumping to the floor made her swing her head around.

Miles pointed his sword at Juno. 'The Lady is calling for you.'

Juno sprang forwards, and with a rapid series of spins from her Jo she knocked Miles away from Naomi's body. She turned to the girls and pointed. 'Take her to the barn.'

Chloe staggered to her feet, picked up her sword and pointed it at Miles. 'Murderer.'

Miles chuckled, raised his sword and looked at Juno. 'Do I have to end the life of another friend, fire child?'

Juno pointed her Jo at the pile of ash and said, 'Harm her, and the wind will take your ashes too.'

Miles snarled, sprang forwards and sent his greatsword

whistling through the air. Ducking the blade, Chloe unleashed a fury of slashing, stabbing and hacking. Juno blocked Chloe's last kill slash with her Jo and elbowed her in the stomach, knocking her aside. With a whip of her Jo, Juno caught Miles in the side of his neck, which sent him to his knees.

'Why did you stop me?' Chloe screamed, spittle spraying everywhere.

Juno removed an antidote and, using the end of her Jo, she lifted Miles's head and poured the contents down his throat.

Miles spluttered and wiped away the purple liquid that covered his lips. 'Pathetic. I expected more, fire child.'

Juno took a step back and willed the heat into her marks, ready to strike. 'Come on,' she said under her breath. 'Please, work.'

Miles took a step forwards, stopped, closed his eyes and shook his head. Confusion spreading across his face, he dropped to his knees and grabbed the sides of his head. With a deep groan, he gritted his teeth as thin tendrils of black smoke escaped from his ears.

'Juno? What is going on?' he said, looking up.

Juno turned to the girls. 'Take Chloe. Go to the barn and fetch the rest. Make your way to Dr Viktor's house.'

'Yes, miss,' a girl said, grabbing Chloe's arm.

'I am going to kill him,' Chloe said, pushing the girl's hand off her arm.

Juno pointed her Jo at Chloe. 'You will do nothing of the sort. Go with your sisters.'

Chloe snarled at Juno.

'Help us carry Naomi, miss,' the girl said, placing her hand back on Chloe's arm.

Chloe, her mouth set in a thin line, turned and joined her team in carrying Naomi out of Fairacre.

'Juno. What is going on?' Miles said, taking in his surroundings. 'Why have I been fighting?'

Juno scanned Miles's brown eyes. 'Are you really with us? Are you back, Miles?'

'What do you mean? Of course, I am with you. Why wouldn't I be?'

Sadness flooding through her, Juno clicked her Jo back into place. 'Pick up your sword, Miles. It is time to go home.'

The red barn lay silent in the afternoon sun. Juno opened the door to find it abandoned. She walked to the water trough, drank deeply, then wiped her mouth with her sleeve.

Miles gazed back at the southern gate. 'What is going on? I remember coming to Fairacre, but nothing after that.'

Juno narrowed her eyes. 'The Lady infected you, Miles.'

'Impossible,' Miles said, his eyes widening. 'She can only infect women.'

'The Lady can infect anyone who wants to be infected,' Juno said. 'She promised you a place in the queen's guard.'

'I don't remember, Juno,' Miles said, his mouth hanging open. 'I don't remember anything.'

Juno clasped her hands behind her back and glared at Miles, her lips drawn in a thin line.

'What?' Miles said, his eyes pleading. 'What has happened?'

Juno dragged her hand through her hair. 'Something bad has happened, Miles. You have hurt people.'

Miles licked his lips. 'Are they okay?' he stuttered.

Juno turned her head away.

'Tell me what I have done,' Miles said, his voice low. 'Look at me and tell me what I did.'

Juno sighed. 'You killed Naomi. You stabbed her through the heart.'

Miles took a step back, confusion rippling over his face. 'No, no, I didn't. I wouldn't.'

'You tried to kill a few of us too. Including me.'

Miles balled his fists by his side, lifted his head and

roared into the night. He opened his hands and looked down at his palms. In one quick movement, he turned and smashed his fist into the side of the barn. Splinters of wood burst into the air.

'You didn't know what you were doing, Miles,' Juno said, taking a step closer. 'You need to calm down.'

'I am going to kill that evil woman,' he snarled. 'I am going to make sure she knows it's me that kills her.'

'That is, if Chloe doesn't kill you first.'

Miles's breath caught in his throat. 'She knows?'

'She was there. She saw it right in front of her.'

Miles dropped to his knees and buried his face in his hands. 'This is not real. This is not who I am.'

Juno placed a hand on his shoulder. 'Come. We need to get back to Dr Viktor's.'

'Where is Chloe now?'

'She is on her way to Dr Viktor's with Naomi's body.'

'How am I going to face her, Juno?'

'I don't know, Miles,' Juno said. 'Maybe she will understand. I just don't know.'

Miles stood and glared at the southern gate. With a growl, he walked up to the trough and splashed water over his face. His face set in stone, he turned to Juno. 'I am going back to Fairacre. I will end this now.'

Juno shook her head. 'That is suicide, Miles. You won't get near her.'

'I have to make this right, Juno.'

'How can you make this right if you give up your life? How does this make things right if you die and the Lady is still ruling Fairacre? Think, Miles.'

Miles thought for a moment then looked down at Juno. 'I will agree for now. But understand this. The Lady is mine to deal with. I will regain my honour.'

Juno looked back at the southern gate. 'I will not stand in your way. We need to get going. They are waiting for us at Dr Viktor's.'

Miles inclined his head. 'Lead the way.'

They headed west past the orchards, into the western forest and through the trees to Dr Viktor's house. Miles opened the front door and walked into a silent entrance hall. A small flicker of light crept underneath the door of the living room. Miles took a deep breath, opened the door and stepped in.

'Brother,' Billy said, grabbing Miles into a hug. 'You are safe.'

Miles unwrapped Billy's embrace. 'Where is everyone?'

'Chloe sent the girls back to the ruins. She is in the back with Naomi. Dr Viktor is in his rooms.'

'I need to speak to her,' Miles said, turning to walk out of the living room. 'I need to speak to Chloe. I want to explain.'

'That is not a good idea, Miles,' Billy said, grabbing his arm. 'She needs to be with her sister.'

Miles clenched his jaw. He walked out of the living room and into his sparring room.

'If you follow the corridor past Dr Viktor's rooms, there is a door on the left. Chloe is in there,' Billy said to Juno.

Juno walked down the corridor, gently knocked on the door and let herself in.

Chloe stared at Juno with hollow red eyes. A sob escaping her lips, she walked over to Juno and collapsed in her arms.

Juno held her tightly while stroking her locs.

A while later, Chloe peeled herself away from Juno and walked over to the table, where Naomi lay. 'I have cleaned her up as best as I can.'

Juno ran her eyes over Naomi's face and down to her crossed hands, where she held a white flower. White silks lay on the length of her still body.

'She looks peaceful,' Juno said, looking at Chloe. 'You have done her proud.'

'Billy supplied these lovely things,' Chloe said, running her hands over the silks. 'Naomi wasn't one for luxury, but that's because she sacrificed so much for everyone else.'

Juno reached out and grabbed Chloe's hand. 'She sacrificed a lot for me.'

'I wouldn't be alive if it wasn't for her,' Chloe said, wiping her nose. 'She made me the person I am today.'

'She did a great job,' Juno said, squeezing her hand.

'I made her go to Fairacre, Juno. She would be alive if I hadn't asked her to rescue that animal boy out there.'

'We both asked her,' Juno said. 'Not just you. And you know she would have done it anyway. She would have done it for Fairacre and the sewer rats.'

Her eyes narrowing, her lip curling, Chloe looked at Juno. 'He doesn't deserve to live. Miles is half the person Naomi was.'

'He remembers nothing,' Juno said, tilting her head to one side. 'And he is beside himself with regret and blame.'

'He should never have let her infect him.'

'That may be,' Juno said. 'But the Lady seduced him with the promise of delivering his lifelong dreams.'

'Where is he now?'

'In his sparring room.'

'I cannot see him now.'

Juno pulled Chloe into a hug. 'Let's try to get some sleep. Tomorrow we can decide what to do.'

'I haven't had a chance to see my Valen,' Chloe said. 'I don't even know where he is.'

'We will find out for you in the morning,' Juno said, giving her a squeeze. 'He is safe. Billy would have told me if he wasn't.'

They left Naomi and climbed the stairs to their room. Juno tucked Chloe into bed, sat on her chair and wrapped herself in her blanket. Chloe laid her head on her hands and closed her red eyes.

CHAPTER 18
ATONEMENT

Juno yawned as she rubbed the sleep out of her eyes.

'Valen, where are you?'

Juno scrambled out of her chair and sat on the side of Chloe's bed. 'Chloe, wake up,' she said, shaking Chloe's shoulder.

'What?' Chloe said, waking with a start.

'Bad dream?'

Chloe shook her head as she ran her hands through her locs.

'It's okay. You are safe here,' Juno said, wrapping her arms around Chloe and giving her a hug.

A soft knock on the door made them swing their heads. 'May I come in?'

'Billy,' Juno said. 'Sure, come in.'

His head appeared around the door. 'Sorry to disturb you. Valen is asking for you, Chloe.'

A bright smile stretching across her face, Chloe swung her legs off the bed, laced up her boots and followed Billy out of the bedroom. Juno laced her own shoes up, left the room and made her way down the stairs and into the kitchen.

'Good morning, fire child,' Dr Viktor said, looking up from his breakfast.

Juno walked over to the cooker, grabbed a bowl and filled it with steaming root soup.

'Thank you for bringing Miles back,' Dr Viktor whispered. 'I am very grateful.'

Juno pulled out a stool and sat facing Dr Viktor. 'I wish it was under better circumstances.'

'I wish it was too. How is your friend?'

'She is having bad dreams. Billy took her to see Valen.'

Dr Viktor pulled out his handkerchief, coughed softly, then wiped his mouth.

'Your cough seems to be getting better.'

Dr Viktor returned his handkerchief, waved a dismissive hand, picked up his bread and dipped it into his soup.

Juno sat in silence while she finished her breakfast.

Dr Viktor opened his mouth, then closed it again.

'What is it?' Juno said, frowning.

Dr Viktor took a breath. 'This may be too much to ask of you.'

'I am listening.'

'I cannot ask anyone to forgive Miles for what he has done. It pains me to know he fell foul of that woman's evil. He is, however, a warrior, who abides by the warrior code. He shall seek atonement.'

Juno placed her elbows on the counter and, resting her chin on her hands, she eyed Dr Viktor. 'If I witnessed Miles murdering Tilly, I don't know if I could forgive him. Even with him being infected.'

'I understand. But it wasn't your Tilly, and it is not you he will be seeking forgiveness from.'

'What are you asking me to do?'

'Not what you are thinking,' Dr Viktor said. 'He will give his life into Chloe's care until she accepts he has done right by her. What I am asking from you is to make sure she doesn't use him as a blunt weapon.'

Juno's forehead wrinkled in surprise. 'You think Chloe would do that?'

'Grief is a powerful emotion that can drive someone to be irrational. Miles may have killed her sister, but he is no murderer.'

Juno thought for a moment. She nodded her head. 'I will do what I can.'

'Thank you. And again, thank you for bringing my boy back,' Dr Viktor said.

Juno inclined her head. She walked to the stove, retrieved a cup and poured herself some strong tea.

'Our second mission was to bring back men who are being held captive in the sewers. From our spies' reports, these men are hollow with sadness and despair. Do you know if there is anything we can do?' she said from the stove.

Dr Viktor grunted. 'The men have shared a part of their essence with the women they love. We can assume, then, that the Lady has infected their essence.'

'The antidote?' Juno said, returning to the counter. 'Will it work on them?'

'They may work. I would try them and see. Billy has been preparing more while you have been away.'

Juno opened her mouth to say something, then closed it as shouting echoed from the entrance hall. She slid off her stool and ran out of the kitchen and into Miles's training room.

'You killed her,' Chloe shouted, her finger inches away from Miles's nose. Eyes staring straight ahead, Miles stood with his back perfectly straight and his arms down by his side.

'You murdered her,' Chloe screamed into his face. 'You murdered my sister.'

'Chloe,' Billy said, walking through the doorway.

Juno held her hand up and silenced Billy with a wave of her finger.

'Say something,' Chloe screamed, peppering Miles's face with small specks of spittle.

The muscles in Miles's jaw twitched as he gritted his teeth.

'I said say something,' Chloe said, jabbing Miles in the chest.

Miles's eyes shifted as he looked at Chloe. His voice catching in his throat, he said, 'I can't remember.'

'Of course you can't remember,' Chloe said, her lip curling. 'Isn't that so very convenient for you? Who cares, right? It's just another girl who got in your way. You murdered her.'

Miles dropped his head. His voice barely a whisper, he said, 'I am not a murderer.'

Her cheeks rising and falling with each breath, Chloe glared at the top of Miles's head.

Dropping to his knees, Miles raised his head and said, 'I submit myself to you.'

'What?' Chloe said, confusion spreading across her face.

His eyes wet with tears, Miles spread his hands. 'I wish to atone, and I will not stop until I destroy the evil that has made me do this. I submit myself to your wardship.'

Her mouth hanging open, Chloe looked at Juno.

Billy took a step forwards. 'It is the warrior's code. His life is yours until the Lady is no more.'

Chloe threw up her hands. 'I don't want this. I will not be responsible for this man.'

'You have no choice, love,' Valen said, appearing in the doorway. 'He will give up his life if you don't accept.'

Chloe shook her head, walked over to Valen, wrapped her arms around his waist and buried her head into his chest.

Valen winced. 'Careful, love.'

Chloe jumped back. Her eyes widened. 'Sorry. I forgot.'

Valen pulled her close and whispered in her ear. 'I know you are hurting. More than I can ever imagine. But I know you will do the right thing by Miles.'

Chloe sighed, her shoulders relaxing. She pulled herself away and walked up to Miles. 'Get up, please.'

Miles stood, placed his hands behind his back and squared his shoulders.

'I accept,' Chloe said. 'On one condition.'

Miles met Chloe's eyes. 'Ask me anything.'

'No man will best me like you bested Naomi. You will train me to be faster than you, more deadly than you, better than you.'

Miles' mouth hung open with surprise stretched across his face.

'Do you understand?' Chloe said, her eyes boring into Miles. 'You will teach me everything you know.'

Miles studied Chloe's face. 'Okay,' he said.

Chloe turned and walked out of the room, dragging Valen behind her.

'Chloe is going to need us more than ever before. We need to make sure we do right by her,' Juno said.

Billy let out a sigh of relief. 'You have our full support. Is she going to lead the sewer rats now?'

'She is the natural choice, but she won't want to. I will speak to her when the time is right.'

Billy walked to the door. 'I am making more antidote. I could do with your help.'

'Miles,' Juno said, joining Billy, 'we need you at your best. Get your head right and get some rest.'

Juno and Billy finished the last batch of antidote, which they packed into the small carrying boxes.

'Do you think we have enough?' Juno said.

'Not for all of Fairacre,' Billy said. 'We will need to carry on tomorrow to get enough.'

The tinkle of a bell echoed through the house. 'What's that for?' Juno said, looking over at Billy.

'Dinner in the living room,' Billy said. 'Miles sometimes puts on a bit of a spread. An extravagant spread.'

Juno's stomach growled. 'This I have to see.'

As they entered the dining room, Billy chuckled at Juno's surprise. 'I told you,' he said with a lopsided grin. 'Have a seat.'

Miles filled the long rectangular table with small bowls of an assortment of steaming food. A glass teapot sat with small glasses inside a circle of freshly baked bread rolls. Juno grinned at Chloe and Valen as they entered the room.

'Well, this is unexpected,' Chloe said, her tired red eyes looking across the table.

'Sit anywhere and help yourself,' Billy said. 'There will be another round of food, so eat as much as you want.'

Juno grabbed a wooden bowl and helped herself to a piece of food from each bowl. Miles walked in holding another tray of steaming food. He knelt, gathered the empty bowls and replaced them with fresh bowls of food from the tray. The thump of Dr Viktor's cane sounded from the entrance hall. He entered the dining room and waited for Miles to pull a chair alongside the table. Billy filled a bowl and passed it over to Dr Viktor.

'Where did you learn to cook, Miles?' Juno said through a mouthful of food.

Miles waved a hand at Billy and Dr Viktor. 'It would not be proper to subject you to the catastrophes of their cooking.'

Juno chuckled and glanced over at Chloe, who sat unmoving with a stony face.

Dr Viktor cleared his throat. 'What will become of the sewer rats?'

'We will leave the day after tomorrow to join them,' Valen said, glancing at Chloe.

'Are you going to be okay to leave by then?' Juno said.

'Billy has performed wonders. And I have my Little Henry if something happens to any of my wounds.'

Dr Viktor jerked his head back with a snort.

Valen ignored Dr Viktor. 'Would it be any trouble to ask for a pot of your salve?' he said to Billy.

'Of course not,' Billy said.

With her third bowl of food finished, Juno poured some tea and listened to the chatter around the table. Her eyes growing heavy, she folded her napkin on the table. 'Thank you for a lovely dinner. I think I am going to go and get some sleep,' she said, standing.

'I think we will do the same,' Chloe said. 'Thank you for the dinner.'

Juno climbed the staircase, entered her room, kicked off her shoes and lay on her bed with her fingers laced behind her head. She turned onto her side and stared at the empty chair next to her bed. Just as her eyes began to close, she frowned at the thumping of feet running up the staircase.

'We need to move,' Billy said.

'What is it?'

'Soldiers approaching the house. Get down the corridor past Dr Viktor's room. Move quickly.'

Juno pulled on her boots, and without lacing them she ran out of the room and down the stairs.

'Open up,' a man said, hammering on the door.

Dr Viktor stood in the middle of the entrance hall and waved Juno towards the corridor. 'Get out of here.'

Juno glanced at Billy. 'What is he doing?'

'He refuses to leave the house, and he says he will slow us down.'

'We can't just leave him here.'

Billy grabbed Juno by the arm and pulled her down the corridor. 'If we don't move, they will trap us in here.'

Juno peered over her shoulder and shook her head as Dr Viktor walked up to the front door.

'Through there,' Billy said, pointing to a small door on the right. 'Pick up one of those packs before you go through.'

Juno threw a pack of antidote onto her back, walked through the door and into a low pitch-black tunnel. She ducked her head, placed a hand on the wall and moved towards the twinkling lights in the distance. At the end of the tunnel, she swung open a low wooden door and knelt next to Chloe and Valen.

'We are not leaving Naomi here, Valen,' Chloe said, her eyes darting back up the tunnel.

'If we go back, love, they will take us, and it won't matter where she is.'

Billy crouch-walked through the small door with two packs of antidote. One pack he threw onto his back, the other he left on the floor ready between his legs. He sat on his haunches and placed his finger on his lips.

'Where is Miles?' Juno whispered.

'He is putting Naomi into a safe place.'

'What place?' Chloe said.

'We have a bunker. We would use it now, but it is too small for all of us.'

'Will she be safe?' Chloe said.

'They will never find her. And even if they did find where she is, they won't be able to get inside the bunker.'

Miles ducked through the door holding two packs of antidote and a long bag filled with practice weapons.

'What have you done with Naomi?' Chloe said, grabbing Miles by the shoulder.

'She is safe. I will retrieve her for you when I can,' Miles said, moving to the back of the room and lifting a trapdoor.

Chloe stared back up the dark corridor.

'Will Dr Viktor be okay?' Juno said.

'They will no doubt search the house,' Billy said. 'If they don't find you, I am sure they will leave him alone.'

Popping his head out of the trapdoor, Miles beckoned for them to follow. One by one they climbed down the wooden stairs into the tunnel. Miles pulled the trapdoor closed, squeezed past everyone and took the lead through the winding tunnels. After a number of twists and turns, Miles stopped at a rusty grate. With a grunt, he threw his weight against it until, with a screech, it gave way. 'Everyone out,' he said, standing aside.

Juno moved the branches of a bush out of the way and hid behind a tree trunk.

'I will burn it down if you don't tell me where they are,' a man shouted in the distance.

Miles gave Billy a worried look before walking through the forest towards Dr Viktor's house. He crouched in front of a bush and parted the branches.

Juno crouched alongside Miles. 'They are hurting him,' she said, releasing her Jo.

Miles placed a hand on her Jo. 'If you go down there, they will have got what they came for. There are too many of them and we will not be able to protect Valen and the antidotes.'

Juno grunted and replaced her Jo.

'Bring him here,' a soldier said. 'Yes, Captain,' another soldier said.

Dr Viktor struggled against the soldiers holding his arms. 'Let me go. There is nobody here.'

'There is a table in the living room that seats six people,' the captain said, walking up to him. 'Where are they?'

'There is nobody here,' Dr Viktor said. 'Search the house and see for yourself.'

The captain lifted Dr Viktor's head and slapped him hard across the face. 'We are searching the house. Tell us where they are and save us the trouble.'

Dr Viktor coughed violently, sending spittle all over the

captain's face. The captain snarled, then for a second time slapped him across the face.

'There is nobody here, Captain,' a guard said, standing at the top of the stairs.

With a ringing of steel, the captain pulled his sword from its sheath and pointed it at Dr Viktor's throat.

Billy stood with a gasp.

Miles pulled Billy down by the forearm and shook his head.

'This is your last chance, old man. Where is the girl?'

'What girl?'

The captain sheathed his sword, shook his head then turned to the soldier. 'Are you sure there is nobody here?'

'Yes, sir. The house is empty.'

'Burn the house, soldier,' the captain snarled.

'Yes, sir.'

'You can't burn my house,' Dr Viktor said, struggling against the guards. 'It has been here for centuries.'

'Where are they?' the captain said again. 'You can save your house if you tell me where they are.'

His voice rising, Dr Viktor said, 'There is nobody here. You searched it yourselves.'

The captain signalled to another soldier. 'They cannot be far. Spread out and search the area.'

'We need to go,' Miles said.

'What about Dr Viktor?' Billy said. 'We can't leave him, Miles.'

'We cannot risk it. All we can do is hope he will be okay.'

'I hear something, Captain,' a soldier said.

'Move,' Miles said, pushing the group to the path. 'Chloe, lead the way and keep us updated on how Valen is doing.'

They jogged in single file down the path towards the south.

'We won't get to the ruins before dawn,' Juno said, glancing over her shoulder.

'Chloe,' Miles said. 'Stop at the next bend.'

The path hooked around a tree, where Chloe stopped.

Billy looked back up the path and shook his head at the burning house. 'Our home. They have taken our home.'

Miles placed his hand around Billy's neck and pulled him in close. The two boys stood in silence. In the distance, the night sky turned orange as the flames devouring the house grew bigger.

Miles took a step back. 'We will not make the ruins by daylight, and it will be easy for them to find us during the day.'

'I will be fine, lad,' Valen said. 'I can keep going.'

'Not at the pace that we need to, Valen,' Juno said.

'What are you suggesting?' Chloe said.

Miles looked south. 'We need protection. Billy and I will stay with Valen while you go and get the sewer rats. Meet us at the fork in the path.'

'Hang on. What about the cave?' Billy said. 'We can head there rather than being exposed at the fork in the path.'

Her eyes darting between Miles and Billy, Chloe said, 'What if they find you in the cave?'

Valen grabbed Chloe's hand. 'We have the rocks to block the entrance. We can go up the well if something happens.'

'It's a good plan, Chloe,' Juno said.

'Here, love,' Valen said, handing her a small metal ball. 'Take Little Jay. Release him if there is a problem and you can follow him to me.'

Chloe slipped Little Jay into a pocket, then threw her arms over Valen. 'Stay safe.'

Valen kissed her on the end of her nose, then pulled himself away. 'Be careful, love. There are soldiers throughout the entire forest.'

'Ready?' Chloe said, turning to Juno.

Juno knelt, checked her laces and gave Chloe a nod. 'Let's go.'

Together they ran south until they reached the fork in the path, then turned west towards the waterfall. The trees turned from kapok to pine, and the forest bed to fern.

With the roar of the waterfall up ahead, Chloe slowed to a walk. 'Let's get off the path. The soldiers patrol and camp near the waterfall.'

'How long are we going to do this, Captain?' a soldier said, hacking at the undergrowth.

Juno and Chloe dropped to their bellies and froze. 'Until the Lady finds this girl,' the captain said.

'And then we get to join the queen's guard,' a soldier said excitedly.

'Not sure I want to leave my home for a big dirty city,' another soldier said. 'A big dirty city with wonders to explore,' the first soldier said. 'You can stay at Fairacre for all I care.'

'The Lady is taking all the women in Fairacre to the City of Lynn,' the captain said. 'Some official business, she says.'

'You see? Even more reason to go to the big dirty city,' the soldier said.

'There is nothing here. Let's get back to the waterfall,' the captain said.

After the soldiers had passed, Juno rose and followed Chloe past the waterfall until they reached the bottom of the valley.

'Why is she sending the women to the City of Lynn?' Juno said, shaking her head.

'I have no idea,' Chloe said. 'Did you hear how they didn't even care? And why should they? They will just get their pick of girls from the schools.'

Images of the young girls happily going about their school day flashed through Juno's mind. She closed her eyes and shook her head in disgust.

'We need to move,' Chloe said. 'From here we throw caution to the wind.'

Juno, running hard to keep up with Chloe, wound her way up

the valley until she turned west onto the cliffs. The moon sank below the tree line in the west just as the sun peeped over the horizon in the east. Weaving through the cliff rocks, they stopped at a soft tweet that sounded from the treetops. Juno searched the trees until she saw the familiar brown eyes of a girl gazing down.

Chloe jumped onto a boulder and waited for the girl to join them.

'Welcome back, miss,' the girl said. 'It is good to see you.'

Chloe gave the girl a quick hug. 'It is good to be back. Report, please.'

'We are close to the temporary camp, miss. Alexa managed to bring a few men back from Fairacre.'

'Any trouble with the men?'

'No, miss.'

Chloe waved a hand. 'Lead the way.'

On entering the camp, Juno turned to the girl. 'Where are the men?'

'Under the makeshift awnings, miss. They only come out once a day to fetch food.'

Chloe grunted. 'It's as if they have given up.'

'We need to try this antidote on them,' Juno said.

'I agree, but not now. We don't know how they will react, and we don't need the distraction while we are trying to get the others back.'

Juno walked up to an awning and moved the flap aside. A man's hollow eyes stared back. She let go of the flap and joined Chloe.

'Where is Alexa?' Chloe said.

'She is in the main camp, miss,' the girl said. 'She has been trying to keep order with Naomi gone, but it has been difficult.'

Chloe sighed and signalled to Juno. 'Let's go.'

Juno followed Chloe across the river and into the chaotic scenes of the ruins. They walked up to the cooking pot, where

Chloe put her fingers to her lips and sounded a sharp whistle. The girls across the camp turned their heads and fell into an uncomfortable silence.

'Alexa,' Chloe shouted.

Alexa popped out of an awning, jogged up to Chloe and gave her a hug. 'It is so good to see you, miss.'

Chloe squeezed her tightly. 'It is good to be back, Alexa. Report, please.'

Alexa cast her eyes around the gathering girls.

Chloe jumped onto one of the logs they used for sitting on. 'Return to your teams and wait in your tents. I will be speaking to you all shortly.'

The girls, seeing Chloe's stern face, dispersed quickly. Chloe frowned. 'Dissent in the ranks, sister?'

Alexa let out a breath. 'With limited information about Naomi, and not knowing whether you would return, they have been restless.'

Chloe ran a hand through her locs. 'I don't blame them. They have all been through enough.'

'You are taking over from Naomi, aren't you, miss?' Alexa said with a look of expectation.

Chloe sighed. 'I am not sure everyone wants that, Alexa. And I don't know if I am ready.'

Juno grabbed Chloe's hand and pulled her off the log. 'You are the natural choice.'

Chloe shook her head. 'Leading isn't something I do, Juno.'

'Yet you have led since Naomi passed,' Juno said. 'Naomi might not have said so, but she acted like you are the next in line.'

Chloe frowned. 'How do you mean?'

'Naomi always had you in her office talking about how she led. She trusted you with all the sewer rat information. And she sent you on the most important missions.'

Chloe looked down and picked at her nails. 'I need to speak to Valen.'

'Speaking of Valen, we need to get moving,' Juno said.

Chloe turned to Alexa. 'Get the weavers, please.'

'Yes, miss.'

'Juno, I need to bring some order here. Can you organise the weavers?' Chloe said.

'Leave it with me,' Juno said, nodding as Alexa approached with the red-headed weaver.

'Alexa, with me,' Chloe said, striding off to the awnings and tents.

Juno sat on a log and beckoned for the girl to sit with her. 'I don't even know your name.'

'Jane, miss. People call me Janie.'

'Nice to meet you, Janie,' Juno said. 'I have an unusual request for you and the weavers.'

Janie rummaged in her shoulder bag and brought out paper and a pencil. 'Yes, miss.'

'Valen is in the caves. We need to pull him from a deep hole. Can we create something to do that?'

Janie, her tongue sticking out, looked down at her paper and scribbled long, sweeping lines.

'And we need it urgently.'

'Yes, miss,' Janie said, tapping the pencil on her lips then continuing to scribble.

'If you need anything, please come and ask me.' Janie raised an eyebrow.

'Sorry,' Juno said, raising her hands. 'I will let you concentrate.'

Janie stood and walked to the rows of tents. 'I will call you when it is ready, miss,' she said over her shoulder.

Juno walked over to her small hay bed. She kicked off her boots, and while massaging her feet she gazed across the ruins.

Chloe strode from awning to awning, speaking to the girls. Smiles leapt to their faces as Chloe spread words of encouragement and hope. Juno lay back on her small bed and laced her fingers behind her head. With a sigh, she closed her eyes as the warmth of the rising sun reached her tent.

CHAPTER 19
THE ANTIDOTE

'It's time, miss,' Alexa said, peering round the tent flap.

Juno laced up her boots, left the tent, walked over to the cooking pot and took the bowl of stew that Jen offered her. Long shadows stretched across the ruins as the late afternoon sun tipped the top of the forest tree line.

Chloe stood on a log, where she placed her fingers on her lips and whistled. The gathering girls fell quiet. 'I have just received a report that Valen has entered the cave. Janie, how are we with the sling?'

'It is ready, miss.'

'Alexa, ready with your runners?'

'Yes, miss,' Alexa said. 'Four here and four at the other camp if we cannot keep up.'

Chloe pulled Little Jay from her pocket and threw him into the air.

With a click, he opened and buzzed angrily in front of Chloe's face before flying towards the waterfall. Four girls sped after Jay into the forest, calling directions to each other.

Chloe walked over to Juno. 'Our spies say they have dropped the rocks to block the cave entrance. We don't have much time.'

'Can we get a group to engage the soldiers at the cave entrance?' Juno said.

'We have, but there are too many of them, and I am concerned they would follow us up the valley.'

'Little Jay has flown towards the temporary camp, miss,' Alexa said.

Chloe broke into a jog. 'Let's get across the river.'

Juno crossed the stepping stones and stopped on the other side of the river, where Alexa was talking to a girl.

'We have found something, miss,' Alexa said. 'It's close to the temporary camp.'

Juno followed Alexa through the forest to the temporary camp, where they turned in to the forest away from the cliffs. At a small clearing, girls stood around a cluster of piled-up rocks.

'The little bug flew down there, miss,' a girl said, pointing to a small hole.

'Let's move these rocks,' Chloe said, rolling a rock out of the way. 'We need a big enough hole to get Valen through.'

The girls rolled the rocks out of the way until the top of a well came into view.

'Hold it,' Juno said. 'Listen.'

They went down to their hands and knees and turned their ears towards the hole.

'Fighting,' Chloe said. 'We need to get down there – now.'

Alexa tied the end of the sling to a tree and threw the harness into the hole. Juno and Chloe climbed over the edge and, using the sling straps, worked their way down the narrow well.

'Valen,' Chloe said, dropping to the bottom. 'Juno, help me get him into the sling.'

'Is that you, love?' Valen said, his eyes half-closed. 'Little Jay told me you were coming.'

'I am here,' Chloe said, pulling his feet through the loops of the sling. Billy appeared through the narrow tunnel, breathing heavily.

'Where is Miles?' Juno said.

Billy bent over and placed his hands on his knees. 'He is at the cave entrance. A few soldiers got through, but he has pushed them back.'

'Chloe, when you have Valen up, drop the harness and give us the signal,' Juno said, pushing past Billy.

Juno unclipped her Jo, slid through the narrow tunnel and ran into the cavern. She sprinted towards the entrance and slammed the end of her Jo against a soldier's shield, sending him backwards into the tunnel. Side by side, Juno and Miles jabbed and stabbed into the cave entrance, keeping the soldiers back.

'Have you got Valen?' Miles said, grunting.

'They are lifting him now,' Juno said.

Juno ducked a flying dagger, then jabbed her Jo into the tunnel. It connected with a soldier's nose.

Sweat pouring from his brow, Miles snarled as a dagger flew out of the entrance and clipped his shoulder. 'We can't keep this up for much longer. It took them minutes to move the rocks. There are too many of them.'

'Let's back up to the cave. We can hold them at the tunnel.'

Miles drove his sword deep into the entrance and connected with a soldier. A scream echoed through the cavern. 'Move now.'

Juno ran through the cavern, down the narrow tunnel and into the empty well. Miles scraped through and faced the tunnel with his sword drawn. A rope whistled through the air. A thud echoed through the small cave as the harness hit the ground.

'Let's go,' Juno said, placing her foot onto one of the harness straps.

Miles sheathed his greatsword, placed his foot onto a harness strap, wrapped his arm around Juno and gave the rope a tug.

On the way up, Juno looked down into the empty well. 'They will have no idea how we got out of here.'

With a grim expression, Miles said, 'They will figure it out eventually. And then there will be soldiers searching the cliffs.'

As the top of the well came into view, Juno reached up and grabbed the outstretched hands of the girls.

Her feet landing on the wall of the well, Juno turned to Alexa. 'Where is Chloe?'

'Already on her way to the camp, miss. Billy moved Valen immediately to deal with his wounds.'

Juno turned to Miles and frowned at the trickle of blood running down his arm. 'Looks like Billy needs to work on you too.'

'Just a scratch,' Miles said. 'Let's get out of here.'

They followed Alexa past the temporary camp, over the river and into the ruins.

Juno walked up to the cooking pot, grabbed a bowl, filled it with stew and handed it to Miles. 'Don't ask me what is in it.'

Miles took a mouthful. 'Rat. We have it sometimes in the winter when food is scarce.'

'Well, I think it's disgusting,' Juno said, pulling a face.

'Juno, Miles, good to see you two are okay,' Billy said, walking over.

'Can you check Miles over?' Juno said. 'He says he has a minor scratch.'

Billy shook his head at the blood dripping from his hand. 'Hardly minor, Miles. Get it cleaned out and apply some salve. You can find it in my bag.'

Miles walked over to the awning that Billy had pointed out.

'How is Valen?' Juno said.

'He will be fine. Overexertion and not having food has made him weak. Chloe is putting him to bed.'

Billy sat on the log and ate quietly.

'We will go back for Dr Viktor,' Juno said.

Billy rubbed his eyes. 'They destroyed our home.'

Juno moved over, sat next to Billy and rested her head on his shoulder.

Billy sighed, wrapped his arm around her and gave her a squeeze. 'I guess this is how you felt when you left your school behind.'

'I miss Tilly and Miss Petra more than the school,' Juno said quietly.

Billy grinned. 'Tilly is definitely one of a kind.'

'Do you think she is alive?'

'Yes. I know she is,' he said. 'And I think you know she is too.'

'I can't bear to think of her being controlled by that evil lady.'

'If Miles and Joanne are anything to go by, she won't remember anything.'

'You like my Tilly, don't you?' Juno said.

'I knew the second I met her,' he said, his lopsided grin growing. 'Are you okay with it? With me and Tilly?'

'I am happy you have found each other. I am not happy that my old school trains girls for men to select them.'

'It is what they have done since the dawn of time, but I also don't agree with it,' Billy said, scratching his chin. 'I didn't choose Tilly. It just happened.'

'And that is how it should be,' Juno said.

'Here comes Chloe,' Billy said, giving her a wave. Chloe sat on the log and let out a sigh.

'How is Valen?' Juno said.

Chloe gave her a half-smile. 'There is colour back in his cheeks. He is sleeping now.'

'Which is something I need badly,' Billy said, rising. 'I will see you both in the morning.'

Juno stood and gave Billy a hug. 'We will find Tilly. I won't stop until we do.'

'Yes, we will,' he said.

Juno sat back down and stretched out her legs. 'Billy mentioned Dr Viktor. I said we would go back for him,' she said, glancing at Chloe.

'Easier said than done. I will send spies into Fairacre to see if we can find him. If he is in the town hall, I am not sure we can get him.'

'We can't keep running, Chloe. They will just keep looking.'

'I don't intend to keep running,' Chloe said, pursing her lips.

Her brow creasing over, Juno looked up into the darkening sky. 'We are so few, and they are so many.'

'We have always been the few fighting the many,' Chloe said, standing. 'I suggest we get some rest. We are trying the antidote on the men tomorrow. It is the key to my plan.'

Juno stood, stepped over to Chloe, gave her a hug, then walked to her tent. She sat on her hay bed, lifted her hands and examined the dormant flame marks. With thoughts of Tilly, she winced at the pins and needles as she willed the heat to enter her marks. Suddenly a deep, throaty rumble sounded from the back of her tent. Juno tilted her head and trained her ears to block out the noises of the camp. A distress call from a bird, followed by the flapping of its flock, reverberated from the forest behind her. The pins and needles grew stronger through her marks, sending an aching heat around her hands. Another deep, throaty rumble sounded behind her tent. Juno stood and walked to the tree line next to the ruins. Two amber eyes appeared through the undergrowth. A smile spreading across her face, Juno sneaked into the forest and crouched next to the knotted trunk of an old tree. Out of the undergrowth Chax ambled up, her tail swishing in greeting. Juno threw her arms around Chax's enormous head and scratched her shoulders. Chax rumbled deep down while rubbing her head against Juno's cheek.

'I knew you weren't too far away,' Juno said.

Chax pulled her head away and licked Juno's face from chin to forehead.

'Disgusting,' Juno said, wiping her face with her sleeve.

Chax tilted her head and stared deeply into Juno's eyes.

'Why are you here? Is something wrong?'

Chax huffed and swung her head to the south.

Juno turned and gazed southwards. In the distance, illuminated by the moonlight, she made out the roof of her school.

'Why do we need to go back there? Is it Tilly?' she said, kneeling next to Chax.

Chax hunched down, opened her mouth and roared.

Juno slapped her hands over her ears and winced. 'Quiet, Chax. The girls might hear you.'

Chax snorted and continued gazing south.

Juno rolled her eyes at the shouting in the ruins. She hugged Chax. 'We will go to the school, but not now. You need to go before the girls get here. Not all of them know you, and you will scare them.'

Chax turned and bounded into the forest. Juno scanned the trees until she found the wide-eyed stare of a girl. She signalled to her that everything was okay, then walked back into the ruins and into her tent. She lay on her hay bed and listened to the nervous chatter of beasts in the forest.

Chloe peeped around the tent flap. 'Have you been out in the forest?' she said with a sly smile.

Juno yawned. 'Chax was checking up on me.'

'Sleep well, young Juno. Tomorrow is an important day.'

. . .

The pitter-patter of raindrops on the top of the tent brought Juno out of sleep. With a shiver she sat up, laced up her boots and stepped out into the gloomy early morning. To the south the thud of practice weapons echoed through the ruins. The ground squelched under her boots as she made her way to the large semi-circle where the amphitheatre had once stood. Miles, his practice greatsword drawn, defended himself from a flurry of jabs from Billy's staff. Juno walked down between the rows of stone seats and sat in the front row. With a keen eye, she studied Miles and Billy's every move.

Billy, breathing hard, swung his staff in a wide arc. Miles side-stepped, dropped his left hip and poked his sword into Billy's shoulder. Billy winced and staggered backwards.

'Why does Billy take such a beating?' Chloe said, walking up behind Juno.

'He is a good fighter, but nothing compared to Miles. And Miles won't let him get away with not training.'

Chloe grunted as she adjusted her short sword.

'Juno, Chloe, good morning,' Billy said, waving.

Miles rapped his sword on Billy's knuckles. Billy yelped, threw his staff on the ground and rubbed his hands.

'Distraction is one of our greatest enemies,' Miles said. 'Never take your eyes off your opponent.'

'Maybe you should fight someone who will hit back,' Chloe said, walking into the fighting circle. 'Do you remember our deal?'

Miles inclined his head and waved his hand at the weapon rack standing on the side of the amphitheatre stage. Chloe strode over and removed a practice short sword, which she whipped around in a figure of eight in front of her.

Billy picked up his staff, left the circle and sat next to Juno. 'This should be interesting.'

Chloe faced Miles, spread her legs and bounced on the balls of her feet. With a sudden burst of speed, Chloe darted in with a furious set of jabs and slashes. Miles, moving like a dancer, slid away from each attack. Chloe faked with her eyes then darted in with a swift jab. Miles stepped aside and slapped her thigh with the flat side of his greatsword.

'Wait,' he said, holding up his hand and walking over to the weapon rack. He hung up his greatsword, selected three short swords and threw one to Chloe, which she caught with her left hand. 'Why wield one when you can wield two?' he said.

Chloe tested the weight of the sword in her left hand.

'The second sword will be a hindrance at first,' Miles said. 'In time it will feel normal.'

Chloe whipped the swords around in a figure of eight.

'Follow these eight basic movements,' Miles said. 'Four are attacking movements and four are defensive movements.'

Chloe stood next to Miles and followed each movement. Minutes later, the sweat formed on Chloe's brow as she breathed heavily.

'Your weaker left hand will catch up with your right hand eventually,' Miles said, casting a critical eye over Chloe.

Chloe panted hard as she strained to hold up the wooden swords, which now felt as heavy as lead.

'You will master these eight basic moves before we continue,' Miles said. 'They will protect your personal space while in combat. If they cannot get through, they cannot hurt you.'

Chloe blew air through her teeth until the left sword clattered to the ground.

'Enough for today,' Miles said, picking up the sword and placing it back on the weapons rack.

Chloe shook her aching arms to increase the blood flow.

'Surprised she didn't try to kill him,' Billy said in Juno's ear.

Juno grinned. 'She knows when to listen. I think she will shock Miles by how quickly she learns.'

Chloe, taking deep breaths, left the semicircle and joined Juno.

'It's time to try this antidote. Miles, can you bring your practice swords? I would rather not have to use steel if things get out of hand.'

Miles strode over to the weapons rack and grabbed his practice greatsword.

'I will get the antidote quickly,' Billy said, running up the stairs.

They squelched through the rain-soaked ground and sat around the cooking pot.

Billy joined them and set the small bag of antidote in front of him.

'How are we going to do this, Billy?' Chloe said.

'Choose the oldest of the camp. If something bad happens, we will easily be able to restrain him.'

'Okay. Let's get over to the temporary camp,' Chloe said.

The rain continued to fall as they made their way through the forest and over the now slippery stepping stones of the slow-moving river. The temporary camp lay silent, with only Alexa and a few girls crowded around the large fire pit.

Chloe pulled Alexa aside and asked her a series of questions. Back at the fire pit she said, 'Third tent along, there is an older man who is less active than the rest.'

Billy stood, walked over to the tent, opened the flap and crouched. After a few moments of conversation, he reached into the tent and led the older man back to the fire pit. 'Sit here, sir,' Billy said, helping him to a log.

'I don't understand what you want me to do,' the old man said, his hollow eyes darting in confusion. 'Do you know where my daughters are? I know I have daughters, but I don't feel them anymore.'

Juno's eyes narrowed as she shook her head in anger.

'It's okay, sir,' Billy said, resting a reassuring hand on his shoulder. 'We have a drink that we hope will make you feel better.'

The man waved a dismissive hand and stared into the forest. 'I have daughters, you know,' he said quietly.

Billy pulled out a vial of purple liquid from his pack, uncorked it and held it to the man's lips. Startled, the man closed his mouth, his lips pressed shut. Billy gently took hold of the man's chin and tilted his head backwards. The man's mouth opened and Billy placed two drops onto the man's tongue. He swallowed, then licked his lips, which left a purple stain across them.

Miles, with his practice sword across his legs, watched the man closely.

'It's not doing anything,' Chloe said into Juno's ear.

Juno held up a hand. The man stiffened, closed his eyes, coughed violently then retched out a black liquid in between his legs. He held his head with his hands and let out a long mournful moan. With a shake of his head, he opened his now bright eyes.

'What have you done to me?' he said, frowning at Billy.

Billy placed a hand on the old man's shoulder. 'What is your name and what are the names of your daughters?'

'My name is Arthur and my daughters' names are Petra and Lena,' the man said, standing. 'My daughters – they kicked me out of my home. Where am I? Where are my daughters?'

Juno stood in front of the man and held her hand up. 'The Lady has infected your daughters. Do you remember who the Lady is, sir?'

'The lady in the town hall,' Arthur said, folding his arms. 'She has my daughters?'

'She has your daughters. She has infected every woman in Fairacre.'

Arthur swore, then kicked out at a log. 'I need to go back and help them.'

'We are planning to do that,' Chloe said, standing next to Juno. 'Please sit, sir, so we can explain.'

The man, eyeing Chloe, slowly sat on a log. Juno and Chloe sat and ran Arthur through the events that had transpired in Fairacre.

His mouth wide open, Arthur shook his head. 'Throughout the winter? This has been happening for that long?'

'Yes,' Juno said. 'The Lady has all the ladies infected. She controls the town guard. She has help from the City of Lynn. And she has forced the men into the sewers.'

Arthur cursed colourfully for a minute. He calmed and looked at Chloe. 'What do you need me to do?'

Chloe moved her arm in a wide arc. 'We need to feed the antidote to the men in this camp.'

Arthur looked down at the purple stain on his finger. 'Is this what you fed me?'

Juno nodded. 'Two drops is all it takes.'

Arthur scanned the awnings and tents. His face turned to grim determination. 'Give me the antidote and wait here.'

Billy handed Arthur the pack of antidote.

'Arthur, I am going to send Miles with you in case there are any problems,' Chloe said, giving Miles a nod.

With a nod, Arthur marched off to the rows of tents with Miles close behind. Juno pulled a face at Chloe as the sounds of retching men filled the camp. One by one the men, following Miles's instructions, left their tents and shuffled to the fire pit.

Arthur returned to the fire pit and handed the bag back to Billy.

Chloe waited for the last of the men to join them. She stood on a log and called for quiet. 'I understand that you are all probably very confused.'

'Who are you and where is my wife?' a man said, stepping forwards, his chin raised. 'Who is in charge here?'

'Please listen to the lady,' Arthur said.

The man turned to Miles. 'Are you the man in charge here?'

Miles frowned and pointed at Chloe. 'Chloe is in charge. Do you have a problem with that, sir?'

The man crossed his arms and lifted an eyebrow at Chloe.

Chloe nodded at Miles. As she had explained the events to Arthur, she repeated them for the men. 'We have a plan to free your loved ones. But to do so, we need to work together.'

The man threw his hands up in the air and said, 'We don't take orders from women. Especially vermin like you who live down in the sewers.'

Chloe wagged a finger at the man and said, 'Is it not men that live in the sewers now? Is it men helping you to get your loved ones back?'

The man shook his head. 'It is women that have put the men down there.'

Miles took a step forwards. 'Was it not the guards of Fairacre that kept you down there?'

'Ordered by the Lady,' the man said, squaring up to Miles.

Miles took another step forwards. 'And yet the guards, who are men, have followed her orders.'

The man's brow furrowed in confusion.

'You will listen to Chloe,' Miles said. 'She is planning to get your loved ones back. Or would you rather do this on your own, sir?'

The man took a step back and rammed his hands into his pockets. Arthur lifted his hand. 'I want to see my daughters. I will help.'

Another man stepped forwards and said, 'My wife. She kicked me out of my home. She would never do that unless something was wrong. I will help too.'

One by one the men stood forwards and agreed to help.

The man with his hands in his pockets stood alone. He stepped forwards. 'I too will help. But let all men know that I do not take orders from women.'

'And let all men know that you, sir, would put the old way in front of your loved ones,' Arthur said, jabbing the man in the chest with his finger.

'I did not say that. I just meant it's not what we usually do.' Arthur raised his voice. 'There is nothing usual about today.'

Chloe separated the two men. 'The sewer rats cannot take on the Lady, the Fairacre guards and the infected alone. We need greater numbers to help us free your loved ones.'

'You want us to rescue the men from the sewers? Like you rescued us?' Arthur said, nodding.

'Yes. Bit by bit we bring them back to the camp and free them from this infection,' Chloe said. 'Once we have enough people, we will launch a full attack on Fairacre and drive the Lady out.'

The men whispered among themselves until Arthur turned to Chloe and said, 'We wish to discuss this amongst ourselves.'

Chloe thought for a second. 'Okay. We will return this afternoon. For now, help yourself to food and water.'

'Thank you,' Arthur said, inclining his head.

Juno watched the men disperse to their awnings and tents. She turned to Chloe. 'Let's get back to the camp. I didn't have breakfast.'

Chloe led the way out of the camp just as the first ray of sunshine broke through the grey clouds. They entered the ruins and sat around the cooking pot. Juno grabbed a bowl of stew and some baked bread.

'Do you think they will help?' Chloe said, sitting next to her with her own bowl.

'Yes. They said they would. I think Arthur needs time to convince that one man,' Juno said.

'Good,' Chloe said. 'We heard Chax last night. Is she okay?'

'She pointed me to my old school. Once we have freed these men, I think I will go and take a look.'

Chloe frowned. 'Why do you need to go back there?'

'I haven't checked the school since I ran away. There may be something there about Tilly.'

'Would you like me to come with you?'

Juno shook her head. 'You have the girls to look after, and I think I need to do this alone.'

'Okay,' Chloe said. 'I will let you go only if you promise to take Little Jay with you.'

Juno shivered. 'Do I really have to? You know how I feel about bugs, and I will have Chax with me.'

'Yes, you really have to,' Chloe said, smiling.

'Oh, if I must,' Juno said, letting out a long sigh.

'Excuse me, miss,' Janie said, standing over them. 'I have a request, if you please.'

Chloe stood and brushed the wet grass and dirt off her clothes. 'Of course, Janie. What can I help you with?'

Janie shyly looked around. 'Miss, the weavers would like to learn how to fight.'

Chloe raised an eyebrow. 'We are not expecting you to fight, Janie.'

'I understand, miss, but we may have to defend ourselves one day.'

Chloe pursed her lips.

'Let's speak to Miles,' Juno said. 'I am sure he will help.'

Chloe thought for a bit, then nodded. 'Follow me, Janie.'

'I am going to get some rest,' Juno said. 'Good luck with Miles, Janie – you are certainly going to need it.'

'Thank you, miss,' Janie said, smiling over her shoulder.

CHAPTER 20
GIRLS CAN FIGHT TOO

That afternoon, Juno left her tent and joined Chloe in the temporary camp. The afternoon sun broke through the thick clouds with beams of sunlight. Rainbows arched over the trees, which still dripped from the morning rain. Arthur sat idly chatting with a few men around the crackling fire pit.

Chloe peered towards the valley. 'Five more rescued men are coming up through the valley. I would like you to explain what is going on once they have had the antidote.'

Arthur stood. 'We are still discussing your plan.'

'We are going to do it regardless, Arthur.'

'Why do you need us, then?' Arthur said, scrunching up his face in confusion. 'It is easier for you to rescue the men. The sewer rats are all girls, and we have limited devices to stop the Lady infecting us. I would rather not put them at risk.'

Arthur nodded. He stood and walked towards the edge of the camp, where the first of the newly rescued men appeared from the trees. He held out his hand. 'Harold, it's good to see you.'

Harold, his eyes hollow and distant, stared at Arthur. He shook his head, walked past Arthur and followed the other men to the awnings.

Arthur pulled back his outstretched hand and scratched his chin. With a shake of his head, he walked back to the fire pit and sat. 'Is that what we looked like yesterday?'

Juno searched Arthur's face. 'You don't remember giving the antidote to the men sitting next to you?'

'I was angry and confused. I wasn't really taking notice of how we looked,' Arthur said.

'Arthur, all the men in the sewers are like that. All of your friends, your colleagues, the people you have known for years.'

Arthur grunted, then turned to Chloe. 'Tell us what we need to do.'

Chloe signalled to Alexa.

'Yes, miss?' Alexa said.

'Arthur has agreed to help us in the rescue. I am going to leave you in charge to organise this.'

Alexa beckoned Arthur with a tilt of her head. 'Please follow me. We need to give the new men the antidote and explain what is happening.'

Chloe watched Alexa and Arthur walk to the awnings. 'That is part one of our plan. Part two is getting Dr Viktor back.'

'We need to find out where he is being kept, while not alerting the Lady,' Juno said. 'If she finds out we are looking for him, it will put the men's rescue mission at risk.'

'That means telling Miles and Billy they can't come,' Chloe said. 'Someone will notice them.'

'Billy will understand. Miles, though, will be a problem.'

Chloe turned and faced the shouts coming from the awnings. Arthur stood with his hands in front of him, asking for calm. Harold, his wild eyes darting around the camp, turned and cursed at Alexa.

'Not having any of that,' Chloe said, standing and walking over to the awnings.

'What did you just give me, Arthur?' Harold said with a shrill voice. 'Calm down, Harold. It's an antidote.'

'These women have possessed us,' Harold said, his fists balled by his sides. 'How dare they keep us hostage in this camp?'

Chloe shoved her face inches from Harold's. 'You are free to go when you wish, Harold. But we won't rescue you if you end up in the sewers again.'

Harold's mouth dropped open.

'Harold, what of your wife?' Arthur said. 'Where is she?'

With a confused look, Harold stumbled backwards. 'Leave me alone. Just leave me alone.'

Chloe caught Arthur by the arm. 'Let him go. He needs time to figure everything out. How are the others?'

'Confused, miss,' Arthur said. 'They are all asking for their loved ones.'

'I have an idea,' Juno said. 'Get everyone to write down who their loved ones are. If we keep a record and show all the men, it will remind them that everyone has lost someone.'

Arthur's eyes lit up. He turned to Alexa. 'May I ask you for supplies?'

Alexa chuckled. 'Let us sit at the fire pit and I will take down your list.'

Juno turned to Chloe. 'There are going to be a lot of men like Harold. I suggest we double the guards in this camp.'

'Let's get to the ruins and I will send a team through,' Chloe said. 'We can speak to Miles and Billy after that.'

At the ruins camp, Chloe handed out instructions to place more guards around the camp on the cliffs.

Juno entered a long awning and sat down next to Billy.

'I hear we have another group of men from the sewers,' Billy said, opening a bottle of antidote and checking its contents.

'One man ran off into the forest after he drank the antidote,' Juno said.

'I can only imagine how confused they are,' Billy said.

'Confused and not liking the fact that they are being led by women.'

Billy corked one of the bottles. 'The more men we rescue, the more we will have to deal with this.'

'Will they not realise that we are trying to help them?'

Billy faced Juno. 'Men have ruled for centuries, and they have always told women what to do. You cannot expect that to change overnight.'

Juno rubbed her eyes with the heels of her hands. 'If they turn on us, there is no way we can free the town of Fairacre.'

Billy grunted as he corked another bottle.

'What are you thinking?' Juno said.

Billy placed the antidote into the small chest. 'There may be a way to maintain order. It will require Miles to take an active role, though.'

'Are we talking about Dr Viktor?' Chloe said, pulling up a tree stump.

Billy shook his head. 'No, but what of Dr Viktor?'

'We will need to go into Fairacre to find him,' Juno said. 'However, we cannot let the Lady know we are there.'

A thin smile formed on Billy's face. 'Which means sticking to the shadows – hence myself and Miles cannot come with you?'

'Yes. Do you trust us to find him?' Chloe said.

Billy chuckled. 'You know I trust you fully with this.'

'I am worried about Miles,' Juno said.

'He is under Chloe's wardship. He will do what she tells him to do,' Billy said, smiling at Chloe. 'Or had you somehow forgotten?'

Chloe rubbed her forehead with her fingers. 'Why do we always have to order him to do something? Why can he not just trust us?'

Billy gave Chloe a lopsided smile. 'As I was explaining to

Juno, you cannot change centuries of conditioning overnight.'

Chloe huffed. 'Even when he knows it's what we are going there for?'

'Conditioning is powerful,' Billy said.

'If I have to order him to stay, I will. What were you talking about before I joined?'

'Juno's concern is that the men in the camp will get out of hand. And I agree with her,' Billy said. 'All it takes is one man to turn the group on you.'

'You were suggesting something about Miles?' Juno said.

'As I think you know by now, Miles is a formidable fighter. I have yet to see him bested. The men at the camp need to know that he is on your side and that he will not tolerate dissent,' Billy said.

Chloe threw up her hands. 'Another order.'

Billy chuckled again. 'Yes, another order.'

'I am going to talk to him,' Juno said, standing. 'Alone.'

Chloe raised an eyebrow. 'Are you sure?'

Juno nodded, left her tent and walked to the amphitheatre. She sat on the top row of seats and watched Miles going through the basic defensive movements with Janie and her weavers. Each of them held a long, thin needle, not unlike the needles they used daily for weaving. They jumped backwards and forwards on the balls of their feet as they stabbed and sliced. Miles walked around coaching each weaver, raising an elbow here, rotating another's hips there. With one last war cry, the weavers' training ended.

'Thank you,' Janie said, blushing.

Miles gave the weavers a small bow, then watched them walk up the steps and out of the amphitheatre. Juno hopped down the steps and joined Miles in the centre circle. With a nod, she walked up to the weapons rack and pulled out a greatsword, which she threw to Miles. She moved to the centre, reached behind her back and snapped out her Jo. The ends of the Jo extended out with a snap. Juno took a deep breath. Thoughts of Tilly and Miss Petra rushed through her mind. Pins and needles sprang into the marks in her hands. Pain erupted through the marks, and with a pop a thin blanket of yellow flames spread out over her hands. Her feet spread and anchored, Juno extended her hand and rocked her finger, beckoning for Miles to attack. Miles shrugged his shoulders and moved into his ready stance. Like a dancer, he moved into an attacking stance and circled Juno. With a feint to the left, he stepped to his right and swung his sword. Juno bounced out of the way and let loose a flurry of attacks, putting him on the defensive. Miles parried her attack and went through his defensive moves, never leaving an opening. Juno darted to her right, and using a one-handed grip she jabbed her Jo at Miles's face. Miles, bouncing on the balls of his feet, sidestepped easily. A pop, and a small ball of fire shot from Juno's free hand. His eyes wide, Miles dodged the small fireball, only to feel the crunch of Juno's Jo connecting with his jaw. Staggering backwards, he narrowed his eyes and let out a deep, throaty growl from deep in his chest. He darted forwards with a blur of slices and slashes. Juno parried each attack while hitting him with stinging shots of tiny balls of fire that exploded around his greatsword. Miles, in full defensive mode, used his greatsword to create a barrier against the fireballs.

Juno extended her Jo, hooked it behind Miles's feet and pulled, bringing him to the ground. Her Jo pointing at his throat, Juno smiled. 'Girls can fight too, you know.'

Miles held both hands up. 'They shouldn't have to fight.'

Juno offered him a hand. 'It is not up to you to tell us what to do anymore, Miles. Chloe is our leader. She leads me, and right now she leads you too.'

Miles grabbed Juno's hand and pulled himself to his feet.

'We are not weak little girls, Miles. Look around you. Who is saving who here?'

Miles placed his hands behind his back and looked up into the sky. After a moment he looked at Juno. 'It is all I know. Dr Viktor taught me I should always protect women and they should never fight.'

A smile spreading across her face, Juno spread her hands. 'And tell me, Miles, who is going to protect you from me?'

A smile crept across Miles's face. He reached up and scratched the back of his head. 'It seems the teacher has become the pupil.'

Juno clipped her Jo back into place. 'Chloe needs you. We all need you. But we don't need you to protect us. We need you to join us.'

Miles sighed. 'I am with you. Teaching the weavers has shown me that girls can fight too. They are quite good.'

Juno threw her arms over his neck and hugged him fiercely. 'Chloe has an important job for you while we go and search for Dr Viktor.'

Miles pulled away and frowned. 'You are going to find Dr Viktor? Without me?'

'Yes, Miles. We need to use stealth and keep to the shadows.' Miles opened his mouth, then closed it.

'Trust,' Juno said, stepping forwards and playfully punching him on the shoulder.

'Let us go and find Chloe and see what this important job is, then,' Miles said.

They left the amphitheatre and jogged through the ruins and up to the cooking pot.

Chloe strode up to the cooking pot and sat on one of the logs.

'I have spoken to Juno and she says you have something for me to take care of,' Miles said, sitting down on the logs.

Chloe folded her arms. 'I am concerned the men in the camp won't work with us. They are showing dissent and confusion after they have taken the antidote.'

'You won't have anything to worry about. I will make sure they know that you are in charge. Billy and I will need to move to the other camp. Chloe, can your girls help move our stuff there?'

Chloe glanced at Juno and said, 'Of course.'

'I will come back during the day to continue the weaver's training,' Miles said.

Miles stood and made his way to Billy's awning.

Chloe turned to Juno. 'Dare I ask what happened?'

Juno shook her head. 'We had a talk. He will keep that camp in order and teach them that you are leading.'

'I will believe it when I see it,' Chloe said, her lips pursed.

'He will surprise you, Chloe.'

Chloe snorted. 'Let's go and see how Arthur is getting on in the temporary camp. Then we are off to Fairacre to see if we can find Dr Viktor.'

Juno stood and followed Chloe to the temporary camp. Jen and Gem worked at the fire pit, where a large side of meat turned on a makeshift rotisserie. Men cautiously approached them with their bowls, bowing in thanks, hoping not to experience a disapproving stare from one of them. Valen and Arthur sat at a table, capturing the names of missing wives, daughters, mothers and grandmothers. A long sheet of cloth hung between two trees, bearing the names of the missing.

Juno walked over to Miles. 'The camp is getting bigger each evening.'

Miles nodded as he cast a critical eye over the camp. 'We are bringing in nearly twenty a night.'

'Lass,' Valen said, his voice booming around the camp.

Juno smiled at the enormous man bearing down on her. 'Hello, Valen. Good to see you have recovered.'

'A few scratches is all,' Valen said, a wide grin stretching across his face. Little Henry appeared on his shoulder and danced while clack-clacking his jaws. 'Get off,' Valen said, waving his hand.

Chloe strode over. 'Ready for another mission into Fairacre?'

Juno nodded. 'If we don't find him in the northern district, we must assume he is in the town hall.'

'Agreed,' Chloe said. 'Let's get some food into us. We will leave straight afterwards.'

Walking up to the cooking pots, Juno looked at Jen and Gem out of the corner of her eye.

'No more rat stew,' Jen said.

'Buck stew,' Gem said. 'Hedgehog likes buck stew but not rat stew.'

Juno took the bowl of stew from Gem, sat on a log, grabbed a roll and watched the stream of men come over for their food.

'One roll,' Jen said, slapping the hand of a man. 'Greedy.'

The man bowed his apologies and jogged back to his awning.

Juno used the last bit of her roll to wipe up the stew as she watched the last sliver of sun disappear over the horizon. She returned her bowl and walked over to the side of the camp, where Chloe and her three team members stood. The girls checked every inch of their outfits before they slunk out of the camp, across the cliff rocks and down through the valley.

At the southern forest tree line, Juno scanned the rows of wheat for any guards. She moved out of the trees and waded through the wheat, stopping at each path to check for movement. The entrance grate to the sewers lay slightly ajar. Juno shuddered at the screech of steel as Chloe pulled the grate open.

They jogged through the sewers until Chloe stopped at a grate that led into the alleys. 'We make our way to the northern district on the rooftops.'

Juno sprang up through the hole into the quiet alley. The girls climbed hand over hand up a drainpipe and crouched on the rooftop. Chloe gave the signal and they sprinted along the roofs, jumping over the narrow alleys. With a signal from Chloe to split up, Juno turned and made her way to the north-east corner of the northern district. She drifted along the roofs, peering through the windows of each house, checking for anything unusual. Juno jumped an alley, walked to the side of a roof and froze. She tilted her head and frowned at the soft whisper that reached her ears.

'Juno.'

She crouch-walked south to the other side of the roof. 'Juno.'

Holding her breath, she remained silent and unmoving. 'Juno, my child.'

Juno jumped off the roof and followed the voice through the alley. 'Juno, where are you?'

At a well-lit street, Juno lay flat against the alley wall. 'Juno, can you hear me?'

A quick peer around the alley corner, and Juno's gasp caught in her throat. Her mouth dropped open and her eyes widened into saucers.

'Come to me, my child.'

Juno stepped out of the alley and into the street. 'Miss Petra? Is that you?' she said, her voice catching in her throat.

Miss Petra spun round and gaped. Her soft brown eyes filled with tears as she walked towards Juno. She spread her arms wide. 'Juno, I knew it was you.'

'You died,' Juno said, her voice a coarse whisper.

Confusion swept across Miss Petra's face. 'I am not dead, you silly child. It is me – Miss Petra.'

Juno reached out and touched the side of Miss Petra's face. Warm tears flowed onto her fingers. 'What are you doing here? How are you alive? We buried you.'

'I don't know,' Miss Petra said, looking around. 'I was at the school and then I woke up here in Fairacre. What are you doing here? And why are you wearing these awful clothes?'

A sob catching in Juno's throat, she reached up and snaked her arms around Miss Petra's neck. She hugged her tightly while nestling her face into Miss Petra's chest.

'It's okay, my child,' Miss Petra said. 'I think it is time we went home.'

Juno lifted her head and smiled into Miss Petra's soft brown eyes. 'Yes. Let's go home.'

Miss Petra's muscles tensed. Her eyes widened. A gasp of air escaped as she stumbled forwards. Her knees buckled as she fell into Juno's arms.

Juno fell backwards, Miss Petra falling on top of her. 'Miss Petra, what's wrong?'

A small trickle of blood dripped from the corner of Miss Petra's mouth. Juno peered over Miss Petra's shoulder and gasped at Erica, who stood with a long, twisted dagger in her hand.

'Erica. What have you done? What have you done?'

Erica's black and white unblinking eyes bore into Juno. Her mouth stretched wide in a sweet smile.

Juno pushed with all her might and rolled Miss Petra onto her back. Juno knelt next to her, gripped her shoulders and shook. 'No, please, no. Miss Petra, please, no.'

'The Lady wishes to see you, Juno,' Erica said, her mouth twisting from a sweet smile into a snarl.

Juno shook Miss Petra's shoulders again. 'No. Miss Petra, can you hear me?'

Miss Petra blinked, then grimaced, showing teeth red with blood. She reached up and snaked her hand around Juno's neck. Eyes turning black and white, Miss Petra's grimace turned into a red-toothed smile. With a tug on her neck, Miss Petra pulled Juno down towards her face. Juno gasped. Her eyes filling with red dots, she looked down at the dagger in Miss Petra's hand. The blade sat deep in Juno's chest. Rolling off Miss Petra and onto her back, Juno turned her head and stared at Miss Petra's black and white eyes. Miss Petra's eyes turned soft and brown. With one last breath, Miss Petra lay silent.

Erica stood over Juno and tilted her head. 'Orphan Juno is dying. So sad. The Lady will fix you. Yes, she will. Or maybe she won't. She doesn't care about you.'

Juno felt the blood trickle into her lungs. She balled her hands into fists and, taking in as much air as she could, she screamed Chloe's name.

Erica threw her head back and laughed. 'Your friends can't help you.'

A whistle broke the eerie silence in Fairacre.

Darkness descended over Juno as she squinted at Erica. She closed her eyes and opened them again. Where Erica had once stood, Chloe stood staring at her with concerned brown eyes.

'Hold on, Juno,' Chloe said.

Juno felt weightless as the girls picked her up. Bubbles of coppery-tasting blood came up into her throat. She closed her eyes as the darkness took her. Consciousness came with a shooting, stabbing pain through her chest. She opened her eyes and squinted as she tried to get the hazy picture of Billy's face into focus.

'That is all I can do, Chloe,' Billy said, his voice quavering. 'I am sorry.'

Juno felt Chloe's wet tears fall onto her face. She opened her mouth and closed it again as the taste of her own blood slammed her senses. A throaty rumble sounded from outside the tent. Juno felt her friends scatter away from her hay bed.

Juno opened her eyes and gazed into Chax's red-flecked amber eyes.

'What are you doing, Chax?' Chloe said, backing out of the tent. 'Leave her alone.'

'Let Chax take her, Chloe,' Billy said.

Juno winced as Chax's sharp teeth bit down into her arm. The world rushed past her as grass and dirt ripped at her arms, legs and back. Her eyes fluttering open, she counted the trees as they flew past. The rough assault of earth tearing at her back, arms and legs came to a sudden stop. Juno sighed as the warmth of Chax snaked around her. The world turned black.

CHAPTER 21
A LIONESS

Juno winced at the throbbing in her head. The blood that crusted her lips bit into her tongue as she licked them. She reached out, placed her hand on Chax's belly and felt the deep, rhythmic breathing. She opened her eyes and winced. The throbbing in her head slightly receding, she rolled onto her hands and knees. The sun's rays sliding through the uneven rows of pine trees sent shots of pain behind her eyes. Chax uncurled herself, stood and stretched. She looked at Juno, then nudged her in the shoulder. Juno sat back on her heels and rubbed her eyes with the heels of her hands. She swallowed and grimaced at the burn from her dry throat. 'I need to find water, Chax.'

Chax huffed, turned and lumbered into the thick, fern-covered undergrowth.

Juno pushed off the ground and stumbled to her feet. She ran her hand along the throbbing ache inside her chest. Her fingers finding the hole in her outfit, she touched the angry red welt on her chest. A grunt escaped her lips as she pushed off a tree trunk to straighten herself. One careful step after another, she shuffled through the undergrowth trying to find Chax.

'Chax, where are you?' she said, covering her eyes from the setting sun.

Amber eyes and a mouth full of ivory-white teeth pushed through a thick fern. Chax tilted her head and puffed at Juno.

'I am coming. Slow down a bit.'

Juno pushed through the undergrowth, her footing getting surer with every step as she followed Chax's flicking tail. The undergrowth turned into a bed of pine needles that crunched under her boots. They snaked through tall, thin pine trees until in the distance an outcrop of rocks came into view. Juno stumbled around the rocks and caught herself on a tree branch. A steep bank fell away to a pool of dark, cool water. In a sitting position, she slid down the bank. At the bottom she got onto her hands and knees, cupped some water, drank deeply and splashed water on her face. She dragged her wet sleeves over her lips to remove the crusty, coppery blood. Juno placed her head into her hands as visions of Miss Petra's soft brown eyes flashed through her mind. With the heels of her hands, she wiped away the tears that cascaded down her cheeks. 'They killed Miss Petra, Chax,' she said, glancing over at the enormous cat who lapped at the water.

Chax cocked her head and whined. With a snort, she bent her head back down and continued to drink.

Juno stood and stretched her arms into the sky to test the muscles in her chest. With her arms spread out, she rotated her hips and felt the stiffness begin to leave her body. 'We need to get back to the ruins. Chloe will be looking for me.'

Chax finished her drink and bounded up the bank and into the undergrowth.

Juno climbed up the bank and began to jog. The lead in her legs disappearing, she broke out into a run. She dodged trunks of pine trees, fallen logs and low branches as she followed Chax's dark brown tail that bobbed in front of her. With a skid, she broke through the trees and stopped on a cobble street. Juno's breath caught in her throat as she looked north at her old school, illuminated by the rising moon.

Chax bumped Juno's hand until Juno draped her hand over Chax's shoulder.

'Why have you brought me back here?' she said, scratching Chax's head with her nails.

Chax looked at Juno, then ambled up the street towards the village. Dim lights shone through the drawn curtains of the village cottages. Juno checked each cottage window to see if she could see inside. At the end of a row of cottages, she peered around the corner at the marketplace. She pulled her head back and dropped to her haunches as a man opened a cottage door. He shuffled across the street and dumped a bucket of dirty water into a drain, then returned to his house.

'I am going to speak to him. You will need to stay hidden,' Juno said, placing a hand on Chax's shoulder.

Chax's nose twitched, and with a snort she padded into the hedges that lined the forest on the opposite side of the street.

Juno walked up to the cottage and knocked lightly on the door. The cottage remained silent, so she rapped harder. With her ear to the door, she listened to the shuffle of feet on wooden floors. Taking a step back, she waited for the man to finish pulling back the door's locks.

'What do you want?' the man said through a crack in the door.

Juno held up a hand. 'Good evening, sir. My name is Juno, from the school.'

The man opened the door a bit more and with distant hollow eyes he gazed through the gap at Juno.

'Mister? Did you hear me?' Juno said.

'There is nobody at the school,' the man mumbled.

'Do you know where they went?' Juno said, tilting her head to get a better look through the gap.

'There is nobody at the school,' the man mumbled again.

Juno took a step forwards, placed her hand on the door and gently pushed it open. The man stumbled backwards into the entrance hall of his house and stood still, his unblinking eyes staring back at Juno.

'Are you okay, mister?' Juno said.

The man stared over Juno's shoulder and frowned. 'Is my Lita with you?'

Juno's forehead crinkled. 'Who is Lita, mister?'

'Lita is my wife. She left to fetch water.'

'When did she leave?'

The man scratched the side of his head. 'Is my Lita with you?'

Juno shook her head in frustration and backed out through the door. She walked to the next cottage and rapped her knuckles on the door.

A man cleared his throat and opened his door. 'Greta, is that you?'

'Who is Greta, mister?' Juno said.

The man peered up and down the cobble street, then scratched the side of his head. 'Have you seen my Greta? My little Greta?'

Juno backed away from the door. 'Sorry, mister, I haven't seen Greta. I have the wrong cottage.'

His eyes narrowing at Juno, the man mumbled under his breath, then closed the door. While walking along the cobble street, Juno peered into cottage windows and sighed at the men who sat staring at their living room walls. She continued to the library where she paused at the open doors. Behind Juno, Chax rustled out of the hedge and padded into the library.

'Hello? Anybody here?' Juno said through the doors.

Chax walked out of the library and up along the cobble road towards her old school.

'Is there nobody in there, Chax?' Juno said, taking a last look through the library doors. With a shake of her head, she followed Chax up the road and up to the tall iron school gates. Juno shivered at the half-open school door that stood atop the steps. A gust of wind picked up a loose page of a schoolbook and blew it against the bars of the gate. A shutter on a third-storey window slammed against its frame. Juno scanned each dark window of the second and third storey classroom windows, looking for lights or any sign of movement. Chax padded up to the gate and butted her head against it. She snapped out her claws and tried to pull it open.

Juno wrapped her arms around herself and shook her head. 'Don't really want to go in there, Chax.'

Chax growled and continued to paw at the gate, leaving deep scratch marks on the metal. Juno walked up to the gate and pulled it open. A squeal of iron shattered the quiet night. She walked through, past the dormant fountain and up the steps to the tall double wooden doors. The handle felt cool in her hand as she pulled the door open. A gust of stale, dry, cold air blew into her face, making her wince.

'If I go in here, you stick with me. If you don't stay with me, I will leave.'

Chax looked at Juno with her red-speckled amber eyes.

'I know you understand me,' Juno said. 'Don't try to pretend you don't.' Juno walked through the door and shivered at the blackness that enveloped her. The tapping of her boots echoed off the walls as she walked down the corridors and into her dormitory. She picked up an oil lamp from Harriet's desk and lifted the glass covering, exposing the wick. With a flick of her finger, she sparked a flame and lit the oil lamp. She closed the glass and turned the dial to 'full'. As the light grew, long, dark shadows climbed the dormitory walls. Juno walked through upturned tables, broken chairs, unmade beds and open clothes chests until she reached her old bed. The bed creaked with a puff of dust as she sat on the edge. With her eyes closed, she remembered the dorm full of smiling and laughing girls. Back onto her feet, Juno walked over to Tilly's bed, where she ran her fingers along the shelves of empty plant pots on the wall. She reached behind two small pots and pulled a framed painting off the wall. A smiling Tilly holding a plant sat next to Juno, who sat tossing an apple into the air. Juno wiped away a tear that trickled down her cheek. She unclipped the frame, took out the painting and tucked it into a pocket.

At Tilly's clothes chest, Juno opened the lid and moved some old clothes aside. She picked up a stack of books and flipped through them while reading each cover. The last book had a pink cover. Juno opened it at the first page and smiled at the neat handwriting that spread across the pages of Tilly's journal. On the last page Juno stopped at a picture of a heart with the words 'Tilly and Billy' written in the middle of it. With a half-smile she snapped the book closed and tucked it into her jacket. Juno looked around the dorm one more time, then left and moved towards the dining hall. The tables, covered in blackened rotten food, turned Juno's stomach. She moved out of the dining room and into the kitchen, where she froze at Chax's sudden growl.

'What is it?'

Her nose twitching, Chax lowered her head and gazed under the kitchen tables. Juno knelt and shone the lamp in the direction Chax was looking. She turned to her right, then jumped as a gigantic rat ran across the floor and under the stoves.

'Disgusting,' Juno said, rubbing her arms.

Juno backed out of the kitchen, and holding the lamp high she walked along the corridor. A door with the label 'Staff' came into view. The door creaked as she pushed it open. A long corridor filled with closed doors stretched out in front of her. Above each door was a plaque with a teacher's name on it. Juno stopped at each door and remembered the teachers as she read each name aloud. At the end of the corridor, her heart jumped into her throat as she read the plaque.

'"Miss Petra. Principal."'

Juno pushed open the door and walked in. To the left, a large unmade bed with four pillows sat snugly against the wall. On the left side of the bed there was a bedside table with two drawers. In front of Juno stood a two-door wardrobe.

Chax, pushing past Juno, walked up to the wardrobe and snarled.

'What is it, girl?' Juno said, walking up beside Chax and resting a hand on her head.

Chax sniffed the air, then bent to the bottom of the cupboard doors and let out another low, rumbling growl.

Juno grabbed the wardrobe handle and yanked the door open. A half-scream escaped her mouth as she fell backwards onto her behind. She scraped her feet on the floor as she tried to get away. In the cupboard, a skull with a wide, toothy grin bobbed forwards, its teeth clattering together. Juno stopped her backwards crawl and took a few deep breaths to calm her beating heart. Her jaw clenching, she got to her feet and slowly crept up to the cupboard.

Juno's eyes widened. 'It's Mr Hargreaves, Chax.'

Chax sniffed the air, then sneezed.

Juno opened the second wardrobe door and scanned Mr Hargreaves's ripped clothes. A long, thin spiral dagger stuck out of his chest.

'The Lady,' Juno said, placing her hand on Chax. 'She must have killed him the night she arrived.'

Chax's nose twitched at the stench that flooded out of the cupboard.

A folded piece of paper with the letter 'J' stuck out of Mr Hargreaves's breast pocket. Juno scrunched up her nose and gently removed the folded note with a finger and thumb. She placed the lamp on the floor, then flicked the note open.

Petra.

. . .

I have cleared the way for our baby Juno. I will leave her by the river tonight.

H.

'What does he mean, he has cleared the way for our baby Juno?' Juno said, looking at Chax.

Chax moved over to the bedside table and scratched at the drawer. Juno sat on the side of the bed and opened the drawer. Small bottles of ink, stacked neatly in a row, sat on top of pristine white paper. Next to the ink sat a stack of envelopes, neatly torn along the seam. She picked the letters up and read them one at a time. Her face creasing in anger, Juno snarled at the men's correspondence. Each one was asking how their future wives were getting on with their training. Juno pulled out the last letter and recognised the same handwriting that was on the note. The words on the page burned into Juno's eyes as she read each line. Her hands shook. She blinked, then started the letter again, reading it through from beginning to end.

'Miss Petra is my mother, and Mr Hargreaves is my father,' she said, pain rippling across her face.

Red mist descended over her eyes. The bed creaked as her entire body shook. 'They are my parents, Chax.'

Chax walked up to Juno and rested her head on her lap. Her enormous amber eyes blinked up into Juno's. She let out a small whine. Juno slid from the bed and onto her knees. She covered her ears with her hands and released a high-pitched scream from deep down inside her.

'Miss Petra had me in Fairacre. Mr Hargreaves got her a job at this school so she could bring me here and hide me from the men of Fairacre,' Juno said through choking sobs.

Chax's growl reverberated around the walls of the rooms.

Juno scrunched up her eyes as she pounded the wooden floor. Pins and needles shot to her marks. White-hot pain exploded from her now cramped, hooklike clawed fingers. The tears in her eyes hissed as they turned to steam. The marks on her fingers replicated and expanded into her palms and up over her wrists. More marks replicated and spread up over her arms, onto her shoulders and down her body. Searing heat followed the marks, making Juno gasp. The marks crawled and slithered up her neck and onto her face. She threw her head back and opened her mouth as the guttural roar of a lioness escaped her mouth. Flames sprang from the marks, creating a thin blanket of bright yellow flames that covered her entire body, neck and face. Her shoulder-length hair singed back into short spikes, the tips turning flame-yellow. Juno stood and gaped as the same bright, thin yellow blanket of flame slithered across Chax's tawny coat.

Chax opened her mouth and let out a roar that

Juno felt deep down inside her. Juno raised her hands and looked at the fire as it shimmered across her skin. With a snarl, she lifted her hands and sent a burst of flames into the wardrobe. She turned and sent another burst of fire into the bed, the bedside table and the curtains.

'This place must burn,' Juno growled.

Fire licking down her long white teeth, Chax let out another almighty roar.

Juno left the room and, walking down the corridors, she sent a blanket of slow-moving flames along the walls and ceilings. Each door she passed she kicked in and sent the flames into the rooms, setting everything inside alight. Waves of fire rolled into the dining room, setting tables and chairs on fire. She strode through the rest of the school and, reaching the staircase to the top floors, she directed the fire up into the second and third storeys. Her face contorted with disgust as she walked out of the front door and slammed it closed. She turned and looked up at the inferno that melted what had once been her school.

'Schools will no longer train women for the needs of men,' she said, looking down at the flames that crawled over her body. 'Do you hear me, Chax? Never again.'

The yellow flames lapping over Chax's body shimmered and shone. She opened her mouth and blasted flames at the school doors.

Juno, the fire shimmering across her body, walked down the steps and out of the gate.

Chax, rumbling deep down in her chest, stopped next to Juno and nudged her towards her back.

Juno grabbed the scruff of Chax's neck and, swinging a leg over, she jumped onto her back. 'Back to the camp, Chax. It is time we end the evil of the Lady,' she spat.

CHAPTER 22
FAIRACRE

Juno, riding atop Chax, ambled along the cobble road, then stopped at the village fountain. She closed her eyes and concentrated on extinguishing the flames that lapped over her and Chax's bodies. Opening her eyes, she watched the flames disappear into the marks. Juno curled her sleeves up and traced the thick flame marks that twirled around her forearms.

Chax came to a halt at the end of the cobble road and turned her head back to Juno.

'Probably not a good idea running through the trees with me on your back,' Juno said, hopping off. She rolled down her sleeves and signalled for Chax to move.

Chax leapt from the cobble road, and with a crunch of pine needles she disappeared into the trees. Juno, breathing in the cool air, stretched her legs as the trees whipped past her face. Chax slowed to a walk, then slid down the steep bank to the same small pool of water. Juno slid down the bank, knelt and scooped a handful of water into her mouth, and splashed more over her face. Chax growled and hunched down on her haunches. Her muscles tensed as she snarled at movement across the watering hole. Juno lifted her head and froze. Up the steep bank, a black timber wolf stood with his head lowered. Dark brown eyes, highlighted by the first rays of the rising sun, peered down at her. Juno scooted to her right and rested her hand on Chax's shoulder. Another soft growl, and a second, light brown, wolf joined the black wolf. They stood side by side and stared down at Juno. The black timber wolf snapped his jaws, backed away and disappeared into the trees. The light brown wolf tilted her head at Juno, her brown eyes searching. The wolf stepped back, turned and ran after the black wolf. Juno let her breath go and stared at the space where the wolves had stood. Chax let out a puff. She bent her head and took another drink. When she had finished, she faced south and waited for Juno to finish her drink.

'Let's get to the camp,' Juno said. 'Lead the way.'

Chax sprang up the banks and into the forest.

Juno climbed up the bank and followed Chax through the forest until, through the thinning trees, they saw the glint of the river that flowed to the great waterfall. They broke the tree line and slowed to a walk along the wide expanse of slow-moving water. Chax dipped her paw into the water and let out a disgusted snort.

Juno knelt and took Chax's head in her hands. 'I am going to need you at a moment's notice. So don't stray too far.'

Chax licked Juno across the face, backed away and bounded off into the forest.

Juno turned south and walked along the riverbank. She found the stepping stones, crossed the river and made her way through the trees and into the ruins. Two girls standing at the edge of the ruins stopped their chatting and covered their mouths. Juno strode past and walked to the cooking pot. Girls gawked with wide-eyed, open-mouthed stares.

Gem and Jen, serving breakfast, both took a step back while peering at Juno. 'Hedgehog is back,' Jen said quietly. 'Wild fire child,' Gem said, tilting her head.

Chloe finished her conversation with Alexa, turned and let out a gasp.

'I guess we needn't have worried,' Billy said with a lopsided grin. 'It seems our Juno is doing just fine.'

Chloe reached out her hand and traced a finger along Juno's cheek.

Juno took Chloe's hand in hers and said, 'I am fine, Chloe. We need to talk.'

Chloe flicked her head towards the amphitheatre, her locs bouncing around her shoulders.

'You too, Billy,' Juno said. 'Where is Miles?'

'He is training the weavers,' Billy said.

Still holding Chloe's hand, Juno strode off to the amphitheatre.

'Miles,' Chloe said, walking down between the seats and raising her hand. 'Look who is back.'

Miles, seeing Juno, called a halt to the practice session. He turned and took the thin sword from Janie. 'Let's continue this tomorrow morning. The weavers can have the day off.'

With a shy smile, Janie inclined her head at Miles and signalled for the weavers to leave.

Juno stepped into the circle and faced her three friends. 'It's time we freed Fairacre from that evil woman.'

Chloe held up a hand. 'Slow down, Juno. Where have you been?'

Juno went through the events of the evening. She finished by reciting the note she had found in the desk drawer.

Chloe sat down and ran her hands through her locs. 'Mr Hargreaves and Miss Petra are your parents? I can't believe it. Are you sure you are okay?'

'I will be okay when I get the woman who killed them.'

Billy sat cross-legged in front of Juno. 'I am really sorry to hear about your parents.'

Juno closed her eyes and shook her head. 'I feel better after burning the school down.'

'You burned the school down?' Miles said. 'You sort of left that out, Juno.'

Juno looked at Miles. 'You know what they were doing at that school, Miles.'

Miles sat next to Billy. 'I know, and after spending time with the girls I can see how wrong it is.'

Chloe choked and spluttered.

Juno slapped Chloe on the back and waited for her to stop coughing.

'I never thought I would see the day,' Chloe said, chuckling at Miles.

The corners of Miles's eyes lifted as he smiled.

Chloe placed a hand on Juno's shoulder and spun her round. 'Juno, do you have any idea what you look like?'

Juno scrunched her face up and shook her head.

'Easier to show you,' Miles said, walking over to the practice stand and retrieving his greatsword. The sword sang from its sheath and he held it for Juno to check her reflection in the shiny steel.

Juno ran a finger along the mark that ran from the outside of each eye and onto her cheek. Marks rose from under her jacket and swirled around her neck. Her shoulder-length hair was now short and spiky, the ends dyed a flame-red colour. Juno pushed the greatsword away and, rolling up her sleeve, she spun her forearm to trace the spiralling flame marks.

'I can see now why everyone was staring,' she said.

Chloe rubbed her eyes. 'I still can't stop staring.'

Miles sheathed his greatsword and sat back down. 'What were you going to talk to us about, oh tattooed one?'

'It is time to go and free Fairacre,' Juno said. 'We cannot wait any longer.'

'We have only freed a quarter of the men,' Chloe said.

'The Lady isn't just infecting the women,' Juno said. 'She is stealing them.'

Billy held up a hand. 'What do you mean, stealing?'

'There are no women in the village and the school,' Juno said. 'Where do you think they are?'

'Are we sure they are not in Fairacre?' Miles said.

Chloe shook her head. 'They aren't in Fairacre. We would have seen something when we were searching for Dr Viktor.'

'So where are they?' Billy said, spreading both hands.

'Only thing I can think of is the City of Lynn,' Miles said.

'We need to move now, Chloe,' Juno said. 'If we wait, there will be no women left to save.'

Chloe rested her chin on her hands. 'We don't have enough people. The girls may take on the city guards, but we won't stand a chance against the knife slingers and the Lady.'

'The men have said they won't fight if it means hurting their women,' Miles said, scratching his chin.

'Not to mention if we give the men in the sewers the antidote, they may turn on us,' Billy said.

Juno walked to the centre of the amphitheatre. She spread her hands and waited for the pins and needles.

'Odd,' she said, tilting her head. 'There are no pins and needles or pain.' She brought up visions of Tilly and Miss Petra. The marks darkened and flames rolled out, covering her hands and arms with a thin blanket of yellow. With a tilt of her head, she grinned at Chloe, Billy and Miles as they sat staring.

'I think you can all see I have more control over my abilities,' Juno said.

Miles stepped closer. 'It doesn't hurt anymore?'

'No, it doesn't,' Juno said. 'Don't come any closer, Miles.'

Miles took a few steps back.

'Everything is okay,' Juno said. 'Remember that. Everything is okay.'

'What are you going to do?' Chloe said.

Juno willed the flames up her arms, down her legs and over her torso. She felt the power of Chax, her lioness, flow through her. The flames slid up her neck and covered her face.

Chloe jumped up. 'Juno!'

Juno extinguished the flames over her head and neck. 'Everything is okay, Chloe.'

'Can you stop it now, please?' Chloe said, her eyes wide with worry.

Juno extinguished the rest of the flames, walked over to Chloe and wrapped her arms around her. 'It's okay,' she whispered into her ear.

Chloe squeezed Juno tightly. 'I am sorry. I thought we had lost you earlier.'

Juno squeezed back. 'I am not that easy to get rid of.'

'That's my line,' Chloe said.

Billy cleared his throat and said, 'Did you find out anything about Tilly?'

Juno knelt, reached into her jacket and pulled out the pink book. 'This is her journal. You can keep it and give it to her when we get her back.'

'She is alive, isn't she?' Billy said, taking the book from Juno.

'Yes, Billy,' Juno said. 'That is why we move on Fairacre tomorrow.'

'I know the girls will be ready. I have serious reservations about the men, though,' Miles said.

'Time to go and have a chat with them, then,' Juno said. 'Chloe, can you get the girls to the men's camp?'

'Of course.'

On the way up the steps, Juno turned to Miles. 'Chax and I ran into timber wolves on our way back from the village.'

Miles frowned. 'It's a bit early in the year to see timber wolves in the forest.'

'What would bring them to the south?'

'Hunting,' Miles said. 'If they cannot find food in the east, they cross to the south.'

'It's the black snow,' Billy said.

Miles pursed his lips. 'If it is the black snow, that is a major concern.'

Billy shook his head and muttered under his breath.

They hopped from rock to rock across the river. Juno pulled her sleeves down and pulled her hoodie over her head. The men turned and stared as the group entered the temporary camp.

'Go to the back of the camp near the cliffs,' Miles said. 'There is a flat outcrop of rocks you and Chloe can stand on.'

Juno, ignoring the whispers and murmurs, walked to the outcrop of rock, climbed up and watched Miles and Billy herding the men towards her. Through the trees that surrounded the camp, the sewer rats appeared and stood on the left side of the rocky outcrop. Chloe, walking through the camp, spoke quiet words to the confused men. She climbed up and signalled for Miles and Billy to join her. They stood together in a line along the rocky outcrop.

Chloe whistled, asking for quiet. 'We have just received information that has us very concerned. We have reports that the Lady may move your loved ones away from Fairacre.'

Wide eyes and worried looks followed hisses and murmurs. Arthur lifted a hand. 'Where are they taking them?'

'We don't know,' Chloe said. 'We were planning to send spies, but we have decided to move on Fairacre tomorrow.'

A chorus of shouts erupted from the crowd of men.

Miles stepped forwards, wagged a finger and yelled, 'Silence!' The camp, falling deathly silent, looked up at Miles.

A rotund man raised his chin. 'We will not follow this woman to our deaths. An attack on Fairacre is suicide.'

With a furrowed brow, Miles said, 'You will not follow the very woman that has freed you from this infection?'

His lip curling, the man said, 'It is a woman that has created this infection in the first place.'

Miles, taking a step forwards, said, 'This woman does not discriminate. She is targeting both men and women. Let me not remind you of the past actions of evil men, sir.'

The man lowered his chin and shook his head.

'It is still suicide, miss,' Arthur said. 'How do you propose that we take on the Lady, Fairacre guard and the city soldiers?'

Murmurs echoed through the camp as men bent their heads and whispered their agreements to each other.

'We will defeat them, but we need your help,' Chloe said. 'You need to stand by us and fight.'

Snorts and huffs replaced the murmuring and whispers.

The rotund man lifted his chin again. 'You expect us to believe that your so-called sewer rats can take on trained guards? This is madness.'

Juno stepped forwards and rested her hand on Chloe's forearm. 'Clear the podium.'

Chloe nodded, then jumped off the rock, with Miles and Billy close behind.

The rotund man threw his hands up in the air. 'Why are we listening to this child? Is she going to scare away the soldiers with her face paint?'

Laughter broke out in waves among the men.

Juno, her voice even and measured, said, 'You will only have to deal with the Fairacre guards. We will deal with the city soldiers and the Lady.'

The men's laughter grew louder. 'You are a child. What would you know about fighting men?' the man said.

Juno lifted her hands and gently sent them alight. Men gasped and pointed while covering their mouths and shaking their heads.

'What is this witchery?' the man said, taking a step back.

'Silence,' Miles hollered, his lip curling.

Her patience running out, Juno whispered Chax's name. The padding of paws sounded behind her. She extended her hand to the left and waited until she felt the top of Chax's head. The rotund man's mouth opened and shut. Wide-eyed men around him took steps backwards, pointing and hissing.

Arthur looked at Miles. 'What is this demon child and her beast?'

'Kill that beast,' a man at the back shouted.

Miles climbed to the top of the outcrop and walked over to Juno. He knelt and held out a hand to Chax.

'Don't go all shy on me now,' Juno said, nudging Chax. 'Go on.'

Miles reached out and scratched Chax behind her ears.

Chax purred and butted her head against Miles's hand.

Miles stood and faced the men. 'Juno and Chax are on our side. They are here to help free your loved ones. We will be moving tomorrow at first light. With or without you.'

Chax faced the men, curled her lip in a snarl and showed her sharp white teeth. Juno placed a hand on Chax's head and increased the flames from her hands onto Chax. Flames licked over Chax's head and over her teeth.

'I will be taking care of the Lady. The girls will take care of the city guard. All we need from you is to take on the Fairacre guard,' Juno said, gazing down at the men.

Chax opened her mouth the rest of the way and roared. Fiery heat blasted out at the men. Juno extinguished the flames from her hands. Chax snorted, shook her head, turned and bounded down the rocks into the forest.

'We will free your loved ones,' Chloe said to the men. 'You either help or stay here and wait.'

Juno hopped off the rocks, walked over to Chloe and embraced her. 'I am going back to the camp to eat and sleep.'

Chloe ruffled Juno's spikey hair. 'We will stay here and get things organised.'

Juno left the loud chattering of the camp behind her. She entered camp, grabbed a bowl of stew and bread, and went straight to her tent. Her laces undone, she kicked off her boots and sank onto the hay bed. Tiredness crept over her as she finished her bowl of food. With a yawn, she placed the bowl on the floor, curled up and fell asleep.

Chloe smiled at her friend. 'About time you showed yourself.'

A wide grin stretched across Juno's face. 'I haven't slept so peacefully in a long time.'

Chloe passed Juno a bowl of food. 'Miles and Billy are in the temporary camp getting things ready.'

'The men have agreed?'

'Miles brought them around. He will be an influential leader one day.'

'How are we doing here?' Juno said.

'Our teams are always ready. The weavers, Gem and Jen will sit this one out.'

'Valen?' Juno said.

Chloe instinctively placed her hand on the small device that sat in her ear. A shadow of worry creased across her face. 'He has had to share his essence for the devices. He is asleep in our tent.'

'Have we got enough devices?' Juno said.

Chloe nodded. 'There are enough. Let's hope that this is the last time we will need them.'

'It will be,' Juno said. She finished her bowl of stew and handed it back to a scowling Jen.

'Hedgehog better get our home back,' Jen said.

'Rat stew for hedgehog if she fails,' Gem said, a sly grin stretching across her face.

'Get, you two,' Chloe said, shooing them away. 'Go on, get.'

'It's time,' Juno said. 'Let's get going.'

Chloe turned and gave Alexa the signal. Alexa turned and signalled for the girls to move. The girls silently melted into the tree line. Juno jogged behind Chloe to the men's camp, where rows of men waited with Miles and Billy. Murmurs escaped the men's mouths as the girls, dressed in black with faces covered, moved through the camp.

Miles turned to Chloe. 'We will follow. Keep it at a steady pace or we will lose most of the men before we get there.'

Chloe moved to the front of the group and led them out of the camp and onto the cliffs. She kept to a slow jog down through the valley and up to the tree line. The unattended fields of wheat swayed in the wind. Chloe turned to Juno. 'Where is Chax?'

'The Lady wants us together. Chax won't risk us both getting caught. She will come if I call or if it's necessary.'

Chloe nodded. She looked to her left and right, then gave the signal to advance. The girls melted into the wheat fields. Close behind, the men, led by Miles and Billy, entered the wheat fields in their designated lines. Juno looked to the east and smiled at the red glow of fire as the sun began to make its entrance over the land of Fairacre. At the last line of wheat, Chloe brought everyone to a halt with a raise of her hand.

Juno peered over the bank. 'A lot more guards from the City of Lynn.'

'No doubt more knife slingers,' Chloe said.

Juno rested a hand on Chloe's shoulder. 'Advance when you see the signal.'

'What signal?'

Juno let go of Chloe's shoulder and stepped out of the wheat field. She stood on the path, with the drawbridge leading to the south entrance in front of her.

'Who goes there?' a guard shouted from across the bridge. Juno, tilting her head to one side, gave the guards a wave.

Shouts from the guards brought more soldiers down through the market district.

'What are you doing?' Chloe hissed from the bank.

Juno unclipped her Jo and extended it with a snap. She took a deep breath and, jogging forwards, she extended it in front of her. At the drawbridge she broke into a sprint, jabbed her Jo into the ground and flicked herself into the air. The marks across her body rippled a deep yellow as the flames covered her entire body in a thin blanket. Juno landed on one knee and slammed her Jo into the ground. A wave of rippling fire blanketed the ground towards the guards. The guards scattered up the southern street and into the alleys. The carpet of flames engulfed the market stalls, setting them ablaze. Juno, hearing Chloe's war cry, extinguished the carpet of flames as she sprinted forwards. With the carpet of flames gone, the guards poured back out onto the southern street. Steel on steel shattered the quiet Fairacre morning as guards engaged the sewer rats and men. Juno extinguished the fire that surrounded her, ran up the southern street and blasted fireballs into the alley to keep the guards at bay. At her side, Chloe and Miles joined her as she sprinted towards the town hall. They entered the town square and slid to a halt. Atop the steps, two men stood in long, flowing cloaks, their hands clasped behind them.

'Knife slingers,' Miles said.

Juno stepped forwards, raised a palm, conjured a fireball and blew it at the knife slingers. Smiles stretching across their faces, they moved to one side and let the fireball explode against the town hall wall. With a fluid movement they reached under their cloaks and flung small, twisted black daggers at Juno, Chloe and Miles. Chloe's two blades whirled in front of her, deflecting the daggers harmlessly away. The knife slingers sprang from the top steps and drew their long, thin twin swords. Juno changed tactic and rained a wave of small fireballs at the knife slingers. Criss-crossing their thin swords, the knife slingers chanted, sending a black, smoky mist over their weapons. The fireballs struck and dissipated into nothingness.

'Time to do this the old-fashioned way,' Miles said.

Chloe stepped forwards and stood shoulder to shoulder with Miles. 'Let's see how well you have taught me, O sword master.'

Twin swords singing, greatsword howling, Chloe and Miles engaged the knife slingers, weaving, dodging and slashing in perfect harmony. Juno moved away from the fight and ran towards the town hall. At the bottom of the steps, she stopped as the town hall doors slammed open.

The Lady stepped out and glared down at Juno. 'Have you brought the cat to me?'

Juno pointed her Jo at the Lady. 'No, and this ends now. Your time here has come to an end.'

The Lady threw her head back and laughed a deep and throaty laugh. Her lip curling and her Jo spinning, Juno let loose a roar of flame that jumped out of each end of her Jo and sizzled and popped towards the Lady.

'Enough,' the Lady said, slamming her hands together.

A shock wave slammed into Juno's flames and put them out.

'Where is she?' the Lady said, tilting her head. 'Where is that fire beast?'

Juno climbed a step. 'She is not here. She will never be yours.'

The Lady snarled. 'Then I will end you and find her myself.'

Juno turned the marks across her body a brilliant yellow and set herself alight.

The Lady took a step backwards. 'This cannot be.'

Juno climbed another step. 'Why are you taking the women? What are you doing with them?'

The Lady took another step backwards. She turned her head to the town hall doors. 'Come to me, my children.'

Juno's school friends exited the town hall, and with hollow black and white eyes they surrounded the Lady. Juno extinguished the flames that surrounded her. 'Tilly,' she said, her voice barely a whisper.

The Lady curled her hand around Tilly's throat. A twisted black dagger extended out of her other hand. 'Come no closer, fire child, or I will end your friend.'

'Let them go,' Juno said, her face contorting in anger.

'We are leaving,' the Lady said, tilting her head towards the eastern gate. 'I am finished in Fairacre.'

Walking up the steps, Juno balled her hands into fists and with a pop she exploded into flames.

The Lady tightened the dagger against Tilly's throat. 'Look around you, young fire child. Soon your pathetic band of sisters will be no longer.'

Juno hesitated, extinguished the flames around her and glanced over her shoulder. To the left, Chloe and Miles, their backs hard against a wall, battled the knife slingers. A long, angry gash on Miles's left side slowed his sword movements. Chloe, her mouth set in a grimace, hacked and slashed with no control. To Juno's right, rows of fallen men lay alive but wide-eyed, holding their sides.

Juno faced the Lady. 'What do you want?'

'We are going to the City of Lynn, and you will not follow today. If you follow, I will end your friend and the schoolgirls.'

'I will come for Tilly,' Juno said. 'You know I will.'

'I am counting on it,' the Lady said, walking down the steps. The schoolgirls surrounded the Lady, their hollow black and white eyes never leaving Juno.

'Stop the soldiers from fighting,' Juno said.

The Lady waved her hand and murmured a command. The two knife slingers disengaged and whistled. The guards broke off their attacks and ran for the eastern gate. The shouts and screams of fighting died down. The groans and cries of men whispered through the air. Juno watched the Lady, Tilly, her school friends and the city guards march towards the exit.

'Juno,' Billy said, running past her. 'She has Tilly.'

Juno grabbed Billy's wrist. 'She will kill her if we follow, Billy.'

'We can't just let her take Tilly,' Billy said, pulling at her hand.

Juno pulled Billy into an embrace and whispered into his ear. 'We will get her, Billy. I promise you that. We will get her back.'

CHAPTER 23
COLD AND EMPTY

'Alexa, close the drawbridges, please,' Chloe said, standing on the steps in front of the town hall.

Alexa signalled orders at the girls, who ran down the streets towards the exits.

'Billy, use the library as a hospital,' Chloe said. 'There should be enough tables in there that we can use as beds.'

Billy bounded up the steps to the library.

'Alexa, take a team and bring Valen and the weavers to Fairacre. The weavers can help with the wounded.'

Alexa sprinted down the southern street with a team of girls.

'Miles, take the antidote. Begin freeing the remaining men in the sewers. Valen will bring the bulk of the antidote with the weavers.'

Miles bounded up the steps after Billy to get the small pack of antidote that Billy carried.

'Arthur, grab as many farmers as possible and tend to the fields. We need to fill our stores in case the City of Lynn retaliates.'

'Yes, miss,' Arthur said, hurrying down the town hall steps.

Juno, standing to one side, smiled as she watched Chloe take control of Fairacre's needs.

A man standing in the square lifted his hand and said, 'Anything we can do, miss?'

Chloe thought for a second. 'Take a group of men and rebuild the market district. We will use it to share out provisions.'

The man signalled to a group of men, who then walked down the southern street.

'There is nobody here,' a man said, rubbing his hands together. 'The houses are empty. Cold and empty.'

Chloe turned to Juno. 'We are too late.'

Juno walked up to Chloe. 'You cannot blame yourself for this. We came as soon as we knew.'

Chloe's brow furrowed. 'They are in the City of Lynn. Why have they stolen all the women?'

Juno turned and eyed the doors of the town hall. 'I am going to go and search the hall. The Lady spent most of her time in there.'

Chloe gave Juno a nod.

The doors of the town hall creaked open. Juno stepped into the dim light and scrunched up her nose at the rows of crumpled blankets that lined the walls of the hall – temporary bedding for the infected women. At the front of the hall, one table stood on a raised stage. Juno climbed the steps onto the stage and sat in front of a thick book. Columns of women's names written in perfectly formed handwriting filled the page. There was a tick or a cross next to each of the names. Juno flipped a page and took in a sharp breath as she traced her finger down the names of the girls from her school. The second-to-last name was Tilly's.

'What are they doing with the women?' Juno said, flipping another page. 'Why have you taken my Tilly?' She flipped the pages back one by one until she found a heading: 'The South'. Juno flipped further back to find more lists of names in neat columns and rows. Another heading had been written in the same bold letters as the previous heading: 'The East'. Each name for the eastern lands had no tick or cross against it. Juno flipped to the first page of the book, then turned to the next page, revealing another heading: 'The West'. Juno sat back in her chair and tapped her chin with her flame-marked finger.

Chloe's boots echoed through the town hall.

'They are taking women from every region,' Juno said with a shake of her head. 'It's not just Fairacre.'

'Every woman?' Chloe said, pulling up a chair.

Juno flipped another page. 'All of them. The Lady started in the south, by the looks of these marks. The other regions don't have marks yet.'

Chloe ran a hand through her locs. 'No clue as to why they are taking them?'

'No. She has just listed the regions and the names,' Juno said. 'I cannot see any order to things.'

'Dr Viktor may have some kind of answer,' Chloe said. 'Miles is looking for him.'

Shouts bounced through the town hall doors and echoed off the walls.

Juno closed the book and pushed her chair out. 'Now what?'

Chloe led the way through the town hall and out into the sunshine. Miles stood at the top of the steps, a hand raised, calling for calm.

'What is going on, Miles?' Chloe said, running her eyes over the growing group of men.

'The men from the sewers are demanding answers,' Miles said. 'As soon as we give them the antidote, they run to their homes searching for their loved ones and they find nobody.'

Chloe stepped forwards and blasted an ear-piercing whistle.

As the chattering died down, a man stepped forwards and said, 'What have you done with our wives? Our children?'

Chloe tilted her head at the well-dressed man. 'What is your name, sir?'

'My name is Leonard. I am the treasurer of Fairacre,' he said, puffing his chest out. 'And I demand answers. Where are our women?'

'The Lady has taken your loved ones to the City of Lynn,' Chloe said.

Leonard frowned, then shook his head. 'Why would she take our women to the City of Lynn? Where is Mr Hargreaves?'

At the mention of his name, Juno winced as the pain jumped through her heart.

'He is no longer with us,' Chloe said. 'The Lady murdered him.'

The pain in Juno's heart dissolved.

Leonard's mouth dropped open. 'I do not believe you. Stand down, lady. As second in line, I will take over from here.'

Her eyes narrowing, Chloe walked down the steps and stood inches from Leonard. 'How do you propose we get your loved ones back, Leonard? I assume you have a plan.'

Leonard lifted his chin. 'I will send an emissary requesting the return of our women.'

'Out of my way,' Arthur said, pushing through the crowd. 'Leonard, is that you?'

'Arthur,' Leonard said, turning and smiling. 'My old friend. How are you?'

Arthur walked up to Leonard and shook his hand. 'I am well, my friend. I see you have met the ladies who have freed Fairacre.'

Leonard blinked, then looked at Chloe, then back at Arthur.

'Yes, my friend. The Lady infected and stole our wives, mothers and daughters. She infected us too, but these ladies have freed us from her poison.'

Leonard snorted. 'I hardly believe that this lady is responsible for freeing the entire town of Fairacre, Arthur.'

'It is true, Leonard,' Arthur said. 'Chloe has taken command and her teams of sewer rats have freed us.'

Leonard's head bobbed angrily. 'You know it is not a lady's place to take command, Arthur.'

'Do you want to tell them otherwise?' Arthur said.

'I do not have to tell them otherwise. I will take over the running of Fairacre from this point forward.'

'Take over if you wish, Leonard,' Chloe said, taking a step back and placing her hands on her hips.

Murmurs whispered out from the men in the town square.

Leonard, his face turning red, snarled at the men. 'What are you whispering about? You know I am next in line to lead.'

Miles walked down the steps, stood next to Chloe and looked at Leonard. 'What are your orders, Leonard?'

Leonard opened his mouth, then shut it again as his face turned a deeper red.

'Who will you send as an emissary to the City of Lynn?' Miles said, his eyes narrowing. 'Is it not the leader of the town of Fairacre who travels to the City of Lynn?'

Leonard spluttered. 'I will choose whoever I see fit.'

Miles took a step closer to Leonard and crossed his arms. 'Make your choice, Leonard. The people of Fairacre are waiting.'

The men spoke in hushed tones as they looked on expectantly.

'Leonard, the men are not happy,' Arthur said. 'Maybe we should ask them what they think.'

Leonard's jaw twitched. 'How dare you speak to me like this! The town of Fairacre is mine to lead.'

'We get a say,' a man shouted from the back of the town square. 'We get to choose,' a man with cap in hand said.

Miles nodded to Chloe and walked up the steps. Chloe followed Miles and stood next to him.

'Let's see what the men have to say, Leonard,' Miles said, beckoning him to the top of the steps.

Leonard cursed, balled his hands into fists and stalked up the steps, where he turned and shouted, 'What is wrong with you? Everybody knows I was to lead this town if something was to happen to Mr Hargreaves.'

A man stepped forwards, removed his cap and inclined his head in a small bow. 'Leonard,' he said. 'I have sent two daughters to the schools above the cliffs. I have seen how it destroyed my wife. Watching them leave destroyed me too. I no longer want to send my daughters away.'

The crowd erupted into a chorus of shouts and cheers.

Leonard snarled down at the crowd. 'It is so because the City of Lynn says it should be.'

'The City of Lynn has stolen our women, taken our food and taken our fine weaver's clothes,' a man shouted. 'And for what? So we can live in drabness? So we can live eating leftovers? So we can lose our daughters?'

Leonard puffed out his chest and slammed a fist into his hand. 'We need to teach our women how to serve. They are inferior.'

A deathly silence descended on the Fairacre town square.

A man stepped forwards, his face contorted in a snarl. 'How dare you speak of my wife so? How dare you, Leonard?'

Leonard stared over to the west side of the town square, where a group of well-dressed men from the northern district stood in silence. 'Will you not help me?' he screamed. 'This is preposterous.'

A well-dressed man lifted his chin and said, 'They have taken my wife and daughters. I wish them returned to me.'

Leonard's mouth hung open, his lips stretched in a thin line as he shook with anger.

Juno stepped forwards and cleared her throat. The men swung round and fell silent as she spoke. 'At school, my mother would hold a vote. A vote to determine what the majority of our school members wanted. I suggest we hold such a vote now.'

The men in the square nodded. 'If it pleases the lady, we would like to vote.'

'All in favour of following Leonard in the old ways, raise your hands,' Miles said.

Leonard lifted his hand high into the air.

'All in favour of following Chloe in hope of a new way, raise your hands.' One by one, the men in the centre lifted their hands into the air. The men from the northern district kept their hands pressed to their sides.

'It's decided,' Miles said. 'We work together with Chloe to rebuild Fairacre and to retrieve our loved ones.'

Leonard growled under his breath as he turned to walk away.

'Stay,' Chloe said, placing a hand on Leonard's shoulder.

Leonard shrugged his shoulder to remove Chloe's hand. 'What do you want?' he said, his lip curling.

Chloe faced the men in the square. 'I will form a Fairacre council. You will choose a representative from each area of Fairacre's district's to sit on this council.'

A girl whistled from a rooftop east of the square.

'Soldiers to the east,' Chloe said.

'Do what you need to do here,' Juno said to Chloe. 'Miles, let's go and have a look.'

They jumped down the town hall steps and sprinted along the eastern street. At the eastern gate, they climbed the steps and stood on the wall.

'Where are they?' Juno said, peering out over the moat.

'They appeared in the orchards, miss,' the girl said.

Miles walked up to Juno and placed a hand above his eyes. 'I see movement. I think they are just observing.'

'Why would they come back if they have all the women?' the girl said.

'Fairacre is its primary source of food,' Miles said. 'And, of course, we have young Juno here, who everyone seems to want.'

Juno placed her hand over her eyes. 'I count six.'

'A scouting party,' Miles said. 'We need to get back to Chloe and report.'

Juno placed a hand on the sewer rat's forearm. 'If they come any closer, come and get us. Make sure we spread the word to all guards on the walls.'

'Yes, miss,' the girl said.

Juno jumped off the roof and joined Miles along the eastern street. 'Do you think they will attack us?'

'If they run out of food, they will. But they will need a bigger army than just a few scouts,' Miles said.

'What do you think of Chloe taking the lead?'

'She has proven herself,' Miles said, placing his hands behind his back as he walked. 'The men will follow. What happens when we finish all of this will be another story. The men of the northern district will want to go back to the old ways.'

Reaching the steps, Juno watched Chloe speak to the men about selecting council members.

'Leonard,' Chloe said. 'I would like you to take a seat on the council as treasurer.'

Leonard frowned, then shook his head in confusion. 'You want me to be on the council?'

Chloe nodded. 'You will count the coffers and report to the council.'

Leonard stood in shocked amazement.

'Well?' Chloe said.

'I am not sure that is a good idea,' Leonard said, glancing over at the well dressed men.

'You heard what the people want,' Chloe said.

Leonard threw another glance at the well-dressed men, sighed, then shuffled off to the town hall entrance.

Miles walked up the steps and stood next to Chloe.

Chloe leaned in closely. 'Trouble at the gate?'

'For now there is nothing to worry about,' Miles said.

Chloe then turned to the men. 'Miles will be my deputy. He will take control of the Fairacre guards while working with Alexa. Alexa will take command of the sewer rats.'

'Lass,' Valen hollered from the southern street, 'what is going on here?' The men in the town square fell silent, then parted to let Valen through. A wide grin spread across Chloe's face as she ran down the steps.

'How are things?' Chloe said, embracing Valen.

'He hasn't been quiet the entire journey,' Janie said.

Valen ruffled Janie's hair. 'I recall you chatting away too, young weaver.'

Janie lowered her head, a shy smile spreading across her face.

'So what is going on here?' Valen said. 'Has anyone given you any trouble?'

'No. Everything is fine, love,' Chloe said. 'We have been working through our next steps.'

Valen's eyebrows shot up into his hair. 'Are you sure none of these men have caused any problems?'

Chloe embraced him again and whispered into his ear, 'No, everything is fine. The Lady has gone, so can you please take back your essence now?'

'Where are the women?' Valen said, gazing across the town square.

'I am finished here. Can we go to your shop? I will fill you in over a nice cup of tea,' Chloe said.

Miles walked through the crowd of men. 'Go. I will make sure the work continues in the town.'

Chloe glanced at Juno and flicked her head towards the manufacturing district. Juno walked down the steps and followed Chloe and Valen to the arts and crafts shop. The familiar tinkle of the bell above the door, ripped open by Valen, brought a grin to Juno's face. Chloe collapsed onto the couch and swung her leg over the armrest.

Juno sat next to Chloe and let out a deep sigh. 'That was all very formal.'

Chloe rolled her eyes, then elbowed Juno. 'Took a leaf out of Naomi's book. I don't know how she did it. I am so tired.'

'Here you go, ladies,' Valen said, holding cups of steaming tea. 'Tell me everything or I will set Little Henry on you both.'

Chloe chuckled at Juno's worried face, then ran through the events of the morning, stopping only to answer Valen's questions.

'The Lady took the women to the City of Lynn,' Chloe said. 'The last of them were Juno's school friends, and Tilly was with them.'

Valen's faced creased with worry as he looked at Juno. 'Are you okay, lass?'

'I know where she is and I am going to go and get her,' Juno said.

'You want to go to the City of Lynn? Alone? That is not going to happen, Juno,' Valen said, raising his hand.

'How else are we going to get Tilly and the women back, Valen?'

Valen shook his head and sighed. 'The City of Lynn is huge, lass. You may get in, but it will take you days to find them.'

Juno clasped her hands together and traced the deep red marks along her fingers. A knock sounded at the front door. Valen heaved his enormous frame out of his office chair, lumbered over to the door and yanked it open.

'Boys,' Valen said, his voice rattling the windows. 'Come in, come in. The ladies are in the office drinking tea.'

'Valen,' Billy said. 'Good to see you again.'

'Have you found Dr Viktor?' Valen said as he walked into the kitchen to get the boy tea.

'No,' Miles said. 'We still have people searching the sewers.'

Valen returned with mugs of tea. 'Here you go, gentlemen.'

Billy and Miles, both standing, accepted the tea with an incline of their heads. Valen reached to the side of his desk and pulled out two folding chairs. He unfolded them and placed them on either side of the couch.

Billy, frowning, cocked his head to one side at the girls. 'What is the matter with you two? Your faces would scare children.'

Chloe playfully punched Billy on the leg. 'Just the minor issue of getting the women back from the City of Lynn.'

Miles grunted. 'I have been thinking about that.'

Juno and Chloe swung round and stared at Miles. Chloe's bouncing leg came to a halt.

'Speak, boy,' Valen said, slapping Miles on the back.

Miles spluttered tea down his front. 'Thanks, Valen,' he said, pulling out a cloth and dabbing his top.

'Well, Miles?' Chloe said.

'You might not like what I say,' Miles said, glancing at Juno.

A smile crept across Juno's face. 'Bait again?'

Miles tilted his head and grunted in surprise. 'Yes. Bait again.'

'No way,' Chloe said, sitting forwards. 'We cannot keep using our friend as some disposable item.'

'Let's hear Miles out, Chloe. We don't have to agree with what he says,' Billy said.

Chloe sat back and folded her arms. 'Go on, then.'

'The issue is simple,' Miles said. 'We cannot go into the City of Lynn. So we bring the City of Lynn out to us.'

'The City of Lynn has an entire army, Miles. The knife slingers are just a small part of the queen's guard. We have no idea what other type of fighters she has. And what about the thousands of soldiers in the normal army?' Chloe said, sitting forwards again.

'We trade,' Juno said. 'Myself and Chax for the women of Fairacre.'

Chloe jerked her head back in surprise. 'Well, that isn't very smart. What is the point of giving all of that power to the Lady?'

'We trade but we don't trade,' Billy said with a lopsided grin.

'We trade but we don't trade,' Miles said, smiling.

Chloe, her brows creasing, sat forwards. 'Are you suggesting we fight?'

'Can you rather pace than this sitting backwards and forwards?' Billy said, shaking his head.

Valen erupted into laughter while slapping his thigh.

Chloe sat back again and folded her arms. 'Well? Are you suggesting we fight?'

'Yes, Chloe. We fight, but with one goal. We rid the world of the Lady.'

'That will release the women from the infection,' Juno said.

'With the Lady gone, the women get to choose,' Miles said.

Valen slapped Miles on the back, sending another wave of tea into his shirt. 'Miles giving women a choice. May the realms speak of this day forevermore.'

Chloe put her hand over her mouth to stifle a laugh. 'Don't let Dr Viktor hear you say that, Miles. He will cough himself into the next life.'

Miles's smile widened as he dabbed his shirt with an already tea-soaked cloth.

'I suggest we call our first council meeting,' Juno said. 'There is a lot to discuss.'

'Arthur and a group of men are setting up the town hall,' Billy said. 'They are getting rid of the blankets and cleaning.'

Chloe stood. 'I will send word that we meet tomorrow afternoon. Let us take the rest of the day to rest.'

The next afternoon, Juno pushed the door open and walked into the town hall. A long table with high-backed chairs sat in the middle of the hall. Chloe, sitting at the head of the table, beckoned Juno over to the empty seat next to her. The town hall door slammed open and Leonard bustled in, holding overflowing files of paper. He sat down and dumped the files onto the table.

Chloe cleared her throat. 'Our council is missing members from the entertainment district and the trader's district. The men will select them in due course.'

Arthur nodded. 'I will see that it's done, miss.'

Chloe turned to the rest of the table. 'We are here today to discuss two things. One, the day-to-day activities of Fairacre. And two, how we get our loved ones back. Arthur, you can begin. How are we doing with food?'

Arthur cleared his throat. 'Yes, miss. We are in the last stages of the wheat harvest, and we will complete the market district rebuild by the end of the week.'

'Will we have enough food for the winter?' Miles said.

'Ample,' Arthur said.

'And that is without the orchards.' Chloe then turned to Janie. 'What of the weavers?'

Janie turned a bright red. 'We are creating winter clothes for everyone in the town and have started mending the girl's clothing.'

Alexa raised a hand. 'Miles and I will work with Janie to design and create the clothes for the Fairacre soldiers.'

'Thank you, Janie,' Chloe said. 'Leonard, your report?'

'Yes. Well, yes,' Leonard said, shuffling papers across the table. 'It seems our coffers in the northern district are intact. The Lady did not touch them.'

Chloe looked through her eyebrows. 'And what of the coins hidden in the houses in the northern district?'

Leonard's mouth dropped open. 'Yes, miss,' he said, shuffling his papers. 'According to my records, they have earned the coins through legal trade, miss.'

Chloe grunted. 'Understand that we know there are coins there, Leonard. We will delve into the matter at a later date.'

Leonard closed his mouth and gave Chloe a nod.

'Anything else on the topic of rebuilding Fairacre?' Chloe said.

'What are we going to do about the orchards, miss?' Arthur said.

'That leads us nicely into our next topic,' Chloe said, smiling at Arthur. 'Miles, if you please.'

Miles gave Chloe a sharp nod. 'We will make a plan to rid the world of the Lady, which will free our loved ones from her infection. We will need to go to the orchards soon to rid them of the scouts. For now, we require that the men of Fairacre start soldier training immediately.'

A pile of files dropped from the table and clattered onto the floor. Leonard, his eyes wide, said, 'You cannot suggest that all of us become soldiers.'

Alexa lifted her chin. 'Are you suggesting that the responsibility of Fairacre's forces falls to the girls?'

'No, no, of course not,' Leonard said, picking his files up from under the table. 'Most men in this town are farmers, artisans and traders. I cannot see them turning into soldiers.'

'Arthur, what do you think?' Miles said, turning his gaze on him.

'The farmers and artisans we should have no problem with. The traders from the northern district and entertainers from the western district will be more difficult.'

'Leonard, how do you feel about training to be a soldier?' Chloe said, her elbows on the table.

Leonard's face turned pink as he stared, unmoving, at Chloe. He shook his head and said, 'I have never tried. I am not a fighter.'

'You will lead by example if you do try,' Chloe said, smiling. 'And you will have excellent teachers.'

'I suppose,' Leonard said, patting the sides of his files so they moved into a neat pile. 'If you think it is necessary.'

'It will be necessary if we wish to return our loved ones,' Miles said.

A loud rap sounded on the town hall doors. 'Come, please,' Chloe shouted.

A girl swung open the door, jogged over to Alexa and whispered in her ear. 'More soldiers in the orchards,' Alexa said.

Chloe scraped her chair back. 'I am adjourning this meeting. We will continue discussions at the next meeting.'

Juno followed Chloe out of the town hall, with Alexa and Miles close behind. The street leading to the eastern gate, bathed in brilliant autumn sunshine, echoed with the noises of men moving food and materials in carts and shoulder bags.

Juno climbed the steps to the top of the wall and placed her hand across her brow. 'More teams,' she said. 'They are getting bolder.'

'We count three teams, miss,' a girl said.

'Are there teams near the other gates?' Chloe said.

'No, miss, every team makes their way to the orchard.'

'It is excellent cover,' Miles said.

'Do you think there is more than we can see?' Juno asked.

'I have no doubt,' Chloe said.

Miles folded his arms and narrowed his eyes. 'It is time to execute the other step of our plan.'

CHAPTER 24
A MESSAGE SENT

Juno crouched on the eastern wall with her eyes set solidly on the orchards. Flickers of flame flashed as the soldiers stoked their cooking fires.

'More soldiers came through this morning, miss,' Alexa said to Juno.

'What about knife slingers?' Juno said, squinting to get a better look.

'None,' Alexa said. 'But we can only see so far into the orchard.'

Juno stood, leaned over the concrete wall and ran an eye over the moat. 'Winter is nearly here, and this moat will freeze over.'

'I think that is what they are waiting for, miss,' Alexa said, peering over the wall.

'They will still need to get over the bridge and through the gates.'

'Then it becomes a numbers game,' Alexa said. 'If more soldiers from the City of Lynn arrive, we might be in trouble.'

Juno placed a hand on her brow and continued searching the orchard.

'What is that black cloud to the north, miss?' Alexa said,

throwing her hand over her eyes. 'I have seen it for a few years now.'

Juno lifted her gaze to the north. 'Dr Viktor spoke of machines in the city that thrust out large plumes of black smoke.'

Alexa shook her head. 'I would hate to live underneath that.'

'Yes, I agree,' Juno said. 'It's noon. We'd best get back to the council meeting.'

The rooftops flew under their feet as they ran and jumped their way to the town hall. Juno skidded to a halt seconds behind Alexa. Alexa stood with her hands on her hips, peering over the roof into the town square. A group of elaborately dressed northern district men huddled and whispered in the far corner.

Juno frowned. 'They haven't lifted a finger since we freed Fairacre.'

'The girls stay away from them, miss,' Alexa said. 'Those men do not say kind words.'

Juno grunted, jumped off the roof and rolled into the square. The men turned and stared as Juno walked up the steps and into the town hall.

'Juno, Alexa,' Chloe said from across the table. 'We have been waiting for you.'

Juno made her way to the seat next to Chloe.

Chloe called the council to order. The members reported on the daily achievements and issues, ending with Arthur giving everyone the good news that the fields were harvested.

'Thank you, Arthur,' Chloe said, nodding her head in his direction. 'What of the plans to get our loved ones back?' she said, turning to Miles.

Miles leaned out of his chair, picked up a roll of parchment and spread it across the table. 'Billy found a map in the library. It is of the area to the south of the City of Lynn.'

Juno, Chloe and Alexa stood and leaned over the worn brown map.

Miles traced his finger from left to right along the great river that ran below the city. 'See this horseshoe section of land here?' he said, tapping his finger north of the river. 'Does that look like a forest to you?'

'A forest on a hill,' Juno said, bending down to get a closer look. 'The river has wound itself into a horseshoe around the hill.'

Miles then tapped his finger right off the horseshoe. 'This is the only bridge that joins the south to the City of Lynn.'

'Do we know anybody that's been to that bridge?' Chloe said.

Leonard cleared his throat and slowly raised his hand.

Chloe beckoned him over. 'Where on this map have you been, Leonard?'

Leonard walked over and squinted at the map. 'I have travelled the road over the bridge and to the city.'

'What about this area?' Miles said, tapping his finger on the horseshoe area.

'It is a hill with a thick forest,' Leonard said. 'It's very dark in there.'

Miles folded his arms and tapped his chin with his finger. 'Perfect place for our defence,' he said. 'Now all we need to do is organise how we trade Juno for the ladies.'

Chloe sat down and shook her head. 'I still don't like this idea, Miles.'

Miles sat, then leaned forwards and placed his elbows on the table. 'It is the only way, Chloe.'

Juno took a step backwards and quietly sneaked out of the town hall. The mid-afternoon sun sent a long shadow over the town square. Northern district men milled about in their fine clothes, their calculating eyes scanning the working men and girls. Juno walked through the square and down the eastern street. Men carrying goods tilted their heads in greeting. Some scuttled away, giving her a wide berth.

At the eastern gate, she walked up to the guard and said, 'I need you to open the gate, then close it when I have crossed the moat.'

The girl frowned. 'Chloe has ordered us to keep the gate closed.'

Juno took the girl's hand. 'Don't worry about Chloe. I will speak to her if she has any issues.'

The girl hung her head. 'Are you sure, miss? I don't want to disobey Chloe.'

Juno squeezed the girl's hand. 'She will no doubt be here when the gate closes. Don't worry. I will make sure nothing happens to you.'

'Okay, miss,' the girl said. She spun the handles to release the gate. As it gently settled on the other side of the moat, the citizens in the eastern street stopped and stared. Juno walked over the bridge, turned and gave the signal to the girl to pull up the drawbridge. The tops of the eastern walls filled with men, who pointed and whispered among themselves.

'Juno,' Chloe shouted from the top of the wall.

Juno turned and gave the sewer rats' signal, telling Chloe to remain where she was. Miles stood next to Chloe with his arms folded and his face set in stone. Juno gazed over the fields at the orchards. Men scrambled around their fireplaces looking for their armour and weapons. In between the soldiers, two slender figures appeared, their cloaks swishing in the soft breeze.

'What are you doing?' Chloe shouted from the top of the wall.

Juno turned and signalled again for Chloe to stay there. She narrowed her eyes in the direction of the orchard, then broke out into a relaxed jog. The captain of the soldiers whistled, bringing his soldiers into a defensive line, their swords drawn, their shields at the ready. Juno lowered her head, increased her pace and smiled at the tingling sensation spreading across the marks all over her body.

A soft padding of Chax's paws sounded behind her. Juno

extended her hand and felt the fur of Chax's head brush her palm. She felt the rippling muscles of Chax's neck, which she grabbed and used to swing her leg over Chax's back. Her hand reaching behind her, Juno snapped out her Jo and held it to her side. The soldiers stood wide-eyed as the captain barked orders for them to hold the line. The twin knife slingers stood with their hands behind their backs. Juno willed the marks until flames licked out of them, covering her entire body. A thin layer of flames rippled over Chax's body, and bursts of fiery flame blew out of her mouth as she breathed. Her Jo spinning, Juno shot bolts of flames into the orchard, setting trees, tents and grass on fire. Soldiers screamed as shields, struck by the bolts of fire, burst into flames. The captain, losing control of the line, took a step backwards, turned and ran into the flaming orchard.

The knife slingers flicked their robes off and drew their stilettos.

'Take the one on the right,' Juno said into Chax's ear. 'Don't kill him unless you have to.'

Chax roared and turned her eyes onto the knife slinger. Juno sprang off Chax's back. The left knife slinger moved into an attacking stance and spun his stiletto, sending thin black daggers at Juno. The daggers hissed and disappeared as Juno spun her Jo in front of her. Juno reached the knife slinger, jumped high into the air and brought her Jo down onto his stiletto. Flames burst down into the knife slinger's face, making him blink rapidly. Backwards and forwards they traded blows, flames bursting and razor-sharp daggers flying. With a feint to her left, Juno rolled and took the legs out from underneath the knife slinger. She thumped her Jo into the knife slinger's chest. The knife slinger gasped and grabbed Juno's flaming Jo. Juno slammed her foot down onto his chest and jammed the end of her Jo under his chin.

'Move, and I will set you on fire,' Juno said, sending another wave of flames down her Jo.

The knife slinger's chin turned blood-red as the flames crackled and spat over his skin. He abandoned his stiletto, spread his arms and held up his hands.

Juno peered over at the second knife slinger, who lay face down with Chax's jaws clamped firmly on the back of his neck.

'Chax,' Juno said. 'Only if you have to, remember.'

Chax let out a deep, rumbling growl. The knife slinger, his eyes wide and mouth open, stared at his twin brother as Chax's jaws flexed.

Juno knelt and held her flaming hand inches from the knife slinger's face. 'I have a message for the Lady.'

The knife slinger snarled. 'I am not your messenger.'

Juno waved her hand over the knife slinger's face until his eyebrows burned off. 'Tell the Lady to meet me at the southern gate of the city, seven days after the first snowfall. Tell her that if any harm comes to any of the Fairacre women I will not only destroy her, I will burn the City of Lynn to the ground.'

The knife slinger narrowed his eyes, then let out a cackle. 'You would never hurt the innocent people of the city.'

A burst of fire from Juno's hand set the knife slinger's hair on fire. His hand shot to his head as he patted frantically to extinguish the flames.

Juno leaned in closer. 'If the Lady harms my friend Tilly, I will feel nothing about burning the city into the ground.'

The knife slinger glared into Juno's flame-specked eyes and eventually gave her a nod. 'I will tell her.'

Juno stood and backed away, her Jo trained on the knife slinger. 'Now go,' she said. 'The seventh day after the first snowfall.'

The knife slinger battled to his feet, then grimaced as he ran his hand over his burnt throat and head.

'Chax,' Juno said. 'Come.'

Chax flexed her jaws one more time, making the knife

slinger's eyes bulge. Releasing him, she backed away until she stood next to Juno.

The knife slinger scrambled to his feet and stood next to his twin brother. 'We will meet again, young fire child.'

Juno flicked her Jo and sent a bolt of fire that hit the ground at their feet. The knife slingers backed away, turned and jogged up through the north of the orchard. Her breath slowing down, Juno brought the fire back into the marks over her body. The flames licking over Chax's body flickered then faded.

She wrapped her arms around Chax's head. 'Rest now, girl,' she said. 'This is nothing compared to what we will need to do soon.'

Chax pulled away from Juno, huffed, then ran towards the eastern forest. Juno walked back to Fairacre. In the distance, she could see the lines of citizens standing and watching from the wall.

'That was so stupid,' Chloe said, her finger waving in Juno's face. 'What if something had happened to you?'

'Everything is fine, Chloe,' Juno said with a half-smile.

'Don't speak to me right now,' Chloe said as she stormed out of the town hall.

Miles's forehead creased over as he leaned forwards with his hands clasped behind his back.

'I had to send a message, Miles.'

'You could have spoken to us.'

'Chloe wouldn't have let me do it if I had.'

'No, she wouldn't have,' Miles said, with a twinkle in his eye. 'Don't worry too much. She will come around.'

The town hall doors crashed open and Valen stormed in with a thunderous look on his face.

Miles slowly backed away. 'You are on your own, fire child.'

'Stupid girl,' Valen said, his face red with anger. 'You put this entire town and its people in danger.'

The air around Juno crackled as the marks on her body turned a dark red. Her chin raised, she narrowed her eyes. 'Be careful, Valen.'

Valen, blinking, took a step back. 'You should have told us what you were doing.'

'No, I shouldn't have,' Juno said, taking a step forwards and jabbing a finger into his chest. 'I do not answer to you, Valen.'

Valen's eyes widened and his mouth fell open.

Juno brought the marks under control. Her face softening, she said, 'I needed to send a message. A message to guarantee the safety of the Fairacre women, my school friends and my Tilly. The knife slingers will deliver that message.'

'We could have helped,' Valen said, his face creasing in confusion.

'You could have, but they needed to see what I could do on my own. The Lady will hear that I defeated her knife slingers and all her soldiers.'

Valen thought for a moment, then let out a long sigh. His hand rubbing his stubbly chin, he eventually nodded. 'I will speak to Chloe,' he said, turning and walking out of the town hall.

Miles walked over to the long table, sat down and waved a hand, asking Juno to join him.

Juno took a seat and folded her arms. Her eyes trained on Miles, she said, 'You think what I am doing is wrong?'

'No,' Miles said, smiling. 'We are a small group of people taking on a city of thousands. We are a pest which they probably think they can exterminate in one go.'

Juno let out a sigh. 'It is me the Lady is after. They are using the people I love against me.'

'You are not the only thing they are after, Juno,' Miles said, resting his hands on the table.

'The women?' Juno said, tilting her head to one side.

'Yes. They need your elemental power for something. But the women seem to be their primary objective.'

'I told the knife slingers I would burn the City of Lynn to the ground if they hurt any of our loved ones.'

Miles chuckled. 'That's going to sharpen their minds.'

Juno's eyes narrowed. 'What if destroying the Lady doesn't work, Miles?'

Miles dragged his hands through his hair. 'Our only hope for escape then, Juno, is for you to stay true to your word.'

'Burn the City of Lynn?'

Miles agreed, with an incline of his head.

Juno placed her elbows on the table and rubbed the temples of her head.

'We are getting ahead of ourselves,' Miles said, reaching over and squeezing Juno's hand. 'Did you tell the knife slingers a time?'

'Seventh day after the first snowfall.'

Miles sat back and thought for a second. 'That gives us very little time.'

'I know, but what will a few weeks extra give us, and how long do we want our loved ones stuck in that city?'

Miles scraped his chair back and stood. 'We need to get to Valen's and discuss this with Chloe.'

Juno let out a long sigh. 'Chloe is going to be very angry.'

'She will come around once she knows that it's going to happen regardless,' Miles said. 'Let's pick up Billy from the library and get to Valen's shop.'

Juno scraped her chair back and followed Miles out of the town hall and into the library.

'How is everyone?' Miles said, walking up to Billy.

'We have one or two critical, but the rest are okay,' Billy said.

'We need you at Valen's,' Miles said.

Billy turned to Juno and gave her a lopsided grin. 'I hear our young fire child went on an adventure.'

Juno folded her arms and glared at Billy.

'Hey, it's fine by me,' Billy said, throwing up his hands. 'Just be careful, okay?'

'I will,' Juno said.

The three of them left the library and made their way down the winding streets of the manufacturing district. The only shop with twinkling lights in the windows was Valen's. Miles knocked on the glass window of Valen's shop door.

'My boy,' Valen said after ripping open the door.

'We need to talk, Valen,' Miles said. 'Is Chloe here?'

Valen eyed Juno, then gave Miles a nod. 'She is on the couch in my office.'

As Juno walked into the office, Chloe glared at her with her arms folded. Her leg, draped over the armrest of the couch, bounced angrily.

Miles, sitting on the foldout chair nearest to Chloe, said, 'We have little time before we need to move on the City of Lynn.'

Chloe spun her head. 'How much time?'

'Juno has given the Lady until the seventh day from the first snowfall.'

Chloe swung her head back to Juno and said through grinding teeth, 'That is just weeks away. We will never be ready.'

'We are ready,' Juno said, her eyes narrowing. 'This will all come down to me and the girls.'

'We need to teach the men of this town to fight,' Chloe said, sitting up on the couch. 'We need the numbers.'

Juno tilted her head to one side. 'These men are artisans, entertainers and traders. We would need months, years, for any of them to match a soldier from the city.'

Chloe fell back onto the couch and rubbed her forehead with her hand.

'Are you suggesting we leave the men behind?' Billy said.

'They will be a distraction. We will end up trying to defend them from the soldiers,' Miles said.

Chloe looked over at Juno. 'What did you tell the knife slingers?'

'That I would burn the City of Lynn if they harmed any of our loved ones.'

Chloe's eyes widened. 'There are thousands of people in that city, Juno.'

Juno spread her hands. 'And there are thousands of women in faraway lands that the city are planning to kidnap.'

The group sat in silence, the only noise being Chloe's leg bouncing on the armrest.

'Tea?' Valen said, standing up.

Billy chuckled, his lopsided grin spreading across his face. 'Tea sounds appropriate.'

Miles turned to Chloe. 'Where is Alexa? We need her here to discuss what we are going to do.'

'She is still searching the sewers for Dr Viktor,' Chloe said, rising from the couch. 'I will send someone for her.'

Valen returned from the kitchen and passed around mugs of piping hot tea.

'She will be here shortly,' Chloe said, returning from the front door and dropping onto the couch. 'Thanks,' she said, taking a mug from Valen.

Billy took a sip of tea, then said, 'I would have liked to see the look on the faces of those knife slingers.'

Juno glanced at Chloe. 'It was the first time I saw fear in their eyes.'

Valen chuckled and slapped Juno on the back. 'That's our fire child.'

Juno looked down at her tea-covered clothes, then shook her head at Valen. 'Thanks for the tea stains.'

A light tap sounded on the shop door.

'Yes, yes,' Valen said, hauling himself out of his chair and down to the shop door. 'Come in, Alexa.'

'Thank you, Valen,' Alexa said. 'Chloe has called for me?'

'She is down here,' Valen said, reaching over the counter for another fold up chair.

Alexa sat on the chair that Valen placed near the couch.

'How are the men coming along with their training?' Chloe said, looking at Alexa.

Alexa thought for a second. 'May I speak frankly, miss?'

Chloe inclined her head.

'They have more chance of hurting themselves than someone else right now.'

Miles snorted into his mug of tea.

Chloe let out a long sigh, then looked at Miles. 'So what is your proposal, Miles?'

Miles placed his mug of tea on the floor. 'Our plan is to draw the Lady out so Juno can face her. We stay hidden in the forest on the hill and let Juno do what she needs to do. If she needs us, we show ourselves.'

'Are we sure the Lady will show herself?' Alexa said.

'I have seen to that,' Juno said.

Alexa lifted a surprised eyebrow at Juno.

'She is going to burn the City of Lynn to the ground if she doesn't show herself,' Chloe said.

Alexa's eyebrows rose even further.

'What we need to know, Alexa, is what else could go wrong,' Miles said.

Alexa placed her hands in her lap and lowered her head in thought. She looked up eventually and said, 'The Lady will use our loved ones against us. She will make them fight.'

'So obvious,' Miles said, slapping his thigh. 'Why didn't I think of that?'

'Even more reason not to have the men with us,' Juno said. 'Only the sewer rats have the skill to fight without killing or maiming.'

'How are you going to fight the Lady if she uses them as a shield again?' Billy said, looking over at Juno.

Juno's face hardened. 'I will do what I must.'

Chloe shook her head. 'I don't like how you are talking, Juno.'

'Do you think I want to do this, Chloe? Do you think I want to choose?'

'There must be another way,' Chloe said.

'What would Naomi do?' Alexa said, her soft eyes looking over at Chloe.

'She would sacrifice the few to save the many,' Chloe said, letting out a long breath. 'But it tore her apart.'

Juno slid out of her chair and knelt in front of Chloe. Taking Chloe's hands in her own, she said, 'I cannot promise that I won't hurt anybody. But think of the alternatives. We will all succumb to the City of Lynn if we do not end her.'

Chloe squeezed Juno's hands. 'You promise you will be careful?'

Juno reached up and hugged her friend. 'I promise I will do what is necessary. And that is all I can promise.'

Chloe let out a deep sigh. She released her friend and nodded.

'How long before the snows come, Valen?' Miles said. 'I estimate we have a week.'

'Aye, lad,' Valen said. 'Maybe sooner if we follow what happened last year.'

Miles turned to Chloe. 'We need to scout the area. Can we send a team?'

'How far is it to the great river, and what type of terrain between here and there?' Chloe said.

'Yes, we need to speak to Leonard,' Miles said.

Alexa cleared her throat.

'Please, Alexa. You are a council member. You don't need permission to speak,' Chloe said.

'Yes, miss,' Alexa said. 'I suggest we keep this all to ourselves. The girls have reported some secretive activity from the northern district.'

Chloe shook her head and sighed. 'Can you assemble a team and go and scout the great river and the horseshoe area?'

'Yes, miss. We will leave tonight.'

'Take provisions,' Miles said. 'And make sure you have your devices.'

'Can you send Janie here, please?' Chloe said.

Alexa turned and left the shop, the little bell tinkling as the door closed.

'It is time our boys have some clothes made for them, Juno,' Chloe said with a wink.

Valen stared at Chloe. 'What is wrong with what I wear?'

'You stick out like a sore thumb, love,' Chloe said, her hand covering her mouth to stifle a laugh.

Valen grunted. 'Not my fault everyone is small.'

A light tap on the shop door sent Valen lumbering out of his chair. Janie walked into the shop and stood behind the folded-up chair Alexa had sat on.

'Please sit,' Chloe said, pointing to the chair.

'Yes, miss,' Janie said, her eyes darting across the office.

'We have decided that only the sewer rats are going to the City of Lynn,' Chloe said. 'The boys here will need some clothes to keep them hidden. Can we make them something quickly?'

Janie's eyes darted to Miles and Billy, and her face turned a bright pink. 'Certainly, miss. I will need to take measurements.'

Juno sat next to Chloe on the couch while Miles and Valen folded up their chairs.

'This should be fun,' Chloe said, lacing her hands behind the back of her head.

'Would you, please, Mr Valen?' Janie said, pointing to the middle of the office. 'Hold your arms out to the side.'

Valen's face turned a bright pink as Janie measured his body. One after the other, Miles and Billy stood with their arms spread wide. Juno placed a hand over her mouth and chuckled as Janie's face turned a brighter shade of pink as she measured Miles's arms and legs.

'They will be ready in a few days, miss,' Janie said, tucking her notebook into her big pockets.

'Thank you, Janie,' Chloe said, watching her walk through the shop and out the front door.

Juno wagged her eyebrows at Miles, then flashed him a grin.

'What?' Miles mouthed at her.

Juno shrugged. 'Oh, nothing.'

CHAPTER 25
FOUR SPHERES

'Are you sure you have everything you need?' Chloe said, resting a hand on Arthur's shoulder.

'Yes, miss,' he said. 'Please bring our loved ones home to us.'

Chloe inclined her head, then turned to the girls and gave them the signal to lower the drawbridge.

'This is absolutely ridiculous,' Valen said as he squirmed in his new clothes. 'These trousers go everywhere they shouldn't.'

Juno and Chloe, walking behind Valen, tried to stifle a giggle.

'I know you are laughing at me,' Valen said, frowning over his shoulder.

'You will get used to it, love,' Chloe said.

Valen threw his hands up in the air and increased his stride to catch up with Miles and Billy.

'The snow has covered the north and east in a black blanket,' Juno said, holding her hand up to her brow.

'Our spies said it's hard going to get through it,' Chloe said.

'How long till we reach the great river?' Juno said.

'It's late afternoon now. If we march through the night we should be there before tomorrow morning.'

Juno pulled her jacket closer as the wind whipped along the

dirt path. The sun in the west fought against the falling black blanket of snow, its rays occasionally finding a way through. The train of girls, their heads down, fell silent as the wind blew in their faces and the darkness enveloped them.

After hours of trudging north through the howling wind, Chloe leaned in and shouted into Juno's ear, 'We are not far off. I can hear the river.'

Juno pulled her hoodie in closer and leaned into the snowy wind. The train of girls came to a halt. The crashing of the river against the rocks whispered through the screaming wind.

A girl from the front walked back to Chloe. 'The bridge is ahead of us, miss,' she shouted.

'Any guards?' Chloe said.

'We haven't encountered any over the last few days,' the girl said. 'Either they are not there or we cannot see each other.'

Chloe nodded. 'It will be daylight in a couple of hours. Let's get moving.'

The girl wrapped her arms around herself and, fighting the wind, moved to the head of the train. Juno walked up to Miles, Billy and Valen and grinned at their chattering teeth. The train moved forwards, and suddenly the dirt road turned into a well-defined road laid with bricks. Juno squinted through the windy snow and could just make out the pillars of the bridge.

'Stay in the middle,' Chloe shouted at a girl. 'We won't be rescuing you from this river if you get blown off.'

Her eyes on Miles's back, Juno placed one foot in front of the other as she fought the gusts of wind. They reached the end of the bridge and turned west, with the great river to their left. A dark shadow rose in front of them as the hill with its tightly packed trees came into view. As the train entered the forest, the trees silenced the wind. Juno turned her head towards the tweet that sounded from high above the trees. They followed the girls' directions until they entered a set of awnings and tents that sagged under the weight of the black snow.

'We are over here,' Chloe said, signalling to a set of tents on the edge of the camp. 'Best we all try to get some sleep. It will be daylight at seven tomorrow morning.'

Miles and Billy disappeared into a tent, and Valen into another. Juno gave her friend a hug and waited for her to disappear into the same tent as Valen. She moved south down the hill towards the crashing river. The trees thinned slightly, and small slivers of the morning sun broke through the thick black clouds. Juno reached the tree line and knelt with her head cocked, listening for Chax. A low, rumbling purr to her left filled Juno with warmth as Chax's wet snout broke out from the bushes.

'I bet you hate all of this black snow, don't you?' Juno said, running a hand over Chax's head.

Chax scrunched up her nose and sneezed. Juno moved to a dry log and sat down, then wrapped her arms around Chax's muscular neck. Chax continued to purr deep down, her mouth blasting white mist into the air.

'You know what we have to do if the Lady doesn't release the women, right?' Juno said, her face buried in Chax's neck.

Chax huffed and butted her head against Juno's shoulder. Juno rested her head on Chax's shoulder. Her eyes, heavy from the long trek, gently closed. Chax grunted and Juno's eyes popped open.

'I think you can come into the camp,' Juno said. 'The girls know you now, and none of the men are here.'

Chax pulled her head from Juno's arms and stared at her with red-flecked eyes. Juno stood and walked back through the thick forest into the camp. She opened the tent flap and waited for Chax to squeeze inside. They crawled inside and lay down in a small ball, Chax's body wrapped around Juno.

. . .

Juno's eyes fluttered open. The warmth of Chax's body around her made her sigh. A hive of activity leaked through the tent as the girls moved around the camp. Juno sat up and moved the tent flap aside. The darkness of the early morning created long shadows that bounced among the trees of the forest. Chax lifted her head, rumbled once, then put her head back down on her paws.

'Time to get up,' Chloe said, her head poking into the tent. 'Oh, hello, Chax.'

Chax opened her eyes, snorted, then closed them.

Juno rolled her eyes at Chloe. 'She will get up when we need her.'

'There is a plate of food out here for you,' Chloe said.

'What time is it?' Juno said, lifting herself up and moving out of the tent. 'It's the morning of the seventh day. We all slept through the day and most of the night.'

'Any movement from the city?' Juno said.

'No. The snow has stopped falling, though,' Chloe said, passing Juno a plate of food. 'We can see the south entrance now.'

Juno sat cross-legged and ate the dried hardtack and cured meat. 'Where are Miles and the others?'

'At the edge of the forest, taking in the city. It's quite a marvel.'

Juno finished her food, took a long drink from a water bottle, then stood and stretched.

A tweet from a girl sounded down from the treetops. Chloe's head spun round and looked up so she could take in the signals. 'Something is happening. We need to move,' she said.

Juno and Chloe darted between the trees towards the edge of the forest. Miles, Billy and Valen crouched at the tree line, their eyes scanning the open expanse between the hill and the city.

'What is it, love?' Chloe said, crouching next to Valen.

'The city gates have opened and a full troop of soldiers have come out,' Valen said, pointing into the distance. 'It looks like they are on their way here.'

Juno growled. 'I told the Lady that she needs to meet me at the city gate.'

'They are testing you,' Miles said. 'Chloe, what are your orders?'

Chloe, her forehead creased in thought, said, 'We do nothing. We wait in the forest.'

Miles nodded. 'Tell the girls to hide. If these soldiers attack, let them come into the forest. We have the high ground.'

Chloe turned on her heel and sent a flurry of signals to the girls in the trees. The soldiers marched in five lines of twenty. The captain, striding out in front, barked orders for them to stay in line.

At the base of the hill, the captain brought his soldiers to a halt and shouted, 'The Lady has a message for you.'

Chloe laid a hand on Juno's shoulder and said, 'Don't show yourself.' She turned to Miles. 'Would you like to do the honours?'

Miles stood, checked his greatsword and walked out of the trees. 'What is the message?'

The captain narrowed his eyes. 'The message is for the fire child. Where is she?'

'You can give your message to me,' Miles said. 'Or you can give no message at all.'

The captain scanned the tree line. 'The Lady has said she will free the women of Fairacre if the fire child and her cat give themselves up.'

'What of the girls from the schools above the cliffs?' Miles said, tilting his head and placing his hands behind his back.

'Only the women of Fairacre,' the captain said. 'That is her last offer.'

Miles shook his head. 'You can tell the Lady there is no deal unless she frees all the women.'

The captain huffed. 'I cannot return without a deal.'

'You are in a difficult situation then, Captain,' Miles said. 'I suggest you return with your men – or I will force you to return without them.'

Juno turned to Chloe. 'We cannot play these games with her anymore. I will need to show her I am not here to bargain.'

Chloe closed her eyes and sighed. 'I understand. I trust you to do the right thing, Juno.'

Juno reached over and grabbed both of Chloe's hands. 'Make sure our sisters are ready. We will need them soon enough.'

'Go, but be safe.'

Juno walked out of the trees and stood next to Miles. The captain's eyes widened at the sight of Juno's spiky red hair and the thick red marks that ran up her neck and onto her face.

'Captain, I suggest you return to the city with your soldiers and tell the Lady what Miles has just said,' Juno said.

The captain scratched the side of his head then cleared his throat. 'That I cannot do, fire child.'

'Then do what you need to do, Captain,' Juno said, spreading her hands.

The captain lifted his hand and in one sweep directed his soldiers to march up the hill.

Juno turned to Miles. 'Time for you to get back into the trees.'

Miles, his hands still behind his back, spun on his heel and walked into the trees. Juno watched the soldiers pick up pace as they began the climb up the hill. Her hand stretched out to one side with her palm facing down, Juno waited for the light touch of Chax's soft fur. A low, rumbling growl echoed through the forest as Chax walked up behind Juno and slid her head underneath her palm. The blood-red marks over Juno's body seeped out a thin yellow fiery blanket of flames that engulfed both their bodies. The soldiers slowed from a trot to a hesitant walk.

'Captain, this is not your fight, and you know this will end badly for you,' Juno said. 'I suggest you go back to the city and give my message to the Lady.'

The captain turned and looked at his men. Their faces etched in fear and their eyes pleading, they gazed at the captain, waiting for orders. The captain's hand shot up, calling them to a halt.

Juno thought for a moment. 'Captain, I will follow you back to the city gate. But I will not enter with you as the Lady has requested.'

The captain looked back at his men, then back at Juno. 'She will punish my men if I don't bring you in with us.'

'No, Captain, she will punish you,' Juno said. 'Your men will be safe.'

The captain stood and stared at Juno while he decided what to do. With a sigh, he said, 'Fair enough.' With a hand signal, the soldiers spun on their heels and marched back towards the city gate.

Juno extinguished the blanket of flames that lapped over Chax and herself. With a swing of her leg, she leapt onto Chax's back. 'Let's go, girl,' she whispered into Chax's ear.

Chax moved forwards at a walking pace, the thick black snow crunching under her enormous paws. The captain, walking behind his soldiers, glanced back several times while muttering to himself at the sight of Juno following. Halfway across the plain, Juno came to a halt and watched the soldiers march to the gate. Her head lifting, Juno took in the city wall and the soldiers standing on its top.

On a platform to the left of the gate, a person held an umbrella over a regal woman. Her sparkling crown, filled with multi-coloured jewels, sat on top of her head. To her right, a tall dark figure stood, wearing a long black hooded cloak that covered his face. In his right hand he held a thick gnarled staff, and in his left hand he held four coloured spheres. The red sphere sitting on top of the other three spheres pulsed a bright yellow. The green, brown and blue spheres sat dark and dormant. The dark figure bent down and whispered into the regal woman's ear. With a nod, the woman looked behind the gate and gave someone a signal. The air around Juno thundered as the gate, pulled by thick metal chains, climbed open. The Lady, wearing a leather tunic, trousers and black boots, marched out of the gate. She walked up to the captain and barked an order. The captain turned to his soldiers and shouted the orders for all to hear. The Lady smiled as she walked towards Juno, with the captain and his soldiers marching close behind.

Stopping a short distance away, the Lady lifted her hand for the soldiers to stop. 'You have my offer, young fire child,' the Lady said, placing her hands on her hips.

'I reject your offer,' Juno said, lowering her chin and looking at the Lady with a furrowed brow.

The Lady gave Juno a beautiful wide smile. 'I see a resolve in you, young fire child. But let's see how much of that resolve is true when you see your loved ones cut down.'

'If you harm any of our women, I will make you and this city pay,' Juno said, her voice a low snarl.

'It is not I that will harm your women. It will be you, fire child,' the Lady said, raising her hand and letting it fall.

The shouts of women and schoolgirls echoed across the plain as they streamed out of the city gate. Their eyes black and white, their mouths contorted, they ran towards Juno. The soldiers behind the Lady drew their weapons, pointed them at Juno and advanced. Juno and Chax burst into a blanket of fiery yellow flames. Chax opened her mouth and roared, signalling to the girls in the forest. The girls burst out of the trees. In one hand each carried a sharp short sword, in the other a blunt practice sword.

Juno let fly a single fireball at the Lady.

The Lady sidestepped and let out a lovely tinkling laugh. 'So predictable, little one.'

A swirling dark grey mist rose around the Lady. As she

extended her hands, two long, jagged black swords materialised. Juno pulled Chax back as the shouting group of women and soldiers bore down on her. A moment later, locs flew past her as Chloe sprang into the fray. Her blunt practice sword struck at the women, knocking them to the ground. Her short metal sword sang at the soldiers, slashing and hacking. Valen lumbered past, his huge club crashing and bashing into the soldiers, the women bouncing off him as if they were nothing but pesky flies. Miles's greatsword sang as the blade cut through the soldiers and the hilt crashed into the women, knocking them unconscious.

'Circle around Juno,' Chloe shouted.

The girls beat the soldiers and women away until a large circle formed, with only Juno, Chax and the Lady standing in the middle.

Juno hopped off Chax and, rubbing the top of her head, she said, 'Bring on the fire, girl.'

Chax sprinted out in a wide arc, then turned back, forming a circle around Juno and the Lady. A circle of fire erupted out of the ground, cutting Juno, Chax and the Lady off from the fighting sewer rats, soldiers and women.

The Lady swung her two swords in circles around her sides. 'I can hear the screams of your loved ones, young fire child. Can you hear them?'

Juno unclipped her Jo and, pushing the buttons, popped out the ends. Fire lapped from her hands and down onto the weapon. 'Why are you taking the women? What are you using them for?' she said, moving into her defensive stance.

The Lady laughed. 'I have nothing to do with the women. I am here for your animal.'

'Then whose orders are they?' Juno said, circling around the Lady. 'Why are you infecting the women and bringing them to the city?'

The Lady tilted her head, then shrugged. 'The women for the

animal. That is the deal with you and that is the deal with the queen.'

Juno lowered her eyes, snarled and sprang forwards, her Jo twirling and sending out slivers of yellow scorching fire. The Lady called up the grey mist with a flick of her hand. The fire sizzled then disappeared as the grey mist ate it. Juno's Jo slammed into the Lady's right-hand sword, sending out a fiery explosion. The Lady's swords countered with swirling grey mist, which sucked in Juno's fire. Juno sidestepped and lashed her Jo against the Lady's shoulder. A burst of flame made its way through the grey mist and burned the side of her face.

The beautiful smile receded. With a curled lip, she snarled. 'Time to finish this.'

Juno sprang back and dodged left and right as shiny black daggers spun out from the Lady's swords. The Lady took a step back, then slammed her hands together, moulding her two swords into one. Her free palm facing Juno, she sent out thick tendrils of smoke. Juno flung fire out from her Jo, but the flames hit the mist and sizzled away. The smoke wrapped around her legs and pulled her feet from underneath her.

'Such a naïve little girl,' the Lady said, walking up to Juno. 'Don't worry – I will look after your magnificent cat for you.'

Juno spun her Jo around and clipped the ankles of the Lady, sending her staggering backwards. The Lady turned and sent a thick cloud of mist at Chax's firewall behind her. The flames parting, Juno's eyes widened as Tilly sprinted through and came to a stop next to the Lady.

'Don't you hurt her,' Juno said, her voice a whisper.

'Give me your animal,' the Lady said, her snarl turning back into a beautiful smile.

Juno, looking at Tilly's black and white eyes, took in a deep breath. 'Forgive me, Tilly,' she said, raising her hands and sending a white-hot fireball at the Lady.

The Lady jumped to her side and watched the fireball scream past her face.

'Juno?' Tilly said, her eyes turning from black and white to a bright blue. 'What are you doing here? Where am I?'

'Tilly, get away from her,' Juno said, pointing at the Lady.

Tilly peered over her shoulder, then turned and ran towards Juno. Juno took a step forwards, her hand reaching out to grab Tilly.

Tilly stumbled and screamed as a thin black dagger ripped through her shoulder.

'No!' Juno shouted as she caught Tilly in her arms and slowly lowered her to the ground. 'Tilly? Can you hear me?'

Tilly's bright blue eyes fluttered open, her breathing coming in quick gasps. 'I don't understand, Juno. What is happening?'

'It's okay, Tilly,' Juno said through gritted teeth. 'Everything is okay.'

Tilly opened her mouth, then slammed it shut. As quickly as her eyes had turned pale blue, they turned black and white.

Juno sprang away as the thin dagger in Tilly's hands grazed her stomach.

The Lady laughed her beautiful tinkling laugh. 'Clever girl. You have been paying attention. But now you have to watch your friend die.'

Juno let out a guttural scream and sprang at the Lady, fire erupting from her marks. Her Jo spinning, jabbing and striking, she pounded the Lady with fire. The Lady whipped her swords apart, and with one stab buried the blade into Juno's thigh, sending her to the ground.

'Or maybe you will die before your beloved Tilly does,' the Lady said, raising her swords above her head.

A war cry sounded as Miles sprang through the fire with his greatsword raised above his head. Juno lifted her hand and burst fire onto Miles's greatsword, setting the blade alight. Miles and the Lady danced around each other, parrying, slashing and stabbing. The Lady feinted to her right, blocked Miles's flaming greatsword, spun him round and sliced across the small of his back. His mouth wide open in a silent scream, he dropped his greatsword, then crumpled to the ground, his legs twisting at an impossible angle.

'Silly boy,' the Lady said as she walked back over to Juno. 'It looks like you are going to have the pleasure of seeing all of your friends die.'

Juno crawled backwards as the Lady lifted her swords.

'Goodbye, young fire child,' the Lady said.

Juno covered her face, waiting for the swords to strike. The Lady screamed. Juno looked up as the tip of Miles's flaming greatsword burst through the Lady's chest. Her eyes wide, the Lady looked down at the sword and blinked in confusion. A deafening roar shook the ground as Chax abandoned her circle of fire. With claws and teeth out, she tackled the Lady and burst into flames, engulfing herself and the Lady. As the Lady disappeared, Juno raised her eyes to the sky and let out a long breath at the sight of the purple liquid, of the antidote, dripping from the corner of Tilly's mouth.

Tilly looked down at the greatsword in her hands. 'What have I done? Juno, what have I done?'

Juno struggled to her feet, hobbled over to Tilly and kicked away the empty vial that lay next to her feet. 'It's okay, Tilly,' she said, wrapping her friend in a hug.

Chax backed away from the smouldering ash that had once been the Lady.

'Still the circle, Chax,' Juno said, releasing Tilly.

The circle of flames that surrounded them hissed and sizzled, disappearing into the ground. Juno scanned the field, then let out a sigh as she saw the eyes of the women return to their normal colours.

'On the soldiers,' Chloe shouted as she passed the girls on her way to Juno.

The girls dropped their practice swords and engaged the soldiers. A horn blasted from the tops of the City of Lynn's walls. Rows of soldiers sprinted out of the gates towards the women in the field.

Juno let go of Tilly, hobbled over to Chax and jumped onto her back. 'Chloe, get the girls to round up the women,' she said over her shoulder.

Chloe let out another whistle. Juno sent a fireball at the soldiers who were fighting the girls. Their eyes wide, they disengaged and back-pedalled to join the soldiers coming out of the gates. The girls, now free, started rounding up the women, who staggered around in confusion. Juno pulled herself onto Chax's back and grimaced as she felt the wound in her leg begin to knit together. Chax, growling under her breath, padded across the battlefield towards the city gate. Juno snapped her Jo onto her back, lifted her hands and sent blasts of fireballs at the soldiers who were still running out of the gate. The soldiers dodged the fireballs but kept advancing across the field. Juno slid off Chax's back, unclipped her Jo, and springing into the air, she slammed it into the ground. A carpet of yellow flame rolled like a wave towards the gates. The soldiers froze as the carpet of fire rolled towards them.

A horn blasted.

The soldiers spun and sprinted back towards the gate. The southern gate, receiving the last of the soldiers, rolled down and slammed shut.

CHAPTER 26
THE COOKS

Juno walked back to Chax and jumped on her back. 'Get to Tilly, Chax.'

Chax bounded back across the battlefield and came to a stop next to Tilly. Juno jumped off Chax's back, knelt next to Tilly and placed her hand over the hole in her shoulder.

'It hurts, Juno. I don't understand. What is going on?'

Juno looked up and searched the field. 'Billy!' she shouted.

Billy, kneeling down next to Miles, waved a hand for Juno to wait.

'He will be here as soon as he can,' Juno said, grabbing one of Tilly's hands. 'I am so glad to see you.'

Tilly gave Juno a thin smile, then shut her eyes with a grimace.

Chloe knelt down next to Juno. 'How is she?'

'I don't know. Billy needs to get here quickly.'

'Miles is in a bad way,' Chloe said. 'Billy thinks he won't be able to walk again.'

'Who are you?' Tilly said, her eyes wide as she stared at Chloe.

Chloe extended her hand. 'My name is Chloe, and I am thrilled to meet you, Tilly. Juno here has told me all about you.'

Tilly shook Chloe's hand. 'I have never seen someone who is a different colour to me.'

Chloe chuckled to herself.

Juno grinned at Chloe. 'We didn't get to leave the school much.'

Chloe smiled, then placed her hand on Tilly's shoulder. 'Don't worry. I am just like you.'

'Tilly,' Billy said, skidding to a stop and dropping to his knees.

Tilly, her face turning pink and eyes softening, looked up at Billy.

'Let me look at that,' Billy said, moving Juno's hand out of the way.

Tilly grimaced as Billy pulled her shirt away from the wound.

'It has gone straight through,' Billy said, pulling a pot of salve out of his pocket. 'You will be fine if we keep it wrapped up and clear of infection.'

'Miss,' Alexa said, running up to Chloe. 'During the fight, soldiers slipped past and crossed the river.'

Juno frowned. 'What did they look like?'

'I couldn't quite see, miss,' Alexa said.

'We need to go, Juno,' Chloe said.

Juno knelt next to Tilly. 'How are you doing?'

Tilly grabbed Juno's elbow. 'Your friend looks very serious. I think you should go with her. Billy will look after me.'

Juno pursed her lips. 'Are you sure?'

Tilly nodded, then let out a yelp.

'Sorry,' Billy said. 'I had to make sure I got the whole wound clean.'

Juno stood. 'Look after her, Billy.'

Billy ignored Juno as he continued working on Tilly.

'Go, Juno,' Tilly said. 'Your friend needs you.'

'Make sure you cover your backs when you bring everyone home,' Chloe said to Alexa.

Alexa turned and strode off to the girls. Juno and Chloe ran towards the bridge, with Chax bounding behind them.

'They have a bit of a head start,' Chloe said. 'Can you and Chax keep up?'

Juno signalled to Chax, who bounded up next to her. With a jump, she landed on Chax's back. 'With the aid of fire. Sure we can.'

Chloe stretched her legs. 'Come on then,' she shouted over her shoulder.

Juno willed the flames through her hands until they covered her and Chax in a thin blanket of fire. They ran together, Chloe in front with her locs bouncing on her shoulders, and Juno and Chax covered in a blanket of yellow fire. As the charred orchards came into view, Chloe slowed to a trot. Juno extinguished the flames, climbed off Chax's back and jogged up next to her.

'Something isn't right,' Chloe said, muttering under her breath.

'What do you see?' Juno said.

'It's quiet. Way too quiet.'

They continued jogging towards the town, then slowed to a walk as the eastern gate came into view.

'Knife slingers,' Chloe said. 'That's why they weren't in the battle.'

Juno squinted her eyes at the two figures standing on top of the Fairacre wall. Chax's tail flicked from side to side as she let out a snarl.

'The gate is closed,' Chloe said. 'No way we can get in there.'

They stopped just short of the wide moat and glared up at the knife slingers. A well-dressed northern district man appeared from the steps and strode over to stand next to them.

Chloe let out a throaty growl. 'I should have left someone here to defend Fairacre.'

The well-dressed man lifted a hand. 'We have heard your

mission to the City of Lynn was successful. Where are our women?'

'They are on their way. Why are these knife slingers here?' Chloe said.

The man glared down at Chloe. 'Did you think your pathetic gang of sewer rats could change the old ways? They are here to help restore order to the town of Fairacre.'

The knife slingers, with their long faces and hooked noses, gazed stony faced down at Juno and Chloe.

'What have you done with the girls?' Chloe said.

The man signalled to his right. Juno's lip curled as they dragged a bruised faced Janie up onto the wall. Chloe stood deathly still as she stared at Janie's blue and purple face.

'The sewer rats have returned to the sewers where they belong,' the man said. 'A few resisted, but you can see our knife slingers took care of them.'

Chloe ground her teeth. 'Be strong, Janie.'

Janie lifted her head and gave Chloe a weak smile.

'What of the men we saved?' Chloe said. 'Where are they?'

'In their homes, waiting for their loved ones,' the man said.

Chloe turned to Juno. 'Sometimes heroes come from the most unlikely places.'

Juno gave Chloe a confused look. 'Who and what are you talking about?'

Chloe looked up at Janie, then back to Juno. 'I am going to give the signal. When I do, I need you to release Janie from that man's clutches and then release a fiery hell into the northern district.'

'You want me to burn Fairacre?' Juno said, her forehead crinkling.

'Fairacre needs a new beginning. And what better way to build a new beginning than from the ground up?'

Juno inclined her head. 'Naomi would be proud, Chloe.'

Chloe's face softened. She turned to the wall and gave Janie a slight nod. Juno draped her hand over Chax's neck.

'Ready?' Chloe said, placing her fingers to her lips. Juno nodded.

Chloe let loose a series of whistles. On the last whistle, Juno shot out a small ball of fire that hit the man holding Janie straight in the chest.

'Run, Janie,' Chloe screamed.

The man let go of Janie as he patted his chest to put out the flames. Janie ran to the steps and disappeared behind the gate. Juno swung onto Chax's back and sprinted northwards around the moat.

The knife slingers flung black twisted daggers at Chloe. 'Try again,' she said, dancing around them.

Screams and shouts from the middle of Fairacre filled the air. The knife slingers stopped their dagger-throwing and disappeared down the steps. Juno rounded the northern side of Fairacre. She lifted her hands and blasted fireballs left, right, left, right, up into the air and down into the northern district of Fairacre. The mansions burst into flames as the roofs, silk curtains and fine materials caught fire. Shouts echoed as the people in the northern district escaped their burning homes. Chloe let go another short whistle.

'Let's go, Chax,' Juno said, spinning Chax around towards the eastern gate.

The chains clicked and the drawbridge came crashing to the ground. Janie waved them through. Juno and Chax sprinted up the eastern street and slowed to a trot when they reached Chloe. She hopped off Chax and walked alongside her up to the town square. The rich men from the northern district, running from the fires, stopped and gawked at the two knife slingers battling two whirlwinds in the town square.

'Very bad man,' Gem yelled, her butcher's knife swinging at the knife slinger.

'Chop, chop,' Jen shouted, her carving knife blurring through the air.

With a kitchen knife in each hand, the twins spun and weaved around the two knife slingers. Juno's mouth hung open as she stared into the town square.

Chloe placed a hand on her hip and chuckled. 'Unlikely heroes,' she said.

The knife slingers' eyes grew wider as each hack and slash hit nothing but thin air.

Juno took a step forwards, then stopped as Chloe laid a hand on her forearm. 'Let the men of Fairacre see,' she said, nodding her head towards the town square.

The knife slingers, standing back to back and breathing heavily, constantly sliced at nothing but air as Gem and Jen darted around them in a blur of blades and insults.

'Evil man,' Jen said, darting in and disarming one of the knife slingers. Gem darted to her left, then dropped and swept the feet from the other knife slinger. His hand flailing, he pulled the other knife slinger to the ground, where they lay in a heap.

Jen, standing over them, sharpened her carving knife against her butcher's knife. 'Slice and dice,' she said.

Gem placed a foot on the knife slinger's chest and lifted her butcher's knife. 'Chopping board for you.'

'Jen, Gem, that is enough,' Chloe said, drawing a short sword and striding into the middle of the square.

Pouting, Jen and Gem stalked off into the crowd while cursing at the northern district men.

Chloe held the tip of her short sword to the knife slinger's throat. 'Go back to the City of Lynn and tell whoever your master is that Fairacre no longer belongs to the city.'

The knife slingers, sweat dripping down their faces, scrambled to their feet with their hands held high.

'Get out,' Chloe said, waving her sword towards the eastern street.

Juno watched the girls surround the knife slingers and escort them out of the town.

Chloe, looking to the north, shouted orders at the men to get buckets to contain the raging fire in the northern district. 'Don't let the fire spread to the town hall,' she said.

The men, forming lines that snaked behind the town hall, passed buckets of water to each other, which they threw on the advancing fires. Chloe and Juno walked up the steps to the town hall and swung open the doors. Leonard sat at the council table, his eyes darting back and forth as he shuffled his files and papers.

Chloe, marching over to Leonard, pointed her short sword at his chest. 'It wasn't me, miss,' Leonard said, his face turning white with fear.

'He is telling the truth,' Arthur said from the other side of the table. 'He objected to the northern district men hiring the knife slingers.'

Chloe lowered her sword. 'Why the change of heart, Leonard?'

With the colour returning to his face, Leonard stood, cleared his throat and said, 'My daughter is missing. I sent her to a school on the northern cliffs.'

'The women and schoolgirls are on their way back from the city.'

'Is my daughter with them?' Leonard said, clasping his hands in front of him, his face pleading.

'What is her name?' Juno said.

His lips trembling, Leonard said, 'Her name is Erica. She is a good girl. My baby girl.'

Juno's head jerked back. 'Your daughter is Erica?'

Leonard nodded frantically.

Juno took in a deep breath, then blew it out while shaking her head. 'She is safe, Leonard. She will be here by the morning.'

Leonard fell back into his chair. Tears streaming down his face, he looked up at Juno. 'Thank you. She is all I have left after her mother passed.'

'She lost her mother?' Juno said.

Leonard nodded. 'She was young. I hated sending her to that school. I missed her every day.'

Juno knelt in front of Leonard. 'Tell Erica that if she needs a friend, she can come to me.'

Wiping away another tear, Leonard beamed. 'Thank you.'

They finally brought the raging fires of the northern district under control. For the rest of the day, the council met to discuss Fairacre's next steps. Night fell, and Juno and Chloe made their way to Valen's shop to turn in.

The next morning, Juno stood on the roof and watched the train of women enter the eastern gate. Shouts of joy bounced off the shop walls as daughters ran to their parents and embraced them.

Chloe stood next to Juno with her arms folded. 'Any news on Tilly and Miles?'

'They are at the end of the train. They should be here soon. How is Janie?'

'Already sorting out the weaving district. She got bashed up, but nothing broken,' Chloe said.

'She is one tough sewer rat,' Juno said.

Chloe turned and grinned at Juno. 'She won't be a sewer rat for long. She will be a citizen of Fairacre.'

Juno bumped Chloe's hip with her own. 'That is going to take some time getting used to.'

'It is going to take time for every woman to feel comfortable in Fairacre. The transition will take time.'

'They will have someone to look up to,' Juno said, eyeing her friend.

'I will be in Valen's shop,' Chloe said, unfolding her arms. 'I am going to get things ready for Miles.'

Juno watched her friend jump off the roof and make her way through the crowded eastern street. Her gaze turned to the eastern gate, where the last women entered the town, running into their loved ones' arms. Juno ran and jumped across the rooftops until she reached the last house. Valen's lumbering frame came into view as he walked alongside six girls carrying a hastily made stretcher, which carried Miles. Billy and Tilly walked arm in arm behind the stretcher. Tilly's arm hung in a sling, her shoulder wrapped in white cloth. She unhooked her arm from Billy and waved at Juno. Juno waved back. As the stretcher carrying Miles came through the gate, Juno jumped off the house and walked alongside, her hand resting on his shoulder. Miles's face looked deathly white.

'Take him to Valen's shop. Chloe is sorting out a place for him to rest,' Juno said.

The girls walked down into the manufacturing district.

Tilly walked up to Juno with a smile spread across her face. 'Miss Petra wouldn't be happy with those marks all over you, Juno.'

Juno pulled Tilly into a hug. 'She certainly wouldn't, would she.'

'Ouch, careful,' Tilly said. 'I have a hole in my shoulder.'

Juno released her and looked down into her big bright blue eyes. 'It is so good to see you.'

Tilly reached up and ran her fingers along the marks on Juno's face. 'Billy has been talking the whole way here. I cannot believe I have been away for two summers and a winter. And I cannot believe what has happened.'

'There is a lot more to talk about,' Juno said. 'Miss Petra, Mr Hargreaves and our school.'

'Billy told me about them being your parents,' Tilly said, her voice breaking.

A twitch of pain shot across Juno's face. 'They did what they could for me,' she said. 'Miss Petra would be proud.'

'Yes, she would,' Tilly said.

Billy walked up, separated the two of them, then looped both their arms into his. 'Let's get to Valen's.'

They walked through the crowds and entered the long winding street to Valen's.

Tilly's eyes burst out of her head as she peered through the windows of the shops. 'So many types of clothes.'

Juno chuckled.

Billy knocked on Valen's shop door and waited for Valen to rip it off its hinges.

'Hello,' Valen said, the bell tinkling wildly above his head. 'Come in, come in. We are in the office. I mean, we are in the old office.'

Juno walked through the shop and stopped mid-stride at the change to Valen's office.

'Miles is sleeping,' Billy said from the far side of the room. 'I knocked him out with a draught.'

Juno walked over to Miles and watched Little Henry scuttle along his back, working away at the long wound.

'Will he walk again?' Juno said.

'I doubt it,' Billy said. 'He may get some feeling back, but the wound is bad.'

Juno sat down on the couch and beckoned for Tilly to sit.

A loud rap sounded on the shop door just as Tilly sat. Valen, grumbling, lumbered through the shop and ripped the door open. Muffled sounds echoed through the shop, then Valen said, 'Billy. They have found Dr Viktor.'

Billy jumped up and ran through the shop.

'Go with him, Juno,' Chloe said. 'Tilly is safe here, and we can get to know each other.'

Juno stood and hurriedly followed Billy out of the shop. They ran through the streets to the marketplace where, in an alley, two girls knelt over an open grate.

A hacking cough echoed out of the hole. 'Can you stop handling me? I can do this just fine.'

Juno slowed to a trot and rolled her eyes at Billy. Billy dropped to one knee and helped pull Dr Viktor out of the hole. Juno gasped as Dr Viktor's black and blue face came through the hole.

'I will be just fine, young fire child,' Dr Viktor said as he wobbled on his feet. 'It's just a few bruises.'

'Get him to Valen's,' Billy said.

'I can walk,' Dr Viktor said as his knees gave way.

'Enough, old man,' Billy said. 'I am surprised you can even see through that swollen left eye.'

Dr Viktor grunted as two girls threw his arms over their shoulders.

'Where have you been?' Juno said. 'We have been looking for you.'

Dr Viktor scowled, then coughed noisily. 'Knife slingers dragged me here from the City of Lynn. They knocked me about and left me in the sewers.'

Juno and Billy followed the girls through the market district and into the manufacturing district. Not bothering to knock, Billy opened the door, grabbed Dr Viktor from the girls and dragged him through the shop and onto a fold-up chair.

'Let me see,' Billy said, pushing Dr Viktor's head back.

'I am fine, you silly boy,' Dr Viktor said, then broke into a hacking cough. Billy grunted then pulled out a small bottle of salve, which he applied to Dr Viktor's cuts and bruises.

Juno sat cross-legged on the floor and grinned. For the first time, she sat with all of her friends, new and old. Tilly, catching Juno's look, gave her a brief smile. Billy finished working on Dr Viktor and moved over to check on Miles. Valen walked in holding mugs of tea, which he handed out to everyone.

Juno cleared her throat. 'Sorry to press, but there is a lot of chaos in Fairacre. What are your orders, Chloe?'

Chloe turned her eyes onto Juno. 'In short, we are going to split up and take on different tasks.'

'I am going to rebuild Dr Viktor's house,' Valen said from his office chair. 'Miles is going to need long-term care, so I want him to be somewhere where he is comfortable.'

'Billy and I are going to start a Fairacre hospital,' Tilly said, her cheeks turning pink as she glanced at Billy.

'We are going to realise Naomi's dream,' Chloe said, looking at Juno. 'Every person, man or woman, will have a say in how we run Fairacre.'

Juno let out a long sigh, then settled her gaze on Dr Viktor. 'Dr Viktor, why is the City of Lynn taking all the women?'

Dr Viktor looked up with his one eye. 'I do not know why. The queen has ordered all women from all regions to go to the City of Lynn.'

Juno frowned. 'As soon as we have finished what we need to do in Fairacre, we will need to find out what is going on.'

Dr Viktor pulled out his handkerchief and, covering his mouth with it, coughed loudly. He replaced it into his pocket. 'With the Lady gone, I think the City of Lynn will have to think of another way to get the women.'

'The people of the City of Lynn rely on Fairacre to feed them,' Chloe said. 'I know we will have contact with them soon. We will have to keep our eyes and ears open.'

Tilly shuffled in her chair. 'What about our school, Juno?'

'Our school is no more. You and I have a lot to talk about,' Juno said.

'Everything is changing,' Tilly said, nervously looking around.

Juno uncrossed her legs, shuffled over to Tilly and placed her hands on her knees. 'We have a lot of evenings to catch up, but know that you are among friends and this is where we want you to stay.'

Tilly threw her arms round Juno and hugged her tightly. The group sat together, telling stories late into the night. Tilly lifted her hand every few minutes to ask a question. At midnight, a small tap on the shop door sounded.

Chloe stood and said, 'It's time, everyone. Please follow me.'

They stood and followed Chloe out of the shop and through the silent streets of Fairacre until they reached the south entrance. The southern fields twinkled and flickered with small candles that surrounded a high wooden pyre. Multicoloured flowers surrounded a lone figure atop the wooden structure. Her arms lay crossed over her chest and her regal head lay peacefully on a silk cushion.

Juno, Chloe, Valen, Billy and Tilly stood arm in arm as they watched the girls, one by one, walk up a small wooden staircase and place an item they wanted Naomi to take with her to the afterlife.

Chloe walked to the pyre, climbed the stairs, pulled out one of her swords and laid it next to Naomi. With a hand on Naomi's shoulder, Chloe closed her eyes and whispered a quiet prayer.

Juno clasped Chloe's hand when she returned. 'Everyone surrounding Naomi is free.'

Chloe, her eyes wet with tears, smiled down at her friend. 'Yes, they are. It is all she ever wanted. Please send her on her way, young Juno.'

Juno willed the marks in her hand alight and, walking around the pyre, she sent a thin stream of fire into the kindle at the bottom. The fire took hold and the night burst into bright orange light. The surrounding girls turned their heads to the sky and watched the tendrils of smoke float gently up into the stars.

CHAPTER 27
MILES

Dr Viktor placed his fingers on his temples and shook his head. 'Does he have to bang all day long?'

Chloe chuckled. 'He is rebuilding your house.'

Dr Viktor waved a hand as he returned from the kitchen pantry. He sat on a stool and dropped the tray of food on the counter. 'How are things in Fairacre?'

'We have our new hospital up and running,' Billy said, smiling at Tilly. 'Our Tilly is a natural herbalist.'

Tilly leaned her head against Billy's shoulder and gave everyone a grin.

'We have had contact from the City of Lynn,' Chloe said. 'Their restricted food supplies created a hard winter. They have opened channels for trade.'

'Who is handling the negotiations?' Dr Viktor said, raising an eyebrow.

'Leonard,' Chloe said. 'He has the art of diplomacy, it seems.'

Dr Viktor grunted. 'Be cautious of side deals and sabotage.'

Chloe pursed her lips. 'The council is aware.'

'And what of our young fire child?' Dr Viktor said.

Chloe glanced over at Tilly. 'She has gone south to clean up the schools.'

Tilly raised her head from Billy's shoulder. 'We only know of the schools in the southern lands. She says there may be more in the north, east and west lands.'

'There are a lot of schools to the south. The east, west and north I don't know much about,' Dr Viktor said.

Valen hollered obscenities from the floor above.

Tilly giggled into her hand. 'Guess he will visit our hospital again tonight. A fresh cut or bruise every day.'

Chloe rolled her eyes up at the ceiling. 'How is Miles doing?' she said.

Billy pressed his lips together and shook his head. 'Nothing has changed. He cannot feel his legs and he refuses to leave his room.'

Dr Viktor laid a gentle hand on Billy's forearm. 'Give him time, my son.'

'Janie has been asking how he is doing,' Chloe said.

'I don't think this is the right time for her to see him,' Billy said with a sigh.

'She might be able to help him, though,' Tilly said, looking up at Billy.

'Let me talk to him about it first,' Billy said.

The kitchen darkened as the sun disappeared.

Chloe stood and readjusted her locs. 'It's time we got back to Fairacre. Valen and I will be back in a few days to help finish the second storey.'

Billy turned to Dr Viktor. 'Tell Miles I will be back soon.'

Dr Viktor nodded his head. The familiar clump of his cane echoed through the new house as he followed everyone into the reception area. Chloe opened the door and scowled at the melting black snow. Valen bounded down the stairs with two fingers stuck in his mouth. Billy turned to Dr Viktor and gave him a swift hug.

'Get out of here,' Dr Viktor said angrily, a small smile playing on his lips.

Billy chuckled, walked through the door and joined the others. Dr Viktor watched Chloe, Billy, Tilly and Valen disappear down the path towards Fairacre.

Miles, hearing the front door close, turned his head and stared out of his bedroom window. The trees, swaying in the wind, were shedding the black layer of tar that the snow had brought all winter long. He reached down and ran his hands over his legs. He felt nothing. The tears refused to show themselves anymore. His hands balled into fists and he pounded the side of his mattress.

'It's okay, son,' Dr Viktor said, walking into his room. 'Are you in any pain?'

'I still can't feel my legs,' Miles said. 'I am worthless if I cannot use my legs.'

Dr Viktor placed a tray of food on the bedside table. 'You are not worthless. They are waiting for you to join them at the council table.'

'And do what?' Miles said. 'Talk all day?'

Dr Viktor picked up a knife and began carving up an apple. 'Talking is just as effective as fighting.'

'I would like to be alone, please,' Miles said.

Dr Viktor placed the knife and apple on the tray. At the door, he turned and said, 'Call me if you need me. Billy will be back soon to check on you.'

Miles waited for the door to close, then let out a long sigh. Small droplets of rain patted against his bedroom window. His eyes closing, he swallowed hard to hold back his rising anger. A moment later, his eyes snapped open as the first howls of the timber wolves broke through the even rhythm of the falling rain.

NEXT UP...

Valen and the Beasts: A Juno and the Lady Novella Book 1.1

Valen plucked the glass box off the shelf and gently placed it on his desk. Inside, a set of handcrafted metal circles linked to form the body of his new beast. He closed his eyes and dreamed of the Fairacre residents buying his latest creations.

A commotion outside Valen's shop brings him back to the present. The Captain has caught the leader of the sewer rats and is parading her in front of Fairacre residents. Her fate will be determined by the townsfolk's demands.

Valen steps in to defend the leader.

A story of discovery, hope and courage, Valen and the Beasts is a journey of an outsider risking everything to stand up for the people he loves. Will Valen save the leader of the sewer rats? Will he show everyone his secret? Or will he buckle under the pressures of the old conventions?

AUTHOR REQUEST

Hello,

Thank you for taking the time to read **Juno and the Lady**. It is the start of an epic fantasy and I really hope you join me for the rest of the journey.

If you have a moment, I would really appreciate a review on either Amazon or Goodreads. The reviews help us indie authors a great deal.

Please feel free to join my mailing list and I will keep you up to date with book release dates, news and upcoming events. https://gjkemp.co.uk/mailing-list/

Again, thank you for spending your precious time reading my book.

Take care,
G.J.

About the Author

A nomad at heart, GJ has lived in nine countries across Africa, Europe and the Middle East. His career has included working as a Divemaster in The Red Sea, a zookeeper in Israel, and a proof-reader in Sweden. Born with cerebral palsy, GJ has spent a lifetime trying to tie his shoelaces while standing up in the hope of not falling over. It is a constant challenge, but sometimes he occasionally succeeds.

Finding the love for writing later in life, GJ spends most of his free time going for walks and dreaming of story ideas. He hopes to one day have a small place on the oceanfront where he can walk his dogs on the beach.

For more information please visit gjkemp.co.uk

- facebook.com/gavin.kemp.92505
- twitter.com/kemp_gj
- instagram.com/gjkempauthor
- linkedin.com/in/g-j-kemp-4a76b03
- bookbub.com/profile/g-j-kemp

Printed in Great Britain
by Amazon